THE LIQUID LOCOMOTIVE

Legendary Whitewater River Stories

D1052629

EDITED BY JOHN
AND
HAI-VAN K. SPONHOLZ

FALCON®

HELENA, MONTANA

© 1999 by John Long.

Published by Falcon® Publishing, Inc., Helena, Montana.

Printed in Canada.

1 2 3 4 5 6 7 8 9 0 TP 04 03 02 01 00 99

All design and prepress work by Falcon® Publishing, Inc., Helena, Montana.

Front cover photo: Lava Falls, Grand Canyon by Wiley-Wales.
Back cover photo: Potomac River, Maryland by Skip Brown.

All illustrations by Gardner Heaton.

Grateful acknowledgment is made to those who granted permission to reprint the selections in this book. A complete list of copyright permissions can be found on pages 255 and 256.

Library of Congress Cataloging-in-Publication Data is on file at the Library of Congress.

CAUTION

Outdoor recreational activities are by their very nature potentially hazardous. All participants in such activities must assume responsibility for their own actions and safety. The information contained in this book cannot replace sound judgment and good decision-making skills, which help reduce risk exposure, nor does the scope of this book allow for disclosure of all the potential hazards and risks involved in such activities.

Learn as much as possible about the outdoor recreational activities in which you participate, prepare for the unexpected, and be cautious. The reward will be a safer and more enjoyable experience.

CONTENTS

INTRODUCTION

John Long

T hroughout history, wherever the water ran, the people came. The Ganges, Danube, Nile (Egypt was know as the "Gift of the Nile"), Mississippi, and countless other rivers provided the lifeblood of all those who settled on their shores. Rivers also served as natural highways. Early boatmen learned to navigate shifting drafts and shoals—or they drowned. Rivers took many shapes, and societies were often cut in half by stretches of wicked rapids. Take Upper and Lower Egypt, which are separated just north of Khartoum by six points of rapids: the famous Nile Cataracts. For centuries people trudged around these fatal waters until someone finally yelled, "Cataract, Smatteract. Hide the children and grab the paddles. We're going for it!"

The so-called Golden Age of Exploration was fueled by humankind's need for shortcuts, our lust for "Cities of Gold," and our refusal to bow before oceans, rivers, mountains, deserts, and frozen wastelands as altars of the impassable. But the exploration itself was often carried out by folks with a **crazy** streak wide as the Euphrates in flood. Places like the Nile Cataracts have always drawn out this crazy streak in both maniacs and the competent few, leading them into encounters with the unknown.

When the earth's great continents were first explored by outsiders, many followed rivers. As the world became increasingly photographed, mapped, and written about, only the most remote and treacherous rivers remained unexplored. For someone exploring such rivers, the hankering to see around the next bend was not enough—if they wanted to stay alive. A shift in psychology, skill, and equipment was required. Though still essential, a spirit of adventure—along with the required boldness—had to be matched with polished skill in wild water.

Enter the modern river explorers—super fit and stark-raving bold, with thousands of miles of big water under their paddles—commanding Kevlar dories, carbon-fiber canoes, self-bailing rafts, and roto-molded plastic kayaks. The goal shifted from exploration in a generic sense to the brave and sometimes lethal sport of seeing just how treacherous was the water a person could possibly survive.

Thus has run the evolution of river exploration—from using rivers as means of transport, to avenues of general exploration, to venues for adventure sport. This collection of stories draws from all these experiences but accents titanic rapids. We've also included a handful of accounts that fall under the category of "clearly mad". Such ventures are not river "trips" in any conventional sense. Some involve descending no-exit canyons through which flow stretches of suicidal whitewater impossible to run in any craft. A team enters the river canyon at point A with the hopes of emerging, alive, at point B. The intention is to run as much river as possible, but often such ventures turn into survival epics involving grueling portages over terrain so grave that one slip brings the curtain down. When the river flows through more open terrain, the most wicked rapids are attempted with friends stationed on shore with throw bags and ropes to haul out folk regurgitating in holes or boils. Only pipe-dreamers expect not to be pitched from kayak or raft at least once during the course of an "impossible" stretch.

This sounds like outrageous fun—at least to those with a weakness for adrenaline. But as with all adventure sports, there's a downside. For example, several days ago I went biking with two friends, both accomplished adventure racers. One mentioned a kayaking accident that had happened recently, when a woman got swamped in a big recycling hole on the American River—and was recycled for two days before her corpse washed free. Most modern river stories are told with a refreshing sense of levity. But believe it: The big water is for keeps. Several of the stories in this collection attest to this fact.

Several of the tales in the following pages can also be characterized as oddball, daredevil pieces simply because dangerous natural phenomena—be they big rocks, big waves, or big rivers—have always tempted kooks and blockheads, and their stories are often as entertaining as the best efforts of "serious" adventurers. In fact, many insist that even the most eminent adventurers are equal parts fool and hero. Sir Francis Drake said that only a fool can conquer the impossible because only a fool would ever try. I believe this foolishness is nothing more than childish restlessness and curiosity channeled through a skilled and unsettled adult. Whatever the case, a sense of fun, wonder, and self-discovery seems always present in these stories, even when the boat flips and people claw to shore while puking up half the river.

Many river trips involve campfires, where people have always entertained themselves with tales of derring-do, romancing the odd fact for effect. River running shares in this tradition, adding a refreshing flavor of self-deprecation absent in most other adventure chronicles. Regardless of their gravity, river stories are almost always infused with a spirit of fun and irreverence. But again, the cutting edge of river running is serious business. It's a business ventured through personal choice. In this sense, all of these stories, both hilarious and grave, are expressions of freedom and the pursuit of experiences that make people feel alive in novel ways. I trust this book conveys the sense of wonder and intensity the writers experienced while riding the "liquid locomotive."

Mutiny on the Yangtze

Michael McRae

D anger dogs the person who fights for dominion over people and over nature. When this hostile, tyrannical part of us pushes us to conquer things with a vengeance, as if these"things" have somehow betrayed us, we violate others' sprits as well as our own. "Mutiny on the Yangtze" suggests that expedition leader Ken Warren was just such a person, a would-be Hannibal torn by the mutiny within. Warren's methods—including the most alarming ones, such as refusing to scout lethal rapids—seem daft and delusional, but perhaps less so than the people who followed Warren in the first instance. When things finally boil over and Warren refuses to face his troops, and later, when he abandons the entire expedition, we understand that whatever else Ken Warren might have been, he was certainly a lost soul. Note how his masquerading caused a sort of enchantment, broken only by some of the biggest whitewater ever rafted (the biggest, some claim). Radical adventure challenges force people to face the truth, and this truth will eventually wash out all pretense and illusion, no matter how strong the original beliefs. Also note that after "lashing the four boats together into an unorthodox diamond-shaped barge, thirty-six feet long and twenty-four feet wide" and bashing through truly monstrous water, Warren spent two days trying to shame and badger his team to carry on. But the enchantment was broken. Warren's team could finally think for themselves, and none were hankering to follow him into the next world.

The upper Yangtze is a river so great and fearsome that only the world's best stand a fighting chance to succeed. Warren's insistence on maintaining absolute control over all aspects of his team's lives precluded world-class talent from ever joining him: Highly skilled boatmen attain expertise through

1

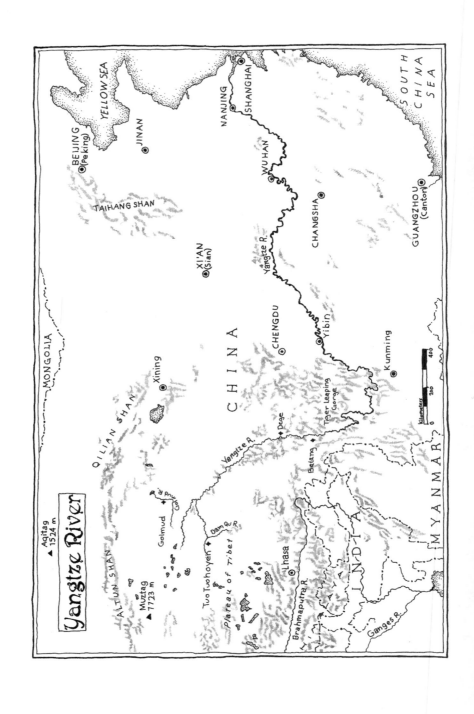

developing self-judgment, not by surrendering it to a despot. Today, as the Chinese mainland continues to open up, we can expect another team to eventually challenge the mighty upper Yangtze. Only then will we know what Warren and company were able to accomplish and what place the Yangtze will take in whitewater lore.

‡　‡　‡

In 1976 a group of Chinese explorers claimed to have discovered the source of the Yangtze River. The world's third longest river, they said, is born on the Qinghai Plateau in western China, a place so high and desolate that, according to legend, it is inhabited by savages who eat hair and drink blood. The expedition had followed the Tuotuohe River, a main tributary of the Yangtze, to the foot of Geladandong, a 21,730-foot peak near the Tibetan border. There, the team said, emerging as a trickle from beneath a glacier, the Yangtze begins its journey to the East China Sea, 3,900 miles away. Only the Amazon and the Nile are longer. Formally, the river is named "Chang Jiang," or the "Long River," but so great is its power that many Chinese call it simply "Jiang,"— "the River."

The year of this discovery, Ken Warren, a tall, swaggering river outfitter and hunting guide from Portland, Oregon, traveled to the source of the Ganges River, in India, and made a first descent of the Bhagirathi, its western arm. He returned to the river in 1977 to run its raging eastern fork, the Alaknanda, accompanied this time by actor Robert Duvall and a TV crew. Two of the expedition's three boats were damaged, but Warren's raft, *What's Next,* survived intact. At the take-out a producer asked Warren, "Well, Ken, what *is* next?" Warren thought for a moment and then turned to gesture at the Himalayas. "The last great unrun river in the world is on the other side of those mountains," he said. "I will run the Yangtze."

This was no idle boast. Indeed, for the next nine years, the goal would be all consuming. Some would call it obsession, saying Warren's pilgrimage to the sacred Ganges had not purified him but only sharpened his hunger for fame and fortune. In any case, Warren's lust for the Yangtze outlasted the years of tribulation he and his wife, Jan, had endured trying to get there. In the spring of 1985 the couple finally received permission to run the river and announced the 1986 Sino-U.S. Upper Yangtze River Expedition.

Scores of people would be swept into the current of Ken and Jan

Warren's lives. One was David Shippee, a young photographer from Boise, Idaho, with ambitions of his own. On July 21, 1986, with TV cameras rolling, the Warrens knelt at the edge of the Yangtze's headwaters and prayed, "Beautiful Yangtze . . . we ask you to take care of us and we promise you no harm." Eight weeks and 1,200 hard river miles later, their prayers had gone unanswered. Wracked by death and mutiny—and, according to several members, tainted by impure motives—the expedition disintegrated, 800 miles short of its goal. And although the Warrens would come home claiming success, few saw it that way, because David Shippee did not come home at all.

In another time, Ken Warren might have been a frontier-town heavy or a backwoods trapper with a name like Leatherstocking Johnson. Warren is a natural for television—six feet four inches tall (six-six in his cowboy boots), with the rugged good looks and blunt manner of a John Wayne. He is sixty but looks fifty. Apart from his sheer bulk (he normally carries 220 pounds), his silver hair is his most striking feature. He wears it swept back, like the spray off the bow of a raft, and it is always impeccably combed. His hands are the size of porterhouse steaks and his grip speaks of years at the oars. When upset or irritated, he curses like a sailor and his resonant voice booms. He is an intimidator.

Warren is opinionated and minces few words. He is a white-bread conservative who once fired off a letter of support to Ronald Reagan on the Iran-Contra arms deal. His heroes are Theodore Roosevelt and test pilot Chuck Yeager: Roosevelt for his dare-to-be-great philosophy, Yeager for his independence and "balls-to-the-wall" approach to life. He also admires them as hunters. "I relate to hunting," he says, "and to men who hunt." A point of pride is that he had never missed a big-game hunting season in twenty-five years until the Yangtze expedition disrupted his life. His study at home, on ten acres outside Portland, is a monument to manliness. A deerskin is draped over the office chair, and his gun rack contains a veritable arsenal: a stainless-steel .44 Magnum, several high-powered rifles and shotguns, an eighteen-inch Bowie knife, and a mean-looking blade that, Warren says, the Gurkhas used to slit the throats of sleeping Argentine troops in the Falklands. The guns are always loaded.

It was actually Warren's love of hunting that introduced him to rafting. In 1948 he bought a one-man navy survival raft to use duck hunting. It wasn't until 1975 that he gave up his job as a broker of drugs and vitamins and went into guiding full time. The next year he found himself on the Ganges, working for Lute Jerstad, one of the first Americans to scale Mount Everest and now a Portland adventure-travel operator. Two years later, with his own business established, Warren met his current wife on the Rogue River. He does not recall paying much attention to her, but she saw him as a "big, bronze river man." At the end of the trip, Warren gave the woman his customary kiss and she saw stars. "I had to sit down," says Jan, "and later I asked him for a second kiss. It seemed like we became one person." Both of them were married at the time—Warren for thirty-four years, she for twelve—and Warren was twenty years her senior, but their romance endured. On July 4, 1982, the two were married on the Snake River.

Sometime during their long courtship, Jan Warren decided that the Yangtze would be the jewel in her river man's crown. "I thought that, for him, it would be the pedestal of his career," she says, meaning "pinnacle." "I was totally in love with him, totally committed to doing this for him." Both speak of their single-mindedness once they have set a goal, but her tenacity may be greater even than his. It was she, in fact, who kept him from giving up his dream after five frustrating and very costly years of dealing with that most inscrutable of Asians, the Chinese bureaucrat.

By 1983, Warren claims, he had invested about $500,000 in the Yangtze project. That year he secured the coveted permit after paying $150,000 to a well-connected Hong Kong film producer acting as intermediary. In the fall, amid much fanfare, Warren's team of fourteen flew to China with six tons of gear. No one showed up to meet them at the airport. The Warrens had confirmation telexes from Peking officials, but no one had sought the permission of the provincial authorities. The team sat in Chengdu, the capital of the Sichuan province, for twenty-eight days, running up an astronomical hotel bill and watching winter slowly settle on the high country. By the time they cleared things up, their "weather window" had closed, and the Warrens limped home, leaving their gear in Hong Kong.

"The Chinese felt very bad about 1983," says Warren. But evidently not bad enough: By the following year the permit fee had risen to $1 million. Warren blames Japanese television, which had run up the bidding to $700,000, yet another likely factor was China's awareness of its new popularity. Long closed to foreigners, the interior was a special plum and the Chinese knew it. Warren was equally aware of the lucrative possibilities in establishing a new branch of Ken Warren

Outdoors, as he had done in India after running the Ganges. He countered with an offer of a joint Sino-U.S. expedition, and the deal was struck at $700,000.

In the spring of 1985 three Chinese athletes—Chu Siming, Zhang Jiyue, and Xu Ju Sheng—moved into Warren's basement apartment in Portland and began training on the rivers of the Northwest as oarsmen for the expedition. It was a natural story, and it caught the interest of many editors, including those at *USA Today*, the flagship of the Gannett newspaper chain. They sent a writer from Washington, D.C., Larry Jolidon, and for a photographer they turned to *The Idaho Statesman*, the Gannett paper closest to Portland. The logical choice there was David Shippee, an eager, creative young photographer with a keen interest in the outdoors.

For Shippee, the Yangtze expedition seemed like a dream trip. Warren had sold first rights to the story to *National Geographic;* and Shippee, though only three years out of journalism school, was, according to a colleague at the *Statesman,* "a guy with a plan . . . [who] was going somewhere." After shooting the feature on the Chinese athletes, Shippee had stayed on to raft the Owyhee River, where he impressed Warren with his energy and enthusiasm. A year later, when Warren invited him to be the primary expedition photographer, Shippee jumped at the offer.

Driving to Portland later that spring for a follow-up interview, Shippee discussed the dangers of the expedition with his wife, Margit. The couple had known each other since junior high school in St. Paul, Minnesota, and had married at about the same time as the Warrens. They also talked about Warren's "difficult" personality, Margit Shippee recalls, but Shippee decided he could deal with that. In Portland, Shippee spent a full morning with Warren and came away reassured. Warren seemed in command of all the details, right down to the helicopter support. "The helicopter especially made him feel better, and me feel better, too," she says. What the two of them did not know, however, was how haphazardly the expedition was coming together.

Things had gone from bad to worse for the Warrens in 1985. Already strained financially, they had learned in July that their film deal had collapsed. Warren then had to borrow $5,000 to fly to Peking to ask for an extension on the agreement. The Chinese gave him until January 1, 1986. By Christmas there was still no backing, and the Warrens grew desperate. "We were sitting here," says Warren, "without any heating oil in the tank, six months behind on the mortgage, and I was cutting down limbs for firewood." Jan continues: "There was no insurance on the car, no registration, bald tires, and the electricity and phone had been shut off. We needed money for bread and milk. We went into Taylor's [her son's] room and emptied the bank and collected two dollars and eighty cents."

Warren was ready to quit. As the deadline crept up, he recalls thinking, "Here I am close to sixty, sinking all my money into this. I don't need to be the first one to run the Yangtze." But Jan Warren would not relent, and in February, just after the couple had filed to reorganize their business to protect them from creditors, the Chinese responded favorably to the Warrens' proposal to reduce the permit fee to $325,000. The following month a television deal dropped out of the sky, with backing from Mutual of Omaha and a film crew assembled by John Wilcox, former producer of ABC Sports's "The American Sportsman," which had carried Warren's Ganges show. The couple then had three months to pull the expedition together. "An awesome task," says Warren.

Warren had hoped to screen applicants by taking them on shake-down trips, but there was no time for that. His only holdover oarsman from 1983 was Ron Mattson, a whitewater rowing-frame manufacturer built like a deep freezer (five foot ten, 205 pounds, sixteen-inch biceps). Mattson had rowed more than a hundred rivers, but no other boatman on the team came close to matching those qualifications. Bill Atwood and Toby Sprinkle were longtime Ken Warren Outdoors employees whom the Warrens regarded as family. (Atwood had once proposed to Warren's daughter and called him Dad; Sprinkle, either willingly or under orders, pampered Warren on float trips to the point of serving him coffee in bed.) Backup boatman Gary Peebles, a thirty-nine-year-old biology teacher and former river guide from Long Beach, California, was chosen only because he'd given the Warrens $2,000 when things were at their grimmest. "We were very touched by that," says Warren, "and we are very, very loyal people." At the same time, Warren refers to Peebles as "the weakest link." The three Chinese were, of course, novices.

Among the completely unknown quantities on the trip were Ancil Nance and Dr. David Gray. Nance was a freelance photographer and climber from Portland. He showed up one day to photograph the Warrens organizing their gear, and the next thing he knew he was the expedition's rock climber—handy to have along if they became stranded in one of the Yangtze's deep canyons. Nance had no rafting experience, but the Warrens liked his spunk.

Gray learned of the trip from an equipment manufacturer whom the Warrens had solicited for free gear. He had never been on such an expedition, and his only direct experience with high-altitude medicine was as a client on adventure-travel trips. But he was chief of emergency medicine at a Texas hospital, and perhaps more importantly, he supplied a $7,000 medical kit for free.

In retrospect it might seem foolhardy that Warren gambled so much on such an unproven team. But his reputation, at least among certain big-water boatmen, is as a hell-for-leather, damn-the-suckholes authoritarian. John Yost of Sobek Expeditions, a competitor for the Yangtze permit, says that in 1985 he considered trying to get a Sobek boatman on the Warren expedition. But after a day with Warren, he abandoned the idea. "His rules of the river were frightening," says Yost. "He had absolute authority. Guides were to follow his orders and could not run rapids the way they felt they should. And he wasn't into scouting rapids." Warren himself pooh-poohs scouting: "You stop and look at some things, and you won't run it. If you run it, you make it."

Yost calls Warren's plan to cover fifty river miles a day "absurd. On exploratory trips we count on ten miles a day. On the Indus in 1979 there were dawn-to-dusk days when we covered only two kilometers [because of portaging]." Yet Warren was so certain of his itinerary that, when he signed his film contract, he thought he was agreeing to a $25,000 penalty if he didn't complete the trip—or at least make a concerted effort to complete it—before his permit expired on September 15. John Wilcox says the contract required Warren only to give the river his best shot, nothing more.

Warren's plan was wildly ambitious, particularly in view of the time-consuming logistics of making a documentary. In mid-July the team was to put in at the source, at about 18,000 feet, and paddle the first 200 miles of shallow headwaters in inflatable kayaks. At Tuotuohoyen, their 14,500-foot base camp, they would switch to 18-foot rafts and begin the 1,700-mile descent to the city of Yibin, the point at which the Yangtze becomes navigable by conventional craft.

Little was known of the river's upper reaches, but it was certain that its character would change sharply below Tuotuohoyen. Tributaries add to its volume, and when it spills off the eastern edge of the Tibetan highlands, its force becomes huge. Lower down, at Tiger Leaping Gorge, one of the world's deepest chasms, it squeezes into a ninety-foot channel bounded by sheer rock walls rising thousands of feet. Boiling down this chute, the river drops 600 feet in ten miles. There are seven major drops, one of which plunges 100 feet in 150 yards. By the time the team reached Yibin, at 1,000 feet above sea level, they would have descended 17,000 feet.

All this in fifty days. As Shippee wrote in a preview story for the *Statesman*, it would be "no mean feat." Accompanying the article was a picture of Shippee, wearing his exuberant, gap-toothed smile, and a headline that read, "Adventure of a Lifetime."

By the time the team of twenty-nine, including the film crew, arrived in Hong Kong, fracture lines had already begun to show. The Warrens recite a litany of transgressions: Peebles arrived "flabby [and] totally out of shape"; Gray had left a medical kit at their house and had to make a "frantic" trip back from the airport to retrieve it; on the flight over, Sprinkle drank until he "totally passed out." Gray, in particular, was becoming "a problem," and the Warrens began taking note of his sins. For the TV news conference at the airport hotel in China, Jan Warren wore a hard and disturbed look and glared at Gray. "All he wanted to do was go shopping," she says. She and Warren began referring to him as their "resident jerk."

There followed the first of many "one-on-one" evaluations that would be held over the next several weeks. Gray was called to the couple's hotel room to face them. "Depending on how you react to this," Warren began, "will decide whether you go on this trip or not." Then his wife lit into Gray. He was lazy, she railed, and scatterbrained—a "playboy." The diatribe was so vicious that Warren took pity and interceded. Gray was stupefied. "After a while," he says, "I realized they were looking for a show of humility," which they got. A fragile peace was formed, but the Warrens held trump: If he did not "shape up," they would replace him with a Hong Kong doctor anxious to be on the trip.

On July 5 the team arrived in Canton with ten tons of gear. At a banquet Warren learned that the helicopter support he'd been counting on had fallen through. Worse, he was told that a number of Chinese teams were already on the river. "They wanted to beat the Yankees," he says, "and that blew us away, because we'd made it a Sino-U.S. thing." In fact, 3,100 university students from Sichuan province had petitioned the government to, as cameraman Edgar Boyles puts it, "not give our river away to these people."

Boyles believes that the Warrens were oblivious to "such strong resentments." Sensitive or not, they did know that the race for the Yangtze had become a *cause celebre*. In 1985 a thirty-four-year-old student and photographer, Yao Maoshu, had asked to join the team. The Warrens turned him down, reasoning that they already had three Chinese. Maoshu mounted a solo attempt, disappeared on the river after 600 miles, and became a national hero. Among the six teams ahead of the Warrens was the Chang Jiang Scientific Expedition, a forty-five-man crew of scientists, sportsmen, and journalists, many of them from the fallen hero's home province of Sichuan. They were ill experienced and poorly equipped (Warren describes them as a "zealous, kamikaze team") but far better off than certain others who were paddling toy rafts and running on pure adrenaline.

Though Warren gave the Chinese scant hope of beating him, he was distressed. How would this affect his film deal? After "considerable thought" he rationalized that it was China's river and that his team would be the first Westerners to descend it.

The team flew to Golmud, a windy dust pit at 10,000 feet, and after two days of acclimatizing they pushed on by bus to the Tuotuohoyen base camp, a day ahead of schedule. That night, almost everyone suffered from the quick elevation gain to 14,500 feet, especially Mattson, who could not stop vomiting. Shippee had a blinding headache and "saw a white ball, like the sun" each time he inhaled and blinked. The next day the crew felt so bad they called it "Black Friday." They made camp on a grassy hill next to the river, stopping frequently in the thin air to sit and survey their surroundings. The river was hardly the mighty Yangtze of everyone's imagination; indeed, it was a disappointment. A maze of shallow channels meandered across the barren tundra, leading the eye downstream to two 7,000-meter peaks in the distance. The low hills around camp reminded Shippee of Idaho, only drier and more desolate. Dust rose with each footstep, and the ravens flying over camp, he wrote in his journal, made a "dry, whooshing sound."

In the evening, a cold rain swept over the highlands. Shippee retired to his tent early and stayed up to alter the size thirty-six wool pants he had been issued. With his thirty-inch waist, they made him look like a willow in a gunnysack. At 2:00 A.M. he lay awake listening to his heart pounding and noticed a slight rattling in his lungs when he exhaled. By sunrise, something told him this was not asthma, as he'd suspected, but something far worse.

"This morning I thought I might die of pneumonia," Shippee would write in his journal. After breakfast he was so weak he had to lie down. He was seeing spots and could not think straight, and his lips and fingernails were cyanotic—blue from lack of oxygen—a symptom that everyone was showing to some degree. Warren was pressing the team to organize their gear for the trip to the source, but Shippee was unable to work. He drifted away from camp and sat alone. Barbara Ries, a *USA Today* photographer assigned to the road team, followed him. "I wanted to know how he felt," she says. "He started to cry and said, 'I'm really scared. I've had pneumonia before, and this is really painful. It feels like a weight on my chest.' I asked why he had not told anyone. He said he was afraid Ken would get mad at him for not pulling his weight."

Though Shippee was worried about being sent home, Ries convinced him to see Gray, who detected crinkling sounds, called "rales," in one of Shippee's lungs. "This feels different from pneumonia," said Shippee. "I thought I should go down." Gray told him, "Okay, you're out of here." Gray thought Shippee had pneumonia, but he was also aware of the similarity between it and high-altitude pulmonary edema, a potentially fatal fluid buildup in the lungs. The only known cure for it is to descend to lower elevation.

Warren went along with the decision but felt cut out. He was the ultimate authority, and he was depending on Shippee. He also believed the doctor to be "an alarmist," according to Gray. Early on, Warren had vetoed his request to erect a medical tent, claiming it would give people an excuse not to work. "Sometimes," says Warren, "doctors can create more fear and paranoia on a trip than the good they do because they get people running to them." He himself was suffering from a severe bout of what he calls "the Preparation H affliction" and had a wracking cough, but he was determined to set an example. "I feel like shit, too," he had told Ries, "but we have to put mind over matter."

Within hours, Shippee found himself rumbling down to Golmud with a Chinese driver, tremendously disappointed that he had missed the "most exciting part of the expedition." That night, lying in a cell-like room at the government guesthouse, he reflected in his journal: "In Ken's eyes I am the real pansy of the bunch. . . ."

"Basically you have two choices," Jan Warren's note began. Shippee read it again, growing angrier and more despairing. "The camera people have made it clear that you are not their problem, and they have no room for you. Based on how you're feeling you can return to base camp and await our arrival or head straight for home."

The camera crew had delivered the note to him the previous

evening, his second in Golmud. They had been his main hope, his escape. He had planned to drive with them down to Yushu, photograph a religious festival there, and then meet the expedition at a resupply point on the river near town. Now, back in his room, he weighed his options and read again the lines that galled him most: "You are not free to rome (sic) around China, and we would be greatly upset to hear about it. Already this has been an added expense." He turned to his journal and wrote hotly, "I don't plan to 'ROME' anywhere in the near future, except possibly back up to base camp."

Jan Warren was right about one thing: Shippee couldn't stay in Golmud for the next three weeks waiting for the resupply convoy. The guesthouse was a stark, surreal place, and he was utterly lonely. The big breakfasts of fried eggs, hearty bread, and sweet peach jam only reminded him of home. A man vomiting noisily in the next room kept him up his first night. On the second, he awoke with a start to a figure looming over him: It was only the mayor, checking on his condition. But his chief worry was money. He had spent $110 on phone calls to his wife—"worth every penny"—and calculated that he could pay his hotel bill and still have just enough for the bus fare back to base camp.

As for his health, it was much improved by the antibiotics he was taking. He decided to return and prove he was not a pansy.

When Shippee arrived at Tuotuohoyen, he was surprised to find that Toby Sprinkle had refused to go to the source. A heavy smoker, Sprinkle was suffering from a persistent cough and was spitting up blood. With the river barely two feet deep at camp and presumably shallower above, Sprinkle had also foreseen 200 miles of certain misery in the inflatable kayaks, which he thought were ridiculous. In the ensuing days, he and Shippee discussed Warren's low-water folly as they prepared the rafts for the source team's arrival and fought the dreadful boredom. Shippee considered starting an exercise regimen to beat the monotony.

Upriver, the ordeal was as bad as Sprinkle had predicted. The river had given the team a brief but wild ride as they spilled out of the shale-and-ice-strewn crater around the source, but then it slackened in pace and volume and divided into a hundred channels that branched out across the austere, flat tundra. The inflatables, some loaded with eighty-four-quart coolers, bottomed repeatedly. Head winds blew the boats backward. Temperatures plunged to ten degrees, and the morning fog coated the moors with ice.

Jan Warren, paddling Sprinkle's kayak, was having a difficult time. At base camp Warren had debated whether she should come at all. "It was possible it would be too difficult physically," he later wrote in a fifty-nine-page manuscript sent to several newspapers, "and I knew that her menstrual period, due in ten days, could affect her difficult task dramatically." In the end, he included her, hoping that her dedication would "rub off on other team members whom I was having concerns about"—meaning mainly Gray.

The Warrens were irked by Gray's "laziness" and "me-me-me attitude." They accuse him of rarely washing dishes or pumping water through the purifiers, as if he were a paying customer on a commercial float trip. They cite evidence that the others felt similarly: The first night out, the Warrens say, everyone stood watching as Gray struggled alone to erect his flapping tent. They also fault Gray for not bringing enough bandages or ointment to dress people's hands. Warren, examining his painful fingers one day, muttered loud enough for Gray to hear, "I wish we had a fucking doctor with us." Another time, when Gray paddled past Warren and into the lead, Warren growled, "So what are you, the fucking leader now?" It was an inviolable law that Warren be in the lead. "That's the goddamn rule of the river, period!" says Warren. "Our rule on every trip is that you don't get out in front of the leader, because he knows better what the hell's coming up."

The final straw came on the last, long day, when Gray refused to take the cooler from Jan Warren's kayak. The immense ice chest acted as a sail in the head winds and barely left room for her in the cockpit. Warren, in a rage, lashed the cooler to his own boat and paddled off like a madman. "I was livid!" he fumes. "I just busted my butt getting into Tuotuohoyen that night." Somewhere out on the tundra that day, paddling alone ahead of the others, he resolved to replace Gray and sack Peebles, whom he deemed physically and mentally unfit for the challenges below base camp.

The next day, back at Tuotuohoyen, Warren called for more one-on-one meetings. Chairs were set up away from camp, and there he held court. "Everyone got raked over the coals before they received any praise," noted Shippee, who eavesdropped from his tent while organizing gear for the departure in two days. Warren savaged Gray, even though he knew he was stuck with him. It would have taken a week for his replacement to arrive, and the film crew's contract stipulated that a doctor be present at all times. Gray would remain for now, but Warren placed him on "probation": If he didn't behave himself, he'd be off the team by Yushu.

The Warrens insist that the probation had nothing to do with Gray's medical decisions, but rather with his failure to pitch in with camp chores. Shippee's journal tells a different story, colored no doubt by Gray's own interpretation (the two had been roommates in Hong Kong, and Shippee referred to him as Dr. Dave): "Gray was put on probation until we got to Yushu. Ken is still furious over Gray's decision to send me down the mountain when I had pneumonia. Ken told me from now on he will make the final decisions concerning the treatment of sickness because he has more experience than Dr. Gray."

The rift between the Warrens and their doctor was now complete, and David Shippee was caught somewhere in the middle.

By July 31 the Tuotuohe had risen slightly but was still barely deep enough to float the seven heavy rafts that would replace the kayaks. After a grand bon voyage celebration, staged by the villagers of Tuotuohoyen, the team boarded their rafts and drifted slowly into the unknown. The next stop was Yushu, 550 miles away.

There had been only one casualty of the one-on-one meetings: Larry Jolidon, the USA Today reporter who covered Warren in 1985. Warren and Jolidon were to have collaborated on a book but had an acrimonious falling-out over how much money Jolidon would receive. Another sticking point, claims Jolidon, was Warren's insistence on doctoring up news dispatches about the expedition. The rest of the crew survived the cut: Peebles had persuaded Warren to keep him on, and Shippee, insisting he was fully recovered, had "stunned" the Warrens with his drive and energy. "You could not put a plate down that he would not be there to wash it," says Jan. Gray deemed him so healthy that he never bothered to put a stethoscope to his chest, and Warren recalls Shippee's "joy and enthusiasm" at being allowed on the trip: "His final words [in the one-on-one meeting] were, 'Ken, no one will outwork me. I promise you that.'"

Each time Warren's heavy raft dragged bottom, Shippee vaulted out to help. He and Dan Dominy, film director for the river crew, pulled "like Clydesdales" across sand bars fifty yards wide, while Warren remained aboard (in order, he explains, to spin the raft off the obstruction with his oars). Shippee was bitterly cold but welcomed the exertion of pulling. At least it warmed him.

The rafts were laden with tons of gear and camera equipment. This was anything but a lean expedition. Warren had approached some 200 companies for sponsorship and many had obliged him. In sorting food before the departure, Shippee had come across about seventy-five pounds of unnecessary spices, including enough monosodium glutamate "to poison the Chinese army." The resupply convoy had such quantities of promotional equipment and clothing that the film crew would later make up goodwill bags for the Tibetans, who were facing the onset of winter. "Warren viewed this expedition in the nineteenth-century tradition of throwing a lot of men and material at it: conquest, and laurels for the victor," says Boyles, an advocate of fast-and-light expeditions. "There is something aesthetic and pure about paring everything down to just what you need. On this trip it was just the feeling of excess. . . . We had enormous crates of stuff we never used. They did not ever sit down and say, 'What can we use?' but 'What can we get?'"

Shippee, despite all the free clothing, was suffering. In a wet snow-storm and driving wind the second day, he wrote, "the cold cut through my neoprene booties, two pairs of socks, my dry suit, jeans and long-underwear top, and thick float coat. The worst part of the day was when Ken took a three-hour jaunt to the right, when he should have gone left. . . . A shallow river is not hard to read, but an old man of the sea is tough to order around." That night he told Gray, "I'm hurtin'." His rales were back.

It happened very fast after that. The next night Shippee's lungs were gurgling, his lips blue. Gray was alarmed. He says that at first Warren scoffed, "It's in his mind," but then agreed to radio for a helicopter. Someone had forgotten the radio's antenna, and a wire one was improvised. Only Russian could be heard. By 11:00 P.M., the drugs Gray prescribed to dry out Shippee's lungs had lost their effectiveness. Lying in a candlelit tent, with an intravenous saline solution hanging above him, Shippee looked up at Gray and said, "I feel funny."

"Do you feel like you're going to die?" asked Gray.

"Yeah," replied Shippee.

Gray needed no further explanation. "It's something you and I don't get to understand," he says.

In the morning, August 3, Shippee needed help to get to Bill Atwood's raft. All day he lay delirious under a tarpaulin, thinking he was in Minnesota. That night, Warren was very concerned and brought hot soup and his heavy survival suit. He got on the radio, this time with the antenna suspended from a kite. "Breaker, breaker. Mayday,

mayday," Warren called. "This is the Sino-American Yangtze Expedition." There was no answer. At 11:24 P.M., Shippee slipped away.

They buried David Shippee on a cold morning, in a grave marked by a lone oar, facing south toward the sun. Warren quoted Theodore Roosevelt, from a passage he keeps framed on his office wall: "The credit belongs to the man who is actually in the arena, whose face is marred by dust and sweat and blood; who . . . at the best knows in the end the triumph of achievement and who at the worst, if he fails, at least fails while daring greatly."

During Shippee's final hours Warren had remained in his own tent, pitched away from the others' on a knoll. For the mourners this became a symbol of Warren's callousness, and several of them considered his effort on the radio to have been superficial. "He was lying in his sleeping bag," says Peebles.

It was Warren's custom to retire to his tent early, but even his recollection of the night points to a remarkable insensitivity. "Toby came in blubbering, 'Dave is dead, Dave is dead,'" he recalls. "I got him shook up and calmed down [Warren reportedly said, "What are you crying for, Toby? People die on expeditions all the time. You could be next."], and then in comes Gray, puts his head on my shoulder, crying, 'I lost Dave, I lost Dave, I lost Dave.'" Warren consoled Gray and reassured him that nothing else could have been done, yet secretly each blamed the other.

Shippee's sudden passing created, says Warren, "a fear you could cut with a knife." But it also became a kind of lens that focused the team's simmering discontent on Warren's authoritarianism and his "divide-and-conquer" leadership, as Peebles termed it.

Floating down to Yushu through a strange and wonderful landscape, each member was left to his own thoughts. Warren was overcome with the passing scenery. In a canyon that cut through "the very peaks of the 18,000-foot mountains," black bears with manes of golden fur lumbered through strange geologic formations. "It was as if we were floating through the top of the world," he marveled in his journal. Farther downstream, the rafts drifted past enormous hills of golden sand set against a backdrop of rugged peaks. Bald eagles, ospreys, and condors flew overhead, and ducks and geese paddled about near the banks. Soon camps of nomadic sheepherders began to appear, and fresh mutton became a welcome addition to the team's diet. At villages, flocks of Tibetans ran to meet them, bringing gifts of bread, yak butter, and yogurt. In exchange, the team passed out Frisbees or yo-yos or empty tin cans. With each passing day, the signs of civilization increased. Prayer flags fluttered from ropes suspended over the river, and the banks were lined with stones chiseled with religious inscriptions.

Tributaries had swelled the river's size, but there was no whitewater to speak of. To pass the time, Gray and others read or listened to tapes. "That's a goddamn affront to Tibet and a desecration of the river," Warren fumed, and he imposed a "ban" on books and boom boxes ("I hate that jive shit"). There was a grudging obedience, but the ban was another irritant in the festering rebellion.

Gray and Peebles, who were tentmates and rafted together, considered quitting the trip. But as they neared Yushu they realized that Gray's position might give him some leverage. The two agreed that they had "quite a bit of power here." They planned to confront Warren and present their demands, but they underestimated the volatility of the situation.

Within minutes of arriving in Yushu, emotions reached critical mass. Warren told Jan of Shippee's death; she told him that several Chinese teams had lost men downstream. Rumors flew. Had six Chinese died? Or three? The river team huddled with the film crew by the rafts, while Warren went off to console his wife. Boatman Bill Atwood, who up to this point had been unusually quiet and brooding, announced flatly that he would not continue with Warren in charge. "Things were happening too fast," says Peebles. Adds Gray, "It was group therapy at its most acute, a huge decompression for everyone."

Feeling a new sense of solidarity, the team explored several options, but deposing Warren seemed the only way to preserve their unity. Ancil Nance, a neutral party, was sent to summon Warren, and Ron Mattson volunteered to be the mutineers' spokesman. He told Warren that the team would not support him as leader. Warren scoffed. "It was the most ludicrous thing I'd heard," he says, "and that was how I reacted." He turned on his heel and went straight to his tent, leaving Jan Warren in the lion's den.

Boyles, observing this scene, thought to himself, "Here is an expedition that's deteriorating right here on this beach, and it has yet to face one objective danger."

Warren had refused to face his men, says Jan, because he felt "backed into a corner. You have to understand that if you want to get somewhere with Ken you sit down man-to-man very quietly. When you start screaming at Ken Warren—and this is true in our personal relationship—he turns around and walks out." Warren's high school nickname was Mute, because of his shyness. "He has a shyness about him now that people misunderstand as ego," she says. "He just doesn't open up to people very much."

Warren wanted more one-on-one meetings but steadfastly refused to meet the group. In the morning he sent his wife to them, with a tape recorder, and the mutineers unloaded on the machine. After another round of individual sessions, four people packed their bags: Gray, Atwood, Sprinkle, and Peebles. Warren regretted losing only Sprinkle; he needed his rowing skills. As for the rest, he says, "at some point they would have to quit anyhow. They just did not have the guts."

Months later, after pondering what was really at the core of the dissolution, Gary Peebles found quite a different reason: "I felt it was because I did not want to be part of Ken Warren being famous. I did not think he deserved to be the first white man down the river."

In the end, he was not, though it wasn't for lack of effort. The expedition, leaner and more cohesive now, consisted of Warren, Nance, Mattson, four members of the film crew, and the three Chinese.

Below Yushu they drifted for a time through the landscape of mist-draped mountains, where ancient monasteries clung to the precipitous green slopes. And then the river seemed to fall off the edge of the world. Nance, who had never captained a raft before in his life, became a star, rowing solo through class V rapids that swallowed all but the snapping U.S. flag in his boat's flagpole. The rapids only grew larger and more ferocious. To prevent a capsize, the team lashed the four boats together into an unorthodox diamond-shaped barge, thirty-six feet long and twenty-four feet wide. But it filled with water and caromed out of control past holes large enough to swallow a steamer. Cameraman Paul Sharpe, paddling a kayak, scouted ahead in the steep-sided, twisting canyons and radioed instructions back upriver. Yet even that method failed them the final two days: The churning river would sweep the rafts past Sharpe on the morning's first rapids, and he would not see the rafters again until evening.

The thrashing became too much when one of the rafts ripped, capsized, then slipped under the other three. Sharpe hiked out to seek help for the dispirited team, wearing only a dry suit and carrying two cans of tuna fish and a water jug. Warren was certain that the worst whitewater was behind them; but despite two days of trying to rally his men and the film crew, he could not convince them to continue. Mattson and Nance were determined to scout the river first. While they were downstream, Warren decided to climb out of the canyon with film director Dan Dominy to get a look for himself. He loaded up an eighty-pound pack and, astonishingly, never returned. From a high vantage, Warren explains, he saw rapids he knew the team would not run and he simply decided to hike out for help. Dominy returned to camp with word that Warren had "lost touch."

During Warren's long march, what was left of the stranded team floated two distress signals downstream: a damaged raft and a life-sized, anatomically correct nude doll that had been brought along as a gag. The Chinese boaters were worried about the doll's propriety, so the team dressed her in a jacket and Speedo bathing briefs and sent her off. On her cheek, she bore the message "The Boys Need Help."

Meanwhile, Sharpe was having an arduous but magical time walking through the exquisite hill country. Warren, wearing a headband emblazoned with a tiger's eye, was often enchanted, too. But he had his low moments. Often he was set upon by dogs, and once by "Tibetan sleaze-balls," whom he took to be robbers. In the village he was baffled to find a raft that the river crew had sent down, stripped bare and stashed in a storehouse. After six days he got a ride to Batang, where his wife was waiting and worrying. On September 12, in a remarkable bit of timing, he arrived a half hour before the river crew straggled in with a rescue team that Jan Warren and Sharpe had sent out. Although several Chinese teams waiting downstream proposed joining forces with Warren to run Tiger Leaping Gorge—and despite Warren's willingness to continue—the ravaged expedition had neither the time nor the strength to go on. Several nights later, under a brilliant full moon, the three rafts that had been left upriver were spotted drifting, unmanned and ghostlike, past Batang.

Nowadays, Ken Warren rises early and slips into his den to pore over his big, blue hardback journals, replay his many tapes, work a little on his memoirs, and knock out a few more equipment testimonials. The epic that began on the Ganges River a decade ago is likely to define him for the rest of his days.

He had returned home full of pride and bluster but expecting to be ambushed by the press. "I've got no regrets," he told reporters at the Portland airport. "Next time, we will take bigger rafts and stronger people."

After leaving the expedition, the four mutineers had gone first to consular officials in China to deliver Shippee's personal effects and to be debriefed, then to the press in this country. Diplomatic cables to the State Department refer to Warren's "disorganized" and "reckless" leadership, and newspaper stories here have made him out to be a latter-day Robert Falcon Scott, the polar explorer who led his men to their death in Antarctica. Gray maintained that Shippee had died of altitude sickness and that a helicopter evacuation would have saved his life. He, Peebles, and Sprinkle visited Margit Shippee, and afterward she held Warren responsible for her husband's death—and said so in print. (The Warrens fault Gray, who they say withheld information from them about Shippee's condition.) Warren's lawyers threatened Peebles and Gray with libel suits; Margit Shippee's lawyers negotiated for Shippee's film, to which the Warrens claimed rights. (*National Geographic* decided against running the feature and released all photos and materials to the Warrens.) Jan Warren wept over being refused the opportunity to meet with Shippee's parents and widow. "We have no guilt feeling whatsoever about David Shippee," says Warren. "None. None."

Yet the couple's days have not been wholly consumed with damage control. They have traveled around Oregon making slide presentations to service clubs and small businesses. During the shows, Warren declaims about "the fear of the unknown": Those who could face it had stayed with him; those who couldn't had left. It was that simple. Shippee, in confronting the river despite his ill health, had been "the bravest of them all."

Having faced the unknown and lived, Warren tells his audience that he is undeterred by the Yangtze's power. The Chinese teams that preceded him, he says, leapfrogged past the river's worst sections. Last month, the Warrens planned to host a Chinese delegation in Oregon and begin the process anew. He plans to complete the unrun portion, from Dêgê to Yibin, sometime in 1988, or possibly even later this year.

In the end, David Shippee had been right: The expedition, in spite of having fallen short of its goal, had been no mean feat. But even Warren's doggedness could not hold it together. "Rivers and mountains have a distinct power of their own, something bigger than us," observes Edgar Boyles. "When people are more concerned with how to work the deal— look good on the film, make a lot from the book—something in the universe will kick back and say, 'You're not worthy.' Call it karma if you will."

Perhaps the three wild asses of the Qinghai Plateau understood this wisdom. "The asses looked as if they were laughing at us as we struggled through the shallow waters below them," Shippee had written in his final journal entry. Or perhaps the river had already told them of the joke it had in store for the Warrens. I quote from *China Daily:*

December 12, 1986. After drifting down the 6,380-kilometer Yangtze River, two Chinese expedition teams finally reached their destination, when they arrived at the mouth of the river near Shanghai last month.

One of the teams, the Luoyang Yangtze Expedition, was the first to complete such a trip and arrived in Shanghai on November 12 after a 175-day effort that left four team members dead [a total of nine Chinese rafters died on the river last year]. Another expedition, the Chang Jiang Scientific Expedition Team, was the first to combine scientific research with the feat and arrived several days later. They discovered, among other things, that the real source of the Yangtze is the Dam Qu River, not the Tuotuohe River as is commonly believed.

THE UPPER KINGS

Jeff Bennett

When a wild river explodes through a no-exit canyon, the distant echo sounds a siren call to those yearning for challenge and commitment with capital Cs. Any team paddling into such terrain is obliged to accept the river on its own terms, terms the team would likely reject outright if other choices existed. In this story, placed on the Upper Kings, grappling out of the canyon is not an option. Rescuers with throw bags cannot be stationed on shore because often there is no shore and, anyway, all hands are needed to negotiate the river. The rapids themselves are mean and unrelenting. As is true for all ferocious rivers, human life is tolerated at best and destroyed at worst. A team does not "conquer" such a river. The most one can hope for is, as Jeff Bennett says, a "tie." With a tie, nature is not diminished. Rather, both the river and the explorers are enhanced—the former in stature, the latter in experience.

‡   ‡   ‡

It was one of the most impressive sights a river runner could ever hope to see. Majestic granite cathedrals rising thousands of feet from the valley floor, carving cool gray patterns against a cobalt sky. Only an occasional cloud broke the pattern of geometric perfection, a silvery ripple in a sea of blue. It was a soothing, enchanting, almost hypnotic sight, having the depth and timeless clarity of an Ansel Adams photograph. It was damn near perfect. Damn near.

The flaw in this fantasy world of marbled grays and ink blues was that it existed only so long as I continued staring skyward. Up toward the birds. Birds and trail walkers. But down here, travel was all but forbidden. There was nothing soothing. Nothing enchanting, or even mildly hypnotic. Only the Upper Kings River. And mile after mile of class V whitewater.

From our bouldery perch above the mighty Kings, I turned to Mark Helmus, a veteran of prior Upper Kings expeditions, and asked what the next half mile of river had in store for us. "Well," he said, "this is a long stretch of class V rapids leading into the bad stuff."

Class V rapids. . . . *Then the bad stuff?!* I returned my concentration to the cliffs, envied the birds, and curled my toes deep into my sandals.

Somewhere above the wind I heard a faint knocking. Kind of like the ticktock of a grandfather clock, but faster. Tracing the sound I looked downward, only to see my knees beating the steady, staccato rhythm that had been dimpling my eardrums.

"Damn," I thought, "If my dog were doing that, I'd get it wormed!"

I started to sweat. That kind of feeling you get when you've got too much adrenaline and not enough action. Then I had an idea. "Mike. Where's Mike? If I strangle Mike I'll feel better."

Our descent had actually started one week earlier, around Mike Doyle's coffee table. It was June of 1987, and a lot of California rivers had already started drying up. A moderate drought was taking its toll. Not only on the rivers but on the rafters that depended on them for their sanity. We were looking for a fix. A thrill. Something that'd get us through the season, if it had to.

We started talking about putting together an Upper Kings trip. Maybe get some guides, a few boats, and see what happened. But it was still pretty early in the season for the Kings. Most boaters— sensible boaters anyway—wait until the deep snows of California's Sierra Mountains melt away, leaving just enough water to "safely" raft the Kings.

Mike was standing in the middle of the kitchen, pondering the Budweiser in his left hand, while listening intently to the phone in his right hand.

"I guess it's running about 2,700 cfs," Mike said, hanging up the phone.

"What's that mean?" I asked.

Mike looked at me and started to laugh. "I don't know. No one's ever rafted it that high."

I'd heard Mike laugh like that before. Usually before we were hammered in some ugly rapid. He's kind of funny that way. But I was sold.

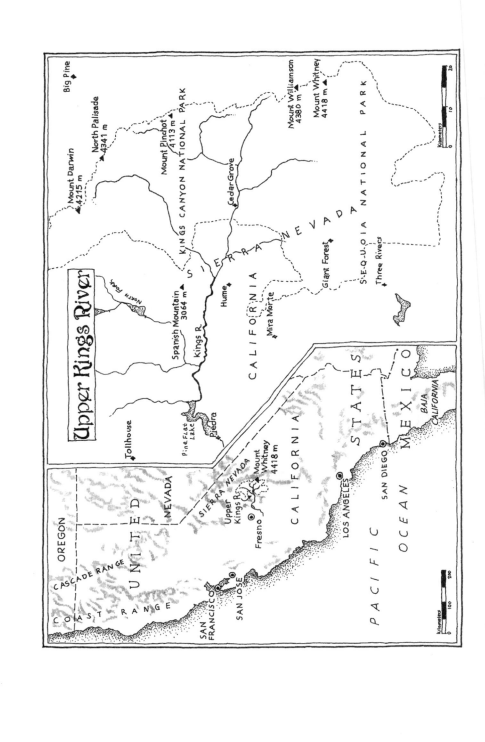

Upper Kings River

Big Pine

Mount Darwin
4215 m

North Palisade
4341 m

Mount Pinchot
4113 m

KINGS CANYON NATIONAL PARK

Cedar Grove

Mount Williamson
4380 m

Mount Whitney
4418 m

SIERRA NEVADA

SEQUOIA NATIONAL PARK

Giant Forest

Three Rivers

North Fork

Spanish Mountain
3064 m

Hume

Kings R.

CALIFORNIA

Mira Monte

Tollhouse

Pine Flat Lake

Piedra

OREGON

CASCADE RANGE

COAST RANGE

UNITED

NEVADA

STATES

SIERRA NEVADA

Mount Whitney
4418 m

Upper Kings R.

Fresno

SAN FRANCISCO

SAN JOSE

CALIFORNIA

LOS ANGELES

SAN DIEGO

MEXICO

BAJA CALIFORNIA

PACIFIC OCEAN

kilometers
0   100   200

kilometers
0   10   20

I'd been itching to do the Kings for a long time, and here was my chance. I canceled some guiding commitments, bought a new paddle, and got psyched.

Two days later we were banging our way across the mountains in a twelve-person van, cursing the heat, and talking about the river.

The Kings is class V from the moment you get in your car. The shuttle is one of the longest kidney-jarring mountain rides you'll ever make this side of Peru's Puacartambo River. Plus, there's no way to minimize the agony. Roll up the windows and the California heat will toast your brain. Leave the windows down and you'll be spitting dust balls before you're halfway to the put-in. I shut my eyes and dreamed of cool Colorado mountains, Alaskan winters, and beer commercials.

Arriving at Yucca Point, we unpacked our equipment and marveled at the spectacular canyon dropping away at our feet. Two thousand feet below us, and just upstream of our put-in, the Middle and South Forks of the Kings emerged from huge granite chasms to form the Upper Kings. It was a refreshing backdrop for the two-mile hike down to the river, carrying our rafts and all the gear for a two-day trip.

Actually, I lucked out during the hike in. I was sharing raft-carrying duties with Mike. Or, to be more precise, I was providing Mike with enough emotional support to get him—and the raft—to the bottom of the trail. His six-foot-seven-inch packhorse of a frame was carrying so much of the weight that it was hardly worth my energy to assist. Anyway, I figured that if God wanted *me* to carry half of that raft, he would have made me six feet seven inches as well.

After rigging the rafts, we made our way down to the first rapid, Butt Hole Surfer, only to find that we had slightly underestimated the river. We dropped over the first ledge into what was supposed to be a class IV rapid and instantly found ourselves getting spun sideways. As we dropped precariously into the next hole, we spun back downstream, pulled hard on the paddles, and barely made it to the first eddy.

This was not a good sign. If we couldn't handle the easy stuff, what would happen when we got to the hard stuff?

We decided to take it easy, pick the least heroic routes through big rapids, and eddy hop when necessary. This method worked fine, except for about 80 percent of the time when there weren't any easy routes or eddies. Then it was paddle like hell, lean into the drops, and hope for the best.

We picked and paddled our way through the next few miles, exchanging heavyweight blows with giant, boulder-strewn rapids like

Grizzly, Nightmare, and The Wall. By the time we'd reached Warp Two and Cassady Falls, just over three miles into the trip, our fun meters were pegged, and our energy levels were low. The mere sight of these two rapids was the last straw. By the time our thirty-minute scout was over ("You gonna run it?" "No, I'm not." "I'm gonna run it. You gonna run it?" "I'm not gonna run it." "Hey, let's get Mikey. He'll run anything!"), half the crew had their sleeping bags spread out and dinner on the stove.

By the time the sun hit camp the next morning, a five-man crew had assembled to run Warp Two. This ten-foot-high waterfall sent rafts sailing into a class IV rapid. Then, after a hundred yards of whitewater, the river plummeted into a horseshoe-shaped cauldron known as Cassady Falls. Though none of us were mad enough to try and run Cassady Falls, Warp Two was too good to pass up.

We paddled the raft round and round the eddy, waiting for the morning's coffee to kick in and reviewing our game plan one more time. Plan A was to come off the bottom of the falls pointing left. That way, we could drive the raft onto a rock and jump out before we were committed to running Cassady Falls. Plan B was to grab onto one of about ten throw bags that would hit us if Plan A didn't work and to pendulum into shore. Fortunately, Plan A worked. The raft pierced the hole at the base of the falls and surged onto the left bank. We were overjoyed to find ourselves shaking hands with the shore crew and walking around Cassady Falls.

Before the excitement of Warp Two had even worn off, we found ourselves at the lip of another big rapid known as That's Dumb.

"I'd say chances are one-in-a-hundred you'll make it through that hole upright."

"Yeah, but what would the consequences be if we flipped?"

"A gnarly swim."

"Yeah, but it's not a killer. At least I don't think it is. You'd flush right out, no? How many throw bags do we have?"

"About six, I guess."

"And it'd make a hell of a picture, wouldn't it?"

"Yeah."

"Let's go for it then!"

Unlike any of the other rapids on the Upper Kings, That's Dumb is brutally short and irresistibly simple. From upstream, the rapid first appears as a horizon line at the far end of a deep green pool. Then, as the river enters the rapid, vertical cliffs and house-sized boulders choke the river down to thirty feet in width. At the same time, the Kings plunges ten vertical feet into liquid cotton candy, traveling all too fast in the wrong direction. Strangely, it doesn't even resound with the boisterous roar typical of such drops. Instead, it sounds more like a trout slurping a fly from the surface. A 14,000-pound trout!

That's all there is. Nothing but swift, green water enters and exits the rapid, and no life-threatening hazards exist beyond the grasp of the hole. All you do is pick a line, hit the hole . . . and hold your breath.

We had good reason to think long and hard about that drop. Everyone on the trip had seen the Cassady and Carlson raft get hammered here in the early video version of *California Whitewater*. And now the river was even higher. Staring deeper and deeper into the hole, I started to feel like a one-legged man heading into an ass-kicking contest.

By the time the same feelings of doubt had run their course through our group, only seven paddlers remained optimistic. Much to my surprise, I was one of them. But the hole seemed plenty survivable, and surely seven strong paddlers in a big SOTAR could punch through. Led by this collective misconception, we boarded our craft.

With people—cameras and rescue bags in hand—once again scrambling along the rocks we divvied up the seats and paddled a few times around the eddy. This time, our game plan was to . . . well . . . end up downstream . . . preferably in the boat.

All too fast, someone gave us the thumbs up, and we were on our way. In a flash we were poised at the lip of the drop, staring into a liquid, foamy, melee of water. In the midst of my excitement, I became a spectator to my own uncertain fate. "They're screwed," I thought, not realizing that "they" included "me." Hopelessness overrode any desire I had to paddle. In fact, paddling seemed as ridiculous a notion as sticking your foot out of a roller coaster to quicken the pace. We were going fast enough.

Suddenly, the crashing jolt of the big hole jarred me back to reality. I dug my paddle deep into the foam and watched the front half of the raft disappear. Then, as if shot from a submarine, our SOTAR's twenty-two-inch tubes soared perfectly skyward like a misguided yellow torpedo. The last thing I remember before joining the crew in a grand swim-along was a rainbow of life jackets streaming through the air like autumn leaves in a windstorm.

Fortunately, I had remembered to keep two hands on the paddle before entering the submarine portion of this adventure. The witch's theme from *The Wizard of Oz* soundtrack rang through my head as I rode the paddle through the tornado of deep currents underlying the surface of the Kings. Had the paddle been a broomstick, I would have surely flown back to shore.

By the time my head popped back into the atmosphere, I had swum past the chorus line of wide eyes and expended throw bags. I turned over on my belly and swam to an eddy downstream.

Having just experienced one of my finest swims, the remainder of our surface activities seemed almost trivial in comparison. As we approached the entrance to the incomparable canyon between Rough Creek Falls and Garlic Falls, other members of our group deemed the river too high for safe passage. We jumped out along the left bank and spent the next half hour lining, portaging, and paddling the canyon. The award for this achievement was a front-row view of Garlic Falls, which plummets a thousand windblown feet into the Kings River.

Past Garlic Falls, the final sets of class V rapids—Body Slam, Pyramid, and Hand-of-God (so named after Chuck Koteen attributed a successful upside-down run of this rapid to an "unseen hand")—laid down beneath the hearty cheers of our paddlers.

Passing Garnet Dike Campground—the uppermost take-out for Upper Kings trips—we found ourselves paddling blissfully through small class II rapids. However, our success in the upper canyons had not gone unnoticed. As one of the rafts casually drifted toward the class III hole at Banzai, the river gods, hell-bent on revenge, lifted their fists one last time and came down squarely on the unsuspecting crew.

As we pulled the upside-down raft and swimmers into an eddy, we smiled, laughed, and praised the river gods. This time, we thought we'd snuck one out. Finally scored a victory against the river. But in the end, it's always a tie. And that's the way it should be.

DAREDEVIL AL FAUSSETT

Whit Deschner

*H*ume said that only the daredevil can confuse us more than a genius
or a fool. What makes a daredevil strive after "deathcom six," the
point at which the rest of us run for cover? And what of the question why? There are no simple answers to these presumably simple questions.
Hardcore adventurers detest the name "daredevil," for it tends to overlook
the often formidable skill of the adventure athlete. And yet once the adventure athlete starts pushing the outer envelope of her ability, she immediately
becomes something of a daredevil. She dares her own skill and mortality with
a devil-may-care abandon. Nothing less will do.

The following narrative covers the strange and dazzling career of daredevil Al Faussett, a sort of whitewater kamikaze. During his time Faussett
astounded many with his cool disposition as he swept toward the lip of another colossal waterfall and another heart-stopping vertical plunge. Gambling
with his life to survive the big drop into hungry waters, Faussett was convinced that these monstrosities could not be tamed but could certainly be
survived. His efforts provide some of the oddest and most amusing river
chronicles in print.

‡   ‡   ‡

Sunset Falls on Washington's Skykomish River drops 104 feet over a
275-foot granite slide. Many a boater has stood spellbound alongside
the roaring explosion of waters and inevitably asked, "Can it be run?"
The answer is a fat ho hum to those who believe they can push the
modern limits of whitewater boating: It was run in 1926. The man's

name was Al Faussett.

And Sunset Falls was only the beginning of Faussett's cataract-jumping career. Over a period of four years, he descended six of the Northwest's most treacherous falls, including 212-foot Shoshone, 45 feet higher than Niagara!

Until 1926 Faussett had been a lumberjack or, as they were known back then, a "dirtyneck." He ran a gyppo operation trying to compete against Weyerhaeuser. Faussett might have kept on running his shoe-string logging outfit had it not been for Fox Studios, which was in the area to shoot a western.

The script for Fox's soundless feature called for an Indian to ride over a falls in a dugout. The choice for the take was Sunset, and the studio offered $1,500 to anyone who would jump the falls.

Faussett was the lone taker of the bait. However, when he saw Fox's canoe he claimed it was far from adequate for such a feat. He would craft his own. Faussett felled a spruce and hand-hewed from it a thirty-four-foot canoe.

But when Faussett added safety features to his canoe, there was little resemblance to an Indian dugout. He had covered the foredeck over with sheet metal, the aft deck with canvas. In the stern he left a small opening where he would strap himself in. To absorb the impact of colliding with boulders, Faussett fastened to the hull five-foot lengths of vine maple at various angles. When Fox saw the finished boat, the company reneged on its offer.

Faussett wasn't going to collect his $1,500, but his friends convinced him that was no reason why his canoe should start gathering termites. Thus it was announced that on May 30, 1926, Al Faussett would run Sunset Falls. A dollar admission would be charged.

Whether or not the enterpriser knew what he was in for, he spoke confidently of the ride, telling the *Everett News*, "It will be a dangerous and thrilling ride. But the people who come will see me make a cool ride, and one they had never anticipated. There is nothing to be afraid of, for I have studied the dangers carefully and believe I can negotiate these falls where twenty men have lost their lives."

On May 30, a crowd of 3,000 gathered along the banks in the cool mist of the falls. It was not an event to be missed. Some had come the night before, and a good share had crashed the gate. The event was to have taken place at one o'clock. At four the crowd had grown impatient. At last word rushed through the crowd that Faussett was adrift in his canoe, floating to the brink.

At a speed upward of eighty miles per hour the canoe crashed through the falls, engulfed in tons of pounding water. The boat grazed over a large granite protrusion and shot almost clear of the water, only to slam back down and disappear. It was several seconds before the boat and its human cargo reappeared, emerging out of the spray and gliding free into the pool below. When Faussett waved to the crowd they erupted, clapping and cheering.

In the *Everett News* Faussett wrote of his descent, "People will never know and little did I dream of the power of those treacherous waters in the falls. When I went under, the water hit me with a crushing force and hurt my lungs. It twisted my body and head. I was hurt inside and could not breathe. The water came so fast it crammed down my nostrils and throat.

"At no time was I afraid of those falls, not even when the water seemed to be crushing the very life out of me. It was all over in a few seconds, and when I saw the light of day as I rode out of the turbulent waters, I thanked God that I had ridden safely through. I have challenged the world to the effect that I can ride anywhere any human can in my good canoe."

As Irv, Al Faussett's son, said of his father, "Dad was another Evel Knievel. He was just born forty years too soon. There just wasn't the instant publicity back then to make him rich and famous."

Three months later and four miles upstream from Sunset, Faussett chose to run Eagle Falls, a series of jagged tiers dropping a total of forty feet. This time the daredevil concluded his longevity might be increased if he rode inside of the boat. For his new craft he hollowed out two halves of a log and banded them together. It was sixteen feet long, cigar-shaped, and had a trapdoor for access.

Due to low water, the Labor Day event was more comical than spectacular. Faussett was bid good luck by his friends, climbed in his boat, shut the hatch, and was shoved into the lazy current.

Halfway through the falls the boat wedged in the rocks. Faussett opened the hatch, yelling for assistance. His friends managed to knock the boat loose with a pike pole, and it and Faussett bounced to the bottom of the falls without mishap.

"On to Snoqualmie and Niagara," he told the press.

Irv said of his father, "In those days people back East still thought of Washington and Oregon as territories. What people did in the Northwest didn't matter to others. Dad wanted to go east and do Niagara. He wanted to put Washington on the map."

Since Niagara was too far away, Faussett announced he would run 216-foot Snoqualmie Falls. But Puget Power, which owned the land adjoining the falls, refused to let the adventurer run, for fear of a lawsuit.

Faussett resolved to run one of the obscure falls upstream from Snoqualmie, but he was foiled again, this time by the King County sheriff, who figured he was saving Faussett's life by stopping him.

The next year Faussett announced he would go elsewhere to run his waterfalls. He went to Spokane to run Spokane Falls. The city officials were not sure whose jurisdiction it was to stop Faussett. The buck was passed to the chief of police, who concluded that it was Faussett's decision whether or not he wanted to kill himself. However, Faussett was not allowed to charge admission.

On June 3, 1927, more than half of Spokane's population crammed along the banks to watch Faussett get swept over the falls. As Faussett climbed in his 775-pound boat, similar to the one used for Eagle Falls, the crowd crammed closer.

Then the river rushed the craft into the seventy-five-foot staircase cataract—a torrent of awesome power. The boat dropped over the first step, somersaulting in the uproar. It then free-fell only to be sucked into a whirlpool, tossed like confetti in a tornado. There it remained spinning around for over twenty minutes until it finally swept close enough to shore to allow several men to pull it to safety. Faussett staggered from the boat with blood dripping down his face and was hurried into an ambulance.

"They've got whiskers on 'em (the falls) an' they sure can give a feller an awful tossing," he told the *Spokesman Review*. He had received a slight concussion along with numerous cuts and bruises about his head. Several hours later the boat worked free of its moorings and went over the lower section of the falls, where it was smashed into pieces and never seen again. Faussett quit for the season. One bump on the head was enough.

But next year he was back, this time in Oregon, to jump forty-foot Oregon City Falls. Faussett's new boat was thirty feet long, essentially a glorified barrel. His plan was to paddle up to the falls, align the boat bow first, duck inside, and close the hatch.

It was the last day of March. A crowd of 10,000 was on hand, and as Faussett and boat reached the brink the crowd was aware that something was drastically wrong. Faussett fought to line the boat up, but gusting winds and a powerful current spun the boat sideways. And that's how it went over. Faussett had failed to get the hatch closed. The boat landed upside down, then disappeared into the froth for over a minute before coming into view.

In the swift current below the falls it took the rescue team six minutes to reach the boat. When they finally righted it, a wet Faussett emerged.

When the *Oregonian* asked Faussett about the ride, he replied, "The canoe is the finest craft on the water. Without it I couldn't have made it. We hit the middle of the falls just right, but the strong wind and current simply made me powerless to shoot the rapids as I had planned. I had no time to close the trapdoor above me so I just hung on. Air under the upturned boat made it possible for me to breathe.

"Going through those rapids sounded like a million cowbells to me. You can't imagine the queer sensation of it. How many times the boat turned over I don't know. About twice, I thought, but others said many times. What I do when I'm buried in water like that I'm not accountable for. I simply hang on. What else is there to do?"

The daredevil's next exploit was to shoot the 186-foot Silver Creek Falls. However, the group of businessmen who owned the property surrounding the falls refused to let Faussett carry out his plans. In order to run the drop, Faussett first had to buy it along with the adjoining hundred acres.

On July 1, 5,000 people crowded into the area to watch the plunge. Dirt roads were jammed with Model Ts. Some of the people never made it to the event, owing to strong drink and traffic.

Faussett's new boat looked like an obese rugby ball. It was made with a wooden skeleton, filled with thirty-six car inner tubes, and covered with orange canvas. It weighed 180 pounds. In order to avoid bouncing off the rock ledge on the way down, Faussett built a ramp protruding twelve feet out past the brink.

Faussett and his boat arched 186 feet into the pool below. Unfortunately, the boat belly flopped instead of landing nose first as planned.

"There wasn't a scared bone in his body," Irv said. But when he crashed into the pool below there were several broken ones; a few ribs, one wrist, both ankles were sprained, and he couldn't move his bowels for four days.

Faussett still wanted to run Niagara, but the logistics of getting there with a boat were too complicated. So Faussett announced he would run Shoshone Falls on the Snake River in Idaho. It was 212 feet high—45 feet higher than Niagara.

The date was July 28, 1929, and the water level on the Snake was low. To make the ride feasible, the Idaho Power Company resolved to open the gates of a diversion dam upstream half an hour before the ride.

Again Faussett used the canvas boat that he had used on Silver Creek. The crowd of 5,000 would be warned with a series of bombs that he was ready to leap—four at fifteen minutes, three at ten minutes, and two at five minutes before the stunt. One bomb would give alarm that Faussett was floating to the brink. A salvo of bombs was to be fired indicating that Faussett was injured and on his way to the hospital.

To deflect the boat from rocks jutting out in the middle of the falls, a wire was attached upstream to a large boulder, then threaded through a three-inch-diameter ring on the boat. The other end of the wire would be held below by someone on the rescue team.

After making adjustments on his boat, Faussett was ready. A single bomb was fired as he was set adrift in the river. Unfortunately the water released from the dam didn't give the boat enough draw, and twice it hung up on the bottom, the last time right on the brink. Two men waded out to the boat and gave it a shove over the falls.

He dropped 212 feet—the highest falls ever jumped.

Faussett emerged from his boat with only a broken right hand. A salvo of bombs was fired off. For the event, Faussett received $733.

The extra forty-five feet didn't mean much to the daredevil, though. "Dad still wanted to run Niagara. It was the falls that had a name to it. Things didn't work out and he never got back there. Even when Dad was in his sixties [twenty-five years later] he still had plans for Niagara."

In February 1948, the man who once described himself as "feeling more at home in a logging camp than in a crowd" "went west." He died of cancer.

"That's not what really killed him," Irv said. "He couldn't stand the regimentation of being in a rest home. It was the first time in his life someone told him what to do: when to turn off the light, when to go to bed. It got him down and he just couldn't take it."

A segment of the obituary in a Seattle newspaper read, "If there are any rivers where Al Faussett is now, he'll be hunting for a waterfall over which to leap."

Irv said of his father, "He lived three lives to most men's one. He got a lot of fun out of life. Funny thing was he never knew how to swim."

FIRST BEND ON THE BARO

Richard Bangs

*P*erhaps no other adventurer in recent years has systematically sought out and bagged so many first descents of wild and often remote rivers as Richard Bangs. From Turkey to New Guinea to Indonesia to Chile to Ethiopia to God knows where, Bangs has been there, lured by a previously unrun river and a thirst for the unknown. Well steeped in the history of exploration, Bangs understood from the start the difference between running a river for mere thrill and running a river that was historically significant. "Purists" have roasted Bangs as a publicity hound spewing all the hype of a circus impresario. To be sure, the same detractors have never tried mounting an international expedition to an obscure region of a backwater country (where most of the world's great first descents remained), or they would understand that only a billionaire could afford to pull off such a trip without hustling the resources to pay for it. Nor do the detractors understand that even with sponsorship, many of Bangs's expeditions were achieved with budgets so slim that less dedicated and savvy folk would never have gotten to the given river in the first place, let alone run it.

This volume contains three Bangs accounts. The other stories present a more formal journalistic handling of significant expeditions. Not to imply Ethiopia's Baro River was inconsequential—quite the opposite. However, the thrust of this narrative is strictly personal and provides readers with a picture of how a world-class adventurer deals with loss. Danger and death lurk behind every wash rock on a fierce river, and all too frequently the reading public thinks continual exposure to these hazards has desensitized the committed adventurer. "First Bend of the Baro" shows us otherwise.

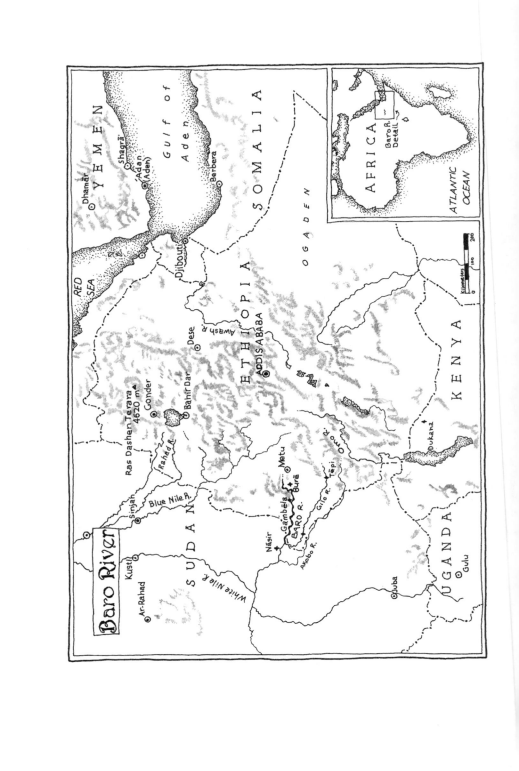

‡   ‡   ‡

Above the jungle was a brawl of flora and vines and roots. Colobus monkeys sailed between treetops, issuing washboard cries.

Below, three specially designed inflatable whitewater rafts bobbed in a back eddy looking, from the ridge, like restless water bugs. There were eleven of us, all whitewater veterans, save Angus. He was in the raft with me, John Yost, and Karen Greenwald. As the leader and the most experienced river runner, I was at the oars.

Our raft would go first. At the correct moment we cast off—then Angus coiled the painter and gripped for the ride. I adjusted the oars and pulled a deep stroke. For a prolonged instant the boat hung in a current between the eddy and the fast water. Then it snapped into motion with a list that knocked me off my seat.

"This water's faster than I thought," I yelled. Regaining the seat, I straightened the raft, its bow downstream. The banks were a blur of green; water shot into the boat from all sides.

Just minutes after the start of the ride, we approached the first rapid. Though we'd been unable to scout it earlier, I had a hunch that it would be best to enter the rapid on its right side. But the river had different notions. Despite frantic pulls on the oars, we were falling over the lip on the far left.

"Oh, my God!" someone screamed. The boat was almost vertical, falling free. This wasn't a rapid. This was a waterfall. I dropped the oars and braced against the frame. The raft crashed into a spout, folded in half, and spun. Then, as though reprieved, we straightened and flumped onward. I had almost gasped with relief when a lateral wave pealed into an explosion on my left, picking up the raft, slamming it against the nearby cliff wall like a toy, then dumping it and us upside down into the millrace.

I tumbled, like falling down an underwater staircase. Seconds later, I surfaced in the quick water below the rapid, a few feet from the overturned raft. My glasses were gone, but through the billows I could make out another rapid 200 yards downstream, closing in fast. I clutched at a rope and tried to tow the raft toward the shore. Behind, I heard Karen: "Angus. Go help Angus. He's caught in a rope!"

He was trailing ten feet behind the raft, a piece of the bowline tight across his shoulder, tangled and being pulled through the turbulence. Like the rest of us, he was wearing a sheathed knife on his belt in anticipation of this very moment—to cut himself loose from entangling ropes. His arms looked free, yet he didn't reach for his knife. He was paralyzed with fear.

With my left hand I seized the rope at his sternum, and with my right I groped for my own Buck knife. In the roily water it was a task to slip the blade between Angus's chest and the taut rope. Then, with a jerk, he was free.

"Swim to shore," I yelled.

"Swim to shore, Angus," Karen cried from the edge of the river.

He seemed to respond. He turned and took a stroke toward Karen. I swam back to the runaway raft with the hope of once again trying to pull it in. It was futile: The instant I hooked my hand to the raft it fell into the pit of the next rapid, with me in tow.

I was buffeted and beaten by the underwater currents, then spat to the surface. For the first time, I was terrified. I saw another rapid speeding toward me. Abandoning the raft, I stretched my arms to swim to shore, but my strength was sapped. This time I was shot into an abyss. I was in a whirlpool, and by looking up I could see the surface light fade as I was sucked deeper. At first I struggled, but it had no effect except to further drain my small reserves. My throat began to burn. I went limp and resigned myself to fate. In the last hazy seconds I felt a blow from beneath, and my body was propelled upward. I was swept into a spouting current, and at the last possible instant I broke the surface and gasped. I tried to lift my arms; they felt like barbells. My vision was fuzzy, but I could make out another rapid approaching, and I knew I could never survive it. But neither could I swim a stroke.

Then, somehow, a current pitched me by the right bank. Suddenly branches and leaves were swatting my face as I was borne around a bend. I reached up, caught a thin branch, and held tight. I crawled to a rock slab and sprawled out. My gut seized, and I retched. A wave of darkness washed through my head, and I passed out.

When my eyes finally focused, I saw figures foraging through the gluey vegetation on the opposite bank. John Yost was one—he had been a close friend since high school. Lew Greenwald, another—he had been in the third boat—and seeing him reminded me that two boats and seven people were behind me. How had they fared?

John paced the bank until he found the calmest stretch of river then dived in: The water was so swift that he reached my shore fifty yards below his mark. He brought the news: The second raft, piloted by Robbie Paul, had somehow made it through the falls upright. In fact, Robbie was thrown from his seat into the bilge during the first seconds of the plunge, and the raft had continued through captainless. The third boat, handled by Bart Henderson, had flipped. Bart was almost swept under a fallen log but was snatched from the water by the crew of Robbie's boat.

All were accounted for—except Angus MacLeod.

The date was Friday, October 5, 1973. I was twenty-three years old. The place was Ilubabor Province, Ethiopia, and our goal had been to make the first raft descent of the Baro River, a major tributary of the White Nile. We had come here, all of us, at my design: I had graduated from the Colorado River and spent four summers guiding rafts and tourists through the rapids there, all the while dreaming of far-off waters. Inspired by accounts of the British army making a raft descent of Ethiopia's Blue Nile in 1968, I'd set my sights on Africa. But where the British had failed—one of their party, Ian MacLeod, drowned while attempting to cross a swollen tributary—I felt certain I could succeed. It had struck me before that Angus had a surname identical to that of the British fatality, and I even mentioned it to Angus, but neither of us was superstitious.

In February of that year—1973—with a small team of conspirators, I had made the first descent of Ethiopia's Awash River. A month later we repeated our success on the classic Omo, a river famous to the world because of Louis Leakey's fossil discoveries on its lower reaches. Both expeditions pitted us against a litany of obstacles, from hippos and poisonous snakes to crocodiles and deadly microorganisms in the water. It was the crocodiles we feared most, so we named our venture Sobek Expeditions, after the ancient Egyptian crocodile god of the Nile. I had returned to Colorado with tales of exotic river running, and now, along with three Africa veterans, seven newcomers had followed me back to tackle another river—the Baro.

As a fervid river runner, I felt I understood the reasons for everyone's involvement in the expedition—except Angus's. He was the odd man out. I'd met him in New Jersey a few weeks before our departure. We were introduced by a neighbor of his, whom I'll call Tom. Tom liked to tell people that he was a "professional adventurer." He'd had a brochure printed up, describing himself as "Writer, Scientist, Adventurer, Ecologist." Something about him seemed less than genuine, but he had hinted that he might invest in our Baro expedition, and we desperately needed money. I agreed to hear him out. He flew me from Arizona, where I'd been guiding, to New Jersey. I was impressed—no one had ever offered to pay airfare to hear my plans, and Tom's family certainly had money. In exchange for what seemed like a sizable contribution to our cause, Tom had two requests: that he be allowed to join the expedition, and that I consider letting his friend, Angus MacLeod, come along as well. I was leery of bringing along anyone outside my tight-knit, experienced coterie on an exploratory mission, but the lure of capital was too strong, so I agreed.

Tom, however, would never make it out onto the Baro. He traveled with us to the put-in, took one look at the angry heaving river, and caught the next bus back to Addis Ababa. He may have been the smartest of the lot.

Angus was altogether different. While Tom smacked of pretension and flamboyance, Angus was taciturn and modest. He confessed immediately to having never run a rapid, yet he exuded an almost irresistible eagerness and carried himself with the fluid bounce of a natural athlete. He was ruggedly handsome and had played professional soccer. After spending a short time with him I could see his quiet intensity, and I believed that—despite his lack of experience—he could handle the trip.

Once in Ethiopia, Angus prepared for the expedition with a lightheartedness that masked his determination. On the eve of our trip to Ilubabor Province—a seventeen-hour bus ride on slippery, corrugated mountain roads—I told Angus to make sure he was at the bus station at 7:00 A.M. for the 11:00 A.M. departure. That way we would all be sure of getting seats in the front of the bus, where the ride wasn't as bumpy or unbearably stuffy. But, come the next morning, Angus didn't show until 10:45. He got the last seat on the bus and endured.

Later, after the accident, standing on the bank of the river with John Yost, I wondered if I'd made the right decision about Angus. We searched the side of the river where I'd washed ashore; across the rumble of the rapids we could hear the others searching. "Angus! Are you all right? Where are you?" There was no answer. Just downriver from where I'd last seen him, John found an eight-foot length of rope—the piece I'd cut away from Angus's shoulders.

After an hour John and I gave up and swam back across the river. We gathered the group at the one remaining raft, just below the falls.

"He could be downstream, lying with a broken leg," someone said.

"He could be hanging onto a log in the river."

"He could be wandering in a daze through the jungle."

Nobody suggested that he could be dead, though we all knew it was a possibility. All of us had a very basic, and very difficult, decision to make, the kind of decision you never want to have to make on an expedition: Should we stay and look for Angus, or should we get out while there was still light? Robbie, Bart, and George and Diane Fuller didn't hesitate—they wanted out. Karen Greenwald wanted to continue searching, but she was hysterical and the weakest member of the group. Against her protests, we sent her out with the others.

That left five of us—Lew Greenwald, Gary Mercado, Jim Slade, John Yost, and me. We decided to continue rafting downstream in search of Angus on the one remaining raft. I had mixed feelings about it—suddenly I was scared to death of the river; it had almost killed me. Yet I felt obligated to look for a man missing from a boat I had capsized, on an expedition I had organized. And there was more: I felt I had to show something to the others: that I wasn't scared of the river.

But the river wasn't through with us. When we were ready to go, I climbed into the seat of the raft and yelled for Jim to push off. Immediately we were cascading down the course I'd swum earlier. In the rapid that had nearly drowned me, the raft jolted and reeled, pitching Gary and me into the brawling water.

"Shit—not again," was my only thought as I vaulted out of the raft into another whirlpool. But this time I had the bowline in hand, and I managed to pull myself quickly to the surface. I emerged beside the raft and someone grabbed the back of my life jacket and pulled me in. My right forearm was torn and bleeding. Jim jumped to the oars and rowed us to shore.

My injury wasn't bad—a shallow cut. But Gary had dislocated his shoulder; he'd flipped backward over the gunwale while still holding onto the raft. He was in pain, and it was clear he couldn't go on. Lew—thankful for the opportunity—volunteered to hike him out.

John, Jim, and I relaunched and cautiously rowed down a calmer stretch of the river, periodically calling out for Angus. We were just three degrees north of the equator, where the sun sets promptly at 6:00 P.M. year-round. It was twilight when we approached another fierce rapid, so we decided to stop and make camp. It was a bad, uncomfortable night. Between us, we had a two-man A-frame tent, one sleeping bag, and a lunch bag of food. Everything else had been washed into the Baro.

The rude bark of a baboon shook us awake the next morning. The inside of the tent was dripping with condensation, and we were soaked.

I crawled outside and looked to the eastern sky, which was beginning to blush. My body ached from the thrashing I'd taken the previous day. I wanted to be back in Bethesda, at my folks' home, warm, dry, and eating a fine breakfast. Instead, we huddled around a wisp of fire, sipping weak tea and chewing wet bread.

The next morning we eased downriver, stopping every few minutes to scout, hugging the banks, avoiding rapids we wouldn't have hesitated to run were they back in the States. At intervals we called into the rain forest for Angus, never expecting an answer.

Late in the afternoon we came to another intimidating rapid, one that galloped around a bend and sank from sight. We took out the one duffel bag containing the tent and sleeping bag and began lining, using ropes to lower the boat along the edge of the rapid. Fifty yards into the rapid, the raft broached perpendicular to the current, and water swarmed in. Slade and I, on the stern line, pulled hard, the rope searing our palms, but the boat ignored us. With the snap of its D-ring (the bowline attachment), it dismissed us to crumple on the bank and sailed around the corner and out of sight.

There was no way to continue the search. The terrain was too rough, and we were out of food, the last scraps having been lost with the raft. We struck up into the jungle, thrashing through wet, waist-high foliage at a slug's pace. My wound was becoming infected. Finally, at sunset, we cleared a near-level spot, set up the tent, squeezed in, and collapsed. Twice I awoke to the sounds of trucks grumbling past but dismissed it as jungle fever, or Jim's snoring.

In the morning, however, we soon stumbled onto a road. There we sat waiting, as mist coiled up the tree trunks. In the distance we could hear the thunder roll of a rapid, but inexplicably the sound became louder and louder. Then we saw what it was: 200 machete-wielding natives marching into sight over the hill. General Goitorn, the police commissioner of nearby Metu, hearing of the accident, had organized a search for Angus. The search party's effort consisted of tramping up and down the highway—the locals, it turned out, were more fearful of the jungle canyon than we were.

I remember very little of the next week. We discovered that Angus had held a United Kingdom passport, and I spent hours at the British embassy in Addis Ababa filling out reports, accounting for personal effects, and communicating with his relatives. John and Jim stayed in Metu with General Goitorn and led a series of searches back into the jungle along the river. We posted a $100 reward—more than double what the villagers earned in a year—for information on Angus's where-abouts. With financial assistance from Angus's parents, I secured a Canadian helicopter a few days after the accident and took several passes over the river. Even with the pilot skimming the treetops, it was difficult to see into the river corridor. The canopy seemed like a moldy, moth-eaten tarpaulin. On one flight, however, I glimpsed a smudge of orange just beneath the surface of the river. We made several passes, but it was impossible to make out what it was. Perhaps, I thought, it was Angus, snagged underwater. We picked as many landmarks as possible, flew in a direct line to the road, landed, cut a marker on a dohm palm tree, and headed to Metu.

A day later John, Jim, and I cut a path back into the tangle and found the smudge—a collection of leaves trapped by a submerged branch. We had run out of things to do. We abandoned the search.

Three months later I was wandering through the recesses of the spice market in Addis Ababa when a vendor I knew approached me. "Mr. Richard. Did you hear about Mr. Angus? They say he is alive. He was found by villagers on the river and he is living with them now. It is the talk everywhere. I do not know from where the story comes."

I went to the British and U.S. embassies. People there, too, had heard the rumor. One consul said he'd heard that Angus was living large as king of a tribe of Amazon-like women. As the story ran, Angus had been visited by outside villagers and invited to leave. Naturally, he'd declined. He was in paradise.

Hearing the rumors was harsh. I wanted to squelch the sensational gossip, to finish business left undone, to determine beyond all doubt what had really happened to Angus. And, most of all, to cleanse my conscience. So in January of 1974, I made another trip to the upper reaches of the Baro. This time the river was ten vertical feet lower than on our last trip: It was dry season in a drought year. What was before a swollen rampage was now a slow, thin trickle. Four of us were in a single raft: Lew Greenwald, Gary Mercado, Professor Conrad Hirsh of Haile Selassie University, and me.

Again, we reached the first rapid within minutes. This time, though, it was a jumble of bus-sized basalt boulders, the bedrock that fashioned the falls during times of flooding. It was unnavigable, so we stood in chest-deep water and wrenched the inflatable boat over and down the rocks, turning it on its side to push it through the tighter passages. A similar configuration constituted the next rapid, and the next, and the next. The routine was quickly established. It was a constant battle against rocks, water, heat, fatigue, and insects. We had naively hoped to run the raft some 150 miles to Gambela, near the Sudanese border, where the river flows wide and flat. We had rations for a week. With all the portaging, we were making less than five miles a day.

Scattered along our course, sometimes in branches high above us where the water once swirled, we found vestiges of the first expedition: five oars, Jim Slade's sleeping bag, a torn poncho, a pack of insect-collecting equipment donated by the Smithsonian, crushed pots and pans, and a ripped sweater that had belonged to Angus, one he had packed in his duffel. But no sign of Angus.

After six days we had made only thirty miles; our bodies were pocked with insect bites, and we had exhausted our food and strength. A trail up the steep slope put an end to our ordeal. We went back to Addis Ababa with no new answers.

I returned to the States and graduate school, running few rivers myself but continuing to manage the business of Sobek (which was growing despite the accident) from my apartment. The following January, Lew Greenwald, my original partner in the business, was drowned on an exploratory run of the Blue Nile in northern Ethiopia. The news shattered me: I burrowed deeper into academia, denounced river running as selfish and insane, and put Sobek aside.

Time softened my edges. By summer I had reenlisted and was once again organizing trips to Ethiopia—though I had no intention of ever going back myself. But the mystery of Angus gnawed. Sometimes in the middle of a mundane chore—taking out the trash, doing the laundry—I'd stop and see Angus's frozen features as I cut him loose. In such moments I would wonder if there just might be a chance that he was still alive. And I'd be pressed with guilt—that I hadn't done enough, that I had dishonorably waded in waist deep, then turned back. I wondered how Angus had felt in those last few minutes—about himself, about me.

In November of that year, 1975, I got a call from a friend, a tour operator. A trip he'd organized to the Sahara had been canceled by the Algerian government, and his clients wanted an alternative. Would I be interested in taking them to Ethiopia? Two weeks later I arrived in Addis Ababa, where I met up with John Yost, Jim Slade, and a trainee-guide, Gary Bolton, fresh from a Sobek raft tour of the Omo River. They were surprised to see me, here where nobody expected I would return.

By late December, after the commercial tour, John, Jim, and I had decided to try the Baro once again. The river pummeled us, as it had before, randomly tossing portages and major rapids in our path. But during the next few days, the trip gradually, almost imperceptibly, became easier. On Christmas morning I decorated a bush with my socks and passed out presents of party favors and sweets. Under an ebony sapling I placed a package of confections for Angus. It was a curiously satisfying holiday being surrounded by primeval beauty and accompanied by three other men with a common quest. No one expected to find Angus alive, but I thought that the journey—at least for me—might expunge all doubt, exorcise guilt. I wanted to think that I had done all that was humanly possible to explore a death I was partly responsible for. And somehow I wanted him to know this.

As we tumbled off the Abyssinian plateau into the Great Rift Valley of Africa, taking on tributaries every few miles, the river and its rapids grew. At times we even allowed ourselves to enjoy the experience, to shriek with delight, to throw our heads back in laughter as we bounced through Colorado River-style whitewater and soaked in the scenery. Again, we found remnants of that first trip—a broken oar here, a smashed pan there. Never though, a hint of Angus.

On New Year's Eve we camped at the confluence of the Baro and the Bir Bir Rivers, pulling in at dusk. A lorry track crossed the Baro opposite our camp. It was there that Conrad Hirsh, the professor from the second Baro attempt, had said be would try to meet us with supplies. We couldn't see him, but Jim thought there might be a message waiting for us across the river. "I think I'll go check it out," he said.

"Don't be a fool," John warned. "We're in croc country now. You don't want to swim across this river."

An hour later, just after dark, Jim had not returned. We shouted his name, first individually, then as a chorus. No answer. Jim had become a close friend in the two years since we had shared a tent on the upper Baro; he had been a partner in ordeal and elation, in failure and success. Now John and I swept our weak flashlight beams along the dark river. We gave up. We were tired, and we sat around the low licks of our campfire, ready to accept another loss, mapping out the ramifications in our minds. Suddenly Jim walked in from the shadows and thrust a note at us.

"Conrad arrived three days ago, waited two, and left this morning," he said, his body still dripping from the swim.

"You fool! I knew you couldn't disappear now—you owe me

$3.30 in backgammon debts." I said it with all the disciplinary tone I could muster.

The following day we spun from the vortex of the last rapid into the wide, Mississippi-like reaches of the Baro. Where rocks and whirlpools were once the enemy, now there were crocodiles and hippos. We hurled rocks, made threatening gestures, and shrieked to keep them away. Late in the day on January 3, 1976, we glided into the outpost town of Gambela. The villagers there had neither seen nor heard of Angus MacLeod.

I never told Angus's relatives of our last search; we didn't find what might have given them solace. What I found I kept to myself, hidden like buried treasure in my soul. It lies there still, dusty, but ready to be raised if needed. It is the knowledge of the precious and innate value of endeavor. Both Angus and I tried, and in different ways we both failed.

I hardly knew Angus MacLeod, not as friends and family know one another. But in the years of searching, wondering, I've gotten to know him in other ways. There are things we tell ourselves. I want to believe that when Angus boarded my tiny boat and committed himself, he was sparked with life and light, that his blood raced with the passion of existence—perhaps more than ever before.

On that first Friday in October 1973, ten of us thought we knew what we were doing: another expedition, another raft trip, another river. Only Angus was exploring beyond his experience. Maybe his was a senseless death, moments after launching, in the very first rapid. I will never forget that look of horror in his eyes as he struggled there in the water. But there are other ways to think about it. He took the dare and contacted the outermost boundaries. He lost, but so do we all, eventually. The difference—and it is an enormous one—is that he reached for it, wholly.

Finally, though it took years, I believe I did the same.

The Upper Youghiogheny River: Fear and Loathing in Friendsville, Maryland

Kevin O'Brien

*A*s the saying goes, if you can make a living doing what you love, you've got the game licked. They key word here is "you." With virtually all adventure sports, there's little chance of getting paid green money for rafting your river or climbing your mountain. Sure, there's a handful of men and women so marvelously crazed and honed as to win sponsorship. But these number roughly a dozen in any given sport, leaving everyone else (including scores of world-class performers) to either work "legitimate" jobs or to teach and/or act as adventure-sport guides. And here lies the rub. What would otherwise be a glorious experience (say, plunging down a spectacular river) can quickly devolve into something hateful when the raft is freighted with inexperienced clients. But not always. Many commercial adventure outings cement lasting friendships between guides and clients. Nevertheless, every guide is certain to eventually encounter clients capable of doing things so spectacularly asinine that only another guide would ever believe them possible. Such encounters often provide hilarious memories—usually long after the fact. The following story is one such example.

‡   ‡   ‡

Whitewater rafting on the rivers of Appalachia has become big business over the last decade. The clientele are for the most part a likeable bunch—New York City cops, auto workers from Detroit, car salesmen from Cleveland, mothers from New Jersey.

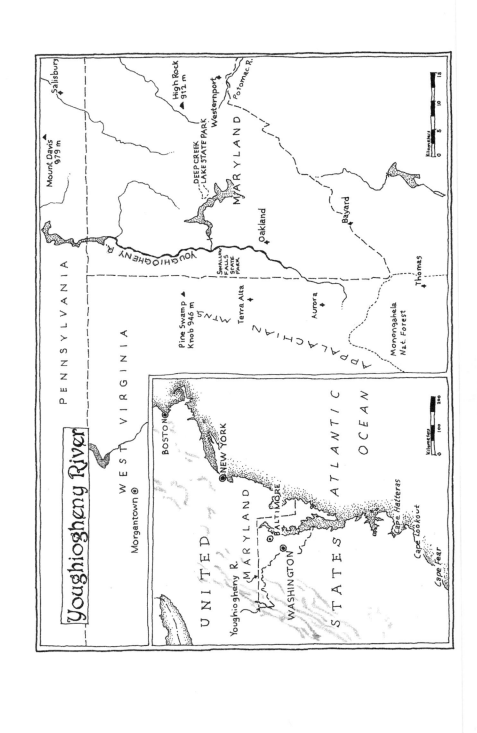

Youghiogheny River

Leaving behind their nine-to-five world, caution to the wind, they flock to the Lower Yough, the Cheat, the New, and numerous other class III and IV runs of the Midatlantic region, heady with the pursuit of adventure.

On moderate rivers, whitewater rafting is a relatively safe, harmless activity, suitable to the masses. Outfitters are quick to point this out in their brochures: "Bring Grandma! Bring the kids! Fun for the whole family!" and so on.

Pitching to the entire spectrum of well-moneyed summer vacationers inevitably leads to the roping in of that uniquely American phenomenon: denizen of the motor home, fugitive of Wally World, vacant-eyed, slack-jawed, bovine. . . .

The *Tour-on.*

The Upper Yough, a steep class V section of whitewater in western Maryland, is no place for Tour-ons. Commercial outfitters have run trips on it since the early eighties and, for the most part, are selective of their clients. It is a demanding run for both guide and passenger, not to be taken lightly.

"Previous whitewater experience required. Guests must be in good physical condition. . . ." Words right out of the company's brochure popped into mind as I stared from the raft at my approaching clients. Obviously they hadn't read it.

"Calvin? Are you Calvin?" the heavy, red-faced man was bellowing at me.

"I'm Kevin," I replied.

"Where the hell's Calvin?" he repeated, looking quizzically down the row of rafts at the other guides. I could see them beginning to smirk.

"There is no *Calvin.* That's *me!*" I answered, unsure of what I'd just said.

Staring blankly at me for a moment, he pointed to the woman tiptoeing down the bank.

"Calvin, this 'ere's my wife, Phyllis."

Phyllis, a large, pink-skinned woman, hair piled high in a spectacular beehive, paused in her descent, tilting her silver-rimmed, bejeweled sunglasses to peer at me over the top, smiling.

"Howdy!" was all she said.

"Glad to meet you, son," hollered Hank as he thundered aboard, extending a hand the size of a ham.

Howdy? Son? I'd heard those words before. An alarm, deep in my brain, began to sound shrilly in my head. My God! I thought. That was it! They're *Texans!*

It's no secret that Texans and whitewater are a lethal combination. Primarily desert dwellers, moving water is alien to folks from the Lone Star State, severely limiting their ability to balance on even the widest cross-tube. Their inherent braggadocio and yahooism prevent them from comprehending the most basic paddle strokes and commands. Their cowboy boots, which they are reluctant to part with, tear holes in rafts.

I'd had Texans in my raft on other rivers. It was never a pretty sight.

Consigned to fate, I helped Phyllis aboard, got the two situated with paddles and life jackets, and shoved off into the current.

Guiding on the Upper Yough makes for a high-energy diversion from my usual work as a free-lance writer and photographer. Given the nature of my career, it also serves as a way of making quick cash, helping to appease the wolves ceaselessly prowling at my door. I'd signed on with one of the larger outfitters that morning, replacing one of their regular, full-time guides who, when last seen, was under the influence of strong drink, fire dancing with customers at about 4:00 A.M.

Floating through the wide, flat section above Gap Falls, the first major rapid of the day, Phyllis began what seemed to be her rendition of a chicken. Hands tucked tightly into her armpits, she began flapping her elbows rhythmically, forward and back. Hank, sitting across from her, stared at the shoreline, oblivious.

"Uh, Ma'am. What the hell are you doing?" I finally asked.

"Ay-robics," she puffed in between flaps. "Twenty-three-foof—twenty-four-foof. . . ." She was counting now.

Hank, with us once again, looked approvingly at his wife, explaining over his shoulder, "She's been doing this for a month, gittin' ready for this trip."

Phyllis puffed on, reddening by the second.

As we entered the small wave train signaling the approach to Gap Falls, I implored Phyllis to get with the program.

"Uh, Ma'am . . . you better grab your paddle," I suggested.

"Seventy-eight-foof—seventy-nine-foof. . . ." Phyllis kept puffing.

"Uh, *Ma'am!*"

"Just to one hundred," she gasped, barely missing a beat.

"Eight-six-foof—eighty-seven-foof."

Hank, picking up the cue as I began paddling hard, dug in his paddle, wailing his Texas battle cry.

"Let's git it!" he hollered, catching sight of the approaching hole.

We punched the corner of the hydraulic and the raft pivoted hard into the eddy on river right. Hank, unprepared for the sudden deceleration, sprawled forward onto the side-tube. Phyllis, her arms frozen in midflap, was hurled to the bottom of the boat. Hovering in the calm eddy, I waved to the other rafts on our trip, congregated just downstream. Satisfied all was well, they disappeared around the corner. It was the last we'd see of them for awhile.

Turning back to the crew, I saw Phyllis righting herself onto her tube, straightening her chrome-rimmed sunglasses. Her conical coiffure now listed forty-five degrees to starboard.

"Hot damn!" Hank cried. "Wudn't 'at a pisser?!"

I wasn't about to argue. Hank's the kind of man that knows a pisser when he sees one.

It seemed obvious from our Gap Falls performance that a rehash of paddling techniques was in order. Weaving our way through the class III below, I went over the commands once more.

Phyllis, listening intently as I described different strokes, practiced them in midair. Attempting a hard hack-stroke, she clipped Hank upside the head.

"Goddammit, Phyllis! Put that dang thing down 'fo' you kill someone!" he shouted.

"You need to practice these strokes," I intervened.

"We know all 'bout oars. We got a canoe back home," Hank assured me.

Undaunted, I continued my hopeless soliloquy as we approached the next drop.

At Bastard Falls the river begins its descent in earnest, dropping over 150 feet per mile. The rapids—Charlie's Choice, Triple Drop, and National Falls—follow one another in quick succession with little room for recovery between them. It's no place for swimmers.

"Now, on the count of three, I need you to give me a really hard forward stroke so we boof into the eddy, okay?" I was going over the method of running Bastard Falls. From our tiny eddy on river left we could hear the rapid thundering below.

"Any questions?" I asked, preparing to push off.

"What's a boof?" inquired Phyllis.

"Never mind. Just paddle hard on three," I replied.

By now I was certain that any attempt to interpret river terminology, no matter how basic, was futile.

We peeled out of the microeddy and headed for the drop. Nearing the top, I began my cadence.

"One." Both paddlers dug in.

"Two." Another hearty stroke.

"Thr. . . ."

Eyeballing the oncoming hole, Hank burst into action, chucking his paddle and diving to the floor of the raft. Phyllis, her mighty third stroke completely missing the water, shouted, "Get up Haaaaaaaaaaa. . . ."

Our momentum gone, the nose of the raft augered into the stiff hole at the bottom of the pourover. Hitting the floor, I caught a fleeting glimpse of Phyllis as she sailed overhead, landing in the foam somewhere beyond.

I clambered over Hank, struggling to unclip my throw bag.

"There she is!" cried Hank, spotting the tip of her breaking the surface.

"Phyyyllliiisss!"

A lucky toss and the rope hit her right in the numbers. Hand over hand I reeled her in. Hank helped me hoist her over the side.

Spread eagle on the floor of the raft, Phyllis lay gasping. Moments later, having caught her wind, she turned to Hank, violently demanding, "Why the hell'd you stop paddling, Slack Ass!"

The ensuing argument continued all the way down the left side of Charlie's Choice, where we emerged, mercifully unscathed.

Eddying out above Triple Drop, both passengers now stonily silent, I described the next series of stair-step ledges, holes, and the wave train, all funneling into the huge hydraulic at the bottom: National Falls. I wrapped up my summary of the rapid with a warning: ". . . and you *don't* want to swim here!"

Rounding the large rock at the top of the channel, we lined up for the series of holes. Sensing the seriousness of the oncoming rapid, both passengers stroked to beat the band.

Slam! We burst through the first hole with plenty of momentum.

Wham! We ploughed through the second, which slowed us only slightly.

Hank, sensing our prowess at having punched the first two holes, decided to throw in a hale backstroke.

Woomph! We slammed into the hole sideways, tilting the boat up on its side, completely vertical.

Hank, formerly on the downstream side, now found himself launched into the air. Deftly latching onto the boat's grabline in midflight, he continued tumbling into the foam, pulling the raft, and us, over on top of him.

"Balls!" I muttered, just as the lights went out. Black faded to green, faded to white . . . and bubbles. Breaking the surface, I looked upstream and saw the raft still caught in the hole. I made out Hank's burred head bobbing on the wave train downstream. To my right, Phyllis rocketed from the whitewater, eyes wide. By now a familiar sight.

As the three of us approached National Falls, I saw Hank set up for the left line. I decided to give him a wide berth and aimed for the right side of the hole.

Tumbling over both edges of the huge hydro almost in unison, we emerged below, bobbing side by side, lucky to have cleared the recirculating backwash. Looking upstream, we watched Phyllis, backstroking furiously, as she got sucked into the maw of the hole.

"Oh, Baby. Oh, Baby. Oh *bayyybee!*" Hank whimpered as he watched his wife disappear into the abyss.

Up . . . down. Up . . . down. Three cycles later Phyllis finally emerged in the green water below the backwash.

The rest of the clients, watching the show from below, rallied around and helped us gather our stray gear.

Back in the raft, Hank stared upstream, the previous quarter mile of whitewater still visible, winding down the valley.

"Ya know," he began philosophically, "I think we may be in a little over our heads."

Phyllis stared blankly into space. Her once magnificent beehive do dangled off her crown like a clump of seaweed. Her sunglasses, both earrings, one false eyelash and three fingernails were gone, floating in the darkness at the bottom of National Falls.

Defeated, I paddled them over to the river-right shore, pointing out the trail to the take-out. I tried to console them. Tommy's Hole, Zinger, F@#k-up Falls, all the rapids below, will still be there, I told them, should they decide to come do battle another day. Tired and relieved, they began the long hike down to Friendsville.

Paddling back across the river, I grabbed the beefiest customer I could find among the other rafts. Paddling R-2, we finished out the run.

Back in Friendsville, I searched in vain for Hank and Phyllis. "Johnny Raygun," the guide whose slot I'd filled that day, waved to me from the liquor store. He caught up with me, reeking of singed hair and Jim Beam.

"Those folks who walked out said sorry they missed you," he told me, handing over a fistful of money. "They left you a twenty-buck tip!"

I counted the money. "There's only $15.50 here," I replied, looking at him accusingly.

"Oh, yeah," he grinned. "I bought a six pack. Want one?"

Sipping my beer, I noticed, out beyond town on Route 68, a huge Winnebago briefly silhouetted against the orange evening sky. Cresting the distant hill, it vanished from sight, bound for Texas.

REQUIEM FOR RONNIE

John Long

*F*ictional *adventure stories take many tacks. The potboiler aims to entertain by coercing suspense out of exaggerated action sequences. Dramatic adventure yarns set intrigues in the adventure milieu, assuming a certain flair is added if the spy or the thief is, say, a Himalayan mountaineer or an ex-Olympian downhiller. Here, the thrill and peril of adventure provide a romantic backdrop into which writers often foist stylized characters bearing little if any likeness to people who run rivers or climb mountains. This formula has produced the odd masterpiece, but all too often such stories misfire because they are written by people who don't know a kayak from a battleship or an ice axe from a rake. Another species of adventure story starts with a character who oftentimes is based on the life of an actual adventurer, or an aggregate of adventurers, and seeks to pull the character to light through a series of awesome trials. Such is the case with "Requiem for Ronnie," which provides a glimpse at the personal dynamics that often fuel adventure prodigies: the stony past; the physical genius and mental steel; the need to touch death to feel alive; and the prodigious passion that can only find expression where "delight and danger grow on one stalk."*

‡   ‡   ‡

This all happened over a dozen years ago, during my last year on the National Whitewater Kayak Team. The Olympic Job Placement Program had arranged a job for me with Finn Properties, a land management outfit in Los Angeles. I worked half days, and aside from changing coffee filters and photocopying documents, I didn't do a

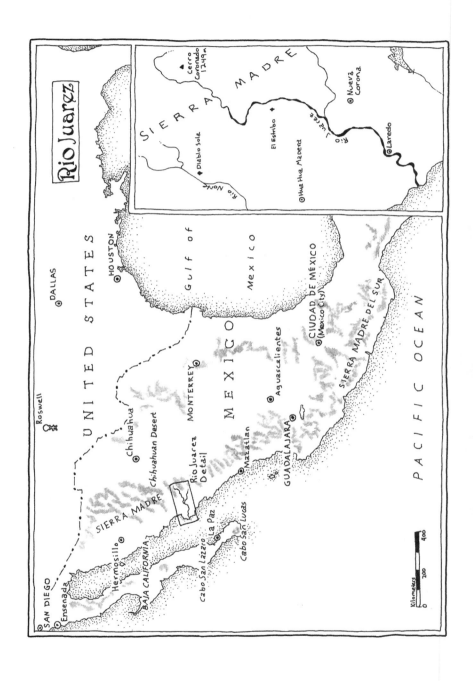

damn thing. Anyway, earlier that summer I'd made a run down the Bio-Bio River in Chile, and one morning while I was going through some photos of it, Hank came over to my little cubical. Aside from casual hellos at the photocopy machine or in the elevator, we'd never said a word to each other.

Hank picked up one of the photos, took a glance, and dropped it back. "I'd heard something about you doing a little paddling."

"A little. . . ." I chuckled. I might not have known much about Hank and the other two dozen Finn employees, but they knew about me—as an Olympian and a slacker.

Hank examined another photo, this one of me cresting a ten-foot wave. "Lined up a little broach-angle here." He sounded as indifferent as if he were noting a typo on a deed. "Probably flipped right after this picture was taken."

In fact, I had flipped. For a moment I sat wondering how a property manager could glance at the photo and know what followed.

"You must be pretty handy on the water to spot my mistake here."

"You run the big water, you make mistakes," Hank said, and picked the photo up again. "But it's been awhile since I made one this silly."

I froze. I'd been the North American whitewater champion for three years running. My entire life was tied to paddling. Hank might as well have kicked me in the balls and told me I deserved worse.

"We'll have to team up some time," I said, "so you can show me how it's done."

Hank reached down and scribbled his address onto a legal pad full of doodles and boat designs. "Swing by the house tonight and we'll talk about it. If you want."

"Count on it." Rolling toward Hank's house that night, I never was so keen to drag a person onto a fiendish river and see him swallow half of it.

Hank lived way out of town, and he answered the door wearing an old pair of Nike gym trunks, his chest and arms glistening with sweat and black graphite dust. He looked extremely fit, like he'd been jimmied off a Roman frieze and struck to life. But along the left side of his back the skin was all scarred and crinkly. An old burn of some kind, and a nasty one.

"Come on in and grab a beer," he said, yanking me inside. He scanned the dark night and quickly closed the door.

His house was not much of a home, rather a warehouse of kayaks, paddles, resin, float bags and tools, every room a workshop except for the one papered in maps and photos. Hank fetched a couple of beers, then showed me his boats. Most were experimental designs. A few were expertly fashioned with Kevlar and carbon fiber, but most were roto-molded plastic. Each bore a little hand-painted design I thought was American Indian—thunderbirds and stuff like that. My eyes ran from the resin fumes.

We'd hardly settled into the chart room when Hank asked, "Can you paddle the desperate stuff or not? And be honest, Lance, or it might cost you your life."

"Where do you get off saying that crazy shit?" I said. "Like I'm some weekend hacker or something."

"I'm talking about big, wild water," Hank said, "not slalom gates. They're very different disciplines, and I don't want to get you killed."

"You know, Hank, you've been talking in circles since you came over to my desk this morning. What's on your mind?"

Hank smiled. "I went down to try and run the Rio Juarez last week-end, but I could see right off it was too much to run alone. You join me on another shot, I'll pay for the copter and all that."

I'd never seen the Rio Juarez, but everyone who had agreed it was suicidal. It occurred to me that Hank was mad. He looked mad, glow-ering there with those laser-blue eyes. But my pride was tied to the business now, which made me worse off than Hank.

"I'll look at it."

"It's perfectly runnable—but not solo."

"Like I said, I'll take a look."

"Fine," Hank said, "but if we're paddling together, you've got to play by my rules."

I couldn't imagine what these rules would entail, but it didn't take Hank long to lay them out.

"You can't mention any of our runs to anybody. It's all a game with me, see—paddling alone, just keeping to myself. That's why I've never had you over till tonight. Now I need you."

Hank went into the kitchen, returned with a couple more beers, and sat back on an old sofa covered with old Navajo rugs.

"Maybe I'll explain it to you later," he said, handing me a beer, "but for now, if you swear to secrecy, I'll have you running rapids you never thought even remotely possible. I can't promise that you'll live long enough to take credit for them, though."

I jumped to my feet. "You got a license to talk like that, or does it just come naturally to you?" So far as I knew, Hank's only credentials were a forceful personality and a knack for outlandish remarks.

"Once we get on the water, I trust you'll understand."

"I trust I will, but it's not going to be on the Juarez—not straight away. And by the way, you know that everyone who's ever seen the Juarez says you'd never get off it alive."

"I've seen it and I say otherwise," Hank came back. "Are we on, or not?"

"I've never seen you paddle a stroke, Hank. We'll do a warm-up first and take it from there."

"Fair enough."

"How 'bout the Tuolumne?" That gauntlet of whitewater was no warm-up, except for the next life.

"Okay," Hank said. His edge had left him in a stroke, replaced by something bordering on relief. There was also a strange, ungraspable feeling of sadness mixed in with it all that confused me mightily. I had the feeling that I could have suggested paddling over Angel Falls and Hank would have said "Okay." Next day, we both called in sick and were on the water before noon.

A week of Sierra storms had drained into the river, and treacherous high water raged west into the San Joaquin Valley. As we slipped into wet suits, I told Hank he'd better be the ace he claimed or he'd be paddling through the pearly gates in about fifty yards. He flashed me that grin of his and cranked out into the stout current. I fell in behind. Over the first quarter mile, I saw that Hank was a superb paddler. After another quarter mile, I realized he was peerless. Then he cut loose.

He would slalom through jagged wash rocks, then bow forward, plunging the nose of his kayak into a standing wave. His boat would submarine in, then pop straight up and flop endwise into the eye of a boiling vortex, where he'd loop around and fire downstream—underwater. He'd crab his boat sideways through steaming rapids, logrolling, over and over. And he ran an entire stretch backward.

Whatever he did, no matter how apparently dangerous and improbable, he did it perfectly. It seemed as though the more outrageous he got, the more the river obliged him. Here I was trying to survive, while Hank clowned through rapids that had snuffed more than one expert. I had never seen anything like it. And I'd seen—and for that matter, beaten—every world champion in the last six years. Hank never stopped for a break or scouted ahead, lest we "cheat the creek of the little it can offer." We powered through a normal day's run in less than four hours.

On the drive home, Hank gripped the wheel and stared ahead silently. A riotous bundle of raw energy on the water, he'd crawled into a funk and had slammed the door behind him. But this mood swing astonished me less than his talent, and I kept wondering where to start and what questions to ask. After an hour on the road he hadn't said a word, hadn't even looked over at me. Finally, I couldn't hack it any longer. Never mind all that paddling in secret business or his ferocious silence. Nobody could possibly get to Hank's level by paddling in a vacuum. Somebody *must* have seen him *somewhere*.

"So who did you compete for, Hank?"

"Never did."

"Well, what other great paddlers have you run with?"

"None. Besides you."

"Fucking hell, Hank! What's with the secret agent bit?"

"We had an agreement. We're going to paddle together, and that's it. That's what we agreed on, remember?"

"Fine, Hank. But if you just saw a guy long jump the Grand Canyon, you'd be curious, too. Believe me."

"This seems like a crackpot way to do things, I know," Hank said, for the first time glancing over at me. "But just bear with me for a while. We'll get to it. We'll get to it all, I hope." That strange, sad energy welled off Hank. We headed on down the road in silence.

Though Hank otherwise stayed strictly to himself, he was dying for company and thought nothing of calling me up at two o'clock in the morning. He'd start talking about rivers we'd just run or were going to run, then we'd move on to flying saucers, reincarnation, and anything else that had a facet of the marvelous in it. Hank was inquisitive in a restless, eccentric kind of way; but I came to recognize in those calls a man reaching out from a place so desolate it has no name in any language. His only salvation came on the water. That devil-may-care grin would creep over his face and three strokes into a run he'd be paddling ten feet off the water and screaming like a kid on a roller coaster. But by the time we'd loaded up the boats and snuck off down the road, he was already crashing back down to zero. It happened every time. I couldn't figure it, but trying to was something I could never give up.

Four months passed before the Rio Juarez came into form, and we were plenty active in the meantime. We hit a score of furious rivers, or "criks," as Hank called them: the Moyle, the Kayan, the Coruh in flood. For a while I wrote off Hank's wizardry to flat-out talent; only later would I understand that he whipped the impossible because he wasn't afraid if the impossible won. He didn't ignore the consequences, rather he loathed them and would taunt and howl at the meanest rapids. Then he'd slip into a run and, once again, the river seemed to be made just for him. The effect was contagious, and over time I fell in behind him and started charging into fuming geysers and hydraulics, rarely opting for sane water on the flanks. The notion was to dare the consequences and trust the river. After a dozen outings I'd picked up several of Hank's stunts, though to a far lesser degree; but I could never fathom how he ran those class VI rapids backward.

Once, when we were driving back from New Mexico, he started talking about the desert, then about a Navajo girl he'd known years before, and I thought he was finally going to bare himself. But something caught in the middle of him—I could feel it—and his drift just floated out over the lone and level sand and blew away.

The things he'd do to avoid other paddlers were incredible. He'd yank his boat off the water and into cover if he saw anybody on the river. Once, on the Lower Merced, we holed up in a reed thicket for more than three hours to avoid passing a camp of rafters in daylight. We ran the last six miles in scant moonlight and completely trashed our boats on rocks we never saw. Whatever his reasons, Hank was terrified of being seen. That much I was sure of. He particularly feared coming upon commercial rafters. From that first trip down the Tuolumne, I knew Hank *had* to have competed at some time. Or some notable had at least seen or heard about him. After our moonlight debacle on the Lower Merced, the mystery grabbed my imagination like grim death. I finally called my old coach, Dan Lamay, and asked him if he'd ever heard of a paddler named Hank Crawford.

"Don't think so," he said.

"Yeah, I figured as much. Dan, I've been paddling with a guy who's about twice as good as anybody you've ever seen. Can you remember any phenoms from way back—this guy's probably in his mid-thirties, at least."

"Well, there were standouts, but not like you're talking about. And anyway, you saw all those other guys: Mittan, Richardson, Bonilla. . . ."

Yeah, I had competed against all of those guys.

The conversation drifted to old friends and what everybody was doing, and just as I was accepting that Hank had actually sprung from the blue, Dan chimed back in.

"You know, before Edwards stopped coaching he used to talk about a kid named Hurt, or Huttle, or something like that. I think he was only with the team a short time before he got tossed in jail. I do know he raced against Accomazzo in a world-cup meet over in Italy and beat him pretty handily."

Accomazzo was a legendary, five-time world champion. By the time I was good enough to race against him, he was almost forty-two years old—and he still beat me.

"Supposedly, he crushed him," Dan added, "but I don't know. That had to be fifteen years ago, at least, and I wasn't there."

It took me two days to track down Edwards, who was living with a daughter in Boca Raton, Florida. His voice was breathy and labored, but the words gushed out of him.

"Hart. His name was Ronnie Hart," the old coach corrected. "He was only with the team long enough to compete in one international regatta, over in Corsica, and he won that one by more than twenty seconds. They thought he ran an illegal boat, or was hopped up on pills, and so on. They just couldn't believe an unknown, nineteen-year-old kid could crush the world's best, but Hart did. And with ease. But let me tell you, as good as he was running gates, his real genius was in big whitewater. We'd take training runs down the Snake and Tuolumne, and the kid was pure magic. Sumbitch would run entire sections backward."

"So where is he, coach?" There was a long pause.

"Oh, he's dead now. Died fighting fires in Sequoia. He was a little wild, Hart was, and he plowed his car off the road and his girlfriend got killed. The judge found him negligent and sentenced him hard— like ten years. You know they got convicts fighting fires these days. Hart and a couple others got caught on a ridge. Ronnie Hart never made it off that ridge."

I smiled.

"So coach, did this Hart ever use any weird gear?"

"And how. He'd run these homemade jobs all painted up with Navajo designs. You know, he grew up with the Indians up by Lee's Ferry, on the Colorado River."

"Probably ran the Grand Canyon a lot, eh?"

"Something like two hundred times before he was eighteen. Hart had himself an Indian girlfriend, and they'd both worked for the raft outfitters since they were kids—you know, setting up camp and cooking and what not. Sometimes there wasn't room on the rafts for all the tourists and junk they strap onto them, so Hart started paddling a kayak behind the flotilla. He got to be a legend with those rafters." There was another long pause, and I could hear the coach's rasping breath over the phone. "Kid was only twenty when that fire got him. Nobody will ever know how good he might have become."

Nobody but me, I thought. Whether Edwards and Hart shared a confidence is something I often pondered but never found out, since emphysema carried the old coach away the following spring.

Several days later, Hank and I spread out the charts and reviewed the topography we'd memorized months before. A thick black line, the Rio Juarez, snaked through the contours passing numerous sections of Piedra Caliza—limestone. The nearest road was a farming track perhaps ten miles east of the river, so we—or rather Hank—planned to charter a helicopter in Laredo. The river was in Mexico, where the air space required all kinds of complicated permits, so the pilot would drop us at the mouth of the canyon, just over the border, but wouldn't go any farther. That meant running the river "blind," without scouting before the big water; and this is like marrying a blind date—and having to live or die with whoever turns up. The charts showed no waterfalls, at least. I wouldn't say Hank seemed worried. Concerned, though.

"Good thing we're honed up. This is going to test us," he said, tapping the circuitous black line with his finger. "Second thoughts?"

"None," I lied.

Despite his thirst for violent water, Hank never pushed me into anything. Through all the crazy, seemingly foolhardy stuff we'd done over the last few months, he always ran a grim section first so I could follow his line and would warn me off certain treacherous bits, though he'd normally run them himself. Sometimes he seemed more paranoid about me getting hurt than he was about seeing other people on the water. And his concern about my hide was something beyond just trying to preserve a paddling partner for another run. Life might have taken the heart out of him, but I counted for something he would always show me but never mention.

"I'd never try this alone," he said, folding up the map. "You know that."

I asked him if he had any more beer.

"It's not like we have to do this."

"We're doing it, Hank."

He shrugged. "I created a frigging monster, here."

"Don't flatter yourself, Hank. I was crazy long before I met you."

"Guess so." And he smiled truly.

Right then I wanted to lift the veil, to put my talk with Coach Edwards out in the open, but the timing was off. I'd know when the moment had come.

We moved from the room with the chart into one just like it but with a TV. A Lakers game was on. We lazed around drinking beer and watching the game and barely talked. Both our minds were already on the Rio Juarez. I'd noticed the little framed photo the moment I came into the room, wondering why Hank had it out like that because he was so private about everything. I went over and looked at the photo. Hank said nothing. The only thing I could figure is that he wanted me to see it.

The photo was a Polaroid—and not a very good one. Hank was in a thrashed, fiberglass kayak all painted up with those Indian designs. Right beside him, hip deep in the muddy water of the lower Colorado, was a girl, her black hair pulled back, her dark eyes locked on Hank. They both looked about seventeen. Hank had been out in the sun so much he looked almost Navajo himself. There was an eerie sameness about them—something much more than simple affinity—that was unmistakable.

"What was her name?" I finally asked.

"Lucy," he said. He didn't need to tell me she'd been in the car Hank had piled up over fifteen years before.

We were on the Rio Juarez the following Saturday. From a nearby sandbar, the river's howl drowned out the roar of the chopper, whirring back to the border. At first sight of the river, my heart leapt into my mouth. A breakneck sluice, the torrent rip-roared directly into a gorge before hooking right and disappearing. For several minutes we just stared. I didn't know water could move so fast. An occasional uprooted oak tore by, barely holding its own above the frothy surface. I kept pushing down the urge to bushwhack out to that farm road ten miles east.

"Looks like a big sled ride," Hank said, studying the flow.

"Should be okay if we stay centered in the current," I said, trying to believe it. Four months back, I wouldn't have entered that river with a .45 at my temple. We had no idea what lay a quarter mile downstream. Hank shoved his kayak to the water line, slithered in, and cinched his spray skirt so taut the draw cord flexed the combing.

"Pull over whenever you can," Hank said, eyes straight ahead.

"We've got to scout this one good." I nodded and tightened my helmet.

We shoved off together. Hank dug a couple of deep strokes, and I fell in behind him. When we entered the current, my head snapped back from the speed. Right off I went over but rolled up okay. We barreled on, knifing through towering rooster tails and haystacks of whitewater, constantly leaning, bracing, trying to follow the inner flow. The river churned so that the top few feet were cream, so we moved principally on feel. The current eased as we entered the true gorge, limestone slabs angling up sharply from the water line. Then we heard it, around the corner: a low rumble, pulsing between the narrowing canyon walls.

"Get left," shrieked Hank, digging hard across the strong current, his boat lunging with each stroke. No eddies meant no stopping. We turned the corner with our shoulders close to the left wall. Just ahead, the entire left side of the river spun into a hideous whirlpool, the very edge of which swirled clockwise up and off the left-hand wall. A halo of mist revolved around the maw, which gained in size and fury the closer we got. The bastard had to be thirty feet across. No doubt about it, we were heading for a no-exit "keeper" hole from hell.

"Hug the cliff," Hank screamed.

Our only chance lay in riding the left-hand lip of the whirlpool, using its downstream momentum to spin us past the cavity. Feeling the circular current yanking me right, I dug my paddle deep left. My boat jumped straight and I caught the white surge flowing off the wall. The force rolled me on edge, the bottom of my boat grinding across the limestone. The mist blinded me, but for one split second the halo parted and I gaped straight into the depths of the gullet, the home of great and grinding boulders. The noise was deafening, the mist thick with the flinty smell of pulverized rock. Just when I thought I might tumble into the eye, my boat slipped down off the wall and I caught the downstream edge of the whirlpool. My bow shot up under the crosscurrent, and I felt it drawing me back in. I teetered, dead in the water, rocking on the very brink.

"Dig!" Hank screamed.

A few atomic strokes put me onto the calm. I screamed until the rock walls trembled, then paddled over to Hank, his face twisted up into that grin of his.

"Buckle up, hombre, we're heading for the Real McCoy."

Below, the river blasted between two walls of living rock that reared vertically off the water. The river bottom was mostly sand and the water ran like glass, though so swift that we covered roughly fifteen miles in the next hour (if the topo map was correct). Twice the river pinched to the merest culvert and passed beneath natural bridges; the ceiling on one was only about five feet above our heads.

Then the river steepened, rifling us through a slalom course of rock pinnacles sprouting from the water like great tenpins on end. From each side of these leapt treacherous wakes, requiring all my expertise running gates to avoid them. Twice the wakes flipped me, and twice I barely avoided a grievous head-on. Smacking a pinnacle might not have iced me outright, but it would have demolished the boat and I would have drowned in spite of my life jacket. There was no shoreline to grope for, no alcove to hide in. When we finally pulled into calm waters, we'd been toiling full bore for more than two hours. We stroked over left to a thank-God shelf, dragged our boats onto it, and collapsed.

Hank had smacked the canyon wall hard enough to cost him the left arm of his wet suit, and he had a nasty rake across the forearm. I'd struck so much debris that my boat leaked slightly from half a dozen spots. From the second we'd entered the canyon there was no going back and no getting out. A look downstream would have turned the stomach of a statue.

One hundred yards below, the river plunged and accelerated into a boiling rage that seemed too savage for mere rock to contain. Fifty yards farther, the canyon pitched like a ski jump before hooking sharply left. At the elbow, the entire river dashed forty feet up the right wall and formed a seething, tsunami-sized perpetual wave with a nimbus of vapors swirling above it.

"Look at that," Hank yelled. A huge log torpedoed past. Stripped bald from its rugged passage, it resembled a giant white bone bobbing atop the whitewater. It disappeared, then popped back up just before the elbow. My guts turned to water as it arced forty feet up and sixty feet across the perpetual wave. At the wave's cresting apex, it tumbled down, end over end, and was washed around the corner.

Staring at that tumbling log, a thousand things welled up inside of me—dreams I was only vaguely aware of, things I wanted to do, a woman I wanted to meet but never had—and I knew these things would never make it past that wave. The moment ruined me, and I sat there dashed and remote. I would have prayed to God if I hadn't hated him so much.

"You see that?" Hank screamed, citing the huge log. "Hell, we can *make* this. The water's so high it'll flush us right through so long as we stay centered in the current. But we've got to come in low on that wave. That's for sure." Hank cinched the strap on his helmet and started for his boat. "No good just staring at it, Lance."

But I might as well have been part of the rock I was sitting on. Hank was setting out to tackle something that combined a forty-foot Makaha wave with a section of Niagara Falls, but none of that mattered and it never had. He'd try the unthinkable because only after he'd slipped through another terminal rapid did he feel that his life was worth living. Then he'd start spiraling down to zero again, and it was back to insane water, then back to zero, and it was just one endless, crazy go-around. But it had to end somewhere. One look downriver told me where.

Hank grabbed my arm and said, "I'm scared, Lance. But we're going to make this. Believe it."

I had to believe him, or try to convince myself I believed him, because I could no more claw over those sheer wet walls and escape the canyon than I could paddle back upriver. The only way out was over that perpetual wave. And the Holy Ghost couldn't survive that wave.

"We're never going to make this," I said.

For the briefest moment Hank seemed ready to admit it, that we were finished. But he caught himself at last and said nothing.

"I guess it doesn't matter to someone who's got nothing to lose," I added.

"I've got you to lose. So quit acting like you're not worth saving."

"Fuck you," I said, glaring back at him. I felt as if the thunderous water below had rushed through my stomach.

We stood glaring at each other—or rather, I glared and Hank looked away. I felt small, because before we ever set foot in Mexico Hank had said we didn't have to run this river at all, and I insisted that we did. And yet I also felt betrayed because Hank's compulsion to escape the wreckage of his life had drawn me into a river of no return. This was unfair to Hank, but my blood still boiled to see him count on my readiness to follow him into the next world. I slouched back on the rock and tried to steady up and even forget, but all I could think about were Hank's early morning phone calls and his fumbling to reach out to me, and the plain fact that I would never meet that woman now and that we were both dust, and all of this made the situation pitiful.

"This is no way for two friends to handle a minor obstacle," Hank said.

"Minor?" I said, looking downstream. "You got to risk your life to save it, fair enough. But paddling into *that*—. Shit, Hank. We're just tossing ours away."

"How can you say that about something you've never even tried?"

"I've never tried blowing my brains out, neither, but I can reckon the outcome if I did. Look at that thing. *Listen* to it." We were 150 yards away from the worst of it, and it still sounded like an Apollo rocket lifting off. The notion of intentionally paddling into that chaos sickened me, more because I had no choice but to do it. We fell back into silence again. I should have hauled out my conversation with Coach Edwards and confronted Ronnie Hart himself, but in dangerous situations you think only of yourself and I wasn't worried about anything but my next breath.

Hank moved about ten feet away, sat down, and stared grimly into a patch of calm water below us. The torment he stoically bore all those years looked to be pushing him into the rock. He surely knew he was finally up against it, and the way he sat there with a numb look on his face, watching the river, I thought maybe he might dive into the current and be done with the whole business. But slowly, as I studied him with a sort of morbid intrigue, I realized—or thought I realized—that he wasn't brooding or groveling at all, rather focusing on what had to be done. And that's what, in a terrible kind of way, made the guy so magnificent: this brute resolve to push beyond the memories to the rapids beyond. That he could never push completely free was beside the point. The marvel was that he didn't know but to try, and to try with the faith of a falling man lunging for a cobweb. It was all a kind of madness, of course, and as usual, a tiny bit of it slowly rubbed off on me. After a couple of minutes I asked, "You think we got any chance here at all?"

"I do," he said, turning toward me and flashing that sly grin of his.

"Well, anything's better than sitting here looking at it." We silently got back into our kayaks, secured the spray skirts, and paddled over to the far right. Danger and delight grew on one stalk for Hank, and even now he acted like our fortune was ensured. I felt that if I had to die, paddling straight into the teeth of it was as good a way as any.

We hit the current and were off.

Vaulting toward the bend, I saw that Hank—just ahead—came in too high as he charged onto the perpetual wave. He sliced across, suddenly dragged his right blade, and shot up to the crest. Momentarily weightless, he dug his right blade deep: The stern of his boat slid around, and he shot down the wave—backward, but perfectly aligned.

Now facing me, Hank plunged down off the wave and into the cataract before us, that inimitable grin all over his face. Then I too dove into the falls and was swallowed.

Locked inside the plunging tube, I fell for what seemed like minutes. The impact ripped me from my boat, and the falls drove me to the bottom and pinned me there face down, like a pinioned stag. Then I was dashed around and my limbs felt like they were being ripped off my body. I surfaced facing the falls, where wakes swamped me over and over. Without a life jacket, I would have been gone. Limp and gasping, I bobbed into calm waters. I spotted Hank downstream, an arm draped over each boat, retching up half the river. But his hacking soon turned to howling. I struggled over to the boats, draped my arms over the bow, and blew about a pint of water out of my sinuses.

"I defy you to find a tougher run!" Hank wailed.

"I don't want to," I coughed out.

"That's it. The ultimate—no one can top it," he rambled on. "I'll never try, I promise you."

"And you took the easy way. . . ." Hank's grin confirmed what I hadn't had time to think through: that he'd intentionally lined up high on the wave and had taken on the falls—backward. And what finally surfaced from the spume was not a fugitive, not a snake-bitten loner, but a kid from an old Polaroid picture. I knew no matter what might happen the rest of the day, Hank could never tumble all the way back down to zero. Later, perhaps. For sure he would. But not that day. That day was his. Was ours.

We kicked over to the narrow shore, dumped the water from our boats, and lay back. Both kayaks were thrashed, and I wished we'd taken the plastic ones instead of the fiberglass boats, which were lighter and faster but fragile in comparison. I noted the last run had ground the little Navajo design off Hank's boat. No matter. Hank kept blubbering and slapping my back in a way I would have sworn was impossible thirty minutes earlier. I was tempted to reveal my secret, but Hank was so high that I didn't want to risk pulling him back down.

Until then, I didn't fully realize how lucky we were because I'd been fretting so hard over trying to survive—or rather, about the fact that we were positively going to die. Now I felt released from some very dark jaws. Though the soggy map showed more limestone below, we had quit the narrowest canyon and by all indications had only twenty miles of easier river to reach El Estribo, the "Stirrup," a town of 9,000.

We'd planned on two days, but it was only midafternoon, so we pushed on. I felt half dead but snapped to at the first whitewater, where Hank clowned through fifteen-foot combers. The guy was paddling a hundred miles above the water.

Then the river suddenly dropped, charging on with the same fury it had above the falls. We cranked around a bend, and just before us the entire river flowed straight into a mountainside. Of course, it went under this buttress, but the only visible breach was a tiny chink, dead center, looking like a doghouse door as we hurtled toward it. This all happened faster than I could panic, and I reflexively lined up behind Hank. Twenty feet before the wall, I saw the chink was wide enough but would clip our heads off. Hank suddenly rolled upside down and knifed into the crack just as I flipped over.

Blazing down a swift river, upside down, inside a mountain, is a sensation I won't try and describe. Fearing I'd get my head torn off if I rolled back up, I stayed upside down till my lungs caught fire. I rolled up only to carom off a wall and plunge down again. Whatever I hit demolished my boat and pitched me head over heels through the darkness. Finally, belched out of the mountain into calm but swift-moving water, I didn't know who or where I was and for several minutes bobbed around in a carbonated pool. Slowly my head cleared. Facing the buttress rising out of the river, the water churned and gurgled from the bowels of the rock like a torrent from a giant storm grate. I couldn't see where I'd come out. Under the waterline, somewhere. I spun around and dog-paddled through fragments of our splintered boats floating around me. I was scraped and battered but otherwise unhurt, still clutching my unbroken paddle. Beyond me, the river crept through open savanna. The difficulties were all behind us now. But where was Hank? Then I spotted him, floating by the right bank. He didn't move as I stroked over to him. He was conscious, though dazed. I grabbed the collar of his life jacket and dragged him onto shore.

I felt around for broken bones, and when I rolled him over, I nearly puked. Two daggers of fiberglass were sunk deep into his back. I drew out the first one, maybe four inches long, directly from his spine. Hank's legs twitched for a second, then went dead. When I removed an even bigger shard from his side, blood gushed out and nothing I could do would stop it. The guy was going to die on me then and there, though I wouldn't admit it to myself. I dragged Hank onto a little rock bench and sat him upright. Only then did I see that blood from a head gash had drained into his eyes.

"Can you get my eyes?" Hank asked calmly. "I can't move my arms." He looked pale. I wiped his eyes.

"You've got some deep wounds in your back, Hank, but we'll just rest up a bit and take it from there."

"I'm history, Lance. I can't even feel my body." I couldn't say anything and must have looked hysterical.

"Relax," he reassured me. I couldn't look at him just then. When I could, he flashed me that grin of his.

"These last few months have meant something to me, Lance. You're the best paddler I've ever seen."

"I'm nothing compared to you, Mr. Ronnie Hart."

He coughed out a chuckle.

"I called old Edwards and he told me everything. Even how you crushed Accomazzo in Italy."

"He wouldn't have made it ten feet down this river."

"Ronnie, you could have been world champ for twenty years. And I should know, because I was the champion for three."

"Sounds good to hear my name." I wiped the blood from his eyes again. "I never really cared about running gates and all that. That was never kayaking to me. What mattered was big water, and we ran the biggest."

"Ronnie, nobody will ever repeat what we've done—ever."

"I won't say never, but we were first."

"You were first, Ronnie. I always followed your lead."

We talked quietly for another ten minutes. I promised to keep Ronnie's secret and to bury him next to the river. His voice waned to a whisper, and though he couldn't raise an arm, his courage never flagged.

"Tell me about the girl," I said. "The one in that photo."

A serenity came over him, as though two strong brown arms had reached out from the void and were bearing him off to a better land. His eyes closed. For several minutes his lips moved in a conversation I was not party to. And smiling slightly, the great Ronnie Hart melded with the purring current and slowly floated away. It all happened so fast.

I broke my paddle in half and used it to dig into the moist soil. In an hour, I laid Ronnie Hart to rest, where his soul could hear the rapids roll so long as the river flowed. As I heaped the ground upon him, I tried to say something pious, but I wasn't making any sense, so I finally quit trying. Still, it was right, me fumbling for a few words, and it was right and fitting that Ronnie had died there. The future held nothing for him. He would never get any higher than he'd been that day, nor would he ever live down his past. For a few brief hours the river had taken him back to a time he'd never wanted to leave. Now, he would never have to. I threw the broken paddles in the river and watched them drift into the night. I had nothing left.

The book had slammed shut on Ronnie Hart, and the fitting end was there, on the river. Unfortunately, I had to get off the river and out of Mexico. I collapsed on shore that night, watched a cold moon inch across the sky, and arose battered, stiff, and exhausted. And starving. I took a compass bearing due east and set off, hoping to gain the farm road in half a day, terrain permitting.

It didn't.

After cresting a hill, the wet dirt turned to mud, ankle deep for a mile, then knee deep for two more. I had to plow a trough through the ooze. The sun beat down, and I kept thinking the mud would turn to quicksand. About noon, the mud gave way to waist-high thicket, each branch bristling with hooked thorns. No use trying to avoid the barbs, since getting free from one meant getting snagged by another. Within ten minutes thorns were tearing straight through my wet suit and into my flesh. Soon, the shrub grew so thick that I had to drag myself over the top on all fours. Branches snapped, dropping me into thorns that slashed my face and arms. My wet suit hung in bloody tatters. I was so weary I could barely focus on my compass. Every time I tried to move on hunch, I found myself going in circles. Hours later I stumbled across a stagnant creek. I was too exhausted to move, much less continue, but the bugs were fearsome and swarmed about my wounds. To escape them, I groveled into the black water, set my head on the rocky bank, and passed out. By morning, the mosquitoes had nearly closed both my eyes.

I pushed on, weak and stumbling. The ground was riven with little trenches that I would tumble into and exhaust myself trying to claw out of. My throat burned, and it took everything I had to read the compass. I would close my eyes, concentrate, then quickly glance down before the needle would fuzz and dance. I entered a half-mile stretch of putrid quagmire, passed by half swimming, half fording through the thick green soup. Every time I touched a log, I thought it was a crocodile or something worse and I struck out with fresh vigor. The final bog ended at a clay bank. But every time I tried to climb out, the lip mushed away, pitching me back into the mire. The reeking water felt like acid on my wounds.

I gave up many times.

On flat ground at last, I crawled under a tree and lay breathless in meager shade. Voices came from nearby, and I looked up and saw—or thought I saw—two men on mules. But I was too wasted to hail them. I must have passed out. When I came to, I spent my last energies crawling over to the road, maybe fifty yards. Of the next few hours I remember only fragments: a sunset, an oxcart, a bumpy ride, and a candle flickering in an adobe hovel.

I came around to find an old Indian woman digging thorns from my nakedness with a dull pin. An old man handed me a wineskin of water and I guzzled it in one long draw. My hands were so torn and swollen I couldn't have even held a kayak paddle—and I never would again. I spent the next day dozing and eating while the old woman applied red mud paddies and caustic herbs to my wounds. I never understood a thing she or the old man said, so I couldn't convey my nightmare. Maybe that was better, because from then on Ronnie's death was strictly my own affair. The next day they hitched up the cart and took me to a highway near the border. I've always meant to go back and thank them. Maybe someday I will.

THE GRAND CANYON

Jeff Bennett

*T*he restless, unstable, or beer-addled mind can conjure many what-if challenges that, when expressed, seem entirely insane. For example, skydiving without a parachute, solo climbing El Capitan barefooted, sailing around the world without a compass, or big wave surfing in an inner tube (provided you first get a tow-in). So what about Bill Beer and John Daggett who, in 1955, decided to swim the Colorado River through the Grand Canyon? "Swim?!" you ask. The modern-day river guide will betray his very mother to avoid swimming a single inch of wild water; yet here, nearly fifty years ago, two young men who had never even seen a rapid decided to swim the biggest water in the land! And remember, back then, rafting the Grand was so rare and considered so magnificently courageous that if you should have met a Grand Canyon veteran in the flesh, you'd be tempted to go up and touch their robes. As so often happens, money—or rather, the lack of it—proved a deciding factor for the expedition. The result was a high-water mark in the history of American adventuring—bold, original, and stark-raving mad. Suffice it to say that Beer and Daggett became completely engulfed in their excellent adventure, one that has never since been considered, let alone accomplished.*

‡   ‡   ‡

The Grand Canyon. Having said those three words—The Grand Canyon—what visions come to mind? Side hikes to Deer Creek Falls? Lunch breaks at Painted Wall Cavern? Or do you conjure images of huge waves and rapids like Granite, Crystal and Lava Falls?

Chances are, whether you've run the Colorado River through the Grand Canyon or not, you've heard about the Grand Canyon experience. Stories of hair-raising flips at Lava Falls, of peaceful drifting among spectacular, timeless rock corridors, and endless nights of world-class camping. The Grand Canyon mystique permeates every facet of modern river running, leaving few of us untouched.

Legends have been borne on the massive waves of the Colorado River, and strong men have perished under the weight of its relentless currents. Even contemporary travelers— nestled among the comforts of Hypalon tubing, welded steel frames, and aluminum shafted oars— display heartfelt respect for the awesome power of the Colorado River. The Colorado's rapids are forces to be reckoned with. Rowed, portaged, or lined. But never swum. Or are they?

This story begins with Bill Beer and John Daggett—two young men set upon the adventure of a lifetime—standing above the raging maelstrom at Soap Creek Rapid. Both men are trying to decide who should have the honor of going through the rapid first.

At first blush, this scene looks little different from many other Grand Canyon trips: 7,300 cfs of unbridled whitewater moving past their feet with all the subtlety of a runaway train. Scouting was a mandatory precursor to survival. A line would be chosen, and the walk back to the top of the rapid would begin.

The only difference was that, this time, their walk upstream would not lead them back to a boat. There would be no reliance upon the massive flotation usually provided by modern rafts. Instead, the bold pair would step right into the river above the rapid, towing their dry bags behind them, and *swim* the mighty Grand Canyon.

I first heard about this adventure from an old Grand Canyon guide and later read about it in Bill Beer's book *We Swam the Grand Canyon: The True Story of a Cheap Vacation That Got a Little Out of Hand*. So remarkable was Beer's tale that I felt it necessary that modern adventurers share a moment of humility while bowing to the courage and audacity displayed by Beer's and Daggett's accomplishment.

By April of 1955, barely 200 adventurers had descended the Grand Canyon. Those that had survived the run were heroes. Venerated river pioneers. But to Bill Beer and John Daggett, simply rafting the Grand was old news. During a small get-together, Bill and John made their disdain know to their friends. They belittled the rivermen's accomplishments. But instead of simply mocking Grand Canyon veterans, John Daggett took the conversation one step further. Knowing full well that

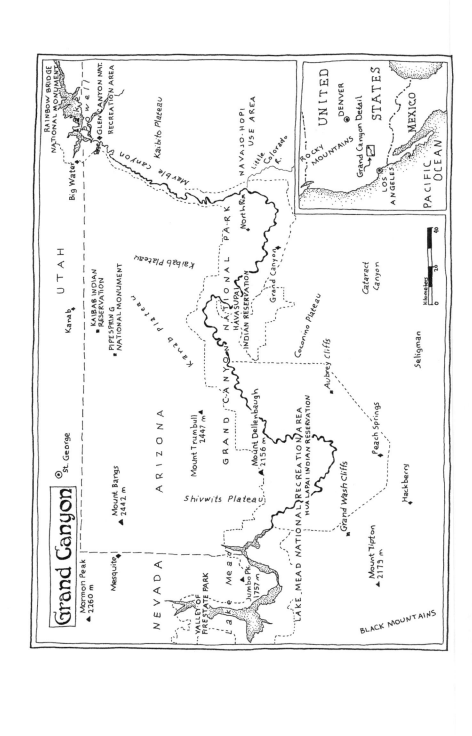

neither he nor Bill had enough money to purchase a raft or buy passage on one, John said that they could—and would—swim the Colorado.

It was a bold if crazy idea, to say the least. Only eighty-six years had passed since John Wesley Powell's historic 1869 descent, and only seventeen years since the first boaters had run all of the rapids without portaging. Plus, neither Beer nor Daggett had ever even *seen* the Colorado before.

But the idea grew. Bill and John spent time at the library, studying maps and reading old chronicles from prior expeditions. They also wrote to the gauging station at Lee's Ferry for water levels and temperatures for different times of the year.

As they continued their research, many of their problems became immediately apparent. Since there was no Glen Canyon Dam in those days, peak flows exceeded twenty times the volume of low flows. Lake Mead, at the end of the Canyon, appeared on the map to be fifty to sixty miles long with no take-out. And the water—regularly in the low fifties—would be numbingly cold for swimmers on an extended trip.

Any doubts about pulling off the trip were shorn when at a party John announced their plans to swim the Colorado. They now had to live up to their proclamation and prove to themselves it could be done.

Though the information from the Lee's Ferry gauging station told them that warmer water would await them in August, Bill and John pressed toward their April launch date for fear of losing momentum. They set out to obtain the necessary gear to sustain their body heat in the chilly spring waters and to keep their gear dry while floating downstream.

Since neither could afford wet suits, they purchased rubber shirts for $15 apiece from a local dive shop and completed their outfits with woolen long johns. They purchased rubber World War II radio boxes for eighty-nine cents apiece, and they crammed them full with sleeping bags, cooking gear, and twenty-four days' worth of food. They even brought along a movie camera given to them by a Hollywood filmmaker. Ironically, the film for the camera cost more than a raft would have!

Before departing for their "vacation," Bill and John were interviewed by local TV stations and the *Los Angeles Times*. The pair made the media promise, however, that news of their trip would not be publicized until they were on the river. That way, it would be too late for the authorities to stop them. They then wrote their wills and headed toward Lee's Ferry.

Their first encounter with the Colorado was at Needles, California. John jumped from the car and tested the water. He proclaimed it too cold for swimming but was reminded by Bill that they had the rubber shirts and long johns to keep them warm.

Their next stop was Pierce Ferry, a small, nowhere place they had spotted on the maps while searching for a possible take-out. There they made camp for the night. That night they were rocked awake by the earth-shattering blast of an atom bomb detonating thirty miles away at a Nevada test site! By morning things were looking better. John walked north from camp and found the river two miles away.

Along their route from Pierce Ferry to the Lee's Ferry put-in, Bill and John stopped along the South Rim to catch a tourist's view of the Canyon, then finished the day's travel at Lee's Ferry.

By morning their gear was double-wrapped in plastic and shoved into the obese rubber boxes. Before entering the river they shot a little pretrip footage of a nearby sign, which read, "No swimming in the Colorado." They then donned their gear, carried their equipment-laden boxes to the water (the boxes now weighed eighty-five pounds each!), and swam into the river. Back on the shore, Dave—their trusty shuttle driver—took a few more movies before waving farewell.

The river, having heard nothing about their grand scheme, bid them a rude welcome. Their first day on the river was fraught with windy blasts of sand and water, leaking boxes, wet maps, and soaking wet camera gear. Even as they made their first night's camp at Six Mile Wash, the river gods hissed and snarled, lifting sand and ashes from their campfire and spewing it all over their gear. The only way they could see their way along the beach, and protect their eyes from the fire's cinders, was to wear their diving masks in camp!

Their first taste of whitewater came at Badger Creek Rapid. Rather than test the main current, John and Bill tried to slip along the bank in the slower, shallower parts of the rapid. This miniature adventure quickly taught them to avoid the shallows, thus avoiding the bruising effects of fast currents and hard boulders.

As John and Bill made their way into Marble Canyon, the immensity of their experience began to impress them. Despite the cold, and the paranoia of what lurked downstream, each man took time to appreciate the majestic beauty that has made the Grand Canyon so famous. They also began to learn more about river hydrology as they jounced their way downriver.

They learned to run rapids feet first and were able to pick out safer routes down big, glassy tongues and around nasty holes. Still, John met a huge, undercut rock face first in President Harding. After a brief bout with the sharp rock, he emerged cut severely on his head and hand. Though the injuries were not so severe as to nix the expedition, it was a quick and harsh reminder of the river's power, and of how far they were from the nearest hospital.

Soon after drifting into the Grand Canyon itself, John and Bill pulled over for a rest just below Tanner Rapid. Looking at the horizon from their camp, they could see Desert View Tower on the South Rim. They talked of hiking out the Bright Angel Trail, eighteen miles downstream, to resupply their soaked food cache and to acquire some much needed repair materials.

After some lunch, they got back in the water and swam to their next camp below Unkar Rapid. There they found they had left their coffee upstream and decided that it was now imperative that they resupply at the South Rim.

The next morning marked the one-week anniversary of their put-in date. It also marked the day they ran the second biggest rapid on the Colorado—Fiancé Rapid (Crystal was not a very large rapid in 1955). After considerable procrastination, and with much trepidation, they made their way into the heart of the current and swam into the rapid. The river proved to be very forgiving and released them unscathed.

Downstream, they cached their gear behind some rocks and made their way from the Kaibab Suspension Bridge onto the Kaibab Trail. One of the first men to come down the trail recognized the duo and informed them that rangers were looking for them. This was their biggest concern—that the rangers would stop them from completing their trip.

At Bright Angel Lodge, high atop the South Rim, they noticed a local newspaper, in which the headline read, "Fear Pair Lost in Colorado Swim Try." Excited by the newspaper reports, their success thus far, and the hope of complete success, John and Bill began talking to the locals about their trip. But their unbridled chatter passed the ears of the rangers, who then cornered John and Bill and held them for a short while in an effort to dissuade them from the trip. Despite threats of jail time, the pair convinced the rangers that they should be allowed to finish the trip so that hoards of daredevils wouldn't arrive trying to complete the trip themselves. Their philosophy worked. The rangers released the pair and even gave them some helpful hints about the next major rapids: Horn Creek Rapid, Hermit Rapid, *and Lava Falls.*

By day twenty, the river had risen to 14,000 cfs. Standing on the right bank above Lava Falls—where the Colorado drops thirty-seven feet through an incredible cataract—John and Bill peered into the river with enormous respect. "At first sight," Bill said in his book, "Lava Falls seemed to deserve its ugly reputation. On second sight, it still deserved it."

They lingered endlessly—as modern river runners still do—before entering the rapid. They talked of possible lines, threw driftwood in the river only to watch it disappear, emptied their full bladders, and ate lunch. Finally, Bill heaved a sigh, grabbed his bags, and entered the river.

With John filming from a rocky perch on the right-hand shore, Bill shot into the great rapid. Though he had picked out a clean line while scouting, the rapid's entrance was nearly invisible from water level. He missed a clean tongue and slipped off the brink twenty feet too far to the left. In the next few seconds he cartwheeled through holes, over waves, past rocks, and, eventually, into the safe haven of an eddy downstream of Lava Falls.

Next, John swam the rapid while Bill took pictures with a 35mm camera. When they rejoined, they agreed that Lava was the worst rapid on the river, but not quite so deadly as people had claimed. They even had enough wit left about them to talk about doing it again! Sometime. . . .

Twenty-five days into the trip, they found themselves drifting through unfamiliar territory. They had not bought the last strip map for the lower canyon because they could not afford it. They were down to one can of peaches between them and were worried that their rations would run out before the end of the trip.

Finally, passing around another bend, they spotted people waving to them from the banks near Pierce Ferry. As they drew closer, they noticed that there were three people, one of whom was quickly snapping pictures while the others beckoned Bill and John to shore. The group included Bill and Buzz Belknap and a ranger sent there to await their arrival. By twilight, Bill Belknap directed them to the mudflat landing at Pierce Ferry. There they exited the river—and entered the legends of river runners.

The full story of Beer's and Daggett's adventure is captured in Beer's book, *We Swam the Grand Canyon: The True Story of a Cheap Vacation That Got a Little Out of Hand.* It's available through The Mountaineers.

THE SELWAY

Pam Houston

"The Selway" is from Pam Houston's superb book of short narratives, Cowboys Are My Weakness. First published in 1992, "Selway" was quickly recognized as a classic in adventure writing. Blow-by-blow action accounts hurl us onto the whitewater where we feel the stout current in our guts; more generalized journalistic deliveries typically add historical background and assorted facts to the venture; literary treatments frame the experience in deft prose. "Selway" conveys all three. But what makes "Selway" a classic is Houston's gift for placing the experience in the broader context of her life—not just as an adventurer but as a woman and a human being on a nameless search. While the river provides the running thread, the focus never strays from the characters and the emotional texture of their experience. This approach—fraught with as many hazards as the wildest rapid—lets us share not just another ride on the "liquid locomotive" but invites us to taste the stuff of her soul. As with all classics, the result is a gift to all who read the tale.

‡   ‡   ‡

It was June the seventh and we'd driven eighteen hours of pavement and sixty miles of dirt to find out the river was at high water, the highest of the year, of several years, and rising. The ranger, Ramona, wrote on our permit, "We do not recommend boating at this level," and then she looked at Jack.

"We're just gonna go down and take a look at it," he said. "See if the river gives us a sign." He tried to slide the permit away from

Ramona, but her short dark fingers held it against the counter. I looked from one to the other. I knew Jack didn't believe in signs.

"Once you get to Moose Creek you're committed," she said. "There's no time to change your mind after that. You've got Double Drop and Little Niagara and Ladle, and they just keep coming like that, one after another with no slow water in between."

She was talking about rapids. This was my first northern trip, and after a lazy spring making slow love between rapids on the wide desert rivers, I couldn't imagine what all the fuss was about.

"If you make it through the Moose Creek series there's only a few more real bad ones; Wolf Creek is the worst. After that the only thing to worry about is the take-out point. The beach will be under water. And if you miss it, you're over Selway Falls."

"Do you have a river guide?" Jack said, and when she bent under the counter to get one he tried again to slide the permit away. She pushed a small, multifolded map in his direction.

"Don't rely on it," she said. "The rapids aren't even marked in the right place."

"Thanks for your help," Jack said. He gave the permit a sharp tug and put it in his pocket.

"There was an accident today," Ramona said. "In Ladle."

"Anybody hurt?" Jack asked.

"It's not official."

"Killed?"

"The water's rising," Ramona said, and turned back to her desk.

At the put-in, the water crashed right over the top of the depth gauge. The grass grew tall and straight through the slats of the boat ramp.

"Looks like we're the first ones this year," Jack said.

The Selway has the shortest season of any river in North America. They don't plow the snow till the first week in June, and by the last week in July there's not enough water to carry a boat. They only allow one party a day on the river that they select from a nationwide lottery with thousands of applicants each year. You can try your whole life and never get a permit.

"Somebody's been here," I said. "The people who flipped today."

Jack didn't answer. He was looking at the gauge. "It's up even from this morning," he said, "They said this morning it was six feet."

Jack and I have known each other almost a year. I'm the fourth in a series of long-term girlfriends he's never gotten around to proposing

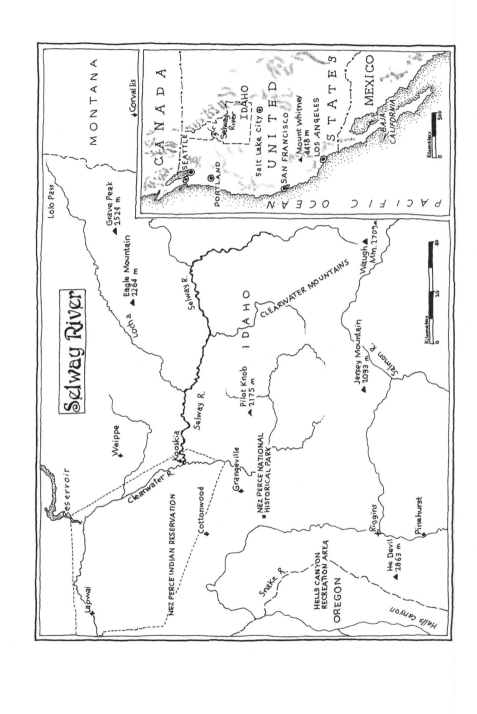

Selway River

to. He likes me because I'm young enough not to sweat being single and I don't put pressure on him the way the others did. They wanted him to quit running rivers, to get a job that wasn't seasonal, to raise a family like any man his age. They wouldn't go on trips with him, not even once to see what it was like, and I couldn't imagine that they knew him in any way that was complete if they hadn't known him on the river, if they hadn't seen him row.

I watched him put his hand in the water. "Feel that, baby," he said. "That water was snow about fifteen minutes ago."

I stuck my foot in the water and it went numb in about ten seconds. I've been to four years of college and I should know better, but I love it when he calls me baby.

Jack has taken a different high-water trip each year for the last fifteen, on progressively more difficult rivers. When a river is at high water it's not just deeper and faster and colder than usual. It's got a different look and feel from the rest of the year. It's dark and impatient and turbulent, like a volcano or a teenage boy. It strains against its banks and it churns around and under itself. I sat and stared at the river and wondered if it was this wild at the put-in what it would look like in the rapids.

"If anything happened to you," he said, and threw a stick out to the middle of the channel. "It must be moving nine miles an hour." He walked up and down the boat ramp. "What do you think?" he said.

"I think this is a chance of a lifetime," I said. "I think you're the best boatman you know." I wanted to feel the turbulence underneath me. I wanted to run a rapid that could flip a boat. I hadn't taken anything like a risk in months. I wanted to think about dying.

It was already early evening, and once we made the decision to launch, there were two hours of rigging before we could get on the water. On the southern rivers we'd boat sometimes for an hour after dark just to watch what the moon did to the water. On the Selway there was a rapid that could flip your boat around every corner. It wasn't getting pitch dark till ten thirty that far north, where the June dusk went on forever, but it wasn't really light either and we wouldn't be able to see very far ahead. We told ourselves we'd go a tenth of a mile and make camp, but you can't camp on a sheer granite wall, and the river has to give you a place to get stopped and get tied.

I worked fast and silently, wondering if we were doing the right thing and knowing if we died it would really be my fault, because as much as I knew Jack wanted to go, he wouldn't have pushed me if I'd said I was scared. Jack was untamable, but he had some sense and a lot of respect for the river. He relied on me to speak with the voice of reason, to be life-protecting because I'm a woman and that's how he thinks women are, but I've never been protective enough of anything, least of all myself.

At 9:15 we untied the rope and let the river take us. "The first place that looks campable," Jack said.

Nine miles an hour is fast in a rubber raft on a river you've never boated when there's not quite enough light to see what's in front of you. We were taking on water over the bow almost immediately, even though the map didn't show any rapids for the first two miles. It was hard for me to take my eyes off Jack, the way his muscles strained with every stroke, first his upper arms, then his upper thighs. He was silent, thinking it'd been a mistake to come, but I was laughing and bailing water and combing the banks for a flat spot and jumping back and forth over my seat to kiss him, and watching while his muscles flexed.

"Are you bailing? I'm standing in water back here," he said, so I bailed faster but the waves kept crashing over the bow.

"I can't move this boat," he said, which I knew wasn't entirely true, but it was holding several hundred gallons of water times eight pounds a gallon, and that's more weight than I'd care to push around.

"Here," he said. "Camp. Let's try to get to shore."

He pointed to a narrow beach a hundred yards downstream. The sand looked black in the twilight; it was long and flat enough for a tent.

"Get the rope ready," he said. "You're gonna have to jump for it and find something to wrap around fast."

He yelled "jump" but it was too early and I landed chest-deep in the water and the cold took my breath but I scrambled across the rocks to the beach and wrapped around a fallen trunk just as the rope went tight. The boat dragged the trunk and me ten yards down the beach before Jack could get out and pull the nose of it up on shore.

"This may have been real stupid," he said.

I wanted to tell him how the water made me feel, how crazy and happy I felt riding on top of water that couldn't hold itself in, but he was scared, for the first time since I'd known him, so I kept my mouth shut and went to set up the tent.

In the morning the tent was covered with a thin layer of ice. Jack got up and made coffee, and we heard the boaters coming just in time to get our clothes on. They threw us their rope and we caught it. There were three of them, three big men in a boat considerably bigger than ours. Jack poured them coffee. We all sat down on the fallen log.

"You launched late last night?" the tallest, darkest one said. He had curly black hair and a wide open face. Jack nodded. "Too late," he said. "Twilight boating."

"It's up another half a foot this morning," the man said. "It's supposed to peak today at seven feet."

The official Forest Service document declares the Selway unsafe for boating above six feet. Seven feet is off their charts.

"Have you boated this creek at seven?" Jack asked. The man frowned and took a long drink from his cup.

"Name's Harvey," he said and stuck out his hand. "This is Charlie and Charlie. We're on a training trip." He laughed. "Yahoo."

Charlie and Charlie nodded.

"You know the river?" Jack said.

"I've boated the Selway seventy times," he said. "Never at seven feet. It was all the late snow and last week's heat wave. It's a bad combination, but it's boatable. This river's always boatable if you know exactly where to be."

Charlie and Charlie smiled.

"There'll be a lot of holes that there's no way to miss. You got to punch through them."

Jack nodded. I knew Harvey was talking about boat flippers. Big waves that form in holes the river makes behind rocks and ledges and that will suck boats in and hold them there, fill them with water till they flip, hold bodies, too, indefinitely, until they go under and catch the current, or until the hole decides to spit them out. If you hit a hole with a back wave bigger than your boat, so long as you're lined up perfectly straight there's half a chance you'll shoot through. A few degrees off in either direction, and the hole will get you every time.

"We'll be all right in this tank," Harvey said, nodding to his boat, "but I'm not sure I'd run it in a boat that small. I'm not sure I'd run it in a boat I had to bail."

Unlike ours, Harvey's boat was a self-bailer, inflatable tubes around an open metal frame that let the water run right through. They're built for high water and extremely hard to flip.

"Just the two of you?" Harvey said. Jack nodded.

"A honeymoon trip. Nice."

"We're not married," Jack said.

"Yeah," Harvey said. He picked up a handful of sand. "The black sand of the Selway," he said. "I carried a bottle of this sand downriver the year I got married. I wanted to throw it at my wife's feet during the ceremony. The minister thought it was pretty strange, but he got over it."

One of the Charlies looked confused.

"Black sand," Harvey said. "You know. Black sand, love, marriage, the Selway, rivers, life: the whole thing."

I smiled at Jack, but he wouldn't meet my eyes.

"You'll be all right till Moose Creek," Harvey said. "That's when it gets wild. We're gonna camp there tonight, run the bad stretch first thing in the morning in case we wrap or flip or tear something. I hope you won't think I'm insulting you if I ask you to run with us. It'll be safer for us both. The people who flipped yesterday were all experienced. They all knew the Selway."

"They lost one?" Jack said.

"Nobody will say for sure," Harvey said. "But I'd bet on it."

"We'll think about it," Jack said. "It's nice of you to offer."

"I know what you're thinking," Harvey said. "But I've got a kid now. It makes a difference." He pulled a picture out of his wallet. A baby girl, eight or nine months old, crawling across a linoleum floor.

"She's beautiful," I said.

"She knocks me out," Harvey said. "She follows everything with her finger: bugs, flowers, the TV. You know what I mean?"

Jack and I nodded.

"It's your decision," he said. "Maybe we'll see you at Moose Creek."

He stood up, and Charlie and Charlie rose behind him. One coiled the rope while the other pushed off.

Jack poured his third cup of coffee. "Think he's full of it?" he said.

"I think he knows more than you or I ever will," I said.

"About this river, at least," he said.

"At least," I said.

In midday sunshine, the river looked more fun than terrifying. We launched just before noon, and though there was no time for sightseeing I bailed fast enough to let Jack move the boat through the rapids, which came quicker and bigger around every bend. The map showed ten rapids between the put-in and Moose Creek, and it was anybody's guess which of the fifty or sixty rapids we boated that day were the ones the Forest Service had in mind. Some had bigger waves than others, some narrower passages, but the river was continuous moving whitewater, and we finally put the map away. On the southern rivers we'd mix rum and fruit juice and eat smoked oysters and pepper cheese. Here, twenty fast miles went by without time to take a picture, to get a drink of water. The Moose Creek pack bridge came into sight, and we pulled in and tied up next to Harvey's boat.

"White frickin' water," Harvey said. "Did you have a good run?"

"No trouble," Jack said.

"Good," Harvey said. "Here's where she starts to kick ass." He motioned with his head downriver. "We'll get up at dawn and scout everything."

"It's early yet," Jack said. "I think we're going on." I looked at Jack's face, and then Harvey's.

"You do what you want," Harvey said. "But you ought to take a look at the next five miles. The runs are obvious once you see them from the bank, but they change at every level."

"We haven't scouted all day," Jack said. I knew he wanted us to run alone, that he thought following Harvey would be cheating somehow, but I believed a man who'd throw sand at his new wife's feet, and I liked a little danger but I didn't want to die.

"There's only one way through Ladle," Harvey said. "Ladle's where they lost the girl."

"The girl?" Jack said.

"The rest of her party was here when we got here. Their boats were below Ladle. They just took off, all but her husband. He wouldn't leave, and you can't blame him. He was rowing when she got tossed. He let the boat get sideways. He's been wandering around here for two days, I guess, but he wouldn't get back in the boat."

"Jesus Christ," Jack said. He sat down on the bank facing the water.

I looked back into the woods for the woman's husband and tried to imagine a posture for him, tried to imagine an expression for his face.

"A helicopter landed about an hour ago," Harvey said. "Downstream, where the body must be. It hasn't taken off."

"The water's still rising," Jack said, and we all looked to where we'd pulled the boats up on shore and saw that they were floating. And then we heard the beating of the propeller and saw the helicopter rising out over the river. The pilot flew up the river till he'd gained enough altitude, turned back, and headed over the mountain wall behind our camp.

"They said she smashed her pelvis against a rock and bled to death internally," Harvey said. "They got her out in less than *three minutes,* and it was too late."

Jack put his arm around my knees. "We'll scout at dawn," he said. "We'll all run this together."

Harvey was up rattling coffeepots before Jack and I had time to make love and I said it would bring us bad luck if we didn't but Jack said it would be worse than bad luck if we didn't scout the rapids. The scouting trail was well worn. Harvey went first, then Jack, then me and the two Charlies. Double Drop was first, two sets of falls made by water pouring over clusters of house-sized boulders that extended all the way across the river.

"You can sneak the first drop on the extreme right," Harvey said. "There's no sneak for the second. Just keep her straight and punch her through. Don't let her get you sideways."

Little Niagara was a big drop, six feet or more, but the run was pretty smooth and the back wave low enough to break through.

"Piece of cake," Harvey said.

The sun was almost over the canyon wall, and we could hear Ladle long before we rounded the bend. I wasn't prepared for what I saw.

One hundred yards of whitewater stretched from shore to shore and thundered over rocks and logjams and ledges. There were ten holes the size of the one in Double Drop, and there was no space for a boat in between. The currents were so chaotic for such a long stretch, there was no way to read which way they'd push a boat. We found some small logs and climbed a rock ledge that hung over the rapid.

"See if you can read this current," Harvey said and tossed the smallest log into the top of the rapid. The log hit the first hole and went under. It didn't come back up. One of the Charlies giggled.

"Again," Harvey said. This time the log came out of the first hole and survived two more before getting swallowed by the biggest hole, about midway through the rapid.

"I'd avoid that one for sure," Harvey said. "Try to get left of that hole." He threw the rest of the logs in. None of them made it through. "This is big time," he said.

We all sat on the rock for what must have been an hour. "Seen enough?" Harvey said. "We've still got No Slouch and Miranda Jane."

The men climbed down off the rock, but I wasn't quite ready to leave. I went to the edge of the ledge, lay flat on my stomach, and hung over until my head was so full of the roar of the river I got dizzy and pulled myself back up. An old Southern woman said men can't really live unless they face death now and then, and I know by men she didn't mean mankind. And I wondered which rock shattered the dead woman's pelvis, and I wondered what she and I were doing out here on this river when Harvey's wife was home with that beautiful baby and happy. And I knew it was crazy to take a boat through that rapid and I knew I'd do it anyway but I didn't any longer know why. Jack said I had to do it for myself to make it worth anything, and at first I thought I was there because I loved danger, but sitting on the rock I knew I was there because I loved Jack. And maybe I went because his old girlfriends wouldn't, and maybe I went because I wanted him for mine, and maybe it didn't matter at all why I went because doing it for me and doing it for him amounted, finally, to exactly the same thing. Even though I knew in my head there's nothing a man can do that a woman can't, I also knew in my heart we can't help doing it for different reasons. And just like a man will never understand exactly how a woman feels when she has a baby, or the reasons why she'll fight so hard to be loved, a woman can't know in what way a man satisfies himself, what question he answers for himself when he looks right at death.

My head was so full of the sound and light of the river that when I climbed down off the bank side of the ledge I didn't see the elk carcass until I stepped on one of its curled hooves. It was a young elk, probably not dead a year, and still mostly covered with matted brown fur. The skull was picked clean by scavengers, polished white by the sun and grinning. The sound that came out of my mouth scared me as much as the elk had, and I felt silly a few minutes later when Harvey came barreling around the corner followed by Jack.

Harvey saw the elk and smiled. "It startled me is all," I said.

"Jesus," Jack said. "Stay with us, all right?"

"I never scream," I said. "Hardly ever."

No Slouch and Miranda Jane were impressive rapids, but they were nothing like Ladle and both runnable to the left. On the way back to camp we found wild strawberries, and Jack and I hung back and fed them to each other and I knew he wasn't mad about me screaming. The boats were loaded by ten thirty and the sun was warm. We wore life jackets and helmets and wet suits. Everybody had diver's boots but me, so I wore my loafers.

"You have three minutes in water this cold," Harvey said. "Even with a wet suit. Three minutes before hypothermia starts, and then you can't swim, and then you just give in to the river."

Harvey gave us the thumbs-up sign as the Charlies pushed off. I pushed off right behind them. Except for the bailing bucket and the spare oar, everything on the boat was tied down twice and inaccessible. My job was to take water out of the boat as fast as I could eight pounds at a time and to help Jack remember which rapid was coming next and where we had decided to run it.

I saw the first of the holes in Double Drop and yelled, "Right," and we made the sneak with a dry boat. We got turned around somehow after that, though, and hit the big wave backward. Jack yelled, "Hang on, baby," and we hit it straight on and it filled the boat but then we were through it and in sight of Little Niagara before I could even start bailing.

"We're going twelve miles an hour at least," Jack yelled. "Which one is this?"

"Niagara," I yelled. "Right center." The noise of the river swallowed my words and I only threw out two bucketfuls before we were over the lip of Niagara and I had to hold on. I could hear Ladle around the bend and I was throwing water so fast I lost my balance and that's when I heard Jack say, "Bail faster!" and that's when I threw the bail bucket into the river and watched, unbelieving, as it went under, and I saw Jack see it too but we were at Ladle and I had to sit down and hold on. I watched Harvey's big boat getting bounced around like a cork, and I think I closed my eyes when the first wave crashed over my face because the next thing I knew we were out of the heaviest water and Harvey was standing and smiling at us with his fist in the air.

I could see No Slouch around the bend and I don't remember it or Miranda Jane because I was kneeling in the front of the boat scooping armfuls of water the whole time.

We all pulled up on the first beach we found and drank a beer and hugged each other uncertainly, like tenants in an apartment building where the fires have been put out.

"You're on your own," Harvey said. "We're camping here. Take a

look at Wolf Creek, and be sure and get to shore before Selway Falls."
He picked up a handful of black sand and let it run through his fingers. He turned to me. "He's a good boatman, and you're very brave."

I smiled.

"Take care of each other," he said. "Stay topside."

We set off alone and it clouded up and started to rain and I couldn't make the topography match the river map.

"I can't tell where we are," I told Jack. "But Wolf Creek can't be far."

"We'll see it coming," he said, "or hear it."

But it wasn't five minutes after he spoke that we rounded a bend and were in it, waves crashing on all sides and Jack trying to find a way between the rocks and the holes. I was looking, too, and I think I saw the run, fifty feet to our right, right before I heard Jack say, "Hang on, baby," and we hit the biggest hole sideways and everything went white and cold. I was in the waves and under water and I couldn't see Jack or the boat. I couldn't move my arms or legs apart from how the river tossed them. Jack had said swim down to the current, but I couldn't tell which way was down and I couldn't have moved there in that washing machine, my lungs full and taking on water. Then the wave spit me up, once, under the boat, and then again, clear of it, and I got a breath and pulled down away from the air and felt the current grab me, and I waited to get smashed against a rock, but the rock didn't come and I was at the surface riding the crests of some eight-foot rollers and seeing Jack's helmet bobbing in the water in front of me.

"*Swim*, baby!" he yelled, and it was like it hadn't occurred to me, like I was frozen there in the water. And I tried to swim but I couldn't get a breath and my limbs wouldn't move and I thought about the three minutes and hypothermia and I must have been swimming then because the shore started to get closer. I grabbed the corner of a big ledge and wouldn't let go, not even when Jack yelled at me to get out of the water. And even when he showed me an easy place to get out if I just floated a few yards downstream, it took all I had and more to let go of the rock and get back in the river.

I got out on a tiny triangular rock ledge surrounded on all sides by walls of granite. Jack stood sixty feet above me on another ledge.

"Sit tight," he said. "I'm going to go and see if I can get the boat."

Then he was gone and I sat in that small space and started to shake. It was raining harder, sleeting even, and I started to think about freezing to death on that tiny ledge that wasn't even big enough for me to move around on and get warm. I started to think about the river rising and filling that space and what would happen when Jack got back and made me float downstream to an easier place, or what would happen if he didn't come back, if he died trying to get the boat back, if he chased it fifteen miles to Selway Falls and got flushed over. When I saw the boat float by, right side up and empty, I decided to try and climb off the ledge.

I'd lost one loafer in the river, so I wedged myself between the granite walls and used my fingers, mostly, to climb. I've always been a little afraid of heights, so I didn't look down. I thought it would be stupid to live through the boating accident and smash my skull falling off a granite cliff, but as I inched up the wall I got warmer and kept going. When I got to the top there were trees growing across, and another vertical bank I hadn't seen from below. I bashed though the branches with my helmet and grabbed them one at a time till they broke or pulled out and then I grabbed the next one higher. I dug my knees and elbows into the thin layer of soil that covered the rock, and I slipped down an inch for every two I gained. When I came close to panic I thought of Rambo, as if he were a real person, as if what I was doing was possible, and proven before, by him.

And then I was on the ledge and I could see the river, and I could see Jack on the other side, and I must have been in shock, a little, because I couldn't at that time imagine how he could have gotten to the other side of the river, couldn't imagine what would make him go back in the water, but he had, and there he was on the other side.

"I lost the boat," he yelled. "Walk downstream till you see it."

I was happy for instructions and I set off down the scouting trail, shoe on one foot, happy for the pain in the other, happy to be walking, happy because the sun was trying to come out again and I was there to see it. It was a few miles before I even realized that the boat would be going over the falls, that Jack would have had to swim one more time across the river to get to the trail, that I should go back and see if he'd made it, but I kept walking downstream and looking for the boat. After five miles my bare foot started to bleed, so I put my left loafer on my right foot and walked on. After eight miles I saw Jack running up the trail behind me, and he caught up and kissed me and ran on by.

I walked and I walked, and I thought about being twenty-one and biking in mountains not too far from these with a boy who almost drowned and then proposed to me. His boots had filled with the water of a river even farther to the north, and I was wearing sneakers and have a good kick, so I made it across just fine. I thought about how he sat on the far bank after he'd pulled himself out and shivered and stared at the water. And how I ran up and down the shore looking for the shallowest crossing, and then, thinking I'd found it, met him halfway. I remembered when our hands touched across the water and how I'd pulled him to safety and built him a fire and dried his clothes. Later that night he asked me to marry him and it made me happy and I said yes even though I knew it would never happen because I was too young and free and full of my freedom. I switched my loafer to the other foot and wondered if this danger would make Jack propose to me. Maybe he was the kind of man who needed to see death first, maybe we would build a fire to dry ourselves and then he would ask me and I would say yes because as you close on thirty, freedom has circled back on itself to mean something totally different from what it did at twenty-one.

I knew I had to be close to the falls and felt bad about what the wrecked boat would look like, but all of a sudden it was there in front of me, stuck on a gravel bar in the middle of the river with a rapid on either side, and I saw Jack coming back up the trail toward me.

"I've got it all figured out," he said. "I need to walk upstream about a mile and jump in there. That'll give me enough time to swim most of the way across to the other side of the river, and if I've read the current right, it'll take me right into that gravel bar."

"And if you read the current wrong?" I said.

He grinned. "Then it's over Selway Falls. I almost lost it already the second time I crossed the river. It was just like Harvey said. I almost gave up. I've been running twelve miles and I know my legs'll cramp. It's a long shot but I've got to take it."

"Are you sure you want to do this?" I said. "Maybe you shouldn't do this."

"I thought the boat was gone," he said, "and I didn't care because you were safe and I was safe and we were on the same side of the river. But there it is asking me to come for it, and the water's gonna rise tonight and take it over the falls. You stay right here where you can see what happens to me. If I make it I'll pick you up on that beach just below. We've got half a mile to the take-out and the falls." He kissed me again and ran back upriver.

The raft was in full sunshine, everything tied down, oars in place. Even the map I couldn't read was there, where I stuck it, under a strap.

I could see Jack making his way through the trees toward the edge of the river, and I realized then that more than any other reason for being on that trip, I was there because I thought I could take care of him, and maybe there's something women want to protect after all. And maybe Jack's old girlfriends were trying to protect him by making him stay home, and maybe I thought I could if I was there, but as he dropped out of sight and into the water I knew there'd always be places he'd go that I couldn't, and that I'd have to let him go. Then I saw his tiny head in the water and I held my breath and watched his position, which was perfect, as he approached the raft. But he got off center right at the end, and a wave knocked him past the raft and farther down the gravel bar. He got to his feet and went down again. He grabbed for a boulder on the bottom and got washed even farther away. He was using all his energy to stay in one place and he was fifty yards downriver from the raft. I started to pray then, to whomever I pray to when I get in real trouble, and it may have been a coincidence but he started moving forward. It took him fifteen minutes and strength I'll never know to get to the boat, but he was in it, and rowing, and heading for the beach.

Later, when we were safe and on the two-lane heading home, Jack told me we were never in any real danger, and I let him get away with it because I knew that's what he had to tell himself to get past almost losing me.

"The river gave us both a lesson in respect," he said, and it occurred to me then that he thought he had a chance to tame that wild river, but I knew I was at its mercy from the very beginning, and I thought all along that that was the point.

Jack started telling stories to keep himself awake: the day his kayak held him under for almost four minutes, the time he crashed his hang glider twice in one day. He said he thought fifteen years of high water were probably enough and that he'd take desert rivers from now on.

The road stretched out in front of us, dry and even and smooth. We found a long dirt road, turned, and pulled down to where it ended at a chimney that stood tall amid the rubble of an old stone house. We didn't build a fire and Jack didn't propose; we rolled out our sleeping bags and lay down next to the truck. I could see the light behind the mountains in the place where the moon would soon rise, and I thought about all the years I'd spent saying love and freedom were mutually exclusive and living my life as though they were exactly the same thing.

The wind carried the smell of the mountains, high and sweet. It was so still I could imagine a peace without boredom.

MIDDLE FORK OF THE KINGS RIVER

Mike Doyle

*"*The proof is in the pudding" has never more aptly applied than to adventure sports. A given adventure can seem to have all the ingredients of a classic and still turn into an epic from hell. Occasionally one can bail midstream; other times we've just got to gird our loins and tough it out. And if we are hugely committed to a sport, odds are we'll eventually end up a half mile down Shit Creek with no option but to try and run the rest of it—and survive if we can. The following story illustrates this point perfectly. The scene: an exciting first raft descent attempted by two bold and experienced guides. From the second they headed for the river they were irreversibly committed to an epic that could and probably should have killed them a hundred times over. Hating life, hating God, hating that his parents ever met, Mike Doyle and partner Mike Hammond found their limits only by surpassing them.*

‡   ‡   ‡

Consider the critical question asked during many ill-fated journeys: At what point do we call it quits? But what do you do when you can't call it quits, when the only way out is down the river? This is the jam we found ourselves in during our attempt to make the first raft descent of the Middle Fork of the Kings River.

We've all heard stories of mountaineering expeditions turning back due to pulmonary edema, rock fall, whiteouts, and frostbite. The decision sometimes results from an incident in which no other alternative exists. Most of the time, though, the decision is subject to a group

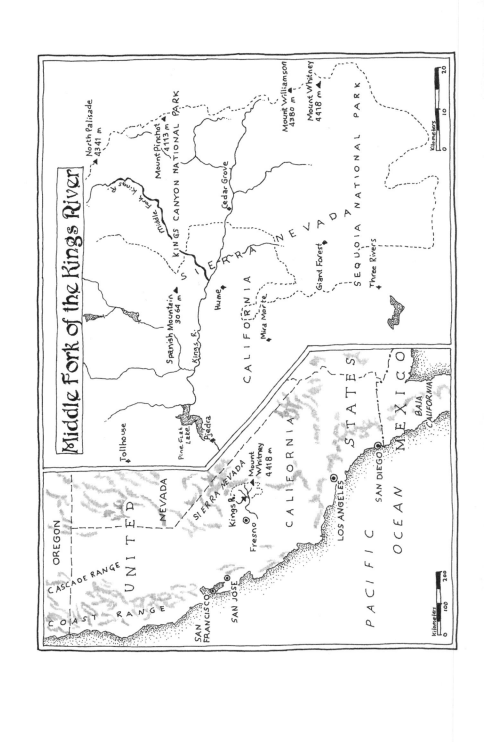

Middle Fork of the Kings River

OREGON

CASCADE RANGE

COAST RANGE

UNITED

NEVADA

SIERRA NEVADA

SAN FRANCISCO

SAN JOSE

Fresno

Kings R.

Mount Whitney 4418 m

CALIFORNIA

LOS ANGELES

SAN DIEGO

BAJA CALIFORNIA

STATES

MEXICO

PACIFIC OCEAN

Kilometers
0   100   200

Tollhouse

Pine Flat Lake

Piedra

Kings R.

Spanish Mountain 3064 m

Middle Fork Kings R.

North Palisade 4341 m

Mount Pinchot 4113 m

KINGS CANYON NATIONAL PARK

Cedar Grove

Hume

Mira Morte

Mount Williamson 4380 m

Mount Whitney 4418 m

SIERRA NEVADA

CALIFORNIA

Giant Forest

SEQUOIA NATIONAL PARK

Three Rivers

Kilometers
0   10   20

decision that isn't always cut and dry. Egos become involved as well as rationalizations like "we may never be this close again."

The options of turning back in whitewater boating aren't always as simple as in mountain climbing. Mountain climbing is a struggle against gravity until the goal is reached. To turn back is an easier option since it's usually downhill. Whitewater boating is the opposite. Gravity is your friend until the point that you decide to turn back, either out of the canyon or back upstream. Only on rare occasions during first descents can one choose to abandon the expedition and exit the river by heading downstream.

Whitewater exploration in California had peaked during the early 1980s. Many groups of kayakers and rafters were bagging first descents at a frenzied pace. Two groups of kayakers were in a head-to-head competition in trying to run the last unrun California rivers. The first group, consisting of Chuck Stanley, Lars Holbek, and a handful of other expert kayakers, were exploring most of the Sierra Nevada rivers at a quick rate. In one week-long period in 1980, they bagged three previously unrun rivers back to back to back.

The other group of kayakers, led by Reg Lake; adventurer, climber, and owner of the Esprit clothing line, Doug Thompkins; and legendary rock climber Royal Robbins had set their sights on the grandest of the Sierra Nevada rivers. They were called the "Triple Crown Boys," and by 1984 they had descended from the headwaters of the three largest rivers in the Sierra Nevada range. The San Joaquin, Kern, and Kings Rivers were all navigated by this group, and tales of the five- to eight-day journeys from 12,000-foot put-ins became legendary among California's boating communities. These expeditions were so extreme that most of them have never been attempted since.

Not far behind the kayakers were the rafting first-descenders. These groups thrived on the belief that "if it can by kayaked, it can also be rafted." Most of the time, the humbling conclusion resulting from these expeditions was that "if it can be portaged with kayaks, it can also be portaged with rafts."

By 1990 the fervor of first descents in California had waned. Perhaps part of the reason was that the "glamour" aspect of first descents had worn off. To many, this looked like way too much work! The other reason was that California had plunged itself into a four-year drought, and the end of it was still nowhere in sight.

By 1990, all of the major rivers in California had been kayaked, and all but one had been rafted. The one that remained unrafted was truly the most intriguing, for it was this one that had been kayaked only once. The "triple crowners" who had run it called it the most spectacular of all their first descents, and it also was by far the most difficult and dangerous. This river was the Middle Fork Kings.

The Middle Kings watershed originates in one of the finest wilderness areas in the United States: the northern portion of Kings Canyon National Park. Peaks rising to over 14,000 feet highlight the area. The foreboding upper reaches of the Middle Kings have names that send chills down the spines of boaters: Disappointment Peak, Disappearing Creek, and the Enchanted Gorge. A distant view of the spectacular lower portion of the Middle Kings can be had from the Kings Canyon Highway at the Confluence viewpoint. It is truly one of the most spectacular river vistas in North America.

After seeing the lower canyon for eight years on the way to many Upper Kings trips, I felt the time seemed right to attempt the Middle Kings. Of course, the California drought had rendered many rivers unrunnable, and the ones that we had been rafting just didn't have the normal "punch" to them. The low water had bolstered our boating confidence levels since most of the rivers don't live up to their fierce reputations unless they're pumping around 2,500 cfs.

I talked to Reg Lake at the San Francisco Outdoor Adventure Fair that spring, and he informed me that the lower gorge of the Middle Kings had no sections that were impassable. There was always a way to portage at river level. Knowing that important fact seemed to set the final plans into motion

By May of 1990, Dave Hammond—my partner in Beyond Limits Adventures, a commercial rafting company in Riverbank, California— and I were training on the West Walker River in a twelve-foot SOTAR in preparation for the first raft descent of the Middle Kings. That spring we also had trained for the expedition on the seldom run Upper Middle Fork Stanislaus, a class V run just north of Yosemite National Park.

Our rafting technique consisted of two paddlers side by side in the middle section of the twelve-foot raft. This R-2 configuration allowed us to quickly catch eddies, jump waterfalls, and punch hydraulics with a comfortable degree of stability. When portaging was necessary, usually one person could schlep the boat over the rocks or line it through the rapid while the other paddler carried gear downstream. After our first descent on the South Fork Merced and its twenty or so portages, we became very proficient at schlep-and-line portaging techniques.

On May 26, Dave and I found ourselves at the Kings River base camp packing gear for our assault on the Middle Fork the next morning. We had talked about doing this run in the office, but now we were face to face with the reality of our conquest. Our general feeling toward this expedition was far from one of jubilation. It was more like "Let's get this trip over with."

By six o'clock the next morning we were in Dave's van heading up to Wishon Reservoir. After a few wrong turns we were lost. We turned back to find the main dirt road. We had to meet our horsepacker by 5:00 A.M. to allow him enough time to get us to the put-in and himself back out by nightfall. We were just about ready to give up when we figured out the right road and sped on.

We arrived at the trailhead by 8:45 A.M. and the packer was waiting for us. "It's getting late," he said, "so pack up and let's get on the trail." The rushed feeling I had as we were preparing to head into the unknown in the middle of the biggest downpour of the year made me think again that maybe we should bail out now. "We're in the middle of a four-year drought," I thought, "and it has to start raining *now?!*"

Deciding to go on with our plan, we hastily threw our gear together and loaded the pack horses with our fourteen-foot raft and equipment. Good-byes were said to my wife Bonnie and Dave's girlfriend Carol. As we headed out, I waved to my ten-month-old daughter Beth and again felt like this wasn't such a splendid idea. Had we really thought this plan through? No. Should we turn back now? Nah, four days later it'll be over, so let's just do it!

It was now snowing, and we were at 8,000 feet. The scenery should have been great, but it was so stormy and misty we couldn't see much of anything except the horses in front of us. The snow was coming down hard. We startled a black bear that was hanging out in a meadow. We'd been on the trail for three hours and our guide announced that he'd never been to Tehipite Valley, our destination put-in, but he kind of knew where the trail was. "Par for the course," I thought to myself.

The snow now covered the trail and the horsepacker had to bushwhack certain sections. At 2:30 P.M. we arrived at what our packer thought was the canyon rim above Tehipite Valley. "Good luck," he said as he quickly dumped our gear, tied up his horses, and disappeared back up the trail. It was pouring rain by now and our gear was soaked. "We've made it this far, so let's pack up and get to the river. It's all downhill from here," said Dave.

The fog was very thick and you couldn't see more than fifty feet ahead. Just as we were leaving, we were surprised by a group of four hikers coming up the trail. They couldn't believe their eyes, seeing the two of us with our raft and equipment.

"What are you guys doing here and how did you get all that equipment this far?" Dave told them about the horses and they asked what we planned to do. As Dave described our plan, I could see a distinct look of disbelief on their faces. Their next statement should have been enough for us to turn around and head back.

"You're more than two miles from the canyon rim, and once you get there you've got five miles down the steepest maintained trail in California to get to the river!" We felt defeated already and again thought about turning back. "If you guys do what you say you're going to do, then you're the baddest fuckers I've ever *seen!*" One guy said, "That river down there is suicidal and it's probably rising as we speak." That wasn't exactly what we wanted to hear at that point.

Not wanting to think about our choices too much, we loaded up, said good-bye again, and struck out up the trail. The next two miles were brutal, with us dragging and hauling the raft mostly uphill, a hundred different ways. About six o'clock that evening we arrived at a place that felt like we were standing on the edge of the earth. From the rock outcropping we couldn't see much, but we could tell that 5,000 feet directly below was Tehipite Valley. From here on it would all be downhill.

The rain kept pounding down, making the trail slippery so I could easily drag the raft behind us. Dave started cutting off the switchbacks and dropping straight downhill to make better time. We would let the boat slide in front of us on a line and then slide after it on our backs 50 to 200 feet. Unfortunately, the last shortcut led us away from the trail and down a gully. About 500 feet later we were stranded in the dark, in the rain, on the face of a waterfall. We decided to set up camp for the night under a manzanita bush.

The next morning I awoke in my dry suit to a moderate drizzle. It had rained all night long and the inflated raft didn't work too well as a shelter. The grommets from the self-bailing floor allowed a constant and annoying trickle of water to drop onto me all night. We quickly packed up, pushed the boat over the falls, and kept going. The gully we were in was becoming a creek, which, according to the maps, would eventually lead us to the river.

My altimeter showed we were still 1,500 feet above the river, but it seemed as though the other side of the canyon wasn't that far away. I had the ugly feeling that this gorge was going to empty into Tehipite

Valley in the same way Yosemite Falls empties into Yosemite Valley—in a sudden 1,500-foot drop. Since we couldn't leave the gorge with the raft because the terrain was too rough, we kept going down. We found that we could just toss the inflated raft over the countless waterfalls and climb down behind it.

We were now 800 feet above the river, and we heard a roar that sounded like twenty-five rocket engines going off. My head snapped to and fro as my eyes scanned the hills for the landslide. I quickly looked for cover, only to find there was none. Luckily, and much to our relief, the slide was happening on another side canyon.

We came to the top of a seemingly bottomless waterfall. Dave crept out to the edge, with me holding his life jacket as he looked over. He saw the bottom a hundred feet below. "No worries . . . it goes," he said, and we pushed the raft out as far as we could. I waited for it to hit. No sound. Dave crept out and saw that the raft was lodged on a four-foot-wide ledge halfway down the falls. The gorge's steep, crumbly granite walls forbade access to our raft. It again seemed as though our expedition was over.

But no, Dave decided otherwise and rigged a seat harness for a descent over the edge. It didn't seem like a smart thing to do, but again it was our best option. After an amazing display of spidermanlike leaps, with seventy-five feet of line attached to him, Dave made it to the raft. I had to belay Dave by hand, with no anchor whatsoever, since there were no tie-offs for the rope anywhere. Dave tugged the line three times and I let it free. The roar of the falls drowned out any verbal communication between us, so I made my way up the canyon wall and traversed out of the gorge down to the valley.

Two hours later I found Dave and the raft at the valley floor. After talking about the amazing ropework that got him to this point, we pushed over the last few hundred yards of gravel on the valley floor to the Middle Kings. "All right! We're here. We've survived the toughest part of the trip," I thought to myself.

I was wrong.

We dropped our equipment and paused by the riverside to look up at the valley walls. As the mist from the storm cleared, spectacular vistas of Tehipite Dome appeared. This impressive rock formation looked like a huge granite thumb towering 4,500 feet above the valley floor. We saw waterfalls, swollen with rainwater, thundering hundreds of feet down to the river. This valley, sculpted by glaciers 10,000 years ago, was truly enchanting.

We packed the raft, got on the river, and took off. The river was flowing about 2,000 cfs, three times what we had hoped for. The first mile dropped 120 feet but it was easy class IV. We came to the end of the valley where the river sliced through a 3,000-foot-high granite wall. All I could see was mist rising from below, so we pulled out and went down to take a look. From our rocky perch we caught our first glimpse of the hell that we were about to experience for the next three days.

To sum up the following epic, I'll say that rafting was the furthest thing from our minds. From the very start we were in a survival mode. The raft and its equipment were nothing more than 300 pounds of high-tech burdens that unfortunately had to be dragged behind us. The Middle Kings wasn't meant to be rafted, or even walked next to. It was a death trap. One slip and you were gone, swept away down raging torrents, over twenty-foot falls, and under house-sized rocks. And it never let up. If anything, it kept getting uglier. There wasn't even a remote chance that any of the next five miles was runnable. It wasn't even worth thinking about. All we could hope for was to try to get ourselves downstream and out of this mess alive.

By day four, we had gone eight miles on the river and had entered level Z on the survival scale. The river averaged a drop of 260 feet per mile with some miles approaching 400 feet. At 2,000 cfs this created a river that was not only impossible to run—it was death defying to portage.

The portages were endless. Most involved climbing down the riverbed with our dry bags while scouting for portage routes, then hiking back up and getting the raft. The rapids, for the most part, were too violent to line. Instead, we'd spend hours portaging the raft aside long, unrunnable cataracts, then the canyon would wall up and we'd have to paddle to the other side of the river. Each ferry required adrenaline-charged paddling as the raft drifted ten feet upstream of more death drops. There were no eddies to catch, so we had to jam the boat on shallow rocks, jump out quickly, and grab the raft before we were swept over the falls.

The really dire part of this portaging was the fact that our bodies became so beaten and tired. Dave had been wearing his dry suit for the past three days when we arrived at a beach for a night's camp. The process of taking the dry suit off at night became very painful due to a bad rash that Dave had developed over his entire body. I told Dave his butt looked like an orangutan's. It did.

We spent our days in the canyon portaging from 5:00 A.M. until 5:00 P.M. Then we'd eat, try to sleep, wake up, and repeat the process. We fought off the frustration we felt as each section became more difficult to portage and as huge boulders broke loose from under our feet. We constantly tried to figure out how far we had come, but every landmark and side creek that we came upon would add doubt to where we actually were. During the steepest sections we would go about two miles for every ten hours of portaging. We couldn't give up, for the alternative would be even harder. No matter how bad it got, to go on was the only option.

On day six we heard a helicopter fly over. I hoped it wasn't looking for us since the worst was now behind us. I figured we had only five miles to go until our take-out. We were already two days behind schedule, and I was sure that everyone back home was freaking out.

By now the river was becoming runnable. Class V+ rapids that I would normally consider unrunnable revealed runnable routes. A typical rapid would be a half-mile-long slalom, with twenty crux moves in it. One rapid took an hour to scout, and as I came back I memorized all the moves. We ran it perfectly, but if we'd missed any position by more than a foot or more, we'd have been history. We were running the best whitewater we had ever seen.

The last two miles went by like a breeze, without even a scout. Stuff we'd probably have portaged two weeks before now seemed like a cakewalk. The end was in sight. It had been six days since we had left the van at Wishon Reservoir. We got to the beach and found a gift from one of our guides, Pat Schimke, who had hiked in and waited for us for a day and a half: two submarine sandwiches and a twelve-pack of beer. We had made it. We hugged each other and cracked open a brew.

Even though our journey wasn't finished, the rest was easy. We hiked up the two-mile Yucca Point Trail to the highway and hitched a ride to Kings Canyon Lodge. A couple from Switzerland picked us up and asked where we'd been. I told them we'd been rafting, and they said that it sounded like fun. Dave and I looked at each other and smiled. Since it was a short ride to the lodge, I chose not to elaborate.

My only mission now was to call Bonnie and tell her we were okay. We got to the lodge, and I placed the call and told Bonnie we had made it. Everyone was glad to hear from us, to say the least!

After I hung up, reality set in and my body seemed suddenly to shut down. The survival mode was over, and now the pain of the past six days was hitting hard. Dave was already checking into a room at the lodge. It was all we could do to open the door and collapse on our beds.

Would I do this trip again? Hell no! This is the kind of experience you have once in a lifetime, if you're smart. Yet, in a way, I'm glad we did it. We were faced with the bail-out point at least a dozen times, yet we kept going. We kept going mostly because we didn't have a choice. The feeling of completion—of victory, you could say—was especially sweet.

Another group of rafters planned to repeat our trip the next month with two rafts and twelve paddlers. They wanted to put in fifteen miles upstream from Tehipite Valley and run the entire Middle Fork Kings. I made sure I called them the next week and gave my recommendation. *"Don't do it!"*

They didn't.

THE BIO-BIO: RIVER OF SONG

Richard Bangs

S ome fifteen years ago I was wandering around Royal Robbins's house, searching the walls for pictures of the countless climbing epics that had forged Robbins into the biggest name in world rock climbing. I found no climbing photos because there were none. But in the hallway hung a big blowup of Robbins in a bright red kayak, airborne as he crested the lip of a tsunami-sized comb of whitewater. Several years before, Robbins had eased out of climbing and taken up kayaking with all the passion and restless energy that had driven him up the greatest climbs of his era. This photo was evidently the fruit of his efforts. "The Bio-Bio," Robbins said, as I gaped at the photo of him flying through the air in that red kayak. A man of few words, and always understated, when Robbins said the Bio-Bio was "some kind of challenge," I took him to mean the now famous river was something extraordinary. Indeed it is. In the years since 1978, when Richard Bangs and friends first ran the "River of Song," the upper Bio-Bio has become a goal for expert river runners the world over, a sort of ultimate feather in the cap for anyone with a paddle, huge talent, and enough money to book passage to Chile.

‡   ‡   ‡

It was a long snore. We knew practically nothing of the river, only that it was Chile's second longest. Yet in a country measuring 2,600 miles long and just 113 miles across at its widest, the odds of finding a navigable whitewater river of any length seemed poor. We had no hydrological data, no flowcharts, not even good maps. For all we knew, the eddies south of the equator spun counterclockwise. But Chile did

107

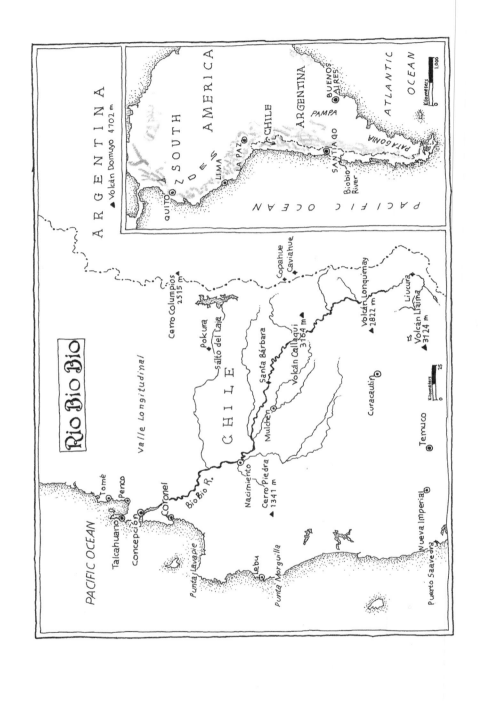

Rio Bio Bio

have a promising source of whitewater: the Cordillera de los Andes, the world's longest mountain range and one of its highest. And the name of our target river, the Rio Bio-Bio, had a fanciful lilt that put a smile on everyone's lips. After struggling with names like Coruh and Tatshenshini, this river sounded like a song.

And that is just what it is: the Mapuche Indian word for the song of a local flycatcher, the Chilean elaenia. The Bio-Bio (pronounced bee-oh bee-oh) springs from Lago Galletue, a shimmering alpine lake at the foot of the 10,000-foot peaks a few miles from the Argentine border. The river flows from near a town called Sierra Nevada in a grand arc, skewing south, then dodging off to the west, passing through the village of Santa Barbara and the town of Los Angeles (near San Fernando) before finally spilling into the Pacific. It all sounds hauntingly familiar to a Californian.

The Bio-Bio had been called to our attention by Bill Wendt, chief ranger at Yosemite National Park. He had spent three years in the area on a United Nations project and had flown over and hiked a portion of the river. Although he knew little of river running and had seen only a fraction of the Bio-Bio, he spoke glowingly of its clear gushing waters and the landscape through which it flowed.

While making plans to run unrun rivers was no longer new to us, committing the time, money, and energy on the basis of so little information made us a little uneasy. Nonetheless, Bill's confidence and excitement were contagious; and six of us were gamblers enough to throw our hats into the ring, including Bill and his cousin George Wendt, owner of a California river-rafting company and a Sobek partner from the beginning; Mike Cobboid, a seasonal Yosemite ranger who also had worked for the Park Service in Chile; and three Sobek river guides: Bruce Gaguine, Jack Morison, and me.

In December 1978 we flew from San Francisco over the equator, reaching Chile at seventeen degrees south, well within the tropic zone. The country we saw below us was barren, sparsely inhabited desert spreading across the western flank of the Andes. By the time we landed at Santiago, Chile's largest city, we had reached the more comfortable temperate zone, and the plain between the Andean peaks and the Pacific tides was full of angular fields devoted to grain and grazing. Santiago is only halfway to Chile's southern reaches, the land's end of South America.

In Santiago we transferred all our gear to the train station: two fat rolls of neoprene that would inflate to Avon Professional rafts sixteen feet long, nine ten-foot-long ash oars, a dozen metal ammo boxes (which never fail to raise a few eyebrows at the customs lines) to keep our gear dry, a couple of eighty-quart coolers, and the six-foot-long aluminum alloy pipes that fit together to form rowing frames. We enlisted a few eager teenagers at the train station to help us load it aboard and took the modern diesel train south to Victoria, a small farming village in the Andean foothills. There everything was unloaded onto the old wooden station platform, and we sat down on the pile of equipment to wait for the arrival of the steam-powered, narrow-gauge engine that would take us up the old spur railroad into the Andes. Finally it arrived, smoking down the tracks like the long-awaited rendezvous with destiny in *High Noon*. We hefted all our gear into a baggage car and took our seats on the antique red-leather bench seats. Then the steam engine belched a cloud of dark smog, sending sparks scattering over the tracks, and lurched and staggered its way out of the station, plunging almost at once into the Andes.

The Andes are one of the most impressive geologic formations on the planet, a single mountain range, predominantly volcanic, over 4,000 miles long, created along the entire west coast of South America, from Colombia to Patagonia. While its highest mountain, Aconcagua (just to the northeast of Santiago, in neighboring Argentina), measures 22,831 feet, which barely joins the top twenty summits, the average altitude of Andean peaks makes it the world's second highest range, behind the Himalayas. A range that long and that high has just about every possible mountain phenomenon: remote and rugged summits that defeat the best mountaineers, sharp glaciated ridges that forbid overland travel, and popular ski resorts surrounding pristine alpine lakes.

The railroad into the mountains followed the line of least resistance and, avoiding the peaks and ridges, took us to Temuco, a small town in the heart of Chile's wine-growing region. Today Temuco is the northern limit of the Araucanians, a native people who have been singularly successful at avoiding conquest. The people derive their popular name from the *araucada*, or Chile pine, known also as the monkey-puzzle tree because its long spidery branches are covered with stiff green needles that remind some people of monkey tails. The Araucanians call themselves Mapuche, however, which means "people of the land." They are for the most part a sedentary, agricultural people who in centuries past hunted guanacos, pumas, and armadillos—and, when their security was threatened, invaders.

In the years of the expansion of the Incan empire, under Tupa Inca's leadership during the years 1463 to 1493, the Incas were stopped in their conquests at the Maule River, some fifty miles north of the Bio-Bio. There, fierce Mapuches armed with bows and arrows showed the Incas that they were, at last, too far from their homeland. In the century that followed, the Mapuches resisted conquest by Spanish forces under Pedro de Valdivia, who solidified the conquest of Chile. Valdivia was slain in battle against the Mapuches in 1553. For 300 years after that, the Mapuches continued to resist conquest and assimilation; until 1882, in fact, the region of Chilean national authority ended at the Bio-Bio, despite the maps that showed but one country. Below that river the Mapuches continued to live apart.

While no Incan, Spaniard, nor Chilean has ever conquered the Mapuches, the slow but inevitable effects of contact and commerce have brought them closer to the modern age. Now they raise wheat and barley as well as the traditional maize and potatoes, and they breed cattle and sheep, like much of Chile's rural population; but the Mapuches continue to be one of the largest functioning indigenous societies in South America.

In Temuco we picked up a seventh expedition member—Alejandro Sepulveda, an administrator in the Chilean Park Service and an old friend of Bill Wendt's from his Chilean sojourn. Alejandro had set up a flight over the Bio-Bio so we could evaluate our destined course before it was too late. We flew from Temuco over the river, soaring over nearly 200 of the river's 240 miles, from Santa Barbara up to its source at Lago Galletue, searching for obstacles that might end our expedition before it got on the water. The river did look runnable, with one series of four big rapids that promised excitement but no major waterfalls or other impassable obstacles. None that we could see, at least, for the river at one point played hide-and-seek in the narrow canyons of the Andes. We congratulated Bill on his choice.

That evening we finally reached the river's source after a half-day's ride in the rear of a cattle truck over back roads. Some Lago Galletue residents killed a lamb, cut its throat, collected the hot blood in a wooden bowl, and dropped in a lemon wedge, which coagulated the blood into chunks that looked like four-day-old cafeteria Jell-O. It is called *nachi*, a delicacy reserved for special occasions. We were honored—and rushed to wash it down with *pisco*, the clear brandy of the Andes.

We spent much of the next morning rigging up for our expedition.

The rafts were rolled out and, with the help of a high-volume pump, assumed their familiar shape. Four separate chambers create the oblong perimeter of the rafts, with two thwarts placed in the center to add stability. Each chamber is inflated to drum-hard tightness, so the raft rides high and firm in the water; the chambers are separated by baffles so that, in the unlikely event one should pop because of a sharp rock, crocodile teeth, or overinflation, the other three will keep the boat afloat. During the twenty-five years of professional river rafting, the standard configuration of the raft—its dimensions, including tube diameter, uplift at bow and stem, and placement of D-rings for tying on gear—has been refined to a very specialized level. Today's riverboat is a far cry from the surplus landing craft that first found its way downriver in the years following World War II.

Next, the two-inch-diameter aluminum tubing was assembled into the rowing frames. They are equipped with the essential oarlocks and also supply stability and rigidity to the raft. When lashed securely into the midsection of the craft, the frame allows gear to be tied onto a wood-panel floor section that is dropped between the thwarts. Coolers, ammo boxes, stove, fuel, water jugs, heavy cast-iron Dutch oven, and other paraphernalia are then all secured to the deck, while the watertight black bags containing dry clothes are tied into the rear bilge section. The weight of the gear, riding low in the boat, adds further stability to the raft in the torquing and twisting of powerful hydraulics. Everything is lashed down securely, either to the boat or frame or both, to prevent its loss in case of a flip.

Finally, all was ready: The oarsman was braced with his feet between the gear on the floorboard, with a spare oar tied by slipknot within easy reach; passengers took their places in the front section for weight balance against the black bags in the rear—and for a thrilling, wet, front-row seat. All the tied-in gear was checked and double-checked; life jackets were pulled snug. Upstream, the snowy crown of Volcán Llaima, scraping the skies above Lago Galletue; downstream, the river. In my dairy I wrote:

As a condor caught an air current overhead, we shoved the rafts into the water, spun into the current, and whirled downstream. The first rapids were shallow, rocky, and couched in a small canyon topped with thick araucaria trees, which cast a magical aura over the river. Twisting through this watery maze, I was struck with the ghostly feeling of unfamiliarity. The river seemed like none other I had experienced. The River Styx, I felt, might bear some resemblance.

The water was crisp, clear as pisco. It almost crackled with each stroke. We pumped and shot through channels and chutes and drank in the scenery. The area we were traversing was called the Switzerland of South America. That does it an injustice. The backdrop was the unique snowcapped Andes, an endless phalanx of three-dimensional points that blends with sky and clouds without clear definition. Closer stood the perfect, snow-dripped cone of Volcán Llaima, poking 10,000 feet into the clouds.

In those first twenty-five miles, the river left the alpine Andean forest of araucaria and flowed across a broad foothill plateau; above the gentle banks, green fields sloped gradually to the bases of the surrounding mountains. Our aerial survey had shown us that later, when the river poured off the escarpment, we would plunge through dark gorges in a fierce region—a junkyard of the spare parts of mountain building. But for now the landscape was smooth and sweet, and we savored its comfort.

Horsemen decked out in silver spurs and leather rode to the edge of the river and gaped at the *gringos locos.* Horses, pigs, and sheep wandered along the cobbled banks, and at one small farm along the river a local cowgirl tried to sell us a live goat for dinner. It was like being in the real Wild West, from the steam engine burrowing into the mountains to the broad-chapped cowboys waving their laconic greetings. And, from what we'd seen of the river from the air, the bronco busting was yet to come.

Our first night's camp was on a broad green velour-textured embankment with a downstream vista of sawtoothed, snow-draped peaks. The night was our real introduction to the Southern Hemisphere: Our latitude was about thirty-six degrees south—the southern equivalent of Carmel, California. We savored a dinner of fresh vegetables and fruit, bantering in shirtsleeve warmth and familiarity beneath a sky spangled with unfamiliar stars.

As we lost elevation, the flora and geology began to change. The towering auracaria pines—which can grow to 150 feet high—gave way to groves of cedars, Lombardy poplars, and cyprus festooned with long shags of Spanish moss. The river began falling into a burnished gorge. Evidence of human habitation began to disappear, and the roots of the Andes were revealed in layers of basalt, pumice, and andesite—the igneous substratum of the great range. There was a sense of leaving behind the commonplace, of gliding toward the unknown.

As we passed a creek mouth, we saw a lone fisherman working a line with a crude sapling pole. This prompted Bill Wendt to try his luck, and he cast his nylon line over the stern. Seconds later he brought a five-pound brown trout flopping into the bilge. He whooped and hollered and threw the line in again. Within seconds he had another strike—and another five-pounder.

All this served to fuel the predator instinct in Bruce Gaguine, and when we passed a giant European hare (the size of a cocker spaniel) loping through the bush like a target waiting to be hit, Bruce got an idea. He had us pull to shore, where he filled the bilge with golf-ball-sized rocks; then we pushed out into the river again, creeping stealthily downstream looking for prey. We saw no more hare, but geese were everywhere. With every turn Bruce sprang to action, spitting rocks from his hands like gunfire.

Preoccupied with the hunt, he didn't notice when the boat was sucked into a rapid littered with boulders and chopped with three-foot drops. While novice river runner Mike Cobbold was at the oars, Bruce was crouched in the bow, still clutching ammunition. Suddenly Mike lost control: The boat rode upon a rock, waffled, and turned on its side, and the river started flushing in. Bruce leapt to the oars and wrestled the raft off the rock and through the rest of the rapid. Since we were the first to negotiate this river, we had the prerogative and privilege of naming rapids. This one became Gaguine's Gauntlet.

We purled past Chilpaca, a ghost town that thrived during a gold strike in 1932. Then we left the inhabited regions behind and were drawn into a forested whirlpool as the sun dropped behind a distant volcano. Camp was at the foot of a tremendous, frothing, white cascade of a tributary.

The next morning was Saturday, and we decided to treat it as such. Scanning our maps, we found a lake just two miles up the tributary, Lago Jesus Maria. We decided to investigate and scrambled up the rocky stream. Before long we reached it, and it was beautiful. The deep-blue, sun-dappled glacial basin was encased by 6,000-foot-high granite points, spires, and flutes, with tears of snow running down steep valleys on its flanks. It looked very much like one of the Twin Lakes at Yosemite, except for the absence of campers. We reveled and sunned in the wildflower meadows; but the promise of rapids downstream on the Bio-Bio called, and we returned to its banks before noon.

Running downstream once again, we splashed and careened through scores of rapids, naming them all as we went. With every passing mile the river was showing us a combination of the best features a river can have: resplendent scenery, powerful rapids, clear water, and good fishing.

That evening we feasted and fested. Bruce got lucky, so a local goose was roasted while the hunter-chef prepared a liver pate. We mixed *pisco* sours for cocktails and spread coals from our campfire beneath and on the lid of the Dutch oven. While heat surrounded the pot and radiated through the cast iron, we awaited the exotic concoction for dessert. Finally, dinner was ready: We uncorked a bottle of Chilean wine (70 cents for the wine, $1.70 for the returnable bottle) and ate corn on the cob, chicken soup, barbecued goose, and, finally, fresh cherry-vanilla pudding—the product of our Dutch oven.

On Sunday we rolled onto the river at 11:00 A.M. At noon we pulled over to a cascading tributary with a promising name, Rio Loco, and noticed some strangely discolored rock: mineral hot springs. "Doesn't this river ever stop?" Jack asked in wonder as we lay back for a soothing soak. "What more can it give us?" If the Bio-Bio heard that question, the river took it not just as a compliment but as a challenge. Downstream we hit the first of the big rapids. We were suddenly in water as violent and complex as any we had met, and it sent pulses thumping and spirits soaring. One rapid had a hole a small hotel could get lost in, dead center in the river. Another had a glassy chute that slid over a twelve-foot drop and ended in a back-rolling column of water, a horizontal tornado. Another was a fifty-yard labyrinth through a team of basalt bone-crunchers positioned like a defensive line.

In the middle of the rock maze, a glacial stream, gray with silt, spit into the river. As we scrambled up the bank to scout, we could see the source of the stream—a fantastic glint of ice pouring down through a mammoth mountain cleft like a huge strand of frozen molasses. It was an unnamed glacier, a stream of brilliant blue light carving through a realm of black basalt and ash. Ignoring for the moment our scout, we climbed higher and the view got better. The glacier hung from the 10,000-foot cone of an active volcano, Volcán Callaqui, a belching, smoking, snow-creamed peak that loomed directly over the river. We paused in amazement and excitedly pointed a route up the broad snowy flanks of the volcano. Perhaps another day; this one was for running the rapids.

Reluctantly we turned our attention to the rapid and descended to walk along its banks. We shook our heads in dismay, then paused in concentration, and finally nodded with understanding. It was, perhaps, possible, and a portage would not be easy. It took half an hour to memorize the run, which zigzagged through the rocks in a broken course. At last we walked quietly back to the boats, checked the rigging, and pulled tight our life jackets. The oarsman slipped on his soft leather gloves.

I began the run, drawing on the oars methodically, trying to match the map in my mind with the frothy view crashing down my bow. The current was fast, and from the river the perspective was disorienting. Almost at once I lost my way. I fell back on my instincts and had to rely on snap judgments and quick action. As I pulled to miss an approaching rock, I suddenly realized I would not make it. Whack? The collision felt like a VW Bug in a head-on with a Mack truck. The boat buckled, rebounded, fibrillated, then snapped around the wrong side of the rock, straight toward a deep-throated hole. Miraculously we were all still in the boat, and we braced for the hole.

We were flushed out immediately and couldn't believe it. But once we were out of the rapid and around the river, before our blood vessels got a chance to relax, the view downstream sent our hearts into our throats. Just 200 yards away was one of the most incredible river sights I have ever witnessed. A 150-foot tributary waterfall leaped in a show of shimmering, reflected light off a sheer cliff of basalt and described a gentle arc as it crashed directly into the river. Most rivers of appreciable length offer tributary waterfalls that can knock the breath out of any mortal; but such falls are usually a long way off the mother river, sometimes a hike of many miles. Never had I seen such a dazzling display of water and light spuming and mixing into a main river. It would have been a crime to continue, so we pulled in directly across from the waterfall to make camp.

After a hypnotic dinner, with the eyes of seven chewing heads trained on the falls across the river, a small group finally broke away and hiked downriver. It was a mistake. The next rapid was the biggest yet, a fuming mad jitterbug of big water dancing and tripping through king-sized holes and against Statue of Liberty boulders. We continued downstream to see if there was a calm stretch into which we could pull flipped boats, should we attempt the rapid. There wasn't. After 500 yards of fast, eddyless water, the river pinched against the south wall creating a quarter-mile-long toboggan run that dumped through a half dozen major souse holes and twice as many pressure waves. Finally, far below, a long, sleepy stretch of water waited, where the pieces could be picked up.

We couldn't remember spotting these rapids from the air, and we had seen some bad ones. But a worse rapid than this seemed unimaginable. To climb out of the canyon would be grim, and to portage half a mile over slippery, uneven terrain would resemble rolling boulders uphill all day. No one slept well that night. Only the spectacle of a shaft of moonlight playing on the milky waterfall across the river distracted us from our worries.

No one was hungry the next morning, so we skipped breakfast and marched down, a funeral procession, to the first rapid. Jack Morison, a ten-year Colorado veteran, commented with a grating crack in his voice that this was the first rapid he had seen that was more difficult than Lava Falls on the Colorado—a rapid considered by many to be the toughest piece of whitewater in the United States. After eyeing the stretch in the warning light of morning's optimism, we decided it was just possible to make the run down what we were now calling Lava South. Besides, it would be far preferable to run it than to portage, though the consequences of a mistake could be dear.

Alejandro looked at it and told us he could round up horses to get us out of the canyon. When we didn't respond to his offers, he told us he had two kids, cute, with brown eyes, and he elected to walk the rapid.

Bruce rowed first, as Bill and I rode the bow. We pivoted past the miraculous tributary waterfall, but all our attention was directed downstream.

Bruce made a good entry but smacked into a lateral wave that turned him the wrong way. The path devised while scouting from shore was the path not taken. We suddenly washed broadside against a boulder bar bisecting the river, and the boat started to ride up on its side, the first stage of a flip. Bill and I threw our weight on the rising tube, and the boat slid off the rock, around the far side into a channel we hadn't been able to see from shore. We were out of control in unknown water. We careened toward a pair of basalt slabs, smashed into one, spun on our side, and flopped down to the rapid's end, right side up. The bilge was brimming with water, and as Bill and I frantically bailed, Bruce pulled to shore on a broken oar. But we made it!

The day continued with a seemingly endless cascade of rapids. At one, Alejandro met a Mapuche Indian who described a recent drowning; and, as it turned out, the victim had been a friend of Alejandro. At the next rapid, Alejandro explained he had three children, just school age, and again he volunteered to walk.

At another sharp rapid, Jack and George were kicked out of the boat. As Jack was thrown out, his tennis shoe caught on the oarlock, and he ended up dangling helplessly upside down in the water, dragged along like a stuntman behind a runaway train. But this was no stunt: He struggled to keep his chin above water and to wrench his shoe free while the boat drifted toward the next cataract, a bad one.

The scene seemed too theatrical to be real, but a watery scream from Jack drove home the reality of the business. George Wendt splashed back into the bilge, grabbed the oars, and wrested the raft back to shore, while Mike plunged out of the boat next to Jack to help pull the caught leg free.

Spitting and hacking, Jack dragged himself up on the beach, a vacant look in his eyes. He'd come close; it was a freakish narrow escape. Some nasty bruises and a deep cut testified the river couldn't be messed with.

Later that same day Bruce, too, paid his dues. After several cautious, successful runs, Bruce decided to take us left through a rapid Jack had already run down the right. It was a mistake.

We suddenly plummeted through space toward a rock at the bottom of a fifteen-foot hole. We smacked, buckled, twisted, and almost flipped, and Bruce hurled overboard. I sprang to the oars just as the raft slammed into a cliff. We bounced off and a few hard pivot strokes spun us into an eddy. No sign of Bruce. A few seconds passed, those steel-cold seconds in which everyone wondered if the man was dead, then we all broke into a chorus of screams. I felt the floor of the boat bump twice and realized Bruce was stuck underneath. I jumped to the side, about to dive in, when a blue-faced Bruce popped up, alive and sputtering next to the boat.

The day had been too intense to continue any farther. We'd run more big rapids in a single day than are run in twelve days on the Colorado, and a couple were as big as the biggest in the Grand Canyon. We camped across from another 100-foot tributary waterfall, one of dozens that grace this canyon, but we were too weary and jaded to give it proper attention. It was like trying to admire a beautiful painting after having been mugged. We slept in exhaustion, unable to worry about what tomorrow might bring.

The next morning, our sixth on the river, was clear as a bell. Alejandro went for a hike during breakfast and came back with information some Mapuche Indians had passed on to him. They said there were twenty-three miles of bad rapids ahead, *worse* than what we'd been through, including a major waterfall. He'd also heard a rumor that another group had tried to raft the river five years earlier, but they had lined their boats for days down to the first big rapid (which we had hit two days earlier) and there they walked out. Prudent, sane men. He concluded by relating the popular local legend of *Chenque*, a cave deep at the bottom of the river where those who drown go. There they live forever, a very good and happy, though perhaps soggy, existence, but they can never resurface.

As was by now the pattern, the morning unrolled a stream of thrilling rapids. At noon, after a surprisingly nasty rapid that we navigated without mishap, we reached a red light. The river pinched into a sliver, barely fifty feet wide, and zigzagged through two tortuous right-angle turns. Most of the water jetted around the first corner, slid down an eight-foot sluice, and crashed into an overhanging cliff on the right. Overhangs—wedges of rock just above the surface—are major risks. Each year they drown a few hapless kayakers and occasionally some rafters. If a boat or body gets swept into an overhang, it easily can get pinned by thousands of pounds of water pressure, making it impossible to escape.

The overhang ahead of us, coupled with the fact that the next three rapids, all in close succession, were horrendous, gave us pause. We were certain we had now reached the series of difficult rapids we had spotted from the air. From high above, they had all looked runnable. Ground level had a different story to tell. After an hour of scouting through the virtually impenetrable brush and after much deliberation, we decided to portage one boat and position it in the water downstream from the falls. There, we hoped it could catch the other boat, should it capsize.

Alejandro had taken little time to decide to walk out to the road and hitch to Santa Barbara, our take-out point. He felt sure his four hungry children would want to see him again. So Jack Morison, who had not upset a boat in ten years of river running, started into the rapid with only one crew member. All the others, save Alejandro, were stationed in the other boat below, with coiled safety lines in readied hands.

"Whatever you do, Rich, stay away from that wall," Jack had warned as we pushed off, as if I might skip out of the boat and splash over to the wall for a playful inspection. Still, the tension in his voice put a lump in my throat.

His setup was perfect. He made it all the way to the top left, where the water was safest, but too quickly the current changed and pushed the raft into the right sluice that rammed into the overhang. The wall bore down on us at an alarming speed; I could see the dark recesses of the overhang getting bigger, enveloping the total picture of possibilities. I jumped back, and bam! We hit the wall at a forty-five-degree angle, and the boat ever so slowly slid up the wall, wedged briefly in the overhang, then tipped over. I jumped clear, as did Jack, and we were flushed safely to the eddy below. His first flip—after ten virtuous years of rafting.

Instinctively Jack and I grabbed the D-rings of the boat and tried to drag it to the right shore. It was as cumbersome as a pregnant hippo, and I found myself quickly exhausted. We made one small eddy but couldn't find a handhold or break in the rock to climb out, so we slid back into the current and down around the corner toward the next rapid. The other boat showed in the nick of time and pulled us in barely twenty-five feet above the angry water. Had we been sucked in, we probably would have lost the boat and gear forever, to say nothing of Jack and myself. Luckily we hadn't sent both boats through the rapid back to back, as we had talked of earlier. The cost would have been high.

This sequence of rapids, each of which was a gamble, was later given the name Royal Flush. The first was the Ace; this second one we called Suicide King. Then we continued through the next rapid, the Queen of Hearts, without mishap; if we hadn't been scared to death, it would have been fun. Shortly thereafter we came to the fourth big one of the day. It was the legendary falls, or *salto,* that the Mapuche had warned us about, and it deserved legendary status. Briefly described, in this rapid—which came to be known as One-Eyed Jack—the river collides with a boulder as big as the Ritz, splits into two channels, then slices, spits, and erupts into 15,000 cfs. We decided to portage.

We unloaded the gear and lugged it a hundred yards down the shore; then we lined the boats through the narrow portions of the river and pushed and shoved them through others. It was difficult to communicate because the roar of the rapid sounded like a rocket at liftoff. In two hours' time we were back in the boats, tossing on whitecapped water as we secured the gear. The lower half of the *salto* was run easily; the stretch is now called the Ten, to complete the gambler's hand. A mile downstream we made camp.

After a long, tough, but satisfying day, we raised a few glasses of *pisco* and vermouth to the rapids of the Bio-Bio and toasted the looming beauty of Volcán Callaqui, still dominating our view to the south. Then we dined on spaghetti, soup, and pudding and laid back for another starry evening with the sound of the water just a few yards from the security of our camp. Our aerial scout and every weary bone in our bodies told us the worst must be behind us.

We pushed off the next day and ran what we thought was a riffle, but it transformed into a class V rapid. George, who was rowing, smacked into every big wave and reversal, and we came within inches of capsizing. Then, without warning, we were in another rapid. This time Jack was swept out of the boat but sprang back in as quickly as he had exited. Next, George repeated the act by being catapulted straight out of the bow. Had we again misjudged the Bio-Bio?

The wildness continued all morning, and despite seven days in the sun, our faces were wan and our knuckles blue. But then the rapids slowly began to ease, and the canyon walls began to taper back. Soon afterward the mountains began to recede and flatten. The first hour of our freedom from the uncertainties of the Bio-Bio's gorge was rich recompense for all the pain and terror. We were through, and the river now rolled in silent majesty.

Here, below the narrow gorge with its small strip of sky and the whitewater that had demanded all our attention, we had a chance once again to appreciate the Chilean scenery. Volcán Callaqui retreated into the maze of the cordillera, the soil around us grew rich from the sediment laid down by the Bio-Bio's floods, and homesteads once again appeared. The branches of the oaks were filled with the songbirds of the south—the Misto yellow finch, the brightly colored red-breasted starling, and the olive-green Chilean elaenia, the bird whose call resonates like a siren's song over the waters of the Bio-Bio.

At 4:00 P.M. we drifted into Santa Barbara, where Alejandro, true to his word, was waiting with a pickup truck. We de-rigged, loaded up, threw a few hands of Frisbee with the locals who had gathered at the small bridge, then drove into town for a final dinner at the firehouse, letting someone else do the cooking for a change.

After celebrating, we wandered to the town square where we were surrounded instantly by dozens of children. They giggled and hovered around us, all smiles and good nature. As the first *Norteamericanos* to ever visit their town, we were instant celebrities. They brought out a guitar, and we played American folk songs while they clapped and cheered; then they played and sang in the haunting accents of the local tongue, and it was our turn to applaud. While the *pisco* flowed and the Southern Cross made its slow pilgrimage across the sky, the Bio-Bio sang its own soft song nearby, a gentle echo of the thunderous symphony of the Andes that had underscored our sleep for the past eight days.

Snake River:
"Can I Keep Your Oars?"

Jeff Bennett

*T*oo much skill and daring can prove dangerous, especially when ace paddlers are constrained to repeatedly apply their talents to a single stretch of water. Even the gnarliest hole or boil will lose its bite after the fiftieth time through. This is precisely when a maniac will start noodling ways to do things differently, for the maniac grows bored through rote. He must find a way to get the juices flowing again. The question is, What way? Blasting through class V rapids in a truck inner tube is one way—the way of the natural-born madman.

‡   ‡   ‡

Every once in a while, one of my river buddies does something so monumentally stupid that I have to ask myself, *"Why didn't I do that first?!"* That was precisely the question running through my head as I watched Mike Blumm blow up his inner tube.

It wasn't the mere act of inflation itself that so bedazzled me, rather the fact that Mike was about to toss this bloated donut into the raging torrents of Wild Sheep Rapid—the longest class V rapid in the Hells Canyon section of Idaho's Snake River.

After a few more minutes of watching Mike force recycled canyon air into his tube, I thought I had the scene figured out. This was a put-on, a practical joke. I was sure of it. But I wanted to play along. So I began walking down the hill, closer to the situation, moving in for a better look.

123

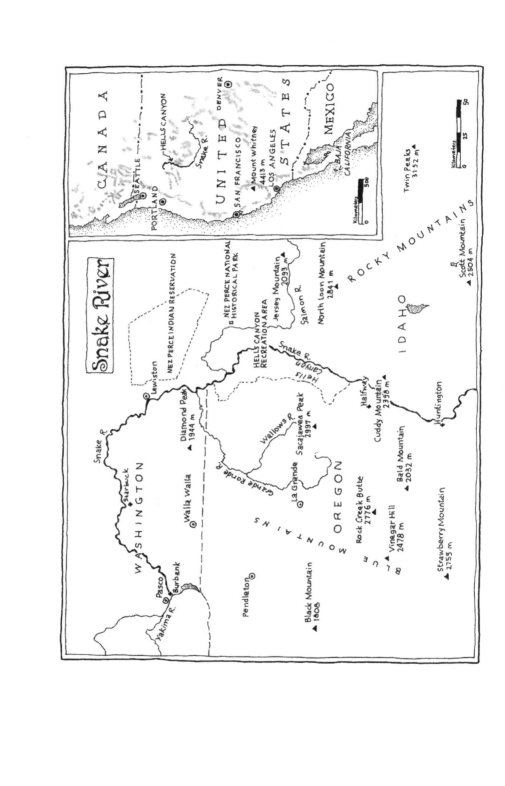

I strained to wipe away my smile as I stepped the final few feet to Mike's side. I put my hand on Mike's shoulder and began to talk. "Things okay at home, Mike? You get fired and not tell us? Wife been backdooring you?" Mike just kept about his business, staring intently at the river.

"Shit," I thought, "this is for real. *He's really gonna do it!*"

It was clear to everyone this little stunt was the brainchild of a madman. Canyon fever. But after a couple of minutes of discussion, Mike was able to convince me that this adventure had been carefully planned.

"Carefully planned?!" I exclaimed. "What the heck kind of planning goes into tubing a class V rapid?!"

First of all, explained Mike, there is the careful selection of the inner tube itself. Don't ask me what that means. I never quite got the theory down on inner-tube selection. Perhaps the key is that the tube holds plenty of air—*hot* air. Next, you have to plan not to forget your helmet or life jacket. No biggie there. Finally, and most importantly, there's the "tell-all-your-friends-you're-gonna-do-it-so-you-can't-back-down" part of the plan. This final point provides some trip insurance in case your mind returns at the last minute. Having overseen all of these fine planning details, Mike was ready.

Watching Mike hike down to the river to survey the rapid one last time, I began to pity the poor sap who would first spot Mike's corpse floating past Heller's Bar. But as one never to let an opportunity slip through my hands, I offered my final words of encouragement: "Hey, can I keep your oars if you don't make it?"

Mike ignored my send-off, dropped his ass into the tube's hole, stepped to the river's edge, and unceremoniously backflopped into an eddy. He then began to backstroke furiously out into the current until, about a thousand backstrokes later, he found his desired entry line for the rapid. I think. Well, either he found his line or his arms gave out.

Mike's knees and helmet began to bob as he accelerated down the slick tongue toward the first line of waves. Soon the river swept him into a confusing riot of foam and current. I felt overwhelmed by the grace of his descent and admired the audacity of his endeavor.

Faster and faster, the river swept him toward the first megahole. As his tube paused, poised above the tip of a huge, gaping keeper, I reached a moment of realization—a realization that I was about to become the owner of Mike's oars.

But it was not to be. For the next few seconds, Mike managed to utilize his inner tube to its fullest capabilities, displaying true tubing finesse whether above, below, or in hot pursuit of his inner tube. And somehow, he survived.

We were finishing up our lunch about the time Mike completed his hike back upriver to join us.

"How was it?" we asked.

"Fun," he said. "A little bigger than I thought it'd be."

As we loaded up the rafts for our own runs through Wild Sheep, Mike seemed extraordinarily calm. It was as if a month of stress and anxiety had been lifted from his shoulders.

We set up camp early that day. Above the roar of the next big rapid—Granite Falls—and beneath overhanging cliffs adorned by ancient Indian petroglyphs, we basked in the late afternoon sun and traded old river lies over cool gulps of beer.

As the conversation turned back to Mike's exploits, we noticed that he was absent from the circle. Gone. Someone mentioned having last seen him walking toward Granite Falls. Scouting perhaps? I mean, Granite *is* the biggest, wildest rapid in Hells Canyon.

Mike stumbled back into camp, exuding that same maniacal glare of intent he'd shown at Wild Sheep. "I'm going to take that inner tube through Granite," he said. "Right through the big hole!"

"All right!" I thought. "A second chance. Maybe *this* time, I'll get some new oars!"

"NO SHIT. THERE I WAS . . ."

Linda Ellerbee

When we choose to take on a challenge, we often do so with a specific outcome in mind—an outcome that rarely plays out. "I had no idea it was going to be like that" or "I didn't know what I was in for till it was over" are common, after-the-fact, refrains. During our journey we naturally start asking "Why am I doing this?" or "How did I get here?" The paradox of being strung tight between fear and desire can produce life-changing experiences if we can flow with a challenge, allowing the "here and now" to lead. Conversely, fighting the unforeseen and struggling to maintain a rigid plan can, and often will, nix the very gifts we might otherwise receive.

The trials of a big river are as unpredictable as the facets of our day-to-day lives and present us with the same array of choices. In the following passage, when strangers, linked by one goal and a neoprene raft, charge down the Colorado River, they discover they can do more than simply survive. In each turn, bump, and roll, they discover more of themselves. Hear the voice of one woman as she, Linda Ellerbee, recounts her experience. The magic begins when we least expect it. And as genuine magic, it is long afterward still strong enough to lift her from the valley of tears and transform her into "a shining thing in a shining place."

⁜   ⁜   ⁜

It is, and I am, cold and damp. Gray sky. Wind. Don't know if it's raining. Don't care. So much river water coming over my head, what's a little more wet? I could be in a warm, dry office in New York City, not

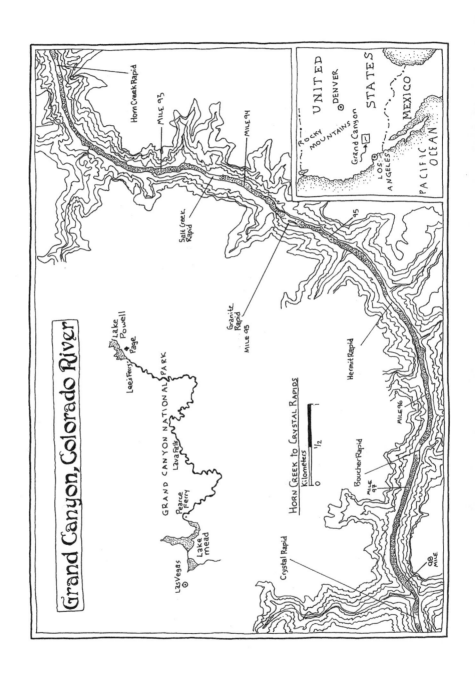

Grand Canyon, Colorado River

crouched in a rubber boat (okay, raft), ankle-deep in forty-eight-degree water, watching a bearded stranger row us down the Colorado River. We round a bend. Lee's Ferry, our starting point for this journey, disappears. Two weeks? I am miserable.

"Bail," yells the bearded stranger.

Twenty-four and one-half chilly miles later, we make first camp. As soon as I set up my tent, it blows up and away and might now be half the distance to Canada but for a big man who jumps into the air and catches it. George is from Covington, Georgia. Quit the navy at thirty-eight and figures if he lives frugally he won't need to job hunt until 2001. Meantime, George is seeing the country, having recently hiked all 2,162 miles of the Appalachian Trail. Now he's doing the canyon. Doing the river thing. I ask George if he's scared of the rapids. I am.

"Nah. You only live once."

Trite, but no less true—for George. What is it I say when I talk about having had cancer? "Smell the flowers." "Take chances." "Live as if. . . ." I wonder: Do people know I might be lying? Right after I was diagnosed, right after I lost both my breasts and all my hair (my hair grew back), I did make time for flowers and chances. It was then I discovered the woods. Soon I came to believe this gift had been waiting years for me, a Gulf Coast gal with a centrally air-conditioned past, washed ashore in the Northeast. I was nearly fifty when I began hiking and, later, backpacking. Whenever I would get to the top of something I thought I couldn't climb, I'd swell with pride and ask myself what other hills in my life might I now take on.

I am drawn to the woods by this challenge, and by solitude, but most of all by beauty. Every year, beauty becomes more important, some magic vitamin, a necessary tonic without which body and soul might wither. This is what the woods and, possibly, cancer have given me. But it's been five years. Life speeds up. Flowers are passed, unsmelled. Chances go untaken. That's partly why this trip appealed. Two hundred twenty-six miles of river. No telephone. No computers. Nothing but flowers and chances. I come to the canyon thinking of it as woods with no trees.

Yet I am frightened of the rapids, even before I see one.

Today there was plenty of whitewater, although the rapids were not, I'm told, large ones. Rummaging in my gear, sorting through the too many things I've brought, trying (uselessly) to brush sand off my stuff, I remember the guy sitting across from me on the plane to Flagstaff. The back of his T-shirt read, "Face your fears. Live your dreams."

Couldn't tell what was printed on the front; at the time, he was bent over, throwing up.

Make this rain stop. My shin is bandaged; I pulled a piece of the Cambrian Period down on it. Hurts, but I won't let on. I'm facing my fears, *okay?* All this talk about rock? Spectacular, but a little geology goes a long way. I'm more of a scenery junkie and the scenery is definitely being rained on. What did the boatman say? "The first day is the worst day."

I am not supposed to be here.

Two mornings later, someone asks if I would like to try the paddleboat. There are five boats. In four, the boatman rows while passengers, uncomfortably seated front and back, ride, talk, look about, and hang on for dear life. In the fifth boat, six people paddle to the commands of a seventh, the paddle captain. Trouble with the paddleboat is there's nothing to hang on to, and you couldn't hang on anyway because you have to paddle. You have to go through big hungry water, actually leaning out and shoving a stick into it at regular intervals. Counterintuitive, says someone. Suicidal, think I.

"Sure," I say. "I would like to try the paddleboat." (Checked the map; there are no giant rapids today.)

Soon I'm reminded how much I like paddling, although until now the experience has been limited to canoes on quiet rivers and quieter lakes. We enter a small rapid. I manage to stay in the boat and keep my paddle in the water. I like the rush, want a bigger rapid. And then we are blessed. The rain stops. By noon, yellow sun dances on green water, bounces off red canyon walls, and shoots back up into blue sky. A crayon day. Feels like falling in love.

Takes a while for the river and canyon to grab hold. But they do. I wake in the night to catch the Big Dipper grinning like a Cheshire cat six feet above my head. *Gotcha.* Hours later, warm in my sleeping bag, the predawn air cool on my face, I say good-bye to the morning star.

On the fifth day, we hike up a side canyon, something we do every day, but this time I hallucinate. I hear Verdi. Another twist of the canyon and there, seated on bailing buckets, are four men, three with violins, one with cello, playing Verdi. Don't know who they are or how they got here. *Play on.* Verdi becomes Dvorak. Without warning, something inside is released. I begin to cry. So much beauty. So little time. Canyon, fill me up.

Our travels are not always the voyages of discovery we say we seek. Often they are rituals of reassurance. This was different. This required one to take physical and emotional chances. Not just the river. The people. *All these strangers? I'm supposed to get to* know *all these strangers?* But isn't one of the gifts of travel the discovery of oneself through other people?

At seventy-three, Wini is a retired professor and genuinely beautiful woman, smart and prickly. This is her fourth trip down this river. One day, on a hike, Wini gets sick. Too much sun? Too little water? John, the trip leader, asks if she needs to be lifted out of the canyon by helicopter.

"No," says Wini. "I don't."

The subject is closed.

Next day, tired from being around too many people, I remain by the river when the others go hiking. Wini has also stayed behind. She stops by my camp, says she's come to realize this is the last time; she will never make this trip again. Since Wini is twenty-one years farther down the road, and because I very much want to know, I ask her what it is like to do something for the last time. I want to cry for Wini. For me, too. No matter what anyone tells you, there's nothing good about getting old.

At the moment, however, I've other worries. *Horn. Granite. Hermit. Crystal.* Bigger rapids. Bigger fears. "You can do it," says Julie, paddle captain and hero. You should see Julie. No matter where we sleep, she sleeps higher, curled up there somewhere, on some rock or another. Mornings, Julie comes down lightly, leaping from boulder to boulder, boat to boat, surefooted as any other wild creature. On the water, her voice is gentle, teaching us to stroke together, turning a group of inexperienced paddlers into a team able to pass through a big rapid and come out thinking they've done it all themselves.

By now, I know the paddleboat is where I want to be. I love the thrill, love the paddling, and find it less frightening if I'm actually involved in my fate, rather than watching someone else row while I hang on and try not to notice a twelve-foot wall of water coming straight at me. But when we climb ahead to scout a big rapid and I look down into this bodacious breaking stuff, my stomach falls away like the rapid itself. *Oh, dear! God, don't make me paddle this! I can't. I will panic. Fall out. Die. Worse, I will chicken out. Drop my paddle and cling, sniveling, to the boat. . . .*

Julie says I can.

I pray a secret prayer and, in case God can't hear me for the water, pray it again, louder. Thus begins the day of big rapids. One boat flips, tossing its occupants into the current. They're pulled out downstream, shivering, teeth chattering, humbled. But as though it were greased, our paddle raft shoots through the beautiful whitewater. We are triumphant. There are no words. Only the song inside me. I am my own band, and I am very much in tune. I, Linda Jane, have successfully paddled the biggest rapids of the grandest canyon of the Colorado River. I feel strong and competent and nineteen. No. I feel strong and competent and fifty-two.

I am supposed to be here.

Can't wait to tell people back home about this. Julie asks if we know the difference between a fairy tale and a river story. We don't. "Well," she says, a fairy tale begins, "Once upon a time," and a river story begins, "No shit! There I was. . . ."

Days of long play. Of water fights and waterfalls. Of skinny dipping alone, in a turquoise pool, then napping in soft grass next to it. Of sun and sunrises. And sunsets. Of climbing boulders I once thought too tall. Of walking ledges I once thought too narrow. Of crude drawings on canyon walls, very old graffiti, left by ancient ones who disappeared. Nights littered with stars. Do the stars know where the people went?

One hot afternoon near the end of the trip, drifting toward more rapids, Julie tells us the reason we're a good paddle team is that we do what she says, when she says it. We nod in pompous agreement. Teacher's pets. "And that is why," says Julie, softly, "I want you to put down your paddles, jump in the river, and swim the next rapid."

"*Excuse me?!*" Have we not spent the better part of two weeks doing our best *not* to fall into this rock 'n' roll river with its cold, cold heart? Now you want us to go in *on purpose?* But nobody says that. We're too busy putting down our paddles and jumping into the river.

Whoosh. Breath knocked right out of me. Whoosh. Don't forget to breathe out. That's what John said. Breathe in at the bottom of the trough. That's what Julie said. Swallowing green and swallowed by green. The world tumbles up and over. I see sky, water, sky, water, sky, water and then it's all one thing: skywater.

The waves end. The ride is over. Julie hauls us into the raft. We are wet and slithery and loud. We are invincible. Soaked in beauty. We are alive.

Overcome with the pure joy of experience, I start thinking how great it would be to be a boatman (even women guides are called boatmen). How fine to live each day, mindful of the world immediately around you, focused on the river, the boat, the passengers, wet and dry, food and drink, sun and sand and sleep. Life 101. I'm about ready to quit my day job when Eric, a real boatman, points out a reality I've not considered. "Every year," says Eric, "I make less money. I'm sort of working toward a cash-free existence." Mmmm. Even that has a certain appeal. It is a life. A good one. But it is not my life. Not this time around.

Weeks later, back in New York City, a phone rings. A woman, someone I wrote a story about, has died from breast cancer. It was the treatment that killed her. I celebrate her courage, mourn her death, and, sorry to say, am relieved it wasn't me. The fear is always there. Although I try to live as if the cancer were never coming back, I know all the nasty little numbers; half the women who get this disease are dead in ten years. I put down the phone, tuck away the fear and go back to work.

But at night, lying in bed, troubled by death and overwhelmed by life, I find I can shut my eyes and whisper. That's all I have to do.

"Take me there," I whisper.

And the magic begins. Gold light slides down a red canyon wall. A green river sings. I am a shining thing in a shining place far, far from here.

THE CHEAT RIVER

James Snyder

*"The amount of time you spend looking at a hole is directly proportional to
the amount of time you're going to spend surfing that hole."*

—Harpo

P icture a tiny, tight-framed damsel with a fresh-out-of-a-salon appearance, pinned under her pink Mercedes sedan. Grimacing with fear and
anguish, she shrieks for help. When all seems lost, a man—and not
just any man, but a superlative "woman's man," with rippling, whip-corded
muscles bulging from his shrink-wrapped T-shirt—turns his angular, freshly
shaven face toward the doomed damsel. He raises an eyebrow, smiles a
gentleman's smile, and with lightning speed dashes over to the rescue. He hefts
the car with his pinky and pulls the damsel free, embracing her to his moun-
tainous chest. They kiss, striking a pose off the cover of one of those gothic
novels hawked in supermarkets. The end. Comically speaking, every man's
dream—but not every man's reality. The ensuing story concerns a hero and
the "hero-ee." However, the initiating hero's luck takes an abrupt turn, and
the fair damsel proves herself to be something much more than a daffy minx
stepped off the cover of a Harlequin romance.

‡   ‡   ‡

Hero stories. You've probably heard a million of them. Usually they're
about someone else, some hotshot river guru with loads of cash and
exotic plane tickets. But this time it's about yours truly—Jim Snyder.

My story is set against West Virginia's incredible Cheat River, where I sat in my kayak at the bottom of Beech Run Rapid, before the Great Flood of '85. The gauge was reading 1.65 feet, the highest level at which we allow unguided rafts on the river. And, at that level, the worst hole on the entire Cheat River lurked at the end of this rapid. The hole at Beech Run Rapid isn't colossal by most paddlers' standards—a low pourover about eighteen inches high—but it is sealed off on all sides by dead-end currents. A bona fide textbook keeper, designed by the river gods to be the exact shape of a four-man raft. The hole curls in at the outer edges and forms a huge, liquid catcher's mitt at its midsection. Rafts stick to the watery mitt like ants to a sucker. And, once they've lost their momentum, rafters can spend fifteen or twenty minutes gyrating and surging in the hole, rarely bursting beyond its powerful round shoulders without some extra assistance. Still, the odds of getting out of the hole increase as the next raft upstream lines up for its ride. Since it's only a one-boat hole, a new boat just provides fresh meat as it knocks the used raft free.

Beech Run Rapid has such a nasty reputation that, when rafts are running it, everyone else on the river tends to pull up to shore to watch the entertainment. But even with the obvious hazards, raft guides are hard pressed to avoid the hole. Since almost every trip sends some unsuspecting crew into the hole, we always post a guide nearby to pick up the pieces, which was exactly my job that day.

Earlier in the trip I had paddled ahead of my group so that I could be in position at the hole when they arrived. As I paddled to the hole, I couldn't help but notice that the trip ahead of ours had already succumbed to the usual riverborne problems. But by the time I arrived, all of the pusher rafts had run by and the last raft was inextricably entwined in the hole's sticky web.

Only one "survivor" was left in the raft—a fine-looking female about twenty-five years old.

The raft beneath her weary body had been bucking so violently that she had finally resigned herself to the safety of the floor. On the shore an irritated guide shouted, *"Paddle hard!"* as she stirred the hole with her paddle. I was the only one in a kayak, and I knew that my group would soon be lining up for their ride through the hole. I quickly appraised the situation and felt that it was time to respond to her distress in some classic manner. After all, I had a heck of a shorebound audience and all the makings of a seasoned veteran. At least I knew what to do.

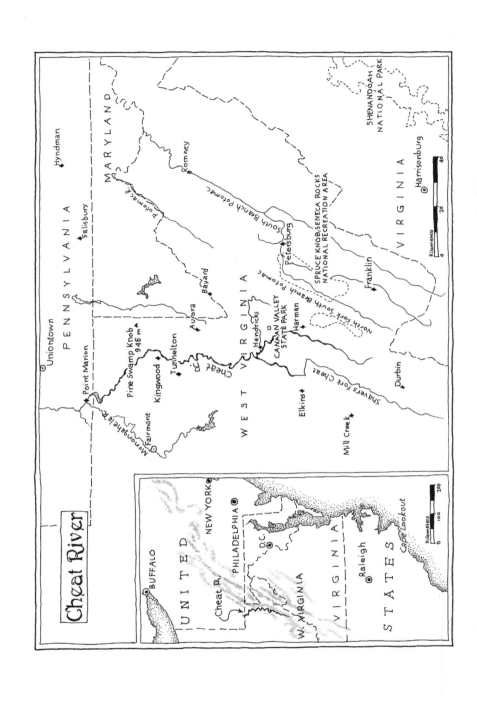

With astonishing deftness, I paddled to the raft from the down-stream side and pulled myself into it. Then I carefully placed my paddle into my kayak and gave it a shove toward safety.

"Let me have that paddle, and I'll get us out," I declared to my newfound admirer. She glanced back at me, exhausted, and gladly re-linquished the helm.

It was now my job to pendulum the little raft back and forth across the hole until it grabbed enough current to jounce free. The only prob-lem was with the paddle. This boat's original owner believed that rafts stay out of trouble on their own and that any major river dilemma is necessarily caused by the passengers. In an attempt, I guess, to coun-teract any passenger's input to his or her own fate, the outfitter had issued little flexible toy paddles. I mean, you couldn't smack a Wiffle ball with one of these things. With my tremendous guide-type muscles, I quickly twisted the paddle into a pretzel while my tired partner rested in the bottom of the raft. Flustered, I paused in the middle of our whitewater rodeo and reevaluated my grand rescue plans.

At this point, the events took a significant turn. In fact, the raft spun 180 degrees, sending me onto the low side of the raft, which was now nestled deep in the trough of the hole. When I stood to get a better po-sition on the downstream tube, the raft bucked and sent me flying feet first between the falls of the hole and the raft itself.

On the way out of the raft, I reached to grab a tube and pull myself back aboard. But instead of making a fittingly heroic self-rescue, I ended up getting my arm caught between the side rope and the raft. It was one of those entanglements Slim Ray and Charlie Walbridge lecture about—the reason why loose ropes don't belong on rafts.

I couldn't believe it. There I was, snagged in the rope while the falls ruthlessly hammered down on my head and shoulders. Even with my free hand on the rope, I couldn't lift myself high enough to get my lips to the surface, or to get some air into my lungs. To add insult to injury, my raft partner had now taken up camp on the downstream tube, pre-venting the raft from flipping and surfing free.

I was hating life. Hating those flimsy toy paddles. Hating the inno-cent woman, the hole, the raft, and my little weenie arms. The situation remained deathly static, giving me plenty of time to realize that, more than anything, I wanted out of the water. Fast! Still, the lady wouldn't move, the raft wouldn't turn, and my arm wouldn't come free. I struggled inches below the surface, fraught with singular desire to breathe. This underwater world was for scuba divers. Jacques Cousteau. Not for river heroes. Not for Jim Snyder.

I peered skyward through the falls, hoping for a change. And just above me I could see the woman peering down, watching me drown beneath the falling water. Damn! This kind of stuff never happened to Superman, Aquaman, and all the other superheroes.

Finally, probably because things could get no worse, my luck began to change. In a moment of glory, my newfound hero stretched across the raft, reached deep into the water, and planted a firm grasp beneath my armpit. Her weary arms pulled and pulled as the falls fought hard to defeat her struggle. The tug-of-war seemed to last forever, but she would not give up. I contributed by lying there, suspended between time and water. Above, her grip strengthened, inching my weary body upward until, in an instant of incredible determination, she leaned into a final, explosive thrust.

Blasting free of the water, my body launched into a rainbow arc across the raft. The torque we created blew the boat straight downstream, free of the hole. I laid in the bottom of the raft exhaustedly admiring my partner as she stared benevolently down upon me.

As my heaving and gasping slowly subsided, I took a few more sweet breaths, looked up at her, and said, "I think you saved my life."

"I think I did," she replied, flashing one of the kindest grins ever to work its way into my memory.

She and her trip paddled away soon after depositing me on the shore. I was never to learn her name or see her again. She had intrepidly shattered the lines of the sexes with her chivalry and valor, leaving me sitting on the bank forever in her debt.

POLIO CREEK

William Nealy

*K*ids do the darndest things in pursuit of fun and novelty. In the process they discover their limits—and those of their parents. Kids' natural sense of adventure typically leads them into sticky circumstances
that most adults, fearing the consequences and lack of control, will categori-
cally avoid. And yet a child's wide-eyed sense of adventure is something to be
recaptured by us adults, who typically have mortgaged our insouciance for a
workaholic schedule, safety in mediocrity, and blubbering about being "too
old for that sort of thing." The person who says he has too much to lose has
already lost the most important things: the courage to take risks and the desire to expand. A yen for exploration is instinctual in us all, but it flows
especially rich in kids. Childhood adventures are everlasting. They return us
to a time when life was younger and open-ended, before we "knew better."
Such stories remind us of the passion alive (or asleep) in all of us, a passion
well represented in Bill Nealy's adventure on Polio Creek.*

‡   ‡   ‡

We kids called it Polio Creek, as in "You better stay out of that ditch or
you'll get polio." It drained from the eastern slopes of Red Mountain,
the southernmost extent of the Appalachian foothills in Alabama's cen-
tral piedmont. It ran through my backyard in Homewood, one of
Birmingham's many bedroom communities. Before World War I, Polio Creek had been a meandering brook with gentle curves and gentler
gradient. By 1950 it had been engineered, channelized, and civilized,

walled on both banks eight feet high, first with sandstone, later with concrete.

Polio Creek was a crack in suburbia, a kid Ho Chi Minh Trail, the forbidden zone. Within its sheer cool walls a youngster could walk for miles without once falling under an adult's reptilian gaze. Here and there were tunnels connecting other neighborhoods to the creek, tunnels big enough to walk upright in and, on occasion, big enough to run like hell in when being pursued by adults or, worse, teenagers. Naturally we were forbidden to play in the creek by the mom and dad units. "Typhoid!" "Rats!" "Snakes!" And, obviously, "Polio!" Practically the worst thing that could happen to one of us would be to slip and fall into Polio Creek. It was a long, sad walk home, dripping with the evidence of a sure whipping offense. Despite the hazards, I lived in Polio Creek.

Once or twice a year a flash flood would pump Polio Creek up eight or ten feet, turning it into a watery freight train whipping through Homewood faster than you could pedal a bike—light speed to a kid. We would be herded into the houses and our parents would stand looking out kitchen windows at the astonishing sight, smoking cigarettes and silently praying the furnace didn't get flooded. To the grown-ups the creek had become a limbless Godzilla, a hell snake unleashed on Homewood, slithering between the houses, hissing and throbbing. Sometimes a section of the retaining wall would get peeled off by the force of the current and entire backyards would be lost, scoured down to the old streambed. Dolls, basketballs, tires, "shine" jugs, paint cans, lumber, lawn furniture, shrubs, and other suburban flotsam would begin the long journey south to the Gulf of Mexico on the crest of the flood. For years I had been contemplating just such a journey for myself.

I had a boat: a one-kid plastic rowboat-looking affair from Kmart. It also doubled as a wading pool, turtle pond, or sled, as circumstances dictated. Conditions had to be just right to run Polio Creek: daylight, mild weather, sufficient water, and absence of adult supervision. One blustery spring day in 1965 everything came together. It had rained all day, and from my sixth-grade classroom I could see parents arriving early to pick up their children, headlights on in the afternoon darkness. A good omen.

My friend Tommy and I rode our bikes home in the rain. Rainwater was gushing out of storm drains, and when we got to the bridge we saw that Polio Creek was high and going higher. We made a plan; I would float the creek and Tommy would stay ahead of me on his

Schwinn Typhoon, checking my progress at each successive bridge. Since this was merely a run-through and not the actual Gulf of Mexico expedition, equipment and supplies were kept at a minimum. A boat, a paddle, and a paddler. I was only going a few blocks.

With Tommy stationed at the first bridge on my home street, I carried my boat upstream through backyards to where a smaller creek fed into Polio Creek through a break in the wall. Moving in a brisk but stealthy manner (a kid carrying a boat anywhere near a flooded creek was fair game for any nosey grown-up), I got into position on the feeder creek and slid down, out of sight. I got in the boat and paddled up to the break in the wall. Polio Creek shot past the breach with a low sucking moan, and as I cleared the wall I was snatched downstream. This was like some demented new ride at the state fair—a Mad Mouse with no brakes and no end, an insane machine. I was falling down a shaft with walls of concrete, water, and air.

The first rapid was a ninety-degree bend to the right with a huge sewage tank protruding from the left wall at the middle of the bend. The entire flow was slamming straight into the tank and folding over itself in its rush to turn right. Despite a frantic stroke or two I was heading straight into a wall of very angry-looking water. Something grabbed the boat, stood it practically on end, and shoved me right at the instant before I hit the tank. Then I was bailing with my hands; water had surged over the transom into the boat as I was tossed to the right. A huge shadow flew over me and someone yelled my name. I looked up toward the sound and saw I had just streaked under the first bridge. I could see Tommy pony-express mounting his Typhoon, heading for bridge number two.

Next bend, ninety degrees left, trying to stay to the inside of the turn. Into the wall instead, nearly vertical, then whipped left just before impact. Bailing frantically now, like those cartoons where Sylvester the cat suddenly has fifty arms. My predicament is dawning on me. First it is a trickle, then a torrent of realization: I am going to drown today. Probably in the next few minutes. The walls are smooth, unbroken. Unless I can somehow stand up in the boat, I can't reach the top of the wall. The water's too deep to stand in and too fast to tread. Ninety-degree bend to the right—stayed inside the turn and only shipped a little water this time. Long curve to the left. The creek is still rising. . . . I can see windows, back porches now. Great. If I don't drown I'm going to get caught. Bridge number two is coming up to meet me . . . it's like sitting in a bathtub of cold water and having the world roll over me. Tommy rides onto the bridge, drops his bike, and runs to the upstream rail. He's crying now. The bridge has a center piling with a tree and some boards stuck to it. The right side would be better because there's a curve to the right just below and that would put me inside the curve. I take the left side, which looks safer, and I'm into the curve before Tommy can run to the other side of the bridge. Boat spinning, I hit the wall this time and I'm full of water. Got to bail.

Third bridge. No sign of Tommy. Water still rising and it will be a squeeze to make it under this bridge . . . less than two feet. For one second I consider grabbing the bridge and climbing up on it. Then I'm scrunched into the bottom of the boat, flying into the penumbra of the bridge. I'm clear, on a long straightaway; ahead is bridge number four. Just below this bridge is a steel water pipe about a foot in diameter that crosses the creek about six feet above the creekbed. I've fished from it. Now it is right at the surface, splitting the flow horizontally like a planer. A huge boil just below where the flows reunite throws steam and froth into the air. It is the end of the world. I remember a concrete storm drainpipe on the right wall just above the bridge. That is how we climb in and out of the creek here when the creek is running a trickle. It's about halfway up the wall. Right now only the top of the pipe is visible, a six-inch ledge curving into brown water. I've got to grab the pipe, roll out of the boat, and climb out. There is silence and I'm looking down a dark tunnel at the top edge of a pipe and the black underside of the bridge. Nothing else exists but that little piece of concrete. I'm there . . . drop paddle . . . grab pipe . . . roll out of the boat. I swing below the pipe, planing on the surface, water tearing at my jeans. Lost a shoe, then the other. I hear a crunch as the boat is cleaved in two by the pipe. I can't bring myself to look downstream. I get a leg in the pipe, then a foot on top and a hand on top of the wall. I bring my head up slowly . . . no fire trucks . . . no Tommy. The coast is clear. I cross to the far side of the bridge. Boat gone. Just brown boiling water. I hope Tommy shows up soon . . . we've got to prepare a good story in case we're interrogated later on tonight. Went wading, slipped and lost shoes. Some other kids swiped boat and sent it down creek, etc.

I see my mom's VW headed toward me, coming fast. There's my mom . . . there's Tommy. Holy crap.

THROUGH THE GRAND

John Wesley Powell

*O*ne hundred and thirty years ago, ten men in four wooden dories *swept down the raging "Colorado River of the West" on the first trip through the Grand Canyon. Extending for 278 miles, more than a mile deep at its lowest point, the Grand Canyon has remained nature's magnum opus since Spanish conquistadors first sighted it in the sixteenth century. The epic "first descent" was led by Major John Wesley Powell, who'd lost an arm to a minnie ball at Shiloh. Contemporary maps indicated terra incognita from the Upper Green River to the confluence of the Colorado and Virgin Rivers. Powell had heard fantastic stories of whirlpools wide as a city block, of bottomless vortices and rapids that would swallow and demolish all craft. And once in the mysterious, unexplored canyon, the river was said to dash through smooth, no-exit granite walls only to plunge underground and resurface "in the aspect of a seething geyser shocking to behold," hundreds of miles downstream.*

A book of whitewater adventures would be lacking if it did not include an account of Powell's incredible voyage. In spirit if not in fact, when Powell, his men, and their four dories cast off from Green River and into the dark unknown of the Grand Canyon, they were embarking on the first great whitewater epic, by which all others would be measured. Seated in a wooden chair lashed to the transom of a wooden boat (the Emma Dean*) smashing through the titanic rapids of the mighty "Grand," Powell was the picture of the brave explorer who, in the middle of the last century, forged into the Western frontier.*

On August 13, 1869, thirteen weeks after the expedition left Green River Station in Wyoming, the Major, with only two crippled boats and six exhausted survivors, emerged from the canyon to find men fishing with nets for their

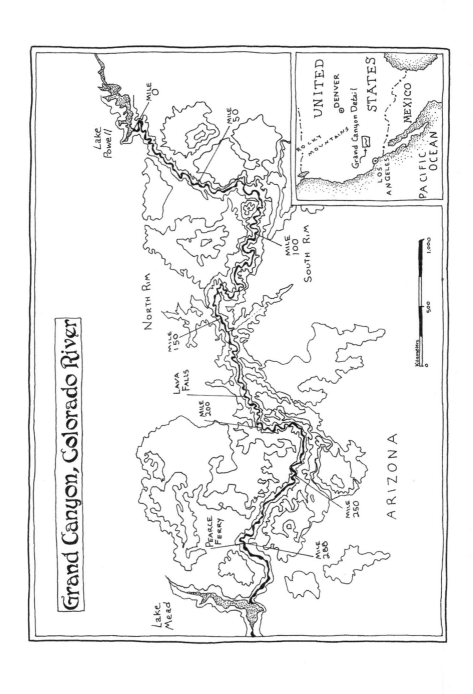

Grand Canyon, Colorado River

Lake Powell

MILE 0

MILE 50

MILE 100

NORTH RIM

SOUTH RIM

MILE 150

LAVA FALLS

MILE 200

MILE 250

PEARLE FERRY

MILE 280

Lake Mead

ARIZONA

UNITED

STATES

ROCKY MOUNTAINS

DENVER

Grand Canyon Detail

LOS ANGELES

MEXICO

PACIFIC OCEAN

Kilometers

0   500   1,000

remains. *One man had left Powell's party near the beginning of the trip and survived; three others left before terrifying rapids in the depths of the Canyon, clambered out onto the north rim, and were killed at once by Paiute Indians.*

Powell's dramatic journal created a sensation when portions first appeared in Scribner's Monthly *in 1874 and 1875. The following, condensed from Powell's original diary, is no less exhilarating today. This excerpt is referred to as "From the Little Colorado to the Mouth of the Grand Canyon."*

‡ ‡ ‡

August 13: We are now ready to start on our way down the Great Unknown. Our boats, tied to a stake, chafe each other as they are tossed by the fretful river. They ride high and buoyant, for their loads are lighter than we could desire. We have but a month's rations remaining. The flour has been resifted through the mosquito-net sieve; the spoiled bacon has been dried and the worst of it boiled; the few pounds of dried apples have been spread in the sun and reshrunken to their normal bulk. The sugar has all melted and gone on its way down the river. But we have a large sack of coffee. The lightening of the boats has this advantage: They will ride the waves better and we shall have but little to carry when we make a portage.

We are three-quarters of a mile in the depths of the earth, and the great river shrinks into insignificance as it dashes its angry waves against the walls and cliffs that rise to the world above. The waves are but puny ripples, and we but pigmies, running up and down the sands or lost among the boulders.

We have an unknown distance yet to run, an unknown river to explore. What falls there are, we know not; what rocks beset the channel, we know not; what walls rise over the river, we know not. Ah, well we may conjecture many things. The men talk as cheerfully as ever; jests are bandied about freely this morning; but to me the cheer is somber and the jests are ghastly.

With eagerness, anxiety, and misgiving we enter the canyon below and are carried along by the swift water through walls that rise from its very edge. They have the same structure that we noticed yesterday—tiers of irregular shelves below and, above these, steep slopes to the foot of marble cliffs. We run six miles in a little more than half an hour and emerge into a more open portion of the canyon, where high hills and ledges of rock intervene between the river and the distant walls.

Just at the head of this open space the river runs across a dike and the river has cut a gateway through it several hundred feet high and as many wide. As it crosses the wall, there is a fall below and a bad rapid, filled with boulders; so we stop to make a portage. Then on we go, gliding by hills and ledges, with distant walls in view; sweeping past sharp angles of rock; stopping at a few points to examine rapids, which we find can be run, until we have made another five miles, when we land for dinner.

Then we let down with lines over a long rapid and start again. Once more the walls close in, and we find ourselves in a narrow gorge, the water again filling the channel and being very swift. With constant watchfulness we proceed, making about four miles this afternoon, and camp in a cave.

August 14: At daybreak we walk down the bank of the river, on a little sandy beach, to view a new feature in the canyon. Heretofore hard rocks have given us bad river; soft rocks; smooth water; and a series of rocks harder than any we have experienced sets in. The river enters the gneiss! We can see but a little way into the granite gorge, but it looks threatening.

After breakfast we enter on the waves. At the very introduction it inspires awe. The canyon is narrower than we have ever before seen; the water is swifter; there are but few broken rocks in the channel; and on either side the walls are set with pinnacles, crags, and sharp, angular buttresses, bristling with wind.

Wave-polished spires jut into the river, their tops sometimes just below the surface, sometimes rising a few or many feet above; and island ledges, pinnacles, and towers break the swift current into ominous chutes and eddies and whirlpools. We soon reach a place where a creek enters from the left, and, just below, the channel is choked with boulders, which have washed down the side canyon and formed a dam, over which there is a fall of thirty or forty feet; but on the boulders footholds can be had, and we make a portage. Three more such dams are found. Over one we make a portage; at the other two are chutes through which we can run.

The granite rises higher; the lower walls alone are over a thousand feet high.

About eleven o'clock we hear a great roar ahead. The sound grows louder and louder as we run, and at last we find ourselves above a long, broken fall, with ledges and rocks obstructing the river. There is a descent of perhaps seventy-five or eighty feet in a third of a mile, and the rushing waters break into great waves on the rocks and lash themselves into a mad, white foam. We can land just above, but there is no foothold on either side by which to effect a portage. It is nearly a thousand feet to the top of the granite, though we can climb to that height up a side gulch and, passing along a mile or two, descend to the river. Such a portage would be impossible, so we must run the rapid or abandon the river. There is no hesitation. We step into our boats, push off, and away we go, first on smooth but swift water; then we strike a glassy wave and ride it to its top, down again into the trough, up again into a higher wave, and down and up on waves higher and still higher until we strike one just as it curls, and a colossal breaker rolls over our little boat. Still on we speed, shooting past projecting rocks, till the little boat is caught in a whirlpool and spun around several times. At last we pull out again into the torrent. And now the other boats have passed us. The open compartment of the *Emma Dean* is swamped and every breaker crashes over us. Our boat is unmanageable, but she cannot sink, and we blast down another hundred yards through ferocious breakers—how, we scarcely know. We find that the other boats have turned into an eddy at the foot of the fall and are waiting to catch us as we come, for the men have seen our plight and know our boat is swamped. They push out as we come near and pull us in against the wall. Our boat bailed, on we go.

The flanking walls rise more than a mile above us, a vertical distance difficult to appreciate. A thousand feet of this is up through granite crags; then steep slopes and arid, perpendicular cliffs rise one above another to the rim. The gorge is black and narrow below, red and gray and flaring above, with crags and angular gargoyles on the walls, which, cut in many places by side canyons, seem to be a vast wilderness of rocks. Down in these grand, gloomy depths we glide, ever listening, for the mad waters keep up their roar; ever watching ahead, for the narrow canyon is winding and the river is closed in so that we can see but a few hundred yards, and what there may be below we know not; so we listen for falls and watch for rocks, stopping now and then in the bay of a recess to admire the gigantic scenery; and ever as we go there is some new pinnacle or tower, some distant view of the upper plateau, or some deep, narrow side canyon.

Then we come to another broken fall, which appears more difficult than the one we ran this morning. A small creek enters on the right, and the first fall washes over boulders, which have been carried down by this lateral stream. We land at its mouth and stop for an hour or two to examine the fall. It seems possible to let the boats down with lines, at least part of the way, from point to point, along the right-hand wall. So we make a portage over the first rocks and find footing on some boulders below. Then we let down one of the boats to the end of her line, where she reaches a corner of projecting rock, to which one of the men clings and steadies her while I examine an eddy below. I think we can pass the other boats down by us and catch them in the eddy. This is soon done, and the men in the boats in the eddy pull us to their side. Just below there is another pile of boulders, over which we make another portage. From the foot of these rocks we can climb to another shelf, forty or fifty feet above the water. On this bench we camp for the night. It is raining hard, and we have no shelter, but we find a few sticks that have lodged in the rocks and kindle a fire and have a meager supper. We sit on the rocks all night, wrapped in our ponchos, getting what sleep we can.

August 15: This morning we find we can let down 300 or 400 yards, and it is managed in this way: We paw along the wall by climbing from projecting point to point, sometimes near the water's edge, at other places fifty or sixty feet above, and hold the boat with a line while two men remain aboard and prevent her from being dashed against the rocks. In two hours we have brought them all down, as far as it is possible. A few yards below, the river strikes with great violence against a rock and our boats are wrenched into a little bay above. We must now manage to pull out of this and clear the point below. The little boat is held by the bow obliquely up the stream. We jump in and pull out only a few strokes and sweep clear of the dangerous rock. The other boats follow in the same manner and the rapid is passed.

It is not easy to describe the labor of such navigation. We must prevent the waves from dashing the boats against the cliffs. Sometimes, where the river is swift, we must hitch a bight of rope around a rock, to prevent the boat from being snatched from us by a wave; but when the plunge is too great or the chute too swift, we must let her leap and catch her below or the undertow will drag her under the falling water and sink her. Where we wish to run her out a little way from shore through a channel of rocks, we first throw in little sticks of driftwood and watch their course, to see where we must steer so she will pass the channel in safety. And so we hold, and let go, and pull, and lift— among rocks, around rocks, and over rocks.

And now we go on through this solemn, strenuous, mysterious way. The river is very deep, the canyon very narrow, and still obstructed, so that there is no steady flow of the stream; but the waters reel and roll and boil, and we are scarcely able to determine where we can go. Now the boat is carried to the right, perhaps close to the wall; again, she is shot into the stream, and perhaps is dragged over to the other side, where, caught in a whirlpool, she spins about. We can neither land nor run as we please. The boats are entirely unmanageable; no order in their running can be preserved; now one, now another, is ahead, each crew laboring for its life. In such a place we come to another rapid. Two of the boats run it perforce. One succeeds in landing, but there is no foothold by which to make a portage and she is pushed out again into the current. The next minute a great standing wave fills the open compartment; she is waterlogged and lurches on out of control. Breaker after breaker rolls over her till one finally capsizes her. The men are hurled out; but they cling to the boat, and she drifts down some distance alongside of us and we are able to catch her. She is soon bailed out and the men are aboard once more; but the oars are lost, and so a pair from the *Emma Dean* is spared. Then for two miles we find smooth water.

Clouds are playing in the canyon today. Sometimes they roll down in great masses, filling the gorge with gloom; sometimes they hang aloft from wall to wall and cover the canyon with a roof of impending storm, and we can peer long distances up and down this canyon corridor, with its cloud-roof overhead, its walls of black granite, and its river bright with the sheen of broken waters. Then a gust of wind sweeps down a side gulch and, making a rift in the clouds, reveals blinding blue skies, and a stream of sunlight pours in. The clouds are children of the heavens, and when they play among the rocks they lift them to the region above.

It rains! Rapidly, little rills are formed above, which soon swell into brooks, and the brooks grow into creeks and tumble over the walls in innumerable cascades, adding their wild music to the roar of the river. When the rain ceases, the rills, brooks, and creeks run dry. The waters that fall during a rain on these steep rocks are gathered at once into the river; they could scarcely be poured in more suddenly if some vast spout ran from the clouds to the river itself. When a storm bursts over the canyon, a side gulch is dangerous, for a sudden flood may come, and the in-pouring waters will raise the river so as to hide the rocks.

Early in the afternoon we discover a stream entering from the north—a clear, beautiful creek, coming down through a gorgeous red canyon. We land and camp on a sand beach above its mouth, under a great, overspreading tree with willow-shaped leaves.

Twelve days and a thousand trials later:

August 27: This morning the river takes a more southerly direction. The dip of the rocks is to the north, and we are rapidly running into lower formations. Unless our course changes, we shall very soon run again into the granite. This gives us some anxiety. Now and then the river turns to the west and excites hopes that are soon dashed by another turn to the south. About nine o'clock we come to the dreaded rock. With great dread we see the river enter these hard, black walls. At its very entrance we have to portage; then we have to let down with lines past some ugly rock. Then we run a mile or two farther, and then the rapids below can be seen.

About eleven o'clock we come to a place in the river where it seems much worse than any we have yet met in all its course. A little creek comes down from the left. We land first on the right and clamber up over the granite pinnacles for a mile or two but can see no way by which we can portage; and to run it would be certain destruction. After dinner we cross to examine it on the left. High above the river we can walk along on the top of the granite, which is broken off at the edge and set with crags and steeples, so that it is very difficult to get a view of the river at all. In my eagerness to reach a point where I can see the roaring fall below, I go too far on the wall and can neither advance nor retreat. I stand with one foot on a little projecting rock and cling with my one hand fixed in a little crevice. Finding I am caught here, suspended 400 feet above the river, into which I should fall if my footing fails, I frantically call for help. The men come and pass me a line, but I cannot let go of the rock long enough to clasp it. Then they bring two or three of the largest oars. All this takes time, which seems very precious to me; but at last they arrive. The blade of one of the oars is pushed into a little crevice in the rock beyond me, in such a manner that they can hold me pressed against the wall. Then another is fixed in such a way that I can step on it, and thus I am extricated.

Still another hour is spent in examining the river from this side, but no good view of it is obtained, so now we return to the side that was first examined, and the afternoon is spent in clambering among the crags and minarets and carefully scanning the river again. We find that the lateral streams have washed boulders into the river, so as to form a dam, over which the water makes a broken fall of some twenty feet; then there is a rapid, beset with rocks, for 200 or 300 yards, while, on the other side, points of the wall project into the river. Then there is a second fall below—how great, we cannot tell. Then there is a rapid, filled with huge rocks, for 100 or 200 yards. At the bottom of it, from the right wall, a great rock projects quite halfway across the river. It has a sloping surface extending upstream, and the water, coming down with all the momentum gained in the falls and rapids above, rolls up this inclined plane many feet and tumbles over to the left.

I decide that it is possible to let down over the first fall, then run near the right cliff to a point just above the second, where we can pull out into a little chute, and having run over that in safety, we must pull with all-out power across the stream to avoid the great rock below. On my return to the boat, I announced to the men that we are to run it in the morning. Then we cross the river and go into camp for the night on some rocks in the mouth of the little side canyon.

After supper Captain Howland asks to have a talk with me. We walk up the little creek a short distance, and I soon find that his object is to remonstrate against my determination to proceed. He thinks that we had better abandon the river here. Talking with him, I learn that his brother, William Dunn, and he himself have determined to go no farther in the boats. So we return to camp. Nothing is said to the other men.

For the last two days, our course has not been plotted. I sit down and do this now, for the purpose of finding where we are by dead reckoning. It is a clear night, and I take out the sextant to make observations for latitude and find that the astronomic determination agrees very nearly with that of the plot—quite as closely as might be expected from a meridian observation on a planet. In a direct line, we must be about forty-five miles from the mouth of the Rio Virgin. If we can reach that point, we know that there are settlements up that river about twenty miles. This forty-five miles, in a direct line, will probably be eighty or ninety in the meandering line of the river. But then we know that there is comparatively open country for many miles above the mouth of the Virgin, which is our point of destination.

This much determined, I spread my plot on the sand, wake Howland, and show him where I suppose we are and where several Mormon settlements are situated.

We talk about the morrow, and he lies down again; but for me there is no sleep. All night long I pace up and down a little path on a few yards of sand beach, along by the riverside. Is it wise, or even possible, to go on? I go to the boats again, to look at our rations. I feel that we can get over the danger immediately before us; what there may be below I know not. From our outlook yesterday, on the cliffs, the canyon seemed to make another great bend to the south, and this, from our experience heretofore, means more and higher granite walls. It seems doubtful that we can climb out of the canyon here. But given that we could, I know enough of the country to be certain that it is a desert of rock and sand, between this and the nearest Mormon town, which, on the most direct line, must be seventy-five miles away. True, the late rains have been favorable, should we go out, for the probabilities are that we shall find water still standing in holes, and, at one time, I almost conclude to leave the river. But for years I have been contemplating this trip. To leave the exploration unfinished, to say that there is a part of the canyon which I declined to explore, having already almost accomplished it, is more than I am willing to acknowledge.

I determine to go on.

I wake my brother and tell him of Howland's decision, and he promises to stay with me. Then I call up Hawkins, the cook, and he makes a like promise, then Sumner, and Bradley, and Hall, and they all agree to go on.

August 28: At last daylight comes, and we have breakfast, without a word being said about the future. The meal is as solemn as a funeral. Afterward I ask the three men if they still think it best to leave us. The elder Howland thinks it is, and Dunn agrees with him. The younger Howland tries to persuade them to go on with the party, failing in which he decides to escape with his brother.

Then we cross the river. The small boat is very much disabled and unseaworthy. With the loss of hands, consequent on the departure of the three men, we shall not be able to run all of the boats, so I decide to leave my *Emma Dean*.

Two rifles and a shotgun are given to the men who are going out. I ask them to help themselves to the rations and take what they think to be a fair share. This they refuse to do, saying they have no fear but that they can get something to eat; but Billy, the cook, has a pan of biscuits prepared for dinner, and these he leaves on a rock.

Before starting, we take our barometers, fossils, the minerals, and some ammunition from the boat and leave them on the rocks. We are going over this place as lightly as possible. The three men help us lift our boats over a rock twenty-five or thirty feet high and let them down again over the first fall, and now we are all ready to start. The last thing before leaving, I write a letter to my wife and give it to Howland. Sumner gives him his watch, directing that it be sent to his sister should he perish on the unknown waters below. The records of the expedition have been kept in duplicate. One set of these is given to Howland, and now we are ready. For the last time, they entreat us not to go on and tell us that it is madness to set out in this place; that we can never get safely through it; and, further, that the river turns again to the south into the granite, and a few miles of such rapids and falls will exhaust our entire stock of rations, and then it will be too late to climb out. Some tears are shed; it is rather a solemn parting; each party thinks the other is taking the dangerous course.

My old boat left behind, I go on board the *Maid of the Canyon*. The three men climb a crag that overhangs the river, to watch us off. The *Maid of the Canyon* pushes out. We glide rapidly along the foot of the wall, just grazing one great rock, then pull out a little into the chute of the second fall and plunge over it. The open compartment is filled when we strike the first wave below, but we cut through it, and then the men pull with all their power toward the left wall and swing clear of the dangerous rock below all right. We are scarcely a minute in running it and find that, although it looked bad from above, we have passed many places that were worse.

The other boat follows without more difficulty. We land at the first practicable point below and fire our guns as a signal to the men above that we have come over in safety. Here we remain a couple of hours, hoping that they will take the smaller boat and follow us. We are behind a curve in the canyon and cannot see up to where we left them, and so we wait until their coming seems hopeless and push on.

And now we have a succession of rapids and falls until noon, all of which we run in safety. Just after dinner we come to another dire place. A stream shoots in from the left, and below there is a fall, and still below another fall. Above, the river tumbles down, over and among the rocks, in whirlpools and great waves, and the waters are lashed into mad, white foam. We run along the left, above this, and soon see that we cannot get down on this side, but it seems possible to let down on the other. We pull upstream again, for two or three hundred yards, and cross. Now there is a bed of basalt on this northern side of the canyon, with a bold escarpment, that seems to be a hundred feet high. We can climb it and walk along its summit to a point where we are just at the head of the fall.

Here the basalt is broken down again, so it seems to us, and I direct the men to take a line to the top of the cliff and let the boats down along the wall. One man remains in the boat, to keep her clear of the rocks and prevent her line from being caught on the projecting angles. I climb the cliff and pass along to a point just over the fall and descend by broken rocks and find that the break of the fall is above the break of the wall, so that we cannot land; and that still below the river is very bad; and that there is no possibility of a portage. Without waiting further to examine and determine what shall be done, I hasten back to the top of the cliff to stop the boats from coming down. When I arrive, I find the men have let one of them down to the head of the fall. She is in swift water, and they are not able to pull her back; nor are they able to go on with the line, as it is not long enough to reach the higher part of the cliff, which is just before them; so they take a bight around a crag. I send two men back for the other line. The boat is in very swift water, and Bradley is standing in the open compartment, holding out his oar to prevent her from striking against the foot of the cliff.

Now she shoots out into the stream and up as far as the line will permit and then, wheeling, drives headlong against the rock, then out and back again, now straining on the line, now striking against the rock. As soon as the second line is brought, we pass it down to him; but his attention is taken up with his own situation, and he does not see that we are passing the line to him. I stand on a projecting rock, waving my hat to gain his attention, for my voice is drowned by the roaring of the falls. Just at this moment, I see him take his knife from its sheath and step forward to cut the line. He has evidently decided that it is better to go over with the boat as it is than to wait for her to be broken to pieces. As he leans over, the boat sheers again into the stream, the stem post breaks away, and she is loose.

With perfect composure Bradley seizes the great scull oar, places it in the stern rowlock, and pulls with all his power (and is he an athlete) to turn the bow of the boat downstream, for he wishes to go bow down, rather than to drift broadside on. One, two strokes he makes, and a third just as she goes over, and the boat is fairly turned, and she goes down almost beyond our sight, though we are more than a hundred feet above the river. Then she comes up again, on a great wave, and down and up, then around behind some monumental rocks, and is lost in the mad, white foam below. We stand frozen with fear, for we see no boat. Bradley is gone, so it seems. But now, away below, we see something coming out of the waves. It is evidently a boat. A moment more, and we see Bradley standing on the deck, swinging his hat to show that he is all right.

But he is in a whirlpool. We have the stem post of his boat attached to the line. How badly she may be disabled we know not. I direct Sumner and another man to pass along the cliff and see if they can reach him from below. Rhodes, Hall, and myself run to the other boat, jump aboard, push out, and away we go over the falls. A wave rolls over us, and our boat is unmanageable. Another great wave strikes us, the boat rolls over and tumbles and tosses, I know not how. All I know is that Bradley is picking us up. We soon have all right again and row to the cliff and wait until Sumner can come. After a difficult climb they reach us. We run two or three miles farther and turn again to the northwest, continuing until night, when we have run out of the granite once more.

August 29: We start very early this morning. The river still continues swift, but we have no serious difficulty and at twelve o'clock emerge from the Grand Canyon of the Colorado.

We are in a valley now, and low mountains are seen in the distance, coming to the river below. We recognize this as the Grand Wash.

A few years ago, a party of Mormons set out from St. George, Utah, taking with them a boat, and came down to the mouth of the Grand Wash, where they divided, a portion of the party crossing the river to explore the San Francisco Mountains. Three men—Hamblin, Miller, and Crosby—taking the boat, went on down the river to Callville, landing a few miles below the mouth of the Rio Virgin. We have their manuscript journal with us, and so the stream is comparatively well known.

Tonight we camp on the left bank in a mesquite thicket.

The relief from danger and the joy of success are great. When he who has been chained by wounds to a hospital cot, until his canvas tent seems like a dungeon cell; until the groans of the maimed and dying who lie about, tortured with probe and knife, are piled up, a weight of horror on his ears that he cannot throw off, cannot forget; and until the stench of festering wounds and anaesthetic drugs has filled the air with its loathsome burden; at last goes out into the open field, what a world he sees! How beautiful the sky; how bright the sunshine; what "floods of delirious music" pour from the throats of the birds; how sweet the fragrance of earth, and tree, and blossom! The first tour of convalescent freedom seems rich recompense for all—pain, gloom, terror.

Something like this are the feelings I experience tonight. Ever before us has been an unknown danger, heavier than immediate peril. Every waking hour passed in the Grand Canyon has been one of toil. We have watched with deep solicitude the steady disappearance of our scant rations, and from time to time we have seen the river snatch a portion of the little left, while we were ahungered. And danger and toil were endured in those gloomy depths; ofttimes the clouds hid the sky by day and but a narrow zone of stars could be seen at night. Only during the few hours of deep sleep, consequent on hard labor, has the roar of the waters been hushed. Now the danger is over; now the toil has ceased; now the gloom has disappeared; now the firmament is bounded only by the horizon; and what a vast expanse of constellations can be seen!

The river rolls by us in silent majesty; the quiet of the camp is sweet; our joy is almost ecstasy.

BARNACLE BILL IN
BURNT RANCH GORGE

Jeff Bennett

"*F*ight or flight" *is, according to psychologists, one of our most basic in-stinctual responses. It goes back to our beginnings, when the grizzly or saber-toothed tiger appeared in the cave entrance. Terror blasted through the middle of us and we said, "Oh, shit" and either picked up a club and prepared to do battle or fouled ourselves and clawed up the walls in pan-icked retreat. But sometimes—when the grizzly's roar is too loud or, in the following case, the swim through the roaring rapid is more than our minds can comprehend—even the fight-or-flight response fails us. Here we simply freeze, rigid as a bronze statue. Once we're "stuck to a thwart like a barnacle to a dock," no amount of cajoling or sweet talk can ease our grip. And by the time our nerves relax and our senses return, another legend has been born. Given the right time and the right scenario, this can probably happen to any of us. Here, it happened just so to "Bill."*

‡   ‡   ‡

Everyone was wide-eyed. Bill was *gone*. I began to think that these are the types of things that you read about in newspapers, or on Charlie Walbridge's river accident statistic sheets. My mood was deteriorating.

"Where's Bill?"

"Sheez, I don't know. I thought he was in *your* boat!"

"Well, he was—but he didn't swim out of the rapid."

We were in the eddy below Lower Burnt Ranch Falls, a nasty class

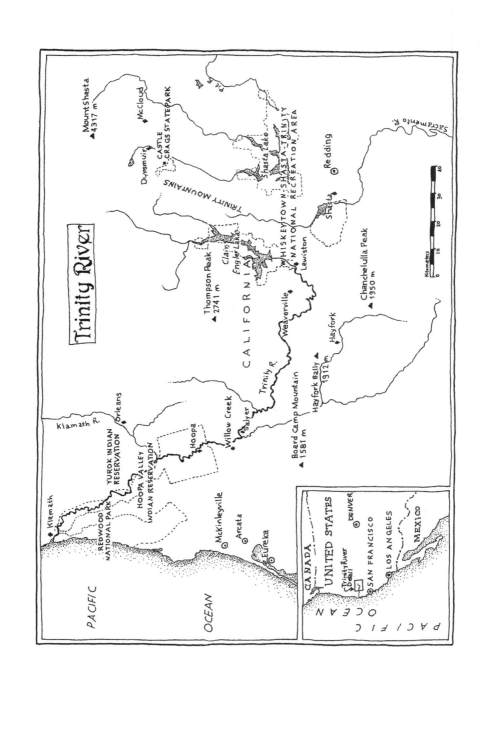

V rapid in the Trinity River's Burnt Ranch Gorge. No, "nasty" doesn't sum it up. Revolting is the word. Here, the river plummets about fifteen feet in fifty yards as big boulders whip the surface into an indecipherable frenzy. To make matters worse, clean runs must start in a narrow chute, then make a big left-to-right zigzag while lurching from hole to hole.

Yet somehow, Lower Burnt Ranch Falls has taken on a reputation as being user-friendly. I mean, I've seen crews practically set up a mid-rapid poker game while blindly slamming through the big drops—and emerge unscathed.

But today was different. Our paddlers were coming unglued in the moves just above the crux, and two out of four boats had flipped. Fortunately, everyone survived the swim with little more than a couple of charley horses and bruised egos. Except for Bill.

Where the hell was Bill?!

A commercial trip down Burnt Ranch Gorge begins unlike any other trip in the nation. After a guide's brief talk at the Cedar Flat put-in, passengers are tossed right into the river—literally! Flipping rafts, swimming rapids, and executing self-rescues in class I and II rapids are *de rigueur* on the pretrip agenda. This is preventive medicine. As much a form of personal insurance as life jackets and helmets.

Strange, you say? Hardly! Burnt Ranch Gorge is on the cutting edge of commercial whitewater, and passengers must be prepared for the inevitable bout with calamity.

I had seen this pattern—flip, swim, flip, swim—repeated many times before at Cedar Flat. And today was no exception.

Following an hour or so of training, the crews appeared shipshape. So we headed off downriver, ready for another day of great river running.

Gliding toward the first rapid—a shallow class IV boulder garden known as China Slide—we marveled at the huge rocky scar etched into the hills on the left bank. Here, in 1890, a half-mile-long, thousand-foot-wide landslide dislodged from the south canyon wall, tore across the river, and backed the Trinity up for twelve miles! We paddled a narrow entry slot through the weathered debris and bounced down the final few feet through channels formed by nearly a century of erosion.

China Slide went by perfectly. Didn't even phase the crew, who had already honed their skills on other class IV and V California rivers. But we hadn't even patted ourselves on the back when the Trinity tossed down the real welcome mat—Pearly Gates—where the Trinity River plunges eight feet into Box Canyon.

One by one, the rafts paddled out into the main current, ferried across to river left, and turned on a powerhouse of forward strokes. With unbridled whoops of excitement spewing from the passengers, the rafts plummeted down Pearly Gates's twisting ramp, and crashed deep into the churning hole at its base. The crews, soaked and smiling, shredded another big Burnt Ranch Gorge rapid without incident and drifted safely into the calm waters of Box Canyon. Here, for the first time, vertical cliffs rose directly out of the deep, swirling currents, transforming the Trinity River's deep V-canyon into a true gorge.

Drifting out of Box Canyon, we found ourselves congealing as teams, sharing not only kinships common among river lovers but also our nervous anticipation for Burnt Ranch Gorge's bigger rapids—Upper, Middle, and Lower Burnt Ranch Falls.

Following a couple of class III drops, the Trinity gave us one more chance to warm up for the falls. Tight Squeeze, a life-sized, aquatic version of bumper pool, clogged the river with car-sized boulders, leaving only narrow chutes and hairpin turns in their wake. Although Tight Squeeze is far from being one of Burnt Ranch's toughest rapids, I had good reason to approach it with caution.

On my first run down Burnt Ranch Gorge, I had miscalculated the current flowing across the entrance drop. In an instant, I found our raft slipping toward a deeply undercut wall. I hadn't even had a chance to shout another command before the raft jammed itself into the wrong chute, tipped up on its side, and planted itself vertically against the wall. The four other crew members and I found ourselves encased between the raft and the wall, standing knee-high in fast water. Two of us were able to push the raft far enough away from the wall to allow the remaining crew members to dive away from the raft and into safer currents; this turned out to be a perfect strategy, since the raft, unburdened by the dead weight from extra paddlers, soon popped free of the wall, landed flat, and finished up the run unscathed.

This time, Tight Squeeze would present no problems.

After another mile of increasingly difficult rapids, we slammed through the final fifty yards of ledges and holes above Upper Burnt Ranch Falls and paddled eagerly into an eddy for a rest. Before we could run Upper Falls's narrow slot, we relieved our rafts of some air.

Running the steep, narrow slot at Upper Burnt Ranch Falls is the ultimate mind bender. You take off on a power ferry from the eddy, dash across the tail waves of the last drop, and spin downstream to face a six- to seven-foot slot. Then you hit a hard forward and wedge the boat into a narrow chasm between two giant house-sized rocks. While your front paddlers stare down a ten-foot slide to the pool below, the raft squirms and buckles as the current tries to slam-dunk it through the drop.

If you let enough air out of the thwarts, you'll simply spit free like a watermelon seed. Leave too much air in your raft, and you're likely to flip. Fortunately, all of our rafts took the melon-seed approach and floated away in the safety of the bottom pool.

Just downstream, Middle Burnt Ranch Falls explodes into a whitewater fanfare that makes Upper Falls look like a carousel ride. Now things begin to get serious. A four-foot entry drop, backed by a strong hole, must be run perfectly to avoid the worst part of the rapid. This means carving a right-to-left track across the face of the ledge and ending up in a microeddy protected by a wall on one side and a boulder sieve on the other side. Then, you must slink the raft through a ten-foot-wide channel before crashing over the two final seven-foot slides.

A clean run through Upper and Middle Burnt Ranch Falls would usually make most any paddler's day complete. But, due to some sort of perverse twist in Mother Nature's sense of humor, all that a successful run of these falls does is get you to the top of Lower Burnt Ranch Falls, definitely the baddest of the bunch.

We scouted Lower Burnt Ranch Falls long and hard, preparing ourselves mentally for the challenge. Psyched up and ready to go, we boarded our rafts and paddled through a narrow entry slot flanked by two leaning slabs of granite. In an instant, the canyon walls melted to a gray blur as the rapid accelerated us through its staircase of raft-pounding holes. We held fast, jabbing our paddles deep into whatever current was available. And as fast as the rapid had started, the storm ended. We floated to the safety of a river-left eddy—hidden from view from the rapid—and waited for the next raft to come through.

In the eddy, it felt as if we'd arrived at our own surprise party. Paddles clacked in high-fives above our heads, and stories of fear and success filled the air like reminiscences at a high school reunion.

Then it happened.

The next raft floated by upside down, followed by four bodies swimming frantically toward the eddy. I grabbed a throw line and pulled one swimmer in while the rest of my crew aided the others.

Once everyone was safely ashore, we made a head count: One, two, three, four—wait, one, two, three, four—*Oh no! Bill! Where's Bill?!*

Our situation below Lower Burnt Ranch Falls turned miserable. Two guides decided to get a closer look at the rapid by climbing the steep cliff that blocked our view of Lower Falls. However, after a few anxious moments, they returned with bad news. Bill wasn't anywhere. Since he had to be *somewhere,* we thought the worst. Maybe, when his raft flipped in the lower falls, Bill wedged a foot in something beneath the surface. While some of the remaining crew started up the cliff to see if they could find some sign of Bill, the rest of the crew simply took it upon themselves to keep yelling his name. This was part hope, part disbelief.

"Bill! Hey, Bill?"

"What?!"

"Hey, did you hear that?!"

"No."

"Listen then—Bill?"

"What?!"

"It's Bill," I thought. "Bill, where are you?!"

"Under here. . . ."

One of the rafts was talking! Well, actually, Bill's voice was coming from one of the overturned rafts.

In the midst of the post-flip chaos, no one ever bothered to flip the final raft back over again. Bill had to be under there.

"Bill, are you under there?"

"Yeah."

He was really there. A hurricane of emotions overtook us. All at once I was relieved, elated—pissed off.

"Bill, come out of there!"

"No."

"What do you mean, no? *Come out!!*"

"*No!*"

Bill had freaked. He must have blown a mental fuse during his swim. He wasn't about to leave the safety of his PVC cave.

"C'mon, Bill, *get out of there!!!*"

"*No!!!*"

We decided to flip the raft over. Then he'd have to come out. We tossed a flip line over the boat, crawled onto a tube, and started pulling.

"Sheez, this feels heavy. I think he's holding on!"

"Bill, let go!"

"No!"

If we were going to get Bill out, we were going to have to pull the raft away from him. Three of us got on the rope and started pulling. Meanwhile, some of the other paddlers started lifting from the other side. It was like opening a gigantic conch shell. The raft was finally coming over.

And there was Bill, stuck to that thwart like a barnacle to a dock. But as the golden California sunshine touched his ashen face once again, his terror began to subside. We choked back some tears of joy, gave Bill a hug, and hiked him back to camp.

As the campfire roared later that night, the tall tales started flying. Bill's story unfolded time and time again, slowly building to legendary status. Even today, the legend lives on—the legend of Barnacle Bill.

BLACK CANYON OF THE GUNNISON

Tim Keggerman

*T*he twelve-mile Black Canyon section of the Gunnison River rips through "the depths of a 2,000-feet-deep gorge." This wicked, interminable gauntlet of whitewater has quenched the most avid river rafter's thirst for rapids, at least momentarily. Huge water reigns. Close calls are the rule. Once committed to the gorge, the only way out is either on the towering water or up the desperate ramparts of the canyon itself, an ascent requiring expert-level climbing prowess and all the requisite tackle. For all practical purposes, ten feet into the gorge and the only way out is aboard the "liquid locomotive." Tim Keggerman's story brings to light the age-old question of who belongs on the liquid locomotive once it reaches terminal velocity. The temptation for experts to drag along friends—especially friends who can snap cover shots and spread the glory—is strong. The power of big water, however, is almost always stronger.*

‡　　‡　　‡

With the rivers of Colorado drying up, our summer guiding season was coming to an end. It was the time of year that river guides neither look forward to nor know how to handle when it arrives. I turned to one of my fellow guides at Crested Butte Rafting and began talking. By the time our conversation was complete, we both had decided that we were ripe for some high adventure and that the Black Canyon section of the Gunnison River was the call.

The Black Canyon of the Gunnison is considered Colorado's number-one scare water. In a twelve-mile stretch, the Gunnison River tears its way through the depths of a 2,000-foot-deep gorge, containing the highest cliffs in the state. Upstream, Crystal Dam provides dam-released flows, leaving enough water in the river for paddling late into the summer.

The Black Canyon's history is as deep as the gorge itself, with heroic feats and boat-smashing failures fueling nearly mythical tales of grandiose proportions.

We were keen to the river's warnings and picked a strong crew of expert boaters, including Aaron Lypps, Kris Pogoloff, and myself. Since this would be an extraordinary trip, we decided that it would be nice to invite a couple of top-notch photographers whom we know, Nathan Bilow and Garry Sprung. Garry Sprung is known affectionately to us as "Gnerps." These guys are hot behind the lenses but lacking in scare-adventure experience—their inexperience would haunt us later in the trip.

It was Friday, and all of us had the next week off. We called the Black Canyon National Monument office to get the permission needed to enter the canyon and were told to sign in at the park office. After gathering our gear, we packed the van and loaded in.

Gnerps and Bilow drove Gnerps's truck from Crested Butte, over Kebler Pass to Hotchkiss, and downriver to where the North Fork of the Gunnison and the Main Gunnison converged. This was to be our take-out. There, we left Gnerps's truck and proceeded with our shuttle.

Our expedition would cover a total distance of thirty miles, so we figured that, at the most, it would take us three days and two nights to complete the descent—well, we hoped it'd be no more than three days.

We put in at the East Portal near the southeast end of Black Canyon National Monument. I read in Doug Wheat's guidebook, *The Floater's Guide to Colorado,* that this trip was for crazies only and was *not* recommended to be run. Plus, the guidebook recommended flows of less than 500 cfs for safety. Today it was running at 2,000 cfs!

We turned to Bilow and Gnerps and advised them that they might want to change their minds. The high water level was a perfect reason not to take the trip. Heck, we were scared ourselves, and if they had any second thoughts, now was the time to sound off. Once we were in the canyon, it would take nothing less than world-class rock climbing to get out. Rad stuff! Regardless, Bilow and Gnerps decided to con-

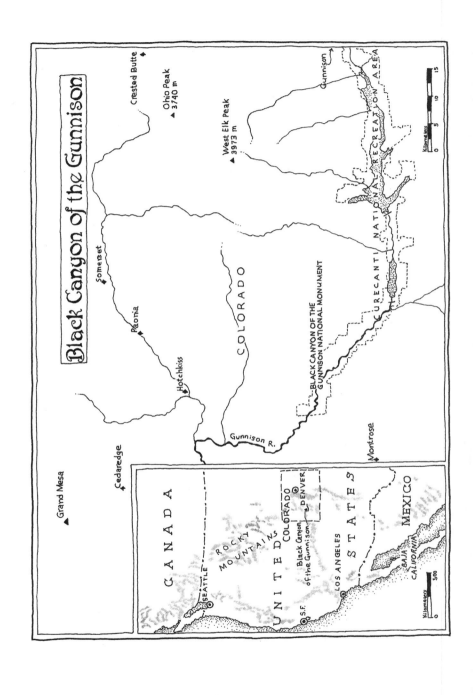

Black Canyon of the Gunnison

Grand Mesa ▲

Cedaredge ✦

Hotchkiss ✦

Paonia ✦

Somerset ✦

Crested Butte ▲

Ohio Peak
▲ 3740 m

West Elk Peak
▲ 3973 m

COLORADO

Gunnison R.

Montrose

Gunnison

BLACK CANYON OF THE
GUNNISON NATIONAL MONUMENT

C U R E C A N T I   N A T I O N A L   R E C R E A T I O N   A R E A

Kilometers
0   5   10   15

CANADA

ROCKY
MOUNTAINS

SEATTLE ◉

S.F. ◉

LOS ANGELES ◉

COLORADO

DENVER ◉

Black Canyon
of the Gunnison

U N I T E D   S T A T E S

BAJA
CALIFORNIA

MEXICO

Kilometers
0   500

tinue with us. After loading the raft with food and gear, we embarked at 3:30 that afternoon. The run began with sweet, easy class III rapids for about the first three miles. When we came to our first class VI rapid, we headed to shore. There, we set up camp under a beautiful full moon and stars that hung like crystal chandeliers amid the towering canyon walls. One of Earth's most awesome canyons caressed all of our worries.

The next morning began bright and sunny. We had scouted the drop below camp the night before and decided we would walk around it. That made me sleep easier. But by morning light, I could see a way to get a thrill by taking my kayak through the incredible drop. I helped carry the raft to a safe launch site, then toted my kayak to the rock cliff next to the fifteen-foot cascade. There, Aaron helped launch me into the massive four-foot boils, fifteen feet below. I did a perfect tail stand in the middle of the next drop and eddied out with the raft.

Now, feeling the adrenaline surge like the river, I knew we were in for an incredible adventure.

The next few miles were fun. Big class IV rapids building into class Vs and getting hairier and hairier. We were having a ball.

After a close call at one of the rapids, we decided we ought to scout the next drop. It was a huge, angry rapid, with a twelve-foot tongue leading into an exploding monster hole on the left, then fuming through a ten-foot lead into a river-wide keeper. This one was pushing the envelope for us, and we all knew it. My first thought was that we ought to walk around it. But as I looked deeper into the rapid, my balls began to grow as my brain began to shrink. We were paddling perfectly, and I knew there would be plenty of rapids to walk downstream. This one had a line. When Kris mentioned that he wanted to go for it, I seized the opportunity. "Why not?" I said, "that's what we're here for!"

I led the way through the drops in my kayak, using the "stay close and keep an eye on each other" technique for safety. That worked—most of the time. But this time I entered just left of center, at the end of a pool, and carved off the top of the tongue. Boof! I slid to such a soft landing that I nearly forgot about the next drop. Water mounded up around me in three- to four-foot boils and slowed my boat's launch off the next drop. I powered right at the crest of a huge surge, slid low down over a ten-foot falls, and promptly back-ended into a keeper hole. *Damn!*

I struck up an impatient conversation with God while the river busily worked me over. I rocked upside down and began setting my paddle when, in a flash of panic, I remembered that the raft was right behind me. I rolled up, still in the hole, only to see the looming figure of the twelve-foot raft falling ten vertical feet directly on top of me. Hastily, I flipped back over just in time for the raft to hit me on the hull and power me out of the hole. A lucky stroke, that.

I rolled up just downstream, feeling better—until I glanced over my shoulder to see the raft stuck in the same keeper hole. Bummer! Kris was washed out of the boat right away as the raft spun in the furious crater. Meanwhile, Aaron clung desperately to the gear to prevent it from being jerked free by the river. I quickly paddled over to Kris and pulled him to shore right above another ten-foot drop, then eddied out in the last available microeddy, which was so small Kris had to hold my bow so that I could get out of the boat. I was no sooner out of my boat before Bilow and Gnerps came floating toward the drop, embracing each other fearfully. Kris and I started yelling, *"Swim! Swim!"* as I raced to grab my throw bag.

We quickly pulled Bilow and Gnerps to shore, then ran upstream to see how Aaron was doing. What a sight! There he sat in the hole, riding the raft's outside tube like a wild bronc. I threw him the rope and handed my end to Kris so that he could pull him in while I raced back to my kayak, going after the gear floating loose from the raft. After deciding not to run the next drop, I scrambled to put in below it and scouted downstream while watching our gear and food floating away. In the midst of the rainbow of gear floating by, the camera equipment caught my eye. I paddled out and struggled to save what I could, but the gear turned out to be too heavy for me to save in the class V+ water.

That's when I started to get scared. No food, no cameras. I restored my composure and snagged three paddles. Kris still had his in hand, so we'd have enough to complete the trip—as though now we had any choice in the affair.

The next mile of canyon contained continuous class VI cataracts. It was easy to talk everyone into a portage-fest. We ran what we could but walked almost everything. It was Rocky Mountain hair water at its extreme. Mandatory eddies, treacherous carries, gnarly poison ivy, and no escape from the remoteness. Strangely, the hard work revived our confidence and restored our cheer. One mile downstream and four hours later, we came to another tough portage around a twelve-foot waterfall. Beneath the falls, a glassy pool ended with what seemed to be the river's end. Beyond that pool, the river seemed to explode into five miles of fifty-degree tilts, undercut flumes, and unimaginable rapids. It was unreal! Like nothing you could ever imagine. Whitewater fantasy land—or a step beyond.

We set up camp and spread out the remainder of our supplies. Dinner was slight: a spoonful of ramen noodles and peanut butter served on a stick. As the sun sank beyond the canyon tops, we retired to our second night's sleep. Lying there, I tallied our losses: one first aid kit ($100), one pump ($50), two paddles ($30), food ($30)—oh, and some camera gear ($4,000!). Still, we had gained one of the most exciting days of our lives.

I stared at the narrow crease of sky glimmering through the gap in the canyon walls. Crossing the starlit sky, I could see a satellite moving up the canyon. I felt humbled, small, and childlike.

The next morning, sun again shook us from our sleep. I ate the last apple and hiked downstream to scout a route for our portage. We decided to carry up away from the huge mounds of house-sized undercut boulders and seek paths along the very foot of the stupendous 2,000-foot cliffs.

Even in the midst of our struggle, the scenery was awesome. Sheer, polished canyon walls dazzled the eye. Painted Wall, one of Colorado's premier rock-climbing walls, loomed above. Bald eagles soared. There was a feeling of magic in the air. High adventure!

The carry was brutal! A portage from hell! It took us eight hours to reach the first beach. The calm pool looked so sweet—and it was sweet, but short.

The rapids that followed were clearly suicidal, and portaging around them was nearly as bad. A narrow ledge led to a dead-end box canyon. We struggled with our equipment, concentrating hard on every footstep. The trail ended just below a monster hole, where I did a rock launch back into the river. We all cheered Kris as he fell into the river on the last hairy move—and survived.

We had made it through the Black Canyon and were now in the class III and IV rapids of Upper Gunnison Gorge. The last drop roared behind us as a huge gray cloud swelled and bellowed in front of us. A storm was setting in. Suddenly it started getting dark, so we made camp at the next beach. By the time we got around to building a fire it had already begun spitting rain.

Thank God for plentiful firewood. A nasty thunderstorm ensued, with high winds and driving rain. We used the raft as a windbreak and kept a huge blaze roaring. We did what we could to dry our stuff out and ate our last "dinner": water and ramen seasoning (our noodles were gone). We were getting used to adversity to the max. Keeping the fire lit called for complete teamwork, and we all performed various shenanigans to keep it going. Though our dinner was meager and our camp primal, our meal seemed to be a celebration feast at the end of what felt like a three-day typhoon.

Our final morning was cloudy and cold. Fourteen-mile-long Gunnison Gorge entertained us with class III rapids interspersed with lots of long pools. A flock of fifteen bald eagles followed us most of the way down the rest of the run. I began to feel that this trip was one blessed by the Big Spirit. These eagles were messengers of peace.

We arrived at the North Fork confluence at noon. Unlike other trips, there was no sitting around, no braggartly reflecting upon the trip. There'd be time for that later. This time we could only think of one thing—*food!*

We packed up our gear and made a beeline for the nearest burger stand.

THE GREAT ZAMBEZI:
A MODERN EXPEDITION

Richard Bangs

*O*nly a few years before Richard Bangs and friends first ran the
Zambezi, the flanking terrain, as well as the lower reaches of the
river itself, had hosted bloody warfare. So the Bangs expedition required considerable political lobbying before the rafts ever hit water. The trip
also required a king's ransom to finance, a problem resolved by a U.S. television crew that tagged along to film the event. In a move consistent with "real"
adventure shows popular in the 1980s, actor LeVar Burton joined the expedition as well. Enlisting a movie star was an old trick used by TV executives to
shore up a "dud" segment, when the given action was, typically, so thin that
a star's presence and reactions were needed to provide interest. On the Zambezi,
however, when Burton was pitched from his raft and flushed like a rag doll
through a class V rapid, TV executives, as well as the general public, knew
that rafting the great Zambezi was a different business from, say, gazing at
polar bears through 10,000-power binoculars. To those who have since run
the Zambezi, many insist that while the rapids are strictly world-class, the
scenery is unsurpassed by any river in the world.

‡   ‡   ‡

A single-span steel bridge links the two African nations of Zambia and
Zimbabwe across a sixty-yard-wide basalt gorge. The view upstream
is of Victoria Falls, plummeting down in a mile-wide curtain, erupting in foam and riot at its base. Downriver, through sinuous gorges, is

171

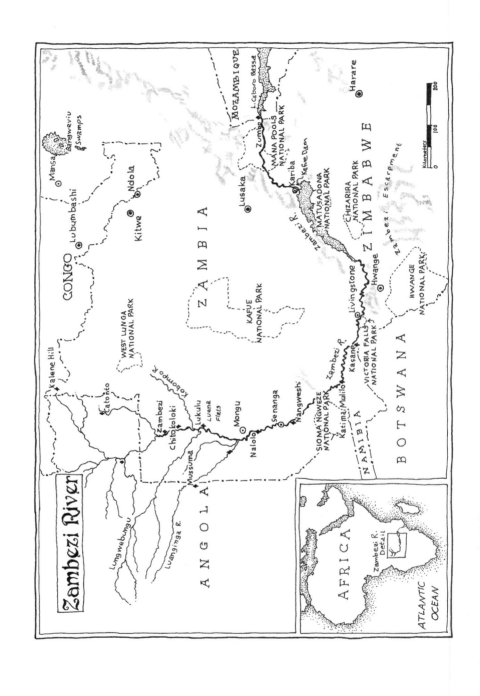

a tableau luminous and arresting, rarely photographed by the tourists, who are distracted by the sublimity of the falls. The bright serpentine-green ribbon of the Zambezi River stretches and tenses between the seven hairpin turns that mark its course from the falls, creating one of the great river corridors of the world. This is the domain of Nyaminyami, the river god of the Tonga people, described in their folklore as a huge snake coiled to strike, with the hungry head of a crocodile.

The fourth largest river in Africa, the Zambezi stakes its claim to greatness at Victoria Falls. From its headwaters at an insignificant spring near the borders of Zambia, Angola, and Zaire, it slowly gains in size and scale until, 720 miles downstream, it is a broad, slow-moving river, surrounding forested islands up to several square miles in size. It seems to have reached senescence there, still 900 miles from its outlet in the Indian Ocean; then it leaps magnificently into an immense rift in its basaltic riverbed and regains the vitality and grandeur that have made its name evocative of the Age of Exploration for over a century.

Throughout 1855, Scottish missionary David Livingstone was engaged in the first extensive European exploration of the African interior to the north of Capetown. He traveled down the Zambezi by canoe, with hopes of finding the African equivalent of the Northwest Passage—that elusive goal of explorers of the New World, a water route through a continent for the sake of commerce. The river had been flowing wide and languid amid an archipelago of beautiful islands teeming with wildlife. On November 16, Livingstone reported distant spray, moving like columns of smoke from a grass fire, though it was still evidently some distance away. Not until the following afternoon did Livingstone land on an island perched in the midst of the spray storm.

Crawling to the edge of the island, he peered into a huge mist-filled rent in the earth's surface. The appropriateness of the local Kololo dialect name for the falls at that moment must have been manifest: *Mosi oa-Tunya*, "Smoke that Thunders." Dr. Livingstone, ever the good champion of civilization and Christianity, renamed the cascade for his queen. We know it today as Victoria Falls.

Now, 130 years later, the sight is still beyond belief. The waters of the Zambezi plunge into the chasm and explode at the bottom, breaking with a roar into a driving mist. The deluge carries down a strong draft, which eddies through the canyon and captures the spindrift, driving it up in tremendous columns several hundred feet high, shot through with iridescence. It was sufficient to inspire Livingstone's most lyrical image in his several accounts of his explorations: "The snow-white sheet seemed like myriad small comets rushing on in one direction, each of which left behind its nucleus rays of foam. . . . [The falls] had never been seen before by European eyes, but scenes so lovely must have been gazed upon by angels in their flight."

Livingstone abandoned his descent of the Zambezi at the falls, continuing instead overland to the east coast of Africa in his search for the waterway that would support commerce, colonization, and the conversion of natives he believed were necessary for the good of the continent (and the British Empire). The impossible turmoil of the river as it twisted through the gorges downstream made passage up or down the Zambezi seem forever out of reach. In my dairy I wrote:

It was Valentine's Day 1981 when I first saw the river, and it was love at first sight. Along with a party of travel agents and tour operators, I had been shuttled between game parks and hotel lobbies for several days, all leading up to this: Victoria Falls. While the other occupants of the Land Rover pressed for a glimpse of the great falls upstream, I looked the other way, out of habit. Some 350 feet below the bridge we were driving over, a mighty river coiled and coursed through a dark basalt gorge. I could see two rapids interrupting this otherwise peaceful stretch, between the hairpin turns that divide the Third Canyon from its cousins. They were pieces of effervescence, feather white, inviting. They looked like they could be run.

The very idea of rafting the Zambezi, picking up where Livingstone left off, was only just becoming possible. For over a decade the river had been the staging area for the majority-rule struggle in Rhodesia that led eventually to the creation of the state of Zimbabwe. In 1966, a year after Rhodesia's unilateral declaration of independence from the British Empire—a move designed to prevent the turnover of power in Rhodesia to majority rule—black nationalist freedom fighters crossed the Zambezi into Rhodesia from Zambia (which had gained its own independence in 1964). The Zimbabwe African National Union (ZANU) was formed to bring down, through armed struggle, the Rhodesian white minority government of Ian Smith. The river and its many side canyons and tributaries, offering a network of passageways and retreats for raids, quickly became a refuge for guerrillas.

The border between Zambia and Rhodesia—the Zambezi River—was closed in December 1973, and land mines and other antipersonnel devices were placed up and down the river by Rhodesian soldiers. As the war heated up and white Rhodesians began to make incursions into the area across the river to raid enemy camps, ZANU also started placing land mines along both sides of the river.

In April 1979 the heads of British Commonwealth nations met in Lusaka, Zambia, and British Prime Minister Margaret Thatcher told the world that her government was "wholly committed to genuine majority rule in Rhodesia." The death knell had sounded for the white government of Ian Smith. Early in 1980, when the new nation of Zimbabwe emerged by treaty and election from fourteen years of conflict, the border once again opened. An effort was launched to deactivate the mines in the more accessible tourist areas, such as around Victoria Falls and Lake Kariba. But no effort had been made to clear the mines within the Zambezi gorges. None had seemed necessary; who would go down into those gorges?

The expedition we proposed in 1981—to raft the Zambezi River, a modern exploration in the tradition of the great river expeditions of the past—sought to take advantage of a unique opportunity, a rare crack in history that would permit an experience unavailable in the past and, quite possibly, in the future. Before the late 1960s, the specially designed inflatable rafts needed to negotiate the rapids in the Zambezi gorges just didn't exist. Throughout the 1970s, when international rafting began to come into its own, it had been impossible to voyage through these gorges because of the war. And a few years hence, if the most ambitious plans of the nations of Africa are fulfilled, a second major dam on the Zambezi will be built midway through the Batoka Gorge (that portion of the Zambezi below its confluence with the Songwe River, some six miles below the falls); nearly all of the free-flowing Zambezi below Victoria Falls will then be backed up by a giant reservoir.

The Zambezi had already been dammed once: At Kariba, downstream from the Batoka Gorge and its rapids, a huge earthen plug built in the Zambezi blocked the river and created one of the largest manmade lakes on Earth. The Kariba Dam was at the time the largest building project in Africa since the Great Pyramids, a wall of restraint 420 feet high and 1,200 feet wide (as long as Hoover Dam on the Colorado River in Nevada, though some 309 feet lower). The lake that resulted drowned some 2,000 square miles of land, including much of the homeland of the Tonga.

The Tonga are, like many of the tribes of southern Africa, cultural and genetic descendants of the aboriginal Bantu culture indigenous to southern Africa. The Tonga worship Nyaminyami, the god of the mighty river that was the focus of their ancient lifestyle of small villages and farms. His lair, they believe, was below the dark water of Kariba Gorge, and they knew he wouldn't stand for a wall across his river.

Construction on the Kariba Dam was proceeding according to schedule when early in March 1957 the Zambezi unleashed a flood of unprecedented ferocity, tearing villages off the face of the earth on its way to the temporary cofferdam erected to allow construction of the larger wall. The surge hit the dam and submerged it, causing thousands of dollars in damage. But in ten months' time a second, higher, cofferdam was built.

The next year, incredibly, the Zambezi above Victoria Falls reached a crest fifteen feet higher than the level of the record 1957 flood. It suddenly seemed that the Tonga beliefs might be more than mere superstition. Nyaminyami had already sent down a spectacular flood, as if to proclaim to one and all that the god of the river still lived. It had failed to dislodge the dam builders; now a second and larger flood hurtled toward Kariba. On February 16, 1958, the cofferdam succumbed to the torrent and burst; yet the water still continued to rise. On March 3 the construction crew's essential suspension bridge was shattered and borne away as the flood finally peaked at more than 100 feet above its low-water level. Nyaminyami had struck a savage blow. But the juggernaut of progress was in motion; construction was resumed and accelerated, and before the river god could again muster his energies, the dam wall was closed in December of 1959. Nyaminyami was tamed—for the time being.

Twenty years later Dr. Kenneth Kaunda, the leader of Zambia since its independence, agreed to our plans for a rafting expedition down the Zambezi, through the twisting gorges below Victoria Falls. More than nine months of preparation went into what would become a nine-day expedition. Reconnaissance included helicopter and fixed-wing flights over the river, intense examination of a series of stereoscopic aerial photographs of the gorge, and a cautious hike along the dangerous mined rim of the first seven gorges, in the company of government "sappers," who are trained to spot and disarm the still-active land mines.

The only possible access for a river put-in was a rugged trail on the Zambian side down to the Boiling Pot, an immense whirlpool at the end of First Gorge, just 200 yards from the base of the falls. Take-out would be at the head of Lake Kariba, sixty miles downstream, at a small Zimbabwean fishing camp. Because sanction and cooperation were needed from both sides of a border so recently the scene of violence, the undertaking took on special significance. President Kaunda agreed to formally launch our expedition, somewhat to the frustration of Zimbabwean government officials who also wanted to sponsor the trip. As if to add the final blessing—sanctification by the international media—an ABC film crew joined to document the venture.

With all these responsibilities and risks in mind, the 1981 Great Zambezi Expedition approached the matter of Nyaminyami and his river with reverence, painting the name of the river god on the prow of the boats. The gesture harkened back to the very first Sobek trips in Ethiopia eight years earlier. There, fearsome tales of the crocodiles on the Omo and Awash Rivers had led to our invocation of Sobek—ancient Egyptian crocodile god—and the name had become indelibly linked with international rafting.

By Monday, October 26, the expedition team had collected in Livingstone, Zambia. Eight of Sobek's most experienced guides arrived first, followed by the ABC film crew and actor LeVar Burton (who portrayed the young Kunta Kinte in the television epic *Roots*), who was to be the principal figure of the television documentary. The team was rounded out with representatives from Zambia and Zimbabwe and several prominent U.S. businessmen. The Great Zambezi Expedition was changing from a century-old dream to a reality.

I squeezed hands with a group of local boys who had scrambled down the steep slope to see us off. Slipping on a pair of studded cotton gloves, I settled in the seat of a five-meter-long inflatable raft. My passengers: photographer Michael Nichols and Joanne Taylor, both as somber as the dark canyon walls. Setting the bowline free, I let the boat drift upstream in the eddy to its confrontation with the rapid known as the Boiling Pot.

Then I dug the oar blades deep, powering out of the eddy and into the main current. The first stroke seemed solid, and I was confidently preparing for the next when the boat canted up a wave. The right oar sliced through air. I grappled with the ill-spent oar and saw, through the heaving water, a black wall looming. With a panicked push on the other oar, I turned the bow toward the wall, which was kicking back water from its face.

Three meters from the wall I dropped the oars and held on. A blast of water pushed the boat up on its side, where it hung for a tense second. Through the wash of white I saw Michael, camera pressed against his eye, still shooting; then I thought I heard Joanne scream. The boat plunged over, upside down, into the rolling mess.

I had capsized in the first rapid, ten minutes after launching our expedition.

It was the first of five capsizes on the Great Zambezi Expedition. Any first descent is subject to flips, swims, and the unexpected, but it was clear that Nyaminyami had not given up his regency. Rapids that looked straightforward suddenly lashed out with furious reversals, while those that seemed like impossible maelstroms, run only on a dare, proved straightforward. Having a television crew along to film the mishaps, as well as the successes, added to the larger-than-life tone of this encounter with one of the great rivers of the world.

A mile downstream from the fourth rapid we made camp for the first night at a peaceful eddy called The Silent Fool. Here, between three 400-foot-high waterfalls created by a Zambian hydroelectric diversion scheme from the river above Victoria Falls, a Zimbabwean military helicopter landed on the bank. It was an Alouette, used not so many years earlier by white Rhodesians for search-and-destroy missions within this very gorge. It was being loaned to us by the Zimbabwean government in case we needed logistical support for emergencies. Michael Arogyaswamy, the Indian-born supervisor of the power station, summed it up: "This must be the first time a helicopter from the other side has landed in Zambia with good intentions in ten years. This proves that the Zambezi is now a river of peace."

During the expedition, the Zambezi was flowing at around 15,000 cfs—a fraction of its rain-season flush but a stupendous current nonetheless. Generally rivers of this scale are best run by oared rafts, with a single guide maneuvering the boat through the large waves and strong hydraulics created by the high water flows, while passengers hold on to whatever safety lines are available. But included in this expedition was a paddleboat—the same size and design as the other rafts but captained by a veteran guide, Dave Shore, and crewed by a mixed group of first-timers and experienced boatmen, all of whom used small canoe-style paddles to power and control the raft. Among the first-timers was LeVar Burton; among the more experienced was sixty-six-year-old Grant Rogers, one of the founders of commercial river rafting in the United States, who had already run many of the world's toughest rapids. The paddleboat had made some excellent runs on the first day of shooting, though Shore and his crew elected to portage one particularly nasty rapid, Number Four.

Based on aerial observation, Number Five had been appraised as "unrunnable" during our pretrip planning, and a portage was anticipated. The current forced its way between a steep drop over a rock on the right side and a huge pourover in the middle of the river, where gushing water barely covered another enormous boulder. But a scout early that second morning revealed a clear run down the right side, if only the first monstrous pourover could be avoided.

John Kramer, one of Sobek's most reliable oarsmen, rowed the first boat; he narrowly missed the pourover and emerged in fine shape. He was followed by the two kayakers, who had come along as safety in case of swimmers, since kayaks in experienced hands are extremely maneuverable. The two oarboats that followed also made it through, and paddle captain Dave Shore decided to test his crew's mettle on this rapid.

He lined up for the crosscurrent traverse to position his boat at the top of the rapid; then to those on the bank—and to viewers of the television special that resulted—he seemed to call an inexplicable "Stop paddling" at a crucial moment. Almost at once he cried out for the crew to dig harder, but it wasn't enough. The raft folded into the hole behind the pourover. One tube was sucked under, while the other rose like a whale. Out washed two swimmers—LeVar Burton and Grant Rogers.

The paddleboat caromed down the right bank, Burton and Rogers following like lost ducklings. The cameras followed them down as LeVar passed beneath the boat into the main current, where kayaker Neusom Holmes picked him up, without a scratch but winded. Grant, however, was swept against a barely submerged boulder, then rolled over a yard-high waterfall. He began to recirculate in the backwash below the falls, popping free just as help neared him. Then the current carried him back toward the middle of the Zambezi.

John Yost and I jumped into an oarboat, cast off, and began the chase, catching Grant almost at once. Barely conscious, Rogers was hauled into the safety of the boat, groaning as he clutched his side—while the ABC cameras kept rolling. The army helicopter accompanying the expedition whined into action, and within an hour Rogers was undergoing treatment at Wankie Colliery Hospital in

Zimbabwe, eighty miles to the southeast.

Four broken ribs and a collapsed lung were no laughing matter, and we were abruptly conscious of our intrusion into a realm long off-limits for diverse reasons—politics, floods, and river gods. Rogers made a complete recovery and a year later was again rafting whitewater rivers; but for both rafters and cameramen continuing through the deep basalt gorge that afternoon, surrounded by hidden land mines, missing a much loved member of our group, vaulting toward unknown dangers as we rowed ever closer to the crocodile feeding grounds of the lower Zambezi, the security of familiar rivers and friends seemed a long way off.

The rest of the second day progressed smoothly. A scimitar-beaked, cinnamon-shouldered bird wheeled above the rafts—the African fish eagle, national bird of Zambia. The sea-green river swept past a pair of limestone alcoves with lush hanging gardens dripping over the yawning entrances. It was the proverbial calm before the storm: After a couple of minor rapids, the body of the river funneled to a narrow chute, then plunged into a hole that seemed to have no bottom. A shambles of white followed until the river reared to a wave that must have been as high as the hole was deep. It was simply the largest rapid most of the party had ever seen. Portaging was the only possible way around rapid Number Nine; it is still a rapid no one has attempted to run.

The process was long and laborious. All gear had to be untied, taken out of the rafts, and carried over the rocky bank to where navigating the river again became practical. Then a crew of four or more had to be assembled to carry the rafts, which although considerably lightened, at over 100 pounds, sixteen feet long, and eight feet wide, were still cumbersome and awkward. Finally, all gear had to be tied into the rafts again, to prevent loss in case of a flip or a rough ride, before the rafts were boarded once more and set loose into the current. But all went well and in less than an hour we were back on the river.

Camp that night was at the end of the Seventh Gorge, only six miles downstream from the falls, where the Songwe River joins with the Zambezi. Alongside a sweeping sandbar and tarnlike lagoon, terraced reefs and irregular bosses of rock marked the tributary mouth. The basalt there was deeply pitted with well-like potholes, ground smooth by whirling, torrent-driven stones. A footpath led up to the canyon rim, one of the few places of access on the sixty-mile route. Downstream from that point, below the most ancient of the eight "Victoria Falls" that have marched back upriver over millennia, lay the Batoka Gorge. The miles ahead were so inaccessible that the fear of land mines was no longer a consideration: Not even the most dedicated guerrilla was willing to climb down into the wild steepness of the Batoka Gorge.

The plateau above and to the north of the gorge was named the Batoka Highlands by Livingstone after the tribe that lived there. Our first day in the Batoka Gorge proper was surprisingly easy. The morning presented a series of thoroughly runnable, thoroughly delightful rapids, not unlike the best of the Colorado: huge standing waves providing classic roller-coaster rides. Only as the expedition approached the last rapid of the day did Nyaminyami strike once again.

The water poured over two gargantuan boulders, fallen in some previous eon from the canyon walls. The current was forced into the twenty meters between the rocks, but it would be easy to bash over or possibly get hung up on the submerged boulders unless the entrance to the fast-moving rapid was exact. The hydraulic effect of the current flowing over a submerged obstacle creates a "hole"—an actual reversal of the downstream flow of the river as the force of the water's abrupt drop literally turns it back on itself in an irregular spinning motion (known to those who have been caught in such a hole as the Maytag Effect).

It was a risky run, but nowhere near impossible, as the first two rafters proved. The third boat through was piloted by John Yost—running alone, since the Zambian wildlife and national parks representative accompanying the group elected to walk around the rapid. Yost missed the entry mark by a yard, enough for the current to sweep him into the second hole sideways. The boat climbed the watery rampart, balanced briefly on its flank, then flopped over almost on top of him. Neusom Holmes, one of the two kayakers, rescued him almost at once; the only injury he received was a nasty bump on the head. When the raft was righted, the only damage it showed was to its spare oar, inexplicably snapped in two. Yost claimed the two casualties, bumped head and snapped oar, were directly related.

At camp that evening Holmes was the last to pull in, having been playing with his kayak in some riffles upstream. His face was waxen as he climbed up the bank to the campsite. "I think I was just chased by a croc," he announced. "It had a head three feet long." His eyes darted uncomfortably up and down the river. We joined him on the bank, searching the turbid waters of the Zambezi. "I must have lost him in that small rapid," he said at last.

The news was heart sickening, since none of us had expected crocodiles yet—the river was too fast, the gorge too abrupt. Crocodiles generally favor slack stretches with gently sloping banks. A consensus was quickly reached that it was probably just a floating log. Nonetheless, everyone bathed in groups that night while one member swept the river with a flashlight for the telltale ruby beads of a crocodile's eyes.

The old Edgar Rice Burroughs image of the crocodile as a man-eating terror of African rivers is, strangely, true. Crocs easily reach fifteen feet in length and half a ton in weight; it takes a lot of protein to support a lizard's system when it's that size. In 1968, for instance, a crocodile was shot in the Okavango Swamp (in nearby Botswana, just south and west of Zambia) whose stomach included the remains of a zebra, a donkey, two goats, and the still-clothed body of a woman who had been missing for seventeen days. Some legendary crocodiles are said to have been responsible for up to 400 human deaths. Experts presently estimate that crocs make a meal of humans once a week in Zambia.

But crocodiles serve their function, and in the Zambezi it's the control of barbel and venu fish, which favor the bream and mormorous that people like to cast for. The Zambezi crocodile population has declined drastically of late, especially along the more accessible stretches of the river below the Batoka Gorge, along the banks of Lake Kariba, and above Victoria Falls in the quiet waters of the upper Zambezi. Croc hides—usually sold to chic French clothiers—fetch up to $100 each these days, perhaps more. But $100 did not seem like fair market value, at least to us, for the creature that had eyed Neusom Holmes's kayak.

The next day was Sunday, and we greeted sunrise with the weekly antimalaria tablet. By this point on the expedition virtually everyone had diarrhea or stomach cramps but no fever. The dry, warm climate of the Zambezi region is not the sort of locale favored by malarial mosquitoes, which are among the most persistent of Africa's threats.

The Batoka Gorge, now nearly 700 feet deep, tapered back a little, revealing more sky and irregular rows of the native mopane trees on the rim. It was the last day on the river for actor LeVar Burton. A willing crew member on the paddleboat despite his harrowing swim, he had been clearly fascinated by the clean lines and quick response of the kayaks throughout the journey. Before the helicopters came in, he asked Neusom for a lesson. Within an hour, he was cutting through the chop of a small rapid with facility, even finesse.

The helicopter landed on the bank, and LeVar and his producer, John Wilcox, bid us farewell. Three members of the ABC film crew remained to continue the coverage of the expedition, which still had to float another thirty unexplored miles to Lake Kariba. Before he climbed aboard the helicopter, Wilcox had a few final reassuring words for the remaining rafters. "Good luck downstream. Don't worry, though. There're no crocs on this river. Old wives' tale."

Fifty-five yards downstream, in the riffle just beyond the one LeVar kayaked, Yost's boat was attacked. A gaping snout lunged from beneath and, sinking two long rows of teeth into the raft, exploded one of the inflated tubes. A veteran of two hippo attacks on rafts he was rowing on the Omo in Ethiopia, Yost lifted an oar out of its oarlock and began slapping the croc over the head with the blade. Amazingly, the croc made a second lunge, then dived and disappeared. Yost frantically rowed the half-deflated raft to shore, and the rest of the boats, rafts, and kayaks made a hasty landing on the nearest beach. If the crocodile had gone for a kayak, low in the water, small and pregnable, it seemed unlikely the paddler could have survived.

Photographer Nick Nichols, a passenger in the victimized boat, estimated the croc at two or three yards; Yost guessed four. This was only the second croc bite in Sobek history, the first being on the Omo. Over the years river runners in Africa had come to expect certain behavior from crocodiles. The reptiles usually displayed their displeasure with charges, their turreted eyes and nostrils riding just out of the water. This usually allowed enough time to hurl a rock or simply to shout at the skittish creatures, who then normally sank to the bottom and hid. Never, however, had a croc attack come unseen from directly beneath a raft. The conclusion was drawn that on the murky rivers of Ethiopia and Tanzania crocodiles approach with eyes surfaced to discern an intended victim. Here the river was clear, and the croc could probably see the boat overhead from the riverbed. Assuming it was a dead hippo, he had shot up for an easy meal.

The tear was too jagged and too big for repair, so the raft was lifted out by one of the Zimbabwean helicopters still escorting the expedition. The two kayaks were also helicoptered out, since neither Neusom Holmes nor Doug Thompkins, the other kayaker, was eager to continue paddling. And though the three members of the ABC team were supposed to continue, they, too, elected to make a hasty exit. Our expedition was reduced to a party of rafters, without media equipment, film stars, or television sensibilities to surround each moment with tangential concerns.

We floated on downstream, quiet and intensely alert, eyes searching the water and shores for crocodiles. Soon we reached Moemba Falls, which aerial reconnaissance had marked as a certain portage. Named for a chief of a nearby tribe, it was a spectacle that Livingstone had viewed from the canyon rim in 1860. He had diverged from his route along the northern plateau on the native report of a waterfall in the gorge, the description of which "seemed to promise something grand." But with the memory of Victoria Falls fresh in mind, he was disappointed. However, G. W. Lamplugh on his 1905 survey actually made it down to the river's edge, and there he formed a different impression: "Insignificant in height, it is true, but when one stands on the brink and sees the whole volume of the great Zambezi converging into a single pass only fifty or sixty feet in width, shuddering, and then plunging for twenty feet in a massive curve that seems in its impact visibly to tear the grim basaltic rocks asunder, one learns better than from the feathery spray-fans of Victoria Falls what force there is in the river, and one wonders no longer at the profundity of the gorge."

Just a couple of miles below Moemba, another spectacular waterfall split the river—only this was a completely uncharted falls. No recorded description of it was found, and no name known. It proved to be an even more difficult portage to reach the calm waters below the falls, including a struggle over sunbaked rocks to lower our five remaining rafts at a ninety-degree pitch over a short cliff. The unanticipated additional time we spent at this portage brought us into late afternoon. At least three unexplored miles lay ahead to the next campsite.

All too soon a huge rapid roared in the waning light. We scouted hurriedly, and fortunately it looked runnable straight down the middle. Neusom Holmes, now behind the oars, volunteered to row first. He rode cleanly over the first wave, then rode sideways up the second and flipped. He and his passengers disappeared in the dusk downstream, swimming for shore. Skip Homer, in the second boat, made it through, barely riding over the wave that had turned Holmes's boat upside down; then Jim Slade capsized in the same place. Two flips in one rapid, and two more rafts to go, with barely enough light to read water.

It was almost black, and it was my turn. I desperately surveyed the rapid for a "cheat" run, but I couldn't even see a hundred yards ahead. I had no idea how the others downstream had fared, whether the water, the rocks, or the crocs had done any damage. I could, however, barely make out the silhouette of Homer's boat tossing in the eddy below, and it gave me an idea. I quickly tightened all the ropes that held the gear in my boat and took out my waterproof diary and camera box. Then I stepped from the boat and kicked it out into the current and watched.

The abandoned boat descended into the maelstrom farther to the left than the others before me, pirouetted in the first wave, and then rode up over the plume of the second wave, right side up. I stumbled down the side of the rapid and found my boat pushing in an eddy, still right side up, with Neusom inside bailing.

The final boat, rowed by John Yost, made it through in almost pitch blackness without trouble, but it was the eerie penumbral run of the empty boat that gave the rapid its name—Ghostrider.

By the beams of our pocket flashlights we proceeded downstream toward the comfort of the coptered camp, but a narrowing gorge, a quickening current, and the rising noise of whitewater forced a bivouac on a rocky ledge.

With the first light of the next day, our seventh on the river, we wearily surveyed the rapid we had elected to shun the night before. It had been a wise move: The river coiled into a thin slot, then rebounded in a white fury off a rock wall. The first four boats were slapped and twisted in the gauntlet, but all made it through. Then Jim Slade, fresh from his capsize the evening before, entered last and was battered by the currents directly into the wall. His aft bucked on its side, rode up the rock wall, and spilled first one passenger, then another, finally the entire crew—and at last flipped over.

It was the fifth flip, and it proved to be the last. A campsite was soon reached and the tepid beer and soda broken out for a much needed lengthy lunch and longer siesta.

The next two days led to a reversal of the first seven: fewer rapids and more wildlife. Crocodiles reverted to more normal behavior and eyed us from afar, and a few bloats of hippos crashed loudly into the water as the boats approached. Over the years hippos have proven to be the greater danger to rafts on the rivers of Africa, responsible for eight attacks on Sobek rafts since the first trip down the Omo eight years earlier. Their reaction was probably the same as the crocodile's had been—that an intrusive hippo was invading their territory.

Finally, in the early afternoon of November 5, the current of the Zambezi died in the waters of Lake Kariba. The journey was over.

I wish I could send a report to Livingstone, so he might have the final chapter on this river he spent so long exploring, so he might close the book.

The Zambezi curls through the final gate into this new lake, Kariba, sparkling like hammered gold. I begin to thank God we made it, then send my prayers of gratitude to Nyaminyami, river god of the Zambezi.

LAVA FALLS—AT NIGHT!

Louise Teal

*L*ava Falls, on the Colorado River, is unquestionably the most renowned rapid in the United States. While smaller, more technical rapids feature dire slalom runs through chutes and wash rocks, Lava Falls resembles the ocean during a tornado—monumental swells and standing waves steep enough to pitch a twenty-foot raft on end and to bust an aluminum oar transit on the way down. The magnitude is second to none, and the same goes for the thunderous racket the big rollers produce. Getting sucked into this cauldron, buck naked, in pitch blackness, riding in one unmanageable raft while fastened to another defiant one, is the subject of the following story—a comically dangerous tale.*

‡   ‡   ‡

Scrawny and unathletic, I was a pretty unlikely candidate to break into Grand Canyon river guiding, the last bastion of the male river god. It wasn't that I was uncoordinated, but in the early 1960s my high school essentially had no athletic programs for girls. My experience in the outdoors was next to nil, except for playing in the vacant lot across the street from our house in the San Francisco Bay area or gaping out the car window while my dad drove through various national parks. I flunked canoeing at Camp Augusta because I refused to memorize the various parts of the boat. My goal in high school, outside of leaving home, was to become a fashion designer; but Dad talked me out of art school because he was afraid I would turn into a communist. "Try

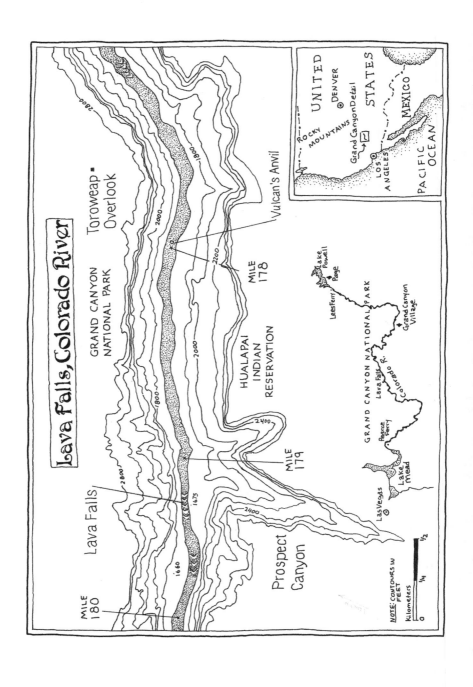

Lava Falls, Colorado River

Toroweap ■
Overlook

GRAND CANYON
NATIONAL PARK

Lava Falls

MILE
180

Prospect
Canyon

Vulcan's Anvil

MILE
178

MILE
179

HUALAPAI
INDIAN
RESERVATION

NOTE: CONTOURS IN FEET

Kilometers
0   ¼   ½

UNITED
● Denver
Grand Canyon Detail
STATES

ROCKY
MOUNTAINS

LOS
ANGELES

MEXICO

PACIFIC
OCEAN

Lake
Powell
Page

Lees Ferry

GRAND CANYON NATIONAL PARK

Grand Canyon
Village

Lava Falls

Colorado R.

Pearce
Ferry

Lake
Mead

Las Vegas ●

UCLA first," he said. So I did, joined a sorority, got married, and moved to Seattle.

But before all that, back in high school, my dad and I went on a commercial river trip through Glen Canyon. I cannot begin to describe the beauty of that place—there was no other canyon like it. It is under water now, thanks to Glen Canyon Dam. Lake Powell is not one-tenth as beautiful as what lies buried underneath. But in 1963, Glen Canyon was still there, and we paddled a canoe down that easy stretch of the Colorado River miles above Lee's Ferry. It is a good thing it was easy because, early each morning, our canoe shoved off before the river guides who were motoring the main group. We were terrified of coming up to a place called Hell's Crossing until we realized we were reading the map wrong—it was Hall's Crossing.

I remember sitting alone one evening on a smooth sandstone boulder by a side creek, with a T-bone steak dripping in my hands. As I watched the swallows work the creek and the sun set salmon colors on the cliffs, I thought, this is the way to live. I want to keep doing this.

Too soon, the trip was over, and I was back to my real life—puberty, high school trauma, and college plans. But I guess your soul has a way of remembering what you wish for, and things have a way of working out.

Years later, when I was living in Seattle, working as a secretary, married to a stockbroker, and sick to death of gray skies, I saw a *National Geographic* article about river trips through the Grand Canyon. Yes! I signed us up for $350 each. When the time came for the trip, my husband Roger couldn't leave because the 1970 stock market was so bad.

I went anyway, a passenger on a thirty-three-foot motor rig. It did not matter how big those boats were; the rapids looked huge and scared me to death. Even so, I loved being down there. The Canyon was beautiful and intense, a completely fulfilling place to be. I wanted to stay. But it did not sound like women worked down there except as assistants to their boyfriends or husbands. No matter: I was still operating from that old frame of mind that you married what you wanted to do. I would just convince my husband to become a boatman.

That was the easy part; he was ready to leave, so we headed south back to the sunshine. Roger wrote various outfitters for work, but none were interested in hiring a stockbroker to run boats. Then Robert Elliott of AZRA wrote back saying that he was running AZRA's first whitewater school and to come along. For a price, of course. The next year, 1972, Roger was running motor rigs down the Grand Canyon, and I was working as his assistant, a soul in bliss.

Our marriage was not to last much longer, but I had found my true love—the river and the Canyon. I had not yet found my boat, though. I never really warmed up to those motors. The next summer, I learned to use oars on the Stanislaus River in California. Roger and I purchased a raft and helped three other boatmen run free river trips for kids. A few wide-eyed juvenile delinquents paid their debt to society as my boat careened down that rocky river. At the end of that summer, Roger went fishing in Alaska for the winter, and I managed to get on another Grand Canyon trip, a snout-boat trip.

A tousled boatman let me row his boat some, and, kind of like Tom Sawyer let his friends paint the fence, he allowed me to catch the eddy below Blacktail Canyon. It's necessary to catch eddies in order to stop on shore. Some of the eddies in the Canyon are huge. In fact, some sections of the Colorado River have more water swirling upstream than current flowing downstream. A few infamous eddies even have names: King Edward, Ever-Eddy, Helicopter Eddy. Rowing into or out of an eddy through the "eddy fence" (a line of small whirlpools where the current is going every which way) can be tricky business if the current is particularly intense. And rowing across a wide eddy fence could be an ordeal in those old heavy snout boats.

Anyhow, the boatman grinned at me while I learned what "busting a gut" meant as I spent at least five minutes rowing through the eddy fence at Blacktail. While my spindly arms pulled on the thirteen-foot oars, he said to me, "If you can make this eddy, you could row the Canyon."

I made the eddy.

But it was more than just the willpower to catch that eddy that started me rowing down there. It was Robert and Jessie, the progressive owners of AZRA. And it was all the boatmen, especially my ex-husband—they were totally supportive. After talking with some other boatwomen, I realize now how lucky I was. Some did not have such an easy time of it, and they always felt under pressure to prove themselves, to always have excellent runs through rapids. But that really wasn't the program back then. As one old boatman put it, "I was really into trying to do good runs, you know, be a hot boatman. But the more trips I did, the more I realized that no one cared about how hot I was. In fact," he grinned, "the heroes were the guys with the wild-ass runs and the great stories."

Those boatmen were almost heroes to me in that they were some of the most clever, capable, giving, and funny people I had ever met. Now I will not say these guys never gave me a hard time. "Well," one boatman said, "we used to give you shit about Lava Falls just to get your goat, but I don't think it was because you were a woman. We razzed everyone about something, and yours happened to be Lava Falls, because you'd twitch when you got there."

As you might expect, there had to be a nightmare among all the dream-filled Canyon days. And for me it involved my old "twitching spot," Lava Falls.

I am still not sure what woke me up. Perhaps it was the odd movement of the snout boat I was sleeping on. What I saw when I peeked out from underneath my tarp made me nauseous. Even in my drowsiness, I realized I had just awakened to a river guide's nightmare—something we had always joked about as a possibility but that had never happened. That is, not until that moment: The boats had somehow broken loose from shore and were floating downriver at night toward Lava Falls.

Lava Falls, that infamous rapid at mile 179. After days of quiet water, it sounds like a 747 jet taking off. Lava pounds, heaves, and froths. Its thirty-seven-foot drop is full of small waterfalls, huge waves, holes, ledges, a folding V-shaped wave, and black lava rocks. Any number of these are capable of flipping twenty-two-foot boats. A windsurfer friend who regularly rides over waves clinging to a flying piece of fiberglass told me that riding through Lava Falls as a passenger was the ride of his life.

If we had been more careful how we tied up the boats that night, I would not have a story to tell. But we had been rowing against the wind for eight hours straight and had to stop, exhausted a couple of miles above Lava. It was all we could do to cook dinner for twenty people, let alone remember details such as tying our boats to tamarisk trees large enough to hold in any change of water or wind conditions. But luckily, we only tied two of the boats to each other, instead of all three.

After the dishes were done, the wind continued to blow, and dark clouds gathered up the Canyon. I headed for the security of the boats to set up a rain shelter. After battling the wind for control of my plastic tarp, I dove under just in time to miss the first raindrops. Soon, I was listening to a full-blown Southwestern storm while being rocked to sleep by the river.

While I slumbered, the water rose (it fluctuates daily due to releases from Glen Canyon Dam upstream). Increasingly stronger current and wind moved the boats back and forth, slowly uprooting the pathetic little bushes holding the boats. Finally, the roots gave way, and the rafts surged out into the current.

That's when I woke up, peered out from beneath my tarp, and realized I was in the middle of the Colorado River, in the middle of the night, heading toward Lava Falls. I did what any girl who can't whistle would do—I screamed. Was anyone awake at camp to hear me?

I wasn't just careening downstream on one boat, but two twenty-two-foot snouts tied together. I quickly squirmed out of my sleeping bag and grabbed my life jacket first, then my channel locks and knife. My rain tarp was tied to my oars and raft frame. I needed to dismantle my temporary shelter enough to get oars in the water and a seat to row on. I cut the bowlines because they were still attached to uprooted tamarisk trees that were now functioning as sea anchors. I didn't want anything keeping me in the current. I wanted to get to shore.

It was wild. Thunder, rain, lightning, and me, naked except for my life jacket, heading toward Lava. Whenever the lightning flashed, I could see enough of the canyon walls to know how close I was getting to Lava. I had flipped boats there in the daylight; I didn't figure my chances were good of getting through with two boats in the dark.

However, I did spend one moment imagining eternal glory in the river-guides' annals if I made a midnight run through Lava. Lightning flashed, and that vision was replaced with a more realistic picture of the boats hitting the first wave and sandwiching me between two snout rigs. Getting this floating disaster to shore seemed like a better idea.

The two boats, tied together at their bows, were being held side by side by the current, making it impossible to use both oars. I turned the boats several times with my one oar, but the current kept pushing the boats back together. I was cruising downstream fast: I needed both oars, and I needed an eddy.

Soaking wet, naked, in the thunder and lightning, with Lava Falls pounding and snorting downstream, it was easy to think of God. Grateful that I was past my college atheist period, I asked for help.

The boats swung apart. In the next lightning flash, I could see a large eddy sparkling downstream. I dug in with both oars and headed for it. I broke through into the eddy, but that wasn't the end of it. The second boat was still in the downstream current and pulled my boat back out again. Downriver the boats went, while I tried to row both back into the eddy. It became a crazy dance in the water. One boat would get into the eddy, and the other would pull it out into the main current. The boats and I spun around. Depending on which boat was nearest the eddy. I pulled or pushed on the oars toward shore.

Finally, both boats were in the eddy. I rowed close to shore and grabbed at small willows to help me stop. When I could see a rock to tie to, I jumped off and wound a line around it. Not taking any chances, I tied the boats to at least three rocks and two bushes. I was high on adrenaline and howled into the wind like a coyote. The storm was starting to move out. Of course, I forgot about thanking God and just felt great about getting the boats to shore all by myself.

My shivering reminded me that I was freezing, so I looked around for some clothes. I thought I would hike upriver and yell across to our camp, but as the adrenaline wore off and I looked at the rough terrain— prickly cactus and sharp travertine rocks—I thought better of that idea. Scrounging around for some calories to warm me up, I discovered our trip's supply of candy. "This is an emergency," I rationalized and ate as many M&M's as I could. After I rechecked my numerous lines tied to shore, I settled down in the boat to sleep.

As it turned out, someone did hear me scream when I made my unplanned departure from camp. A passenger had been up late gazing into the campfire. She was a bit puzzled by the boatmen's reactions when she woke them up: They spent the next five minutes rolling around in their sleeping bags, laughing hysterically. They gleefully pictured me sound asleep under my orange tarp, floating toward the brink of Lava Falls.

I probably would have reacted the same. Finally, my ex-husband hiked downstream to look for the boats.

Again, I woke up. This time to someone shouting across the river and shining a flashlight my way.

"Is that you, Louise?" Roger shouted from the opposite bank.

"Yeah," I shouted back.

"How many boats do you have?"

I shot back, "How many do you have?"

"One," he replied.

I laughed across the river. "Well, I've got more than you!"

Eventually, I got tired of pushing those old snouts around and went somewhere I could row more responsive boats—working as a Grand

Canyon National Park Service river ranger. It was a stellar crew that 1979 season, but even so, I am afraid I was too much of an anarchist at heart to work for the government. Plus, I really missed my old crew and the commercial passengers. By the end of the summer, I was back with my old crew. Fortunately, by then Jessie had convinced Robert that it was financially viable to row smaller boats—eighteen-foot rafts with ten-foot oars, rafts that could actually pivot.

No matter how river equipment, the river-tour industry, or the Canyon changes, that ancient pile of rock never stops its song. And as one retired boatman said, "When you stick your oars in the water, you're feeling the whole story. There's no words, but it's the full language of the formation of the earth."

My life, too, is full of changes, but one thing that remains constant is coming back to the Canyon every summer, even if only for a partial season. It is an addiction that some people—employment counselors, my relatives, and a few mates—might say has been a curse. But to me, it has been my greatest blessing.

GORE CANYON:
THE RIVER OF FEAR

Timothy Hillmer

A river only knows herself to be a river, a run of instinctive waters—
sometimes turbulent, restless, indomitable. She is brutally frank,
never discriminating between a crack kayaker and a rotten log. Per-
haps this is why rivers are so attractive. She puts nothing but her undivided
might into every swirling whirlpool and pourover. Her many selves are there
for every boater to dread and, in turn, enjoy. Picture yourself surviving a fren-
zied water ride then easing into a placid eddy. Is there a greater moment of
grace for any paddler? I suspect that author/rafter Tim Hillmer would insist
that when he was tumbling through a class V rapid and finally got his hands
on a throw bag, that this *was the truer grace. You be the judge.*

‡   ‡   ‡

Butterflies in the stomach; a sixth sense foretells that today my luck
will vanish like a beacon in the fog. Call it paranoia or call it honest
fear. This is what any canoeist, rafter, or kayaker feels before running
a class IV rapid for the first time. An atheist in a world inhabited by
river gods.

And this is how I feel as I stand at the top of Colorado's Gore Canyon Rapid on the upper Colorado River. It is the challenge of meeting
the unexpected, much the way a blind man might feel traveling across
unfamiliar terrain. No matter how many rivers I run or how well I train,
there is always a fear that perhaps these skills are not enough. My nerve
trembles. Failure lurks.

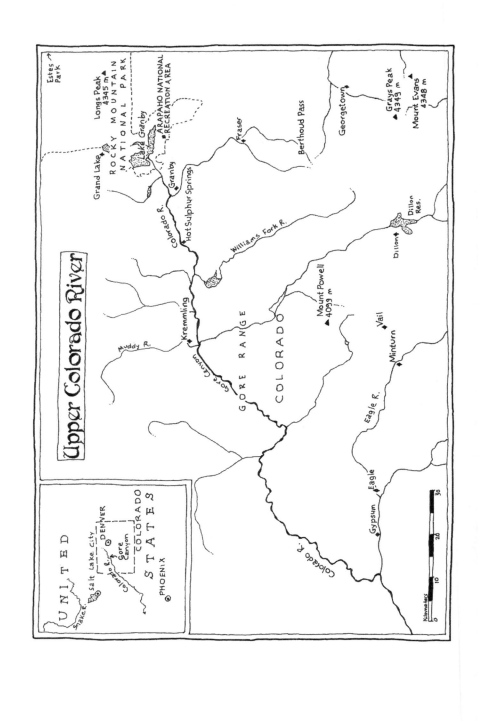

Upper Colorado River

UNITED STATES
Snake R.
Salt Lake City
Colorado R.
Gore Canyon
DENVER
COLORADO
PHOENIX

Estes Park
Longs Peak 4345 m
Grand Lake
ROCKY MOUNTAIN NATIONAL PARK
Lake Granby
ARAPAHO NATIONAL RECREATION AREA
Granby
Fraser
Berthoud Pass
Georgetown
Grays Peak 4349 m
Mount Evans 4348 m
Hot Sulphur Springs
Colorado R.
Williams Fork R.
Dillon Res.
Dillon
Kremmling
Muddy R.
Mount Powell 4093 m
Gore Canyon
GORE RANGE
COLORADO
Vail
Minturn
Eagle R.
Eagle
Gypsum
Colorado R.

Kilometers
0   10   20   30

I am here with an exploratory team from the Boulder Outdoor Center (BOC), a Colorado-based rafting company. Only two weeks earlier, the BOC made the first successful paddle-raft descent of Gore Canyon without portage. We have returned to attempt it again, only this time at a lower and more technical water level of 1,500 cfs.

For two years I have listened to other boaters tell vivid horror stories about this brief six-mile run. In Doug Wheat's excellent book, *The Floater's Guide to Colorado,* he begins and ends his description of Gore Canyon with these words of caution: "If you are looking for an enjoyable raft or kayak run, Gore Canyon is not for you . . . it is not recommended." And in *Rivers of the Southwest* by Fletcher Anderson and Ann Hopkinson, the authors describe their horrifying kayak descent of the Gore at 10,000 cfs, one in which Ms. Hopkinson was nearly killed after being pinned by an undercut rock. As their guidebook simply states, "Gore Canyon is the most difficult paddlable whitewater in the Colorado River. Ill-informed rafters have twice attempted this run. Both attempts failed dramatically in the first mile."

Gore Canyon Rapid roars on. Located only a mile into the canyon, it is the first real challenge of the trip. I watch now as Eric Bader, the twenty-five-year-old owner of the BOC, heads back upstream to make the first attempt on Gore Rapid in an open canoe. I do not question his skills, merely his sanity. Only two hours earlier, I had watched him unload his green Perception HD-1 canoe at our put-in west of Kremmling, Colorado. Next to our self-bailing rafts, his boat looked like a dehydrated nightcrawler. But I realize that no one is better suited to attempt this than Eric, a veteran of over fifteen kayak descents of Gore Canyon. As he passes my safety position on his way upstream, I smile and send a psychic sign of the cross his way. Go in peace, my friend, and paddle like hell.

I am doubtful of his chances of success as I wait below, throw bag in hand. A canoe is a canoe and this rapid is a meat grinder no matter what vessel challenges it. My thoughts are broken by a shout and I look up to see Eric paddling into the first drop. His entrance is pinpoint precise, perhaps made easier by the narrowness of his canoe. He surfs the inside curve of a pillow, then drops straight into the maelstrom. Like a scalpel in a landslide, he slices through the main hole, pauses on the boil surging upstream of the undercut rock, then slides like an eel around it, carefully slithering through the remaining obstacle course. It is a flawless run and Eric paddles into the eddy, smiling.

Our crew hikes upstream to raft it. Brian Brodeur, a veteran guide for the BOC, will captain. We studiously scout the entrance drop, then climb into our Riken self-bailer and head out. I feel pumped up and ready; it's full speed ahead. We approach the rapid with an upstream ferry, carefully maneuvering across the river and through a class IV rock garden directly above the entrance drop. We pivot around a boulder, spin, and charge toward the first turn. Our boat slides agonizingly into a rock just left of the chute, then hangs at the lip of the falls. Then we are in it. My body arches out into the cascade, reaching for current. The moment flashes by as our boat plows into the hole, stops with a sledgehammer blow, then rises perilously up like a drunken tightrope dancer pointing at the sky. I am slammed backward out of the raft, thrust into a huge reversal, and surrounded by a violent whirl of green and white. Like being shot out of a rocket silo, I am flushed away and under. I pop up, gasp for air, then am yanked down again.

No mercy. I am aware of my feet downstream, of being hit by a barrage of rocks and straining to break the green surface and swim left. It is a mad, topsy-turvy waterslide of a ride as I try to swim and cover up for protection. Suddenly I see a throw rope and latch onto the line. I feel my battered weight swing into the slim eddy with a pendular motion. I see Eric smiling above me. I rest in the shallows on a rock, spitting out water and coughing. I probe for a bruised knee, give thanks for the shore under my booties, and curse Gore Rapid. I was not the lone swimmer. After talking to Eric, I learn that Kim, a strong paddler from Steamboat Springs, Colorado, had also popped out of the raft and had somehow managed to pull herself out on a rock. The boat and remaining crew nearly capsized in the hole but were mercifully spit out into the current where they wedged upon a boulder. After paddling over to retrieve Kim, they proceeded to slide their way down the remainder of the rapid. Our second crew, in an oarboat rowed by Gene Dennis, wisely decides to portage after witnessing our epic. Their self-bailing SOTAR is hoisted up the talus slope with ropes, then it's carried around by way of the railroad tracks high above the run.

I am exhausted from my swim, but Gore Canyon doesn't care. The river does not let up. The bottom section of the half-mile Gore Rapid consists of two class IV+ boulder gardens, then a violent, six-foot drop over a mass of razor-sharp rock. We proceed with caution. All boats negotiate the final falls without mishap, then spill into a beautiful jade pool. It is our first chance to look back, take a deep breath, and be aware of the immense canyon we are floating through. In contrast to the relentless rapids, the high rust-colored walls rise peacefully on either side like slabs of gleaming bronze—isolated magnificence in the heart of the 11,000-foot Gore Mountain Range. To rest in the pool at the bottom of this gorge almost makes my harrowing swim worthwhile. We are here where few have been, all believers in a world of river gods. With our sense of adventure renewed, we plunge ahead.

The pace is furious as we paddle through uncountable and un-named class IV and V rapids. We stop two miles past Gore Rapid on river left to scout Tunnel Falls. As I move along the shore I am greeted by a roar from beyond the horizon line. What I see upon moving closer forces me to doubt my purpose here. It is breathtaking, as if the entire riverbed had been smashed away with earthquake force to create a twelve-foot curtain of seething froth. It is a terrifying, illustrated ex-ample of a keeper. As I study the waterfall, I spy a possible run on the far left where the river makes a slight turn and pours over and off a rock slab jutting from shore. Here the reversal is less violent and al-most forgiving, but it contains a corkscrew turn with zero room for error. To not pirouette to the right at the brink of the falls would mean floating sideways or backward over the drop, into the jaws of the dragon. May the river gods be with us.

We set up safety lines along the shore for Eric, then watch as he sneaks down on river left with his canoe. He drawstrokes around an annoying rock and approaches the brink of the falls. He hangs on the inside bend of the turn. Amazingly, like some cosmic daredevil, he is smiling as he plummets down. His green canoe bucks up violently, then slips past the boiling foam of the main falls. I am envious of the ease he exhibits. I dream of narrow rafts and winged life jackets. Paddle or fly.

Our crew returns to the raft in silence. We will follow Eric's route and hope that our wide boat can squeeze down the narrow chute. Life jackets are cinched tight. Helmets adjusted and snapped on. The wind howls upstream.

We hug the left shore and slide through the rocky upper section. I draw left, trying to keep our raft away from the main current tugging toward the falls. As we approach the horizon line, panic sets in. Instead of turning right and into the corkscrew bend, we plow head on into a rock knifing out from shore, bounce off, spin, and slide over Tunnel Falls backward.

Falling. Like ripping down a roller coaster blindfolded and out of control. I feel the boat surge up on its side and cover me in a shadow as I am enveloped by the dark veil of the falls. My body is sucked down and under. Then, like being shot out of a cannon, I am hurled downstream underwater. I pull myself out of the river just above the next rapid and kneel prayerfully in the shallows. On the opposite side I count heads and see that our paddle crew is safe. Even our flipped raft has been pulled to safety. Eric paddles up in his canoe to check on me. Humiliated and stunned, I wave okay, get a throw bag from him, and head upstream to set up safety for Gene Dennis's oarboat.

I perch alone on a truck-sized boulder near the mouth of Tunnel Falls. The wind whips up the constricted canyon and I must brace against a rock or be blown from my position. I try to forget my exhaustion and fear. In times such as these it is best to trust one's experience acquired from running other class V rivers. Don't think; react. Go with the flow. Forget the dragons.

I hear a shout from across the river and see the second boat approaching. Gene Dennis is rowing while Ivan Schmitt, another Steamboat guide, paddles up front. As they draw close to the main drop, I see Gene is having trouble with his oars in the narrow channel, bumping and scraping them against rock. He is momentarily popped out of his rowing seat as Ivan continues to paddle. Their boat approaches the falls backward, then attempts to pivot around and forward. With sickening familiarity, I see their raft ricochet off the shore, whirl helplessly around, and dive head on into the horrible mouth of the main falls. Ivan is buried in a torrent of water as the raft flips. Gene is sent flying through the air with one hand clasping an oar, like a flailing acrobat who has missed his trapeze.

Red throw bags arc out across the water, aimed at the bobbing heads of the swimmers. Ivan and Gene each snag a line and are quickly reeled in. Eric helps nose the flipped boat over to shore with his canoe. I pause momentarily and gaze at Tunnel Falls, thankful that no one has been sucked back into the killer reversal.

With the afternoon fading and the canyon bathed in shadow, I rejoin my dazed paddle crew and we push on. Passing hurriedly through a series of minor rapids, we stop to scout Toilet Bowl, a river-wide ledge hole. It was here, nearly three years ago, that Eric almost drowned while attempting to rescue a fellow kayaker trapped in the reversal.

As we reach the scouting point to study the drop, we suddenly see Eric hurrying in his canoe along the river's left side, attempting to sneak down a rocky slot that hugs the shore and avoids the hole. We scramble for throw bags as his canoe successfully squeezes through the boatwide cavity, then overturns and is sucked back into the reversal. Eric somehow dives from his boat at the last second and swims to shore. We watch in horror as the green HD-l is battered and tossed like driftwood in the power of the hydraulic. Eric scrambles up to our perch, wet and out of breath.

"No way was I going back into that hole," he says.

Throughout the fifteen minutes that the canoe recirculates in Toilet Bowl, I push out of my mind any thought of what this killer hole would have done to my friend. I only give thanks he is alive and next to me on shore.

A decision is made to line the rafts around Toilet Bowl, and we do so, using carabiners and climbing ropes. Suddenly the canoe pops out of the reversal and is sent downstream unmanned. We give chase with Eric now paddling in our raft and run the last major rapid of the day, Kirshbaum, in the gold light of sunset. We holler through each wave, paddling in unison. Finally, we catch up to the canoe below Kirshbaum, where it has miraculously lodged intact between two rocks.

As we float the remainder of the run down to the take-out at Pumphouse Beach, I look around and see the tired faces of our crew, exhausted by Gore Rapid, Tunnel Falls, and the innumerable rapids between. We are together here in the twilight, a small procession heading home. I think of ancient ships returning at dusk from distant lands with their holds full of gold, silver, and spices. I think of the early explorers I studied as a child—Balboa, Cabrillo, and Drake—those who discovered new worlds and returned home to the welcome of kings and queens.

There will be no royal welcome or feast at our take-out. Dinner will consist of leftover lunchmeat and a few cookies eaten as we pack our gear in the dark and wait for the shuttle vehicle to return. I only know that come next summer I will once again be scouting Tunnel Falls and perhaps plotting a new route over this twelve-foot abyss. I know that at night I shall dream of current, of rivers, of a beautiful wave endlessly curling back, repeating the sharp cycle of water and motion and return. I know I am a river runner, as far from any historical limelight as Pizarro was from discovering El Dorado. But I have learned that within myself, a landscape has been surveyed and charted, a dark continent explored.

CATARACT CANYON

Jeff Bennett

*W*hen watching masters in action, their talent seems so polished, so sure and steady that it's hard to imagine them as hackers flubbing the most basic maneuvers. But nobody ever appeared on the scene ready-made, gliding through malicious rapids like so many boat wakes. All masters go through a break-in period during which they are green, incompetent, and clumsy. Many experts are loathe to recount their early blunders, when naked fear turned their minds to mush and they did things so daft as to furnish grist for legends—legends of terror and folly. For over a decade our man "Arnie" (whom the following story concerns) rowed the Grand with the best of them. But there was a time. . . .

‡   ‡   ‡

Get in a raft with a river guide and you're liable to hear enough tall tales to write a novel. Some of them true. For me, it always helps to keep a healthy supply of enduring stories in my repartee to fill in quiet moments, flat stretches, and to avoid questions like "How deep's this river?"

While the best river stories usually stem from firsthand experiences, a good secondhand tale can't be overlooked. Such is the case with the following story.

During my early days as a raft guide, I had the good fortune of befriending an ex-Colorado River guide named Arnie. All his boating skills were acquired while getting his raft stomped by the big rapids of Cataract Canyon, which, during high water, is one of the most treacherous sections of the Colorado River. Though the end result was a fine set of well-honed big-water skills, his initiation to the business of running rivers was downright embarrassing.

The swamper is the low man on the guiding totem pole. Swampers load and unload rafts, set up porta potties, and fill the position of all-around gofer. In Cataract Canyon, swampers hang out by the guides, watching their every move, sometimes waiting years for the moment when they can take the helm. Arnie had just bluffed his way into his first river job, swamping for a big outfitter of marginal repute. His verbal resume had consisted of trips from the Rogue down to the Stanislaus, with a few rivers in between.

Arnie spent the beginning of his first season swamping during highwater trips through Cataract. During the peak of runoff, raft companies sent motorized pontoon boats or triple-rigs through the big drops. This allowed for a greater margin of safety but imparted nothing upon the swamper. After a couple of these trips, Arnie split for the Colorado Rockies for a few weeks of backpacking.

Upon his return to Utah, he was surprised to find things had changed. A guide strike was on and the company was understaffed. The top two-thirds of the totem pole had been hacked off. Arnie was now a head boatman.

A trip was heading out the next day, and Arnie's services were badly needed. "You want to guide it?" asked the owner. "The river's still high. It's a real scream in there. But these folks really want an oarboat trip. You up to it?"

Arnie hadn't expected that question quite so fast. His expertise was dishwater, not whitewater. But Arnie was quick on his toes. This was an opportunity that had to be grabbed. "Uhm. Well, uhm. . . ." If he was going to do this trip, he'd have to say yes before his throat totally sealed off. "Err, yeah."

Arnie was now locked in. No turning back. He dragged his knotted stomach over to a friend's house and bummed some beer.

"Hey, Arnie, I heard you're gonna row it tomorrow. One trip just got back. A real nightmare. They lined up wrong at Satan's Gut and flipped, big time. Everyone held onto the raft. And with the oars and ammo cans and all, some folks got pretty banged up. A couple of broken arms or legs or something. Yeah, a real nightmare."

Arnie's mind was spinning. *Flips . . . oars . . . broken arms.* He was starting to wish he had been on the level about his experience. Or lack thereof. But it was too late. By the time morning arrived, he found him-

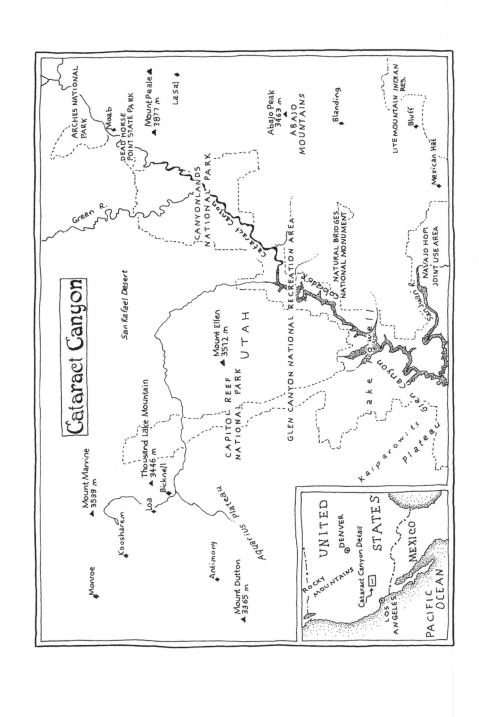

self on a bus heading toward the put-in.

The first couple of days of most Cataract Canyon trips take in miles of peaceful water, easy rapids, and glorious canyon scenery. While the passengers relished these experiences, Arnie honed his rowing skills. He pulled on the left oar, then on the right. Anyone who knew anything would have wondered what the hell Arnie was doing working up a sweat in class II water. But he was pulling it off. He told stories from his first Cataract trips as if he'd done it for years. Everyone was convinced of Arnie's prowess—except Arnie.

After a couple of days on the river, they had reached the lip of the inevitable. The mother of Cataract Canyon rapids—Mile Long and The Big Drop. Arnie's heart was wrestling his stomach for a position in his throat. A creeping fear began to seize his brain. "What the hell am I doing here?" he thought. Meanwhile, his mouth moved with the disguise of confidence that he had perfected over the course of the last two days of guiding.

Flying through Mile Long, Arnie's oars danced along the surface like wounded crickets, catching the current and the tops of waves and flailing in the troughs. But he was doing alright. Hanging tough and keeping the raft straight.

Before long it was all over. Arnie and his crew had survived Mile Long, slurping down their victory like so many shots of confidence. But more rapids—worse rapids—waited downstream.

Arnie's biggest moment came way too soon. Quivering with excitement and terror, he went into a short guide's speech he'd heard the old-timers say before: "Okay, down there is Satan's Seat and Satan's Gut. The Big Drop. It's what we're here for. Remember everything about what I said when we started this trip. Don't panic, hold on tight, and *don't fall out.*"

Following final preparations, Arnie tugged heavily on the oars, straining hard to get the boat out into the main current. Soon, truck-sized walls of water began dancing like angry spirits on the river's surface. Arnie's mind was becoming overloaded. *"A real nightmare . . . lined up wrong . . . flipped . . . held onto the raft . . . broken arms . . . broken legs . . . broken necks."* His friend's words rang loudly above the roar of the rapids. Then it happened.

"Snap!" An oar broke with a sickening pop. *"Kaploosh!"* The first set of waves exploded over the boat, nearly capsizing the raft. Paralyzed with fear, Arnie could do nothing. Huge diagonal waves reached

skyward, forming ever narrowing corridors of doom, funneling the raft and crew toward extinction.

"Jump!"

The crew looked startled.

"C'mon! Jump!!!"

Arnie had gone berserk. No one could have guessed what was running through his mind. The perceived inevitability of a flip in Satan's Gut had warped Arnie's sense of judgment. He felt that it would be better to simply swim the Gut than to hold onto a tumbling raft full of arm-breaking oars and ammo cans.

"Ju-u-u-ump!"

No one budged an inch. For many of the passengers, this was their first taste of wilderness adventure. This was supposed to be fun. Exciting. Not a Hollywood version of "Arnie Goes Psycho." They hunkered lower and lower into the raft, holding onto ropes and frames with white-knuckled vengeance.

"Jump!"

Arnie dove overboard. No kidding! Right out there in the middle of Mother Nature's personal drowning pool. Out there under the vultures and Utah's blazing sun.

It took a few seconds before Arnie found the surface again. He came up within earshot of the raft. Seeing his crew glued in place, he shouted his final words of misguided encouragement before concerns for his own well-being became paramount.

"Jump!" Blub, blub, blub, blub. . . .

Now the raft, totally unguided, floated perilously toward Cataract Canyon's biggest, ugliest holes. Nearby, Arnie bobbed through the churning brown waters like a cork in a sea storm. Both raft and Arnie had the worst of possible lines. A big hole drew near. The roar of the water was sickening.

In a moment it was all over. Somehow, the raft had slipped through unscathed. The crew was safe. A perfect run. But Arnie was nowhere to be found.

"There he is!" shouted someone from the raft.

Arnie had taken an awful swim. He had entered the hole straight on, dead center. He was no match for its powerful grasp. He was sent deep into the bowels of the Colorado once, tumbled and released, and sucked back down for another ride. By the time he had reached the calm pools below, he had expended all the energy he had in his fight for survival.

"Arnie, hang in there. Just a second." One of the least adventurous passengers—a genuine city slicker—had unstrapped a spare oar and set about rescuing Arnie.

By that time, other boats had converged for the rescue, but Arnie's crew reached him first. They hauled him over the gunwales and laid him on the pile of gear, letting the sun revive him.

By the time he came around, there was little left to Arnie's Cataract Canyon trip. The peaceful calm of Lake Powell waited downstream. There would be no opportunity for vindication. No chance to replenish his ego. Just hour after hour of the longest days of Arnie's life.

His story has reached near legendary proportions in some circles. Quite an unwelcome infamy. Fortunately, his real name is seldom revealed because the fact is, embarrassing things happen to almost all river guides during their first crack at paddling big water.

But Arnie stands alone in suggesting that one and all *"Jump!!"*

WHITEWATER RELATIVITY: ON THE NEW AT FORTY FEET

Barry Tuscano

*N**ovice paddlers can show remarkable boldness; however, the sight of a thunderous class V rapid is generally sufficient to loosen their bowels. But not always. Every so often someone shows up who seems entirely fearless. Given the aptitude, the fearless novice is the first to gain expert status—if he doesn't kill himself in the process. During the initial phases, when courage is huge but skill and judgement are small, the bold neophyte is guaranteed to face disaster. If survived, the disastrous event instills the healthy fear that was missing in the first place. Thereafter, the novice can either quit the sport and devote his life to Jesus—as happened to several of the principals in the following potboiler—or settle into a saner learning curve. Either way, that first encounter with catastrophe is burned into memory and often provides grist for legendary stories.*

Barry Tuscano's diabolical "Theory of Whitewater Relativity" led him— a fearless, know-nothing rafter—to the brink of extinction. I trust other readers will find his deliverance as spectacular as I did.

‡ ‡ ‡

My whitewater career began in 1971 on the Youghiogheny River. Riding the rapids in a little raft was an instant hit with me. Riding them outside the raft was even better. Twenty-five years ago, there was no one on the river to show us differently. In our complete absence of common sense, my friends and I thought the only way to approach a rapid was full speed ahead, right down the middle. That's why our early raft trips involved more swimming than paddling. We didn't have the foggiest notion what a hole or an eddy was. If the raft flipped, which it normally did, the ensuing fun simply made the venture that much more memorable.

In 1973 I was introduced to the Pittsburgh Explorers Club, a social organization that regularly scheduled outdoor activities such as rock climbing, parachuting, and whitewater rafting. For the most part the activities served as an excuse for going to exotic locations and getting drunk. The activities were always strenuous, but the parties afterward were killers.

Explorers Club members were undertaking some monumental expeditions and always had great stories to tell. In reality, most of them were in way over their heads. I fit right in with their rafting program. They ran trips to the New and Gauley Rivers. That first run on the Gauley still lives in club lore.

Some of us had shown up late and had to take our little Sears raft. The older members had all secured spots in the club's big rafts. The club's archives contain a slide of us, upside down and airborne at Pillow Rock, that is still shown at Christmas parties. We swam every rapid on the Gauley that day.

For the next couple of years we made trips to the New River two or three times per summer. We owned two Sears specials—$99 on sale—as well as horse-collar life jackets and wooden canoe paddles. We camped at Fayette Station, where our nighttime activities became legendary.

Once our party was bigger than we could fit into the rafts, so we got a truck inner tube and took turns riding the rapids in the tube. Pretty soon we were fighting over who got to ride in the tube.

The New was perfect for tubing—deep, with few rocks. We rode inside the tube with our feet hanging down and our arms over the sides. It was amazing how the tube caught the deepest current and skirted the holes. Not that we knew what a hole was. We'd learned that there were rapids named Keeneys and Greyhound. These were places where we could count on having fun, usually outside the raft. Occasionally we would encounter a commercial raft trip—the industry was in its infancy then—and the guide would get a troubled look and ask us if we knew what was coming up.

What a sight: two little yellow rafts with four people in each, straddling the tubes, riding the raft like bronc busters. We had lost so many paddles that we began tying ropes from the handles to the raft. Some-

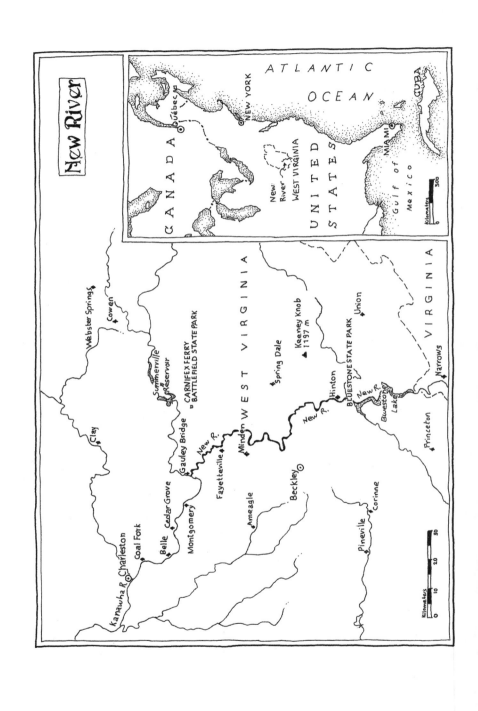

New River

times my dog rode in the front of the raft. The inner tube would tag along behind. Those guides had every reason to be concerned. But there's no doubt in my mind that we had more fun than their customers.

It was about this time, huddled round the campfire and the keg, that I came up with my asinine theory of "whitewater relativity" that can be summed up as "It's only water."

To illustrate the finer points of this theory, I regularly invited my friends with the worst hangovers to join me for a sunrise swim through Fayette Station Rapid (a big-wave class IV). This morning ritual not only broadened our insights into the dynamics of rivers; it also cleared the cobwebs associated with the previous night's debaucheries. I've long since dumped my theory of "whitewater relativity." Knowing what I now know—or even what the greenest whitewater novice knows by heart—it's incredible my theory didn't get us all killed. One time, it nearly did.

It was a dark and stormy weekend in October 1976, exactly one month before my wedding. I was twenty-five. I was madly in love. I was irrational. We were at Summersville Dam.

My bride-to-be and I were having a tough time with my theory of whitewater relativity. It was only water, but it was six inches deep and it was inside my tent. We spent the early morning hours crammed in our VW Bug, writhing in wet sleeping bags. It was raining as hard as I've ever seen it rain and the water was everywhere. Shortly after daybreak I downed a couple of Rolling Rocks and went looking for the other Explorers. I found them at the base of the dam, hypnotized by the sight of the water blowing out of the dam. It had rained four inches overnight, and the lake was overflowing. The water was lapping at the railing above the put-in. The others, who all had come to take on the mighty Gauley, gaped at the flood with respectful awe.

I can't imagine now what I was thinking.

"Where's the rafts? Come on, let's get going."

I was greeted with blank stares and stern admonitions. Not a single other person was even contemplating getting on the river. I had never considered that we wouldn't.

Later that day I formulated a new rule to live by: Never make a life-and-death decision on a morning that your breakfast came from a brewery.

I didn't shove off down the Gauley, by myself, at 15,000 cfs. Instead, I talked some of the Explorers into driving down to look at the New.

At the Fayette Station bridge, twenty miles south, it was still pouring. Our group stood and stared at the New River. The campsite above Fayette Station Rapid was under water. Fayette Station Rapid was gone. The water rushed by at fifty miles per hour, about ten feet below the bridge deck. The painted gauge on the bridge pier was under water.

There was some discussion by the Explorers as to what it would be like to put in on the New at this level. I'm looking at where the take-out rapid, Fayette Station, used to be and arguing that it will all be washed out. Several of the more experienced Explorers kept mentioning *"big holes."* I quoted the theory of whitewater relativity: It's only water.

Final result: Four of us decide to take a Sears special and an inner tube and give it a whirl. Where, you ask, did I find three other maniacs to risk this with me?

Number one: Kitty, my wife. She loves me and has no choice. Number two: Joady, my sister. She trusts me and has a touch of my love of adventure. Number three: Ron, Joady's husband. He loves Joady and has no choice.

Now we're rolling. We load the gear and head up the road to Fayetteville. These are prebridge days. Halfway up the Gorge Road, we're turned back by a mud slide. I have since made this a rule to live by: When shuttle roads are washed out, the river gods are trying to give you one last warning.

The detour was thirty miles back through Gauley Bridge to Fayetteville. We stopped at a gas station to blow up the raft, then proceeded to Cunard, the put-in.

We donned our heavy two-piece hooded diving suits and primitive life jackets. We also wore cheap plastic helmets. Our paddles were dutifully lashed to the raft. Kitty and I were using homemade paddles that I had crafted in wood shop. I had used a wood canoe paddle for a pattern, lengthened the shaft, and enlarged the blade. For strength I used solid red oak. The paddles were heavy but unbreakable. Each had a hole drilled in the grip, and we knotted a piece of parachute cord long enough for freedom of movement. No one ever considered that the cord was also long enough to strangle someone.

I don't remember any talk about what to expect once we were on the river. We did discuss the possibility that the powerlines below Railroad Rapid might be in the water. We had no contingency plans if they were. We hoisted the raft and began the long descent to the gorge. Our trusty inner tube was in the raft and the raft was on our heads.

If anyone had any reservations about the river, surely we would have turned back when we got to the part of the hill where a colossal mud slide had obliterated the road. We were knee-deep in very unstable mud and rock and could easily have triggered another major avalanche. But I guess the gods were saving us for the river.

The water was so high that the put-in was on the lower road. The river here looked like the ocean—so very, very wide, with huge, smooth waves rushing by. For fifty yards along each bank, trees sprouted up through the current. I realized that whatever happened, it was going to be fast!

I have since paddled countless high-water runs. I was on the Lower Yough the day of the 1985 flood. I paddled the Grand Canyon, the Cheat at ten feet, the Tygart at thirteen feet, the Ottawa in the spring. But this, by a long shot, was the fastest sustained current I can ever remember seeing. In the time it takes to describe this debacle, we were at the take-out. Maybe fifteen minutes.

We jumped on the raft, straddled the tubes, got a good knee grip, and paddled like hell to get out through the trees. Once into the current, everything was smooth sailing. The swells were fifteen feet high and a quarter of a mile long. No need to paddle; we were traveling too fast already. Down past the railroad bridge in three swells—about two minutes.

Luckily we ducked under the powerline, just short of the crest of the wave. A few feet higher and we would have been "wired!"

Having negotiated what I thought would be the only threat on the river, I began a short discourse on how easy this was going to be. Probably even boring. Meanwhile, as we roared around the next bend, there appeared a new feature in the distance, one that none of us had ever seen before. The same smooth swells were visible to the horizon, but then the horizon was fairly abrupt. In the center of the river a spout of water was shooting some thirty feet into the air.

It took a few seconds for this to register. Then Joady piped up with the first rational idea of the day.

"Hey, that looks pretty big. Maybe we better try to get over to the side."

My reaction was less rational. "Just paddle hard. It's only water."

At any rate, we could never have gotten over in the seconds that were left before we crested the lip of that huge caldron of exploding white froth. That instant will be forever etched in our memories, perhaps more in mine, since I was the one responsible for the folly. Looking down forty feet into the bottom of the hydraulic, which stretched from tree line to tree line, there was no doubt in anyone's mind that we were about to die.

I remember thinking, "Now I know what a hole is."

That raft never even slowed down on impact. I think we rode it all the way to the bottom of the river. Suddenly I was being tumbled and cartwheeled through a chaotic mass of foaming and wrenching water.

The force was indescribable. Any resistance was out of the question. This river was going to do what it would to me, and all I could do was submit. I tried to curl into a ball, but centrifugal force kept my limbs splayed.

Suddenly, I was clobbered by a huge flume of water and was carried with it. I tucked into a ball again and the noise faded. The water became black and I was sure that I was on the verge of eternity. I closed my eyes and waited. I was being swept away with such force that I felt like a tiny insect. Finally, my lungs forced me to attempt something. I opened my eyes and for the first time could see light in one direction.

"That must be up!"

I broke into a strong breaststroke and seconds later surfaced. Simultaneously, I began gasping air and surveying the surface for other survivors. The first thing I saw was the raft. It was floating upright about ten feet downstream. A couple of strokes brought me to it, and I managed to flop over the side.

Upstream and off to the right, I spotted the inner tube, and I almost collapsed with relief when I realized that Ron and Kitty were clinging to it. I thought I could see Joady's yellow helmet and orange life vest farther downriver, toward the right shore.

My first job was to get to Kitty and Ron and haul them back into the raft. I grabbed my paddle rope and pulled in a splintered oak shaft. Another rope had nothing at all. All of the paddles were either broken or gone. Being in the raft seemed less than secure. I began hand paddling toward the tube, making very little progress.

Kitty and Ron were about twenty feet away from me when we came to the second hole. This time I recognized what was coming from the signs—another abrupt horizon line, with a spout of water geysering high into the air.

I glanced toward the tube for a second and then, terrified, I threw myself spread-eagle across the raft and grabbed the oarlocks with both hands. I don't know what I thought the raft was going to do, but I was determined not to relinquish those oarlocks. From this position in the raft I wasn't able to see much, but after my experience in the first hole, that suited me fine. I closed my eyes.

I never did let go of those oarlocks. But at some point, not far into my second hole ride, the raft was torn free. The oarlocks were my only connection to reality, and I held them like my life depended on it.

I finally surfaced, spitting up water and sucking in air. Miraculously the tube was right beside me, and I latched on to it. A short distance away I could see the shredded remnants of the raft floating downstream. I had no desire to retrieve it.

Feelings of security are by all means relative. Floating a 70,000 cfs river with two other half-drowned people on an inner tube suddenly felt great. I started yelling for everyone to stroke for shore. We were exhausted and terrified. One more hole would certainly have killed us. Letting go of the tube and swimming would have been easier, but none of us were about to relinquish that tube. We made very slow progress to the right shore, but, thankfully, we made it.

As we crawled up the bank, my first reaction was to collapse. But I was so worried about Joady that I scrambled up to the railroad tracks and started running, scanning the river, and calling. I did this for almost a mile and was despairing of ever seeing my sister again when I rounded a bend and spotted her casually strolling down the tracks.

I couldn't believe it. We had all survived! I should have been overjoyed, but I was overcome with exhaustion. I collapsed right there and began retching. Joady had to help me walk back to Kitty and Ron. She explained that she had surfaced from the hole near the right shore, grabbed a tree, then made it to shore.

I hadn't realized it, but I was the only one to hit the second hole. Kitty and Ron neatly skirted it, close enough to see my terrified face as I plunged in.

We landed less than a half mile from Fayette Station. It had taken us fifteen minutes to get there, most of it spent swimming or hanging on to the inner tube. Later I learned that the big holes that did us in were formed by Whale Rock in Upper Keeney and the undercut in Double 2. I have since paddled the New at fifteen feet and had a close look at each of these holes as I drifted by. At fifteen feet those features look very impressive, but there is no comparison to the way they looked that fateful day from the brink—at more than thirty feet—with more than twice the flow.

What effect did this amazing experience have on us? For a time I had a difficult time finding folks to take rafting. Everybody knew that some, or all of us, should have died that day.

Did whitewater lose its charm? I got a kayak the next summer, which opened up a new chapter in my notorious career of aquatic mis-adventures. Kitty did indeed marry me the next month and has also mastered the kayak. We now have a fifteen-year-old son who has mastered the Upper Yough.

Joady and Ron never got in another raft and try not to think about whitewater. Shortly after our debacle they found God and dedicated their lives to Jesus.

These days I have a deep respect for rivers. Over the years I've been taught many a valuable lesson by these powerful teachers, but that first one remains the most memorable of all.

RUNNING THE AMAZON:
THE ACOBAMBA ABYSS

Joe Kane

S tretching for 4,200 miles, the mighty Amazon River carries a volume *of water unmatched by any river in the world. Located in the northern end of South America, the Amazon flows east from the Peruvian Andes through northern Brazil and eventually spills into the Atlantic Ocean. Though it's known mostly for its awesome deltas the Amazon's upper reaches—and many tributaries—feature massive whitewater previously unrun before the expedition related here. The team started with eleven members, but by the time they reached the Acobamba Abyss only eight remained: Zbigniew (aka Zbysz) Bzdak, Piotr Chmielinski, Tim Biggs, Francois Odendaal, Jerome Truran, Jack Jourgensen, Pierre Van Heerden, and Joe Kane. The adventure began at the headwaters, high in the Peruvian Andes, and continued for six months until the team finally reached the Atlantic. Theirs was a journey of "death-defying encounters: with narco-traffickers and Sendero Luminoso guerillas and nature at its most unforgiving." The following excerpt captures the crux run through the Acobamba Abyss on the Aupurimac River near the source of the Amazon, where the rapids, contained by sheer canyon walls, emerge like a charging army, relentless and wrathful, one after another. It is clear from the following excerpt why Joe Kane's* Running the Amazon *became a best seller.*

✦   ✦   ✦

Below us lay three bad rapids, a short stretch of calm water, and then, where the gorge suddenly narrowed, a single, twenty-foot-wide chute through which the whole frustrated Apurimac poured in unheeding

217

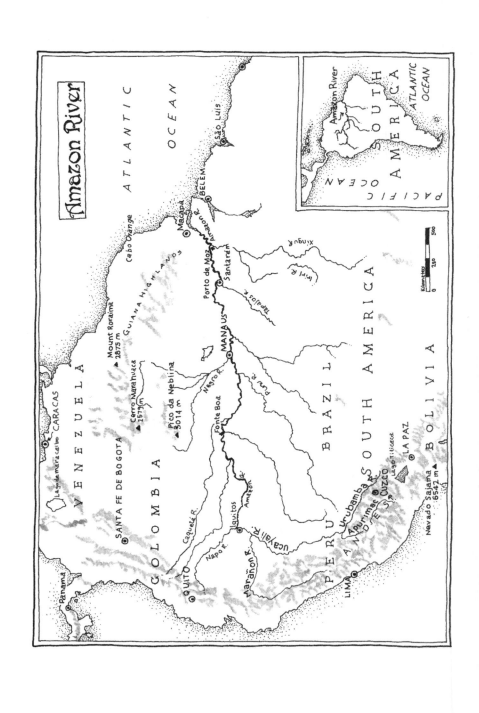

rage. The river was whipped so white over the next half mile that it looked like a snowfield. The thrashing cascades raised a dense mist, rendering the dark canyon cold and clammy. Their roar made my head ache.

"You swim in that," Bzdak shouted in my ear, "you don't get out!"

But the gorge walls were nearly vertical. We could not portage, we could not climb out, we could not pitch camp. Even had we found a relatively flat area, as the gorge cooled through the night boulders would pop out of the ramparts. The rock shower would be deadly.

We had no choice but to attempt to line the raft, a tedious, nerve-racking procedure in which we sent the raft downriver unmanned at the end of Chmielinski's 150-foot climbing rope—a length at a time.

While I stood on a boulder on the left bank and held the Riken in place by a short, thin line tied to its stern, the two Poles affixed the heavy climbing rope to the bow and worked downstream with it as far as they could. At Chmielinski's signal I dropped my line and kicked the raft into the first rapid. Within seconds the boat was hurtling through the rapid at what must have been twenty knots, leaping wildly. I shuddered when I imagined riding it.

In the middle of the second rapid, the raft flipped. As it passed the Poles, half the bowline snagged underwater, tautened, and, though rated with an "impact force" of more than a ton, snapped as if it were mere sewing thread.

Unleashed, the raft sped down the river. Truran, who had run the first rapid in his kayak, was waiting on a boulder near the calm water above the terrible chute. When he saw the raft break free, he dove into the river, swam for the raft as it drifted toward the chute, and managed briefly to deflect it from its course. He scrambled aboard, and as the raft accelerated toward the chute he caught a rescue line thrown like a football by Chmielinski. The Pole arrested the raft as it teetered on the chute's lip and slowly hauled Truran back from the edge of disaster. (Chmielinski later described Truran's effort as one of the bravest he had seen on a river.)

Draining as all that was, we still had to get the boat through the chute, somehow hold it to the wall and board it, and then run the ugly water below. The lower rapid could not be scouted. We could only hope that it held no surprises—no waterfalls, no deadly holes.

Jourgensen and Van Heerden slowly worked their way down to the chute, creeping along the boulders that sat at the foot of the gorge's left wall. When they arrived, Chmielinski told them to rest. Then he and Truran anchored the raft with the stem line while Bzdak took the bowline, now shorter by some forty feet, and climbed hand over hand up the two-story boulder that formed the chute's left gate. From the boulder Bzdak then climbed to a foot-wide ledge that ran along the left wall.

At Chmielinski's command I followed Bzdak. I ascended the boulder easily enough, but negotiating the wet, slick wall was something else. It was so sheer that I couldn't find a solid grip, and I quickly developed what rock climbers call "sewing-machine legs," an uncontrollable, fear-induced, pistonlike shaking. I felt cut off and alone. One misstep and I was in the river, which now churned angrily fifteen feet straight below.

Bzdak stopped on the ledge three feet in front of me and looked back. He shouted to me, but I couldn't hear him above the river's tumult. He inched his way back and put his head next to mine.

"Don't look down!"

We wormed along the ledge until we could lower ourselves onto a one-foot-square rock at the base of the wall and a few feet in front of the gate boulder. We squeezed onto that small rock, each of us with one foot on it and one in the air, and braced ourselves as best we could, trying all the while to ignore the exploding river next to us.

Bzdak twirled the climbing rope up off the top of the gate boulder and tugged on it, signaling Chmielinski to send the raft. I wrapped my arms around Bzdak's waist and leaned back like a counterweight. The raft vaulted the chute. Hand over hand, Bzdak reeled in slack line as fast as he could. I tensed, anticipating the jolt we were about to receive. The raft approached us, shot past, and *boom!* the line straightened and stretched, the raft hurtled down the rapid. I tried to calibrate my backward lean.

"Hold me, José!"

I couldn't. We were going in.

Yet somehow Bzdak was hauling the raft toward us, fighting it home inch by inch. Then the line was in my hands and he was in the raft, tearing a paddle loose from beneath the center net. The raft smashed up against the left wall. The river pounded through the chute, curled into the raft, knocked Bzdak flat, and buried him.

Trying to hold the raft was like pulling against a tractor. I couldn't do it. But the raft bailed itself quickly, and Bzdak rose from the floor and paddled toward the rock. When he was five feet away he leapt for it. How he managed to land on that tiny space I do not know, but we made our stand there, anchoring the bucking raft from what seemed like the head of a pin.

We watched Van Heerden help a ghost-white Jourgensen over the boulder and along the wall, then down the wall into the raft. The two men took up positions in the front of the raft. Then Chmielinski climbed over the gate boulder with . . .

. . . I read Bzdak's lips: "Shit!"

. . . Odendaal's kayak.

Its owner appeared behind Chmielinski and stared at us. Chmielinski took aim and shoved the kayak down the boulder's face, dead on into the center of the lurching raft. Then he signaled me into the raft, but the rope had sawed my hands to bloody pulp and I couldn't uncurl them. Bzdak shook the rope loose. I dove the five feet from the wall to the raft and crawled to the left rear. Chmielinski worked his way down the wall and took Bzdak's spot. Bzdak jumped into the raft. With Jourgensen squeezed between them, he and Van Heerden got their paddles ready up front. I reached beneath the center net and yanked out a paddle for me and one for Chmielinski.

"What are we doing?" I yelled to Chmielinski.

He yelled back, "Francois goes alone, he dies!"

Biggs and Truran had managed to traverse the river above the chute and sneak down the far side of the rapid, but it was too risky for Odendaal. Were he to make a single mistake during the traverse he would plunge through the chute and into what we could now see was a deadly hole a few feet below it. Instead, Chmielinski intended to mount Odendaal and his kayak on the raft and run the rapid.

Chmielinski had tried that strategy with an overwhelmed kayaker once before, in Colca Canyon. Like Odendaal's, that kayak had been almost as long as the raft, and with it strapped over the center net the wildly top-heavy raft had flipped moments after it entered the rapid. Everyone had taken a bad swim, Bzdak the worst of his life. If that happened here, we would drown in the hole. But Chmielinski reasoned that it was better that six men risk their lives than that one be condemned to a near certain death.

I looked up at Odendaal, standing atop the boulder. His eyes were frozen. He looked paralyzed. I knew the feeling.Chmielinski screamed at Odendaal. He inched his way to the raft and into it and mounted himself spread-eagle on top of his kayak, facing to the rear.

"Squeeze on that kayak like it is your life!" Chmielinski yelled.

Chmielinski could not hold Odendaal's added weight. He leapt and landed in the raft as it bucked away from the wall. Seconds later, even before I could thrust Chmielinski's paddle at him, we were sucked into the heart of the current. With Chmielinski screaming at the top of his lungs—"*LeftLeftLeft!*"—we managed to turn hard and get the nose of the boat heading downstream. We skirted the ugly hole, but it shoved the raft sideways. We found ourselves bearing down on a "stopper" rock no one had seen, a rock that would upend us if we hit it.

Chmielinski screamed, "*RightRightRight!*" and we were sideways, then "*InInIn!*" a steering command intended for me, and I hung far to my left and chopped down into the water and pulled my paddle straight in toward me so the rear end of the boat swung left and the front end right. Then a wall of water engulfed me and all I saw was white.

Somehow we shot around the stopper rock's left side but we were still sideways in the rapid—"*GoGoGoGo!*"—paddling hard forward and fighting in vain for control, and the river slammed us up against another rock, this one sloping toward us. Chmielinski's side of the raft shot up on the rock, mine lowered to the river coming behind us, the water punched at the low end, drove it into the rock, and stood the raft up on its side, teetering—"*UpUpUpUpUp!*"—and I fought to climb the high side, to push it back down with my weight, but Odendaal and his kayak had me blocked and I saw Bzdak trapped the same way on the front end. The water pouring in knocked me off my feet, the boat started to flip—"*GoGoGoGoGo!*"—and all I could do was try to paddle free of the rock digging blindly with my paddle—"*GoGoGoGoGo!*"— and *Boom!* we were free and bouncing off the left gorge wall and then heading straight for the gentle tail at the end of the rapid and the calm flat water beyond.

Just above the rapid's last hundred yards we found an eddy and put Odendaal out of the boat to walk along a sandy bank that ran almost, but not quite, to the end of the rapid. We ran the rest of it, two small chutes, *boom-boom,* and met Truran in the softly purling water below. He pointed overhead to the narrow crack of sky between the gorge walls. Storm clouds were snagged on a dark peak. We had to find a campsite quickly, before the boulder-loosening rain hit.

But Odendaal had run out of walking room and stood stiff as a statue thirty yards upstream of us, at the rapid's tail. Biggs sat in his kayak in an eddy near Odendaal, shouting at him to jump in the rapid and swim. Odendaal refused. The exchange continued for ten, fifteen minutes. Then, as the sky darkened, we all began to yell at the

Afrikaner. He looked up. He slipped. He was in the river. He bounced through the rapid unharmed and Biggs fished him out at the bottom. After we put his kayak on the water Biggs escorted him downstream.

We got lucky—the gorge widened and we found a generous expanse of sandy beach. But after we unloaded our gear, Odendaal lambasted Biggs over the scene at the last rapid, saying that as the expedition leader it was his right to have stood there two hours if he so chose. Disgusted, Biggs walked away and joined the rest of us around the fire. When Chmielinski had dinner ready, Odendaal sat down but did not speak, choosing instead to play Biggs's harmonica softly to himself.

Chmielinski guessed that we had covered barely a mile that day. This was disappointing, but for the time being we relaxed. The storm clouds evaporated and we sat by the fire on that fine beach and watched a star show in the thin opening overhead, the river that short hours before had been a deafening monster now bubbling along tranquilly beside us.

During the morning run on our second day in the Abyss, the gorge walls closed in on us once again, narrowing to perhaps thirty feet. At first this was a shock, but the river ran smooth and fast, and we calmed down. Truran, Biggs, and Odendaal paddled their kayaks ahead of the raft and disappeared around a bend.

Fifteen minutes later a gnawing worry gripped the five of us on the raft. Four hundred feet ahead of us the river appeared simply to stop. The gorge turned left, and the wall that crossed in front of us seemed to swallow the river. We expected to see a white line between the river and the wall, a line of riffles, the tops of rapids. The absence of such riffles suggested a waterfall.

We drifted, tense and uncertain. In the front of the raft Bzdak and Van Heerden shipped their paddles. I used mine as a rudder, keeping the bow pointed downstream while Chmielinski stood up and studied the river before us. After a few minutes he said, "Okay, I see a white line." Then we saw it, too, but it looked strange, too hard and unwavering to be riffles.

Jourgensen, sitting between Chmielinski and me, asked, "What if that line is part of the rock formations on the wall?"

We drifted in silence. After about a minute, Chmielinski said, "Shit!" I had never heard him use the word. "It is a rock formation! To the bank, fast!"

We paddled urgently for the left wall, and when we gained it Bzdak and I dug in the slippery rock for fingerholds. While we held the raft, Chmielinski stood up and tried to determine what lay below the natural dam we assumed we were now approaching.

"This is the thing you are always afraid of," he said. "You cannot go back, you cannot portage, you cannot climb out, the water is dropping away in front of you. Even if that is a waterfall, the only thing we can do is go."

We set off uneasily, no one speaking, all eyes on the water line. Where were the kayakers? Now the river ended fifty, now forty, feet in front of us. We went to the wall again, found a crack, inserted fingers. Chmielinski climbed the crack, but when he was fifteen feet above us he fell, returning to the river in a dark blur that ended with a splash and his red-helmeted head bobbing toward the falls.

Bzdak and I paddled furiously. Van Heerden unclipped a rescue line and threw it downstream. We hauled the raft captain aboard just as we began to shoot over the falls . . . but it was not a waterfall at all, just a long, gentle rapid. Steep—hence no riffle tops—but straight, no boulders, all lazy, harmless waves. And luck.

Then our luck ran out. We reentered pinball country. We lined the raft through a cluster of gargantuan boulders, hour after hour of whipsawing rope, bloody hands, and bruised shins, and at the end of the day had to negotiate an ugly rapid that took an hour to scout and half a minute to run.

Something happened to me in that half minute. The rapid was a tricky one. It had three chutes and a dozen turns, the last around a broad hole. We handled the first two chutes well, but the third had a ten-foot drop—a small waterfall. At the top of that last chute Chmielinski yelled, "*Out!*"—a signal to me to set the raft's nose straight—and I managed two correcting strokes before we hit the chute's left wall.

Then the raft burst through the chute, a wave broke over the top of the raft, I saw nothing but water, and I heard Chmielinski screaming "*OutOutOut!*" I dug with my paddle and managed three more strokes before we hit the edge of the big hole and the force of the currents spinning around the hole jerked the raft and threw me into the center net.

Or had I jumped into the net? I could not honestly tell. The rapid had been a difficult one, that much was clear, and when we completed it Biggs and Truran shouted congratulations to us. Chmielinski was jubilant, beaming, charged with adrenaline. "Perfect," he said as he shook my hand.

I wasn't so sure. I suspected I was beginning to crack.

In general, however, that run buoyed our hopes—perhaps we would break free of the Abyss the next day. There was a good feeling in camp that night, except for my self-doubts and a blowup between Biggs and Odendaal over Odendaal's failure to follow Biggs's instructions in a difficult rapid.

"Tim's in a terrible spot," Truran said to me as we sipped tea before dinner. "He's like a veterinarian injecting his own dog. If Frans drowns, the responsibility is on Tim. People will say to him, you were the river captain, why didn't you take Frans off the water? But Tim really cares for Frans. He wants him to have a good outing, so he's reluctant to send him off. Maybe the lesson in all this is that if you can't do the job yourself, you don't put a friend in charge. You look for someone impartial."

That night Odendaal came to my tent. He was smoking his pipe and seemed pensive and subdued.

"Is my behavior on the river causing you rafters worry?" he asked.

Speaking for myself, I said, I was concerned mainly with running each rapid, with getting through the Abyss alive. He was an afterthought, except when we had to carry him on the raft.

"That's good," he said. "I was afraid . . . well, Tim's being too emotional. I am paddling at my best, but Biggsy is overworried. In a good way, of course. I know he acts as he does because he cares for me."

I said Biggs certainly did appear to care for him. Then he wished me good night.

Thinking about it later, I found his assertion that he was "paddling at my best" surprising. As far as I could tell he was portaging any rapid he could. However, I did not think less of him for this. If anything I admired his prudence, and at times I was envious that he could portage his kayak around many rapids that, with our much bigger raft, we had no choice but to run.

I worked on my notes, but this did not distract me from questioning my own behavior on the river, especially on that last rapid. I had always assumed (without ever really testing that assumption) that the one thing I had control over was my nerve, my ability to act under pressure. Now I wondered if I had misled myself.

We had advanced one mile our first day in the Abyss, two miles the second day. Our third day started off with no more promise. A hard rain had fallen through the night, and by morning the river had risen six inches. Biggs estimated that it had come up 20 percent overnight, from 4,000 cfs to 5,000. We were awake at dawn and on the water by 8:00 A.M. By 11:00 A.M., lining the raft through three unrunnable rapids, we had progressed a grand total of about 400 yards.

And then we encountered a chute almost identical to the one at the entrance to the Abyss. The Apurimac compressed to about twenty feet wide, and the walls rose not just vertically but in fact narrowed—the powerful river had cut its gorge faster than gravity could bring the upper ramparts tumbling down. The kayakers found what they called a "sneak" along the right wall, a small chute next to the main chute that was an easy run for them but too small for the raft. Meanwhile, we couldn't scout the rapid and we couldn't line the raft through it.

Once again Bzdak and I climbed the gate boulder, inched along a thin ledge on the left wall, and retrieved the raft after Chmielinski shoved it through the chute. Once again Van Heerden and Jourgensen worked their way down the wall and into the raft. Once again we bore down on a monstrous hole. In fact, it was the biggest hole I'd seen, a gargantuan churning turbine easily thirty feet across, its eye sunk a good five feet below its outer lip. With Chmielinski screaming furiously, we managed to skirt the hole, but as we did I had the distinct impression of it as a demon lurking over my right shoulder.

We shot past the hole, bounced off both walls, and spun clockwise in a circle. With the portly Jourgensen riding on my corner of the raft, we sat low in the water and the river pelted us constantly over the stem. Now, as we spun, he lost his balance and with an assist from the water beating me on the back sent me flying out of the raft. On my way out Chmielinski reached across and jerked me back in.

Just as I got back into position I saw that we were bearing down on Biggs, who was in his kayak, in a tiny eddy right in the middle of the rapid, poised to rescue one of us in the event of a spill. Bzdak screamed a warning, but in the narrow gorge Biggs had nowhere to go—we had come on him too fast. We ran him down, trapped him beneath the raft, and hauled him fifteen yards before his boat popped out, riderless, from beneath ours. Then Chmielinski managed to reach under the raft, grab Biggs by the life jacket, and yank him free, alive but distraught.

We broke for lunch exhausted and demoralized. After five hours of work we had advanced perhaps 800 yards. Food went down hard, because each man felt within his gut a stone of fear and fatigue. To our right, in the east, the sight of snowcapped 21,000-foot Auzangate hovering over the gorge brought little joy, for it reminded us that we were still some 6,000 difficult feet above sea level.

After lunch Chmielinski, Truran, and I scouted downriver and discovered our worst rapids yet. Four thundering drops, each at least 200 yards long, with so much whitewater that at first they appeared to be one continuous froth.

Bzdak joined us on the rock and appraised the river. "What do you think?" I asked. He turned to me. "Whatever you do, keep paddling. Keep control of the raft. And do not swim!"

He and I climbed back to the raft and sat on it, waiting for Chmielinski. From utter emotional exhaustion I fell asleep and awoke to Chmielinski splashing water in my face. He ordered Van Heerden to accompany Biggs, Truran, and Odendaal, who had found a portage route too tight for the raft but adequate for their kayaks. The cover was that Van Heerden could film the rapid. The reality was that by now Chmielinski did not trust Van Heerden. The Afrikaner would not respond to Chmielinski's commands, and his habit of smoking on the raft, and of tossing the empty cigarette packages in the river, had already led to harsh words between the two.

After the kayakers and Van Heerden left, Chmielinski said to Bzdak, Jourgensen, and me, "Okay, guys, looks good. All we do is keep straight in the top chute." He paused. "If you swim, try to go to the right." I had never heard him suggest the possibility of swimming a rapid.

We paddled upstream, turned into the current, maneuvered above the chute, and slowed slightly as we dipped into it. Then the river picked us up and heaved us forward. We were airborne. The only time I had felt a similar sensation was as a teenager, when I had ridden a motorcycle off a small cliff.

The raft hit the water, jackknifed, and spun 180 degrees. We went backward into the Ballroom. Chmielinski and I cracked heads and then I was on my way out of the raft. I grabbed netting as I went over the side.

"Jack!" someone screamed, and for a split second I saw Jourgensen in the heart of the rapid. He was under, up, under again, helpless, his life jacket his only hope, for he could barely swim. His face looked bloodless and frozen, his eyes blank. But he wasn't struggling. It was as if he had resigned himself to the inevitable.

The raft pitched, heaved, scooped me up. Chmielinski lay sprawled across the net and at first I thought the force of our collision had knocked him out. The raft bolted up, then down. Bzdak, standing in the bucking bow like a crazed warrior, reached into the river and with one hand plucked Jourgensen back from eternity. He dropped the big man on the floor of the raft as if he were no heavier than a trout.

Two seconds later we plunged into Milk Shake.

"ForwardForwardForward!" Chmielinski yelled as he scrambled back into paddling position. We paddled hard to try to regain control of the raft, but it was too late. The front right rose and we began to flip. Jourgensen struggled up from the floor, climbed Bzdak's back, and nearly knocked him out of the boat. Bzdak wrestled him off and threw himself at the high side with Chmielinski. The raft leveled for a moment, then started to spin left to right.

"Switch!" Chmielinski yelled. That was a new one. He and I turned on the tubes and became front men, Bzdak the lone driver.

We handled the third rapid, Liquidizer, but lurched out of control as we tumbled over a short waterfall into Dead Man. We bounced off the left wall, hit a rock, spun a three-sixty, hit the right wall—and somehow ricocheted right across the hole. I got one terrifying glance at its ugly swirling eye, and then we shot into the calm water below it.

We paddled to some boulders along the right bank, climbed out of the raft, and sat in silence. You could almost hear the nerves jangling. Then Bzdak said, slowly, "Those were the biggest holes I have ever run."

Chmielinski agreed but didn't elaborate, which was unusual for him. Jourgensen said nothing, but with shaky hands tried to light his pipe. After a while Bzdak said, "We call that Wet Pipe Rapid, Jackie."

And then the laughter started, nervous titters at first, then low howls, then wild insane roaring.

Having once again advanced but a mile over the course of an entire day on the river, we finally began to understand how long a distance forty miles could be. On flat land you could walk that far in two days. We might well need two weeks to travel it on water. We resigned ourselves to a long haul.

That night Chmielinski instructed me to cut our already lean rations by half. We would fill out the cookpot with our one surplus ingredient, water. Nobody was happy with this, but none opposed it.

As bats wheeled above us we ate a thin gruel—three packages of space-age chili, one package of powdered soup, water, water, water, eight bowls—then huddled on a granite slab along the river, watching the stars in the slit overhead, following them down to the top of the gorge wall, which in turn was lit up with fireflies. It seemed as if the stars fell right to the river.

"I don't think I've ever seen a more brilliant canyon," Tim Biggs said. Grunts along the rock affirmed that all shared his thought. We were scared and tired, but those emotions concentrated our attention, told us that we were in a sacred place, a place untouched by humans and perhaps, until then, unseen.

"Rivers have their own language," Truran said. "Their own culture. We're not in Peru. We're in a place that speaks in eddies and currents, drops and chutes and pools. So we only made a mile today. Can you think of a finer mile?"

I walked back to my tent and worked on my notes. An hour later, when I crawled into my sleeping bag, I heard the heavy breathing of Jack Jourgensen, who had pitched his tent near mine. I could not forget the look on his face that afternoon when he'd fallen into the rapid, the blankness of it, the resignation.

Jourgensen was nearly fifty-two—and at a crossroads. He'd been reading Leo Buscaglia's *Personhood* and wondering, as he put it, "What does it mean to get in touch with the world and yourself?" He wanted to be more than a man who got rich selling highway paint. His presence on the Apurimac said he was a filmmaker, an explorer, an adventurer—"Viking" was the word he liked to use in the diary he kept for his seven children, the youngest of whom, Leif, was only five months old.

I think all of us were inspired by the fact that Jourgensen would attempt a journey that scared the wits out of men two decades younger and in much better condition, but I know that I, for one, felt guilty about his being there. The cold truth was that he did not belong on the river. He was overweight, with a degenerating disc, arthritic hips, and a history of gout, and the swimming and climbing taxed him much more than it did the rest of us. Back home, he had a huge family depending on him. Yet in Cuzco, when our expedition doctor, Durrant, had said that she considered it imprudent to allow him on the raft—"What will you do if he breaks a leg, or has a heart attack? You could kill him trying to get him out of the canyon"—no one had responded. No one had wanted to lose the golden goose.

I slept fitfully that night, my body bruised from the bad rapids. At first light I got up and checked the food bags for mildew. Bzdak was up, too, on breakfast duty. He made a pot of instant coffee and poured me a cup, although anticipation of the impending confrontation with the Apurimac already had my stomach in knots. We ladled the rest of the coffee into cups and distributed them to the tents.

"Bzdak," I said when we had finished, "if we have another rapid like those ones yesterday, will you run it?"

"If there is no choice. Otherwise, no. What if someone breaks his leg? No way out. We put him to the raft and keep pushing. Not so good."

That morning the river's gradient increased, and supported by the rain that had fallen over the last three days, the water rose another six inches and grew more volatile. We encountered rapid after rapid that was off the scale of difficulty—class VIs. For five straight hours the kayakers portaged and we worked the raft downriver on the end of Chmielinski's mountain-climbing rope.

This time, however, Chmielinski added a new twist to the lining procedure. He directed Bzdak to ride the raft and paddle it as we tethered him from shore. Chmielinski provided the bulk of the brains and muscle, but it was Bzdak who took the brunt of the risk. These were rapids a man could not swim and survive. The velocity of the water, let alone the rocks and boulders into which it would drive one, would crush a skull as easily as an eggshell. Yet all Chmielinski had to say was, "Bzdak, go there," and point to a boulder in the middle of the river or to an eddy far downstream, and Bzdak was in the raft and flying, with no more response than a hand signal to ask, "At which eddy should I stop?"

During six years in some of the wildest, most unforgiving places in the Western Hemisphere, these two disparate men had learned to depend on each other utterly. Despite the terrible risks they were running, despite our dire straits, it was wonderful to watch them work the precious raft down the beastly river. The only sign of the tremendous emotional pressure they were under was an occasional frenzied exchange in Polish.

By the afternoon of our fourth day in the Abyss (and our sixth since leaving Cunyac Bridge), Bzdak was exhausted. His eyes were red and puffy and his paddle responded too slowly to the raging water. I felt I should spell him on the raft, but Chmielinski would not hear of it. "This is a special thing between me and Zbysz," he said. "We have many years together. It is correct for me to ask him to go, but not to ask you."

Chmielinski's reply came as a relief. I was more than grateful to scramble along the boulders behind him, hauling in slack line, paying out line as the raft took off, anchoring him so the speeding raft did not drag him into the river. I preferred the feel of rock under my feet, for by now fear of the river dominated my thoughts. My nerves were so raw from the whitewater that each afternoon, when the word came down that we were stopping to make camp, a wave of gratitude, of recognition that I had survived one more day, washed over me with a feeling that was palpable—it felt as if my body, one big knot of fear the day through, had suddenly come untied. The simple act of sipping my evening cup of coffee gave me immense pleasure.

Part of my fear was due to the fact that I could not get comfortable on the raft, which was packed in such a way that the nonpaddling man, either Jourgensen or Van Heerden, was crammed into my left rear quadrant. When Jourgensen rode next to me, weighing down our corner of the boat, I always felt that I was about to be pitched into the river. Van Heerden rode in back when he wanted to film and jumped around constantly. Once, as we bounced through a rapid, he hit me with his camera, knocking me out of the boat and stamping my right temple with a wound that quickly turned purple. The tiny Riken, the agent of my salvation, of my deliverance through the terrible river, now seemed dangerously overburdened.

In all, it appeared that we might never escape the Abyss, that it would never end. There was simply no flat water. It was rapid after rapid, mile after mile, driven by what Joseph Conrad described as nature's "sinister violence of intention—that indefinable something . . . in unheralded cruelty that means to tear out of [a man] all he has seen, known, loved, enjoyed or hated . . . which means to sweep the whole precious world utterly away from his sight by the simple and appalling act of taking his life."

"What do you think, Tim?" I asked Biggs later that day.

"I don't know, mate," he said. "But I'd be lying if I didn't say the river had me a bit scared."

Rainy season had begun in the high Andes. Influenced by tributaries miles above us, the river changed color daily. At times she appeared a coffee-and-cream brown, at others emerald green, still others a glacial gray. In the early evening she might run smooth and unthreatening past the camp, yet by morning, having come up a foot during the night, be thundering and powerful. In some places she was studded with three- and four-story boulders, in others her banks were packed with crushed gravel. Given these changes in mood, in appearance, it was impossible not to think of the river as having a will and intent of her own. In the end, however, it was sound, a voice, that most gave her life—she roared as she charged through her canyon. She seemed not only willful but demonic, bent on the simple act of drowning us. You could shout at her, curse her, plead with her, all to the same effect: nothing. She barreled on indifferent, unrelenting.

And so, inevitably, we turned our frustrations inward. On the river a shouted instruction might end as a yell and a grumbled epithet. In easier times, choice tent sites had been shared or left for another; now, as soon as we found a camp each man scrambled for the best land. Food was eyed greedily and served in strict portions.

In the Abyss the competition between Chmielinski and Odendaal festered into open hostility. The Afrikaner's insecurity over his titular role as expedition leader manifested itself as a kind of delight when the Chmielinski-led raft encountered trouble. This attitude, though hardly admirable, was understandable. Several times a day Truran, Biggs, and the raft team would run rapids that Odendaal couldn't, and his solitary portages seemed to set him apart, to isolate him.

Chmielinski, for his part, had no respect for Odendaal as a riverman and did not go out of his way to hide his disdain. "He is afraid of the water," he would mutter on the raft as he watched Odendaal portage yet another rapid he considered easily runnable. He did not regard Odendaal as his equal, let alone his superior, in any way.

At the end of our fourth day in the abyss, when it appeared that both Odendaal and the raft team would have to make a long portage, Odendaal's face cracked in satisfaction. "I'll be in camp two hours ahead of you!" he said and laughed. Then he clambered up a boulder, hauled his kayak after him, and set off.

This goading was more than Chmielinski could stand, for the raft carried all of Odendaal's food and most of his gear. After the Pole scouted the route, we portaged the food and equipment bags downstream in three backbreaking trips, heaving them up and over boulders and nursing them along jagged crags. Odendaal did not see us and did not know that we had managed to put the lightened raft on the river instead of portaging it.

Kayaking downriver ahead of us, Biggs had found a tiny cave with a soft, sandy floor. We reached this camp well ahead of Odendaal. He looked shocked when he arrived and without a word left to set up his tent.

The next morning I awoke to the sound of Odendaal's voice at Biggs's tent, which was pitched near mine. Odendaal wanted Biggs, the river captain, to command Chmielinski to deflate the raft and portage it over the next few kilometers. This, he argued, would be faster than lining. Biggs was noncommittal.

On the face of it, Odendaal's was a strange bit of logic. We lined the raft much faster than we could portage it, and as we had demonstrated the day before, we portaged our equipment and lined the lightened raft faster than Odendaal portaged his kayak.

However, if it came down to portaging the raft without the option of lining—if we deflated the raft—Odendaal would certainly move faster than we. And for Chmielinski, there was a world of symbolic difference between carrying a deflated raft overland and working an inflated one down the river. Deflating the raft would be humiliating, an admission of defeat.

Biggs fetched Chmielinski, who had a mumbled exchange with Odendaal that quickly escalated into a shouting match. Chmielinski told Odendaal that he knew nothing about whitewater. Odendaal threatened to throw Chmielinski off the expedition at Cachora.

I left then and went to the cave. Truran was making coffee. "If anyone goes at Cachora it should be Francois," he said. He was silent for a moment as he filled my cup, then said, "It's a constant game of one-upmanship with those two. They've got to get over that, or we'll put ourselves in even more danger than we already are.

Chmielinski did not deflate the raft, but that morning, as we attempted to line it through a rapid, it lunged around a boulder and pulled up short, teetering on its nose. Using one of our rescue lines, Bzdak, Truran, and I lowered Chmielinski thirty feet down the boulder's face. He freed the raft by slashing the snagged climbing rope, but the rope then ricocheted into aquatic oblivion. Suddenly, all we had left in the way of rope was our five short, thin rescue lines, which were dangerously frayed from overuse. Soon, unable to line the raft, we would be forced to portage. It would be slow, difficult, nasty work.

By lunch we had not advanced 500 yards. Chmielinski sat by himself and spoke to no one.

Unbelievably, that afternoon the rapids got worse. We would fight through a few hundred yards of bad water, lining some rapids, running others, but always hoping that beyond the next bend we'd find a calm, clear stretch. Then we'd peek around the bend and think, "This is getting ridiculous." The rapids only got bigger, meaner, and longer.

Late in the afternoon we faced yet another monstrous rapid around which we could not portage the Riken. Chmielinski picked a rafting route, and then, in an attempt at conciliation, consulted with Biggs and Odendaal, who concurred. "You'll do well," Odendaal said to us as he set off to portage his kayak along a thin ledge on the canyon's left wall. Biggs agreed: "You've run much worse." He and Truran shouldered their boats and went with Odendaal, and Chmielinski instructed Jourgensen to follow them. (He feared that Jourgensen's next swim would be his last.) Bzdak, Van Heerden, and I waited for Truran to reach the bottom of the rapid and position himself to rescue us. Then we took up our paddles.

No one had read the current moving left to right just beneath the top of the rapid. I'm not exactly sure what happened when we hit it. One moment I was in the boat, the next all was darkness and silence. I grabbed for what I thought was the raft and got river. The water grew cold, colder, frigid. I tried to swim, but I couldn't tell if I was going up or down, and in any case my flimsy strokes were useless against the powerful current. Something squeezed the wind out of me like a giant fist. Again I tried to swim, searching for light, and again I was dragged down and flipped over and over and over.

I had taken some bad swims before, but this one was different. In a moment of surprising peace and clarity I understood that I was drowning. I grew angry. Then I quit. I knew that it was my time to die.

Suddenly, as if rejecting such sorry sport, the river released her grip. I saw light. Kick. Pull. Pull toward the light. A lungful of water. Pull.

Air!

Then the river sucked me back down again. Blackness, tumbling, head crashing off rocks.

Air!

Light!

I surfaced to find the gorge wall hurtling past me. I hit a rock, snagged for a second, and managed to thrust my head out of the water long enough to spot Truran in his kayak at the foot of the rapid, holding in an eddy.

"Swim!" he yelled.

A blast in the back and I was in again. Everything went black. I sucked water up my nose and into my lungs. I bounced off something hard and surfaced next to Truran.

"Grab my waist!" he shouted. I wiggled onto the stern of his kayak and clamped my arms around him. He deposited me near a sandy bank on the river's left side and told me to wait there.

I knelt in the sand and puked. When Truran returned, I waded into the river, stopped, and turned back to shore.

"Get in the water!" he yelled. "Now!"

Then we were in the rapid, and I was hugging him with whatever strength I had left, and the river was beating over me, as if angry she had not claimed me. Long minutes later I stood at the foot of the gorge's right-hand wall.

Van Heerden was smoking a cigarette rapidly and shaking. Chmielinski looked at me as if at a ghost. When the raft had flipped, the alert Poles had grabbed onto it again immediately and been yanked from the hole. Van Heerden had been tossed clear and driven toward a flat-faced boulder. The river went directly under the boulder. If Van Heerden had gone with it he would have been shoved under the boulder and killed, but as he was about to hit it, Truran, scouting in his kayak, had yelled to him. Van Heerden had turned and reached for the raft, which was trailing him. The raft had slammed into the wall and pinned him. Van Heerden had been sucked under, but Chmielinski had managed to grab a hand, and Bzdak his head. When the raft bounced off the wall they wrestled him free. They assumed I had gone under ahead of him.

Chmielinski said, "Guys, in the boat." Either we got right back in or maybe we would never have the nerve to get in it again.

It was dark when we made camp, on tiny patches of sand hidden among boulders. We managed to eat about half our thin dinner before Truran accidentally upended the cookpot. No one spoke, except Chmielinski, to announce that we had advanced all of one mile that day.

Cold, hungry, and scared, I doubted whether I, or any of us, would survive the Abyss. And though I knew it was self-pity, I resented the fact that everyone in that sad little camp but me had at least one partner with him, someone who would have to face family and friends and say, "This is how he died."

The skies opened up and rain fell hard. We bolted for our tents. I hurried into mine, lit a candle, and stared at it until it had burned almost all the way down. When I blew it out the darkness terrified me—it reminded me of the darkness inside the river. I searched frantically for matches and burned two more candles one after another. I lit a fourth, my last. When it burned out I lay awake in the dark, eyes open, and felt my body tumbling, tumbling, tumbling.

CAUGHT UP IN A HELL OF WHITEWATER

by Walt Blackadar

*W*ith the first ascent of Everest in 1953, Tenzing Norgay and *Edmund Hillary climbed into a mythical realm of achievement and experience. Successive generations would refine the style of ascent, but the venue itself was the biggest nature had to offer and could never be topped on this earth. Kayakers first paddled into their own mythical realm in the early '70s, when a handful of boaters successfully ran some of the biggest and wildest rivers on the planet. At the leading edge of this bold new breed was Walt Blackadar, a transplanted eastern physician living in Salmon, Idaho. Like Norgay and Hillary, Blackadar was less a technical genius and more a visionary with the courage to challenge psychological barriers in search of the physical limit—a limit Blackadar passed, at the remarkable age of 49, with his solo first descent of Alaska's mighty Alsek River, a feat which ranks amongst the greatest coups in the history of adventuring. Author Ron Watters, in his biography of Blackadar* Never Turn Back, *wrote that the Alsek would "in time represent the Everest of the whitewater world. It took years of probing Everest with teams before it was climbed, and then decades of team ascents before it was climbed solo. Walt Blackadar made the first ascent of whitewater's Everest, and he made the ascent alone."*

‡   ‡   ‡

(Original introduction to article, Sports Illustrated, 1972)
The Alsek River flows in a torrent into the Gulf of Alaska. So fierce are its whitewater rapids and so menacing the huge icebergs that break

away from glaciers along its banks that no man had ever run the river in a boat. There were reports of an especially treacherous gorge named Turn Back Canyon with 300- to 1,000-foot vertical granite walls, numerous waterfalls, and dizzying whirlpools. The water was flowing at 50,000 cubic feet per second. In comparison, the mighty Colorado, the ultimate in whitewater rivers of the continental U.S., moves through the Grand Canyon at 10,000 to 20,000 cubic feet per second. The run entailed many worst-case scenarios and went far in confirming the Blackadar legend. What follows are Blackadar's journal entries.

‡   ‡   ‡

August 13
My birthday—49! Looked in the mirror and realized I wasn't getting any younger. Decided to paddle the Alsek alone, though it is against sanity and all safety codes. I've tried for six months to get others to join me. I'm not suicidal but get depressed watching so many patients with incurable diseases. Take-off date next Thursday.

August 19
Busy week. A close friend, who is a former national kayak champion, phoned from Boston this morning and gave me hell, as has everyone else who knows of my plans. But I'm going anyway. Took out a two-week accident policy for $50,000, which would pay off all my debts and leave a reserve.

August 20
After an all-night drive to Seattle, flew to Juneau and sent my kayak air freight on the same flight. The boat is a Mithril Vector, made of fiberglass and other flexible plastic material; a little over 13 feet long and 23 inches wide. The sea, footrests, and hooks over my thighs are all molded to my body so that I wear the boat rather than sit in it. A watertight spray skirt closes the cockpit around my waist so that no water can enter the boat, even when I'm upside down.

When I reached Juneau, the bow of the kayak was caved in, dented like a Ping-Pong ball. I took two three-pound coffee cans, rammed them forward with a paddle and popped the dent out. There is no visible damage.

I've weighed—in every sense of the word—what I'm taking on this trip: the boat (26 pounds); food (17.5 pounds); sleeping bag (3.5

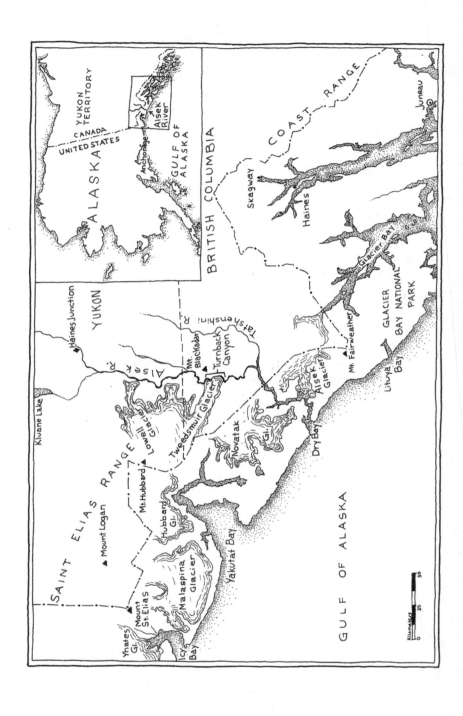

pounds); tent and air mattress (8 pounds); life jacket, clothes, wet suit, and boat repair equipment (14.5 pounds); my 86-inch paddle and take-apart spare (5 pounds); float bags (3 pounds); toilet kit, fishing rod, and two-way radio (7 pounds)—a total of 84.5 pounds. I'm another 175 pounds.

There was a terrible storm in Juneau during the afternoon, but at 5:20 P.M. I was able to take off in a chartered plane piloted by Layton Bennett to overfly the Alsek and examine Turn Back Canyon. We flew over the river between storms, a three-hour round trip. Started flying up the gorge at 500 feet. Then after two trips at 200 feet with the wing tips nearly touching the canyon walls, I called a halt to the low flying. A kayak would be safer.

The severest part of the canyon looks to me shorter than the 12 miles previously reported. I would guess just five miles long. But it's as tough as I imagined. There are two or three good stops for a kayaker, but there is no way to walk the riverbank and scout the worst rapids. There are too many cliffs that are too severe to climb. From the air I saw a way to portage around the toughest spot in the gorge. Also saw several very impressive boiling pots with water spouting 10 to 20 feet high. I think I can avoid these. There is one eight-foot roller wave all the way across the river that will be a sure flip, but I don't believe it will trap a kayak sideways. A roller like this is caused by a ledge that acts as a dam. The water streams down the nearly vertical spillway and, as it meets tur-bulent water at the bottom, a huge wave forms and curls backward like a surfing wave. If a kayak turns sideways and doesn't crash through the crest, it will tumble over and over and be held fast in the wave. There are several sure flips but no holding holes and no danger, unless I swim.

Except in the gorge, there are sandbars all along the river, so I feel I can make a landing field for a rescue plane every five miles if I am stranded. Layton Bennett has told me how to do it. I am not sure of the size of the waves; they look big. I was told there is a waterfall in the canyon. I saw a couple but feel they are runnable. There is nothing in the Grand Canyon, however, with as much violence or power.

I'm glad I'm going solo. I wouldn't want the responsibility had I talked somebody else into making the trip. I know any sensible per-son will say I shouldn't run this river, but it is in my blood. I must prove things to myself.

Now for my plans: the pilot will pick me up at the mouth of the Alsek 10 days after I set out. I think I can paddle the 230 miles downriver (the first 22 miles of the trip will be on the Dezadeash, not the Alsek) in seven days, but I have allowed myself extra time. If I am late, the pilot is authorized to spend $1,000 overflying the river before calling my wife. Should he find something suspicious like a tent, boat on shore, etc. and no sign of me, he will land if possible or send a helicopter. I have left a letter with instructions to spend up to $5,000 to prove me alive or dead, but if my boat is found swamped and there is no sign of me for 14 days, I am dead.

If stranded I will stay with the river—there are enough flat and open places so there's little chance of grizzlies attacking me in camp. If I am found dead, the pilot has been told to bury me there and not bring me home but to take positive identification to my wife.

I feel the gorge is tough but paddlable. The left bank rises 6,000 or 7,000 feet; there is no exit because the terrain slopes up into snow country. The right side is vertical rock, not ice, and about 500 feet high. One can climb out in a couple of places without rope, if necessary.

August 21
A friend took me up the inside passage to Haines, 80 miles northwest of Juneau, in his 50-foot launch. Lovely relaxed trip. I go inland tomorrow to Haines Junction, 150 miles away.

August 22
Got a ride with a schoolteacher in his truck. Checked with the Mounties. They plan to fly a helicopter down the Alsek to the British Columbia junction on August 24 to count game and will check on me.

I am carrying one week of full rations and another week of half fare. The food is all dehydrated but common supermarket stuff—breakfast of dry cereal, powdered milk, and instant coffee. Lunch—dry fruit, nuts, and candy. Supper—Lipton's one-pot meals like ham cheddarton and chicken supreme cooked over an open fire in a coffee can.

Wish I had company through the canyon; after that I'll be glad I have only myself to take care of. Water is clear up here and not too cold. Weather is bad.

Well, I'm off!

August 22, later
Left the road at 7 P.M., after sending the above notes to my wife. Camped at 8:30 P.M., with a headwind of 40 mph and waves at two feet high.

Tent up and flapping. All secure. Boat tied to a tree along with my life jacket. Four big beaver dams. Have seen two of the animals, plus four ducks. In bed by nine.

August 23
Camping in a driving rain. Started fire with four matches and two birthday candles. Cooked beef stroganoff and am sitting in tent eating it now while I dry off. My watch stopped last night so I reset it by the sun. I'll have to guess the time from now on. Today I paddled down the Dezadeash to the Alsek. The current is flowing faster—6 mph. Fished twice with my eight-foot rod. I was hoping for salmon but no strikes— water muddy. One golden eagle, six ducks, a porcupine, and a beaver.
    Rain quit during the night. Slept well.

August 24
Good camp, sheltered by an overhanging bank, but since wind and tent are facing upstream, a grizzly coming from the rear will surprise us both.
    Big water today. No stops needed to scout rapids. Stayed in the center but constant maneuvering necessary to avoid rocks and holes. No flips, but my heart pounded once or twice as I passed cliffs with boils and huge hydraulics—violent currents that twist and turn and grab from all directions at once. The water is now icy, and I can't force myself to practice rolling up and thus psychologically prepare myself for the canyon ahead. I feel a flip would present at least a 30 percent chance of a swim, what with the difficulty of rolling in such water. The water is brown, similar in color to the Grand Canyon. I can still read the water confidently since the crests of the waves are white, but the glacier silt adds power to the rapids.
    Lowell Glacier, off to the right, is tremendous. It is a mile of bright blue ice wall over 100 feet high and extending out into the Alsek, which undercuts the cliff. As I passed, huge blocks of ice two-thirds the size of a football field would crack free from the wall and drop 20 feet to the river bottom, then tip outward and slap the water with a frightening sonic boom. These were followed by tidal waves that tossed earlier ice blocks (calves) and my fragile kayak sky high. Fortunately, I never was within 200 yards of an ice fall and tried to stay in the open so I could maneuver the waves. An active glacier is an amazing spectacle. And I've got three more ahead!

Became lost in the floating calves but continued on to the end of the iceberg lake, where the river turned abruptly. Must have paddled over 50 miles today so quit early but could have gone all the way to Turn Back Canyon, where the worst rapids begin. Plan to sleep late in the morning and proceed gradually, but if I get to the canyon before 2 P.M. I'll tackle it then; otherwise, will rest until noon the next day. I have been paddling in my full wetsuit, including boots and gloves, but nothing to keep my head warm, only my regular protective helmet. I want to remove my gloves in the gorge, if the icy water is not unbearable, so that I can grip the paddle more firmly. I'm three days ahead of schedule and going strong—very relaxed. My 25 ounces of vodka will see me home with spare. Am less tense being alone. In a kayak I never rely on others to get me out of trouble, so I wear a 33-pound floatation life jacket. Water that can separate me from my boat would be so big no other kayaker could help. He'd be too busy staying up himself.

I have matches and emergency supplies sewn into my life jacket. No sign of the helicopter, perhaps because I have traveled so fast. Saw two golden eagles and a friendly shorebird fatter than a tern—small beak, gray-brown with a banded tail.

August 25

In the gorge and stranded—almost directly across from a creek that gushes off the mountain on the left, forming a roaring waterfall. My boat is on the bank in the rocks and my tent 100 yards upstream on a sandbar. This has been a day! I want all kayakers to read my words well! The Alsek gorge is unpaddlable! Unbelievable. After carefully scouting the rapids, I found it's twice as bad as it looks. There's one huge horrendous mile of hair (the worst foamy rapids a kayaker can imagine), 30 feet wide, 50,000 cubic feet per second, and a 20-degree downgrade going like hell. Incredible! I didn't flip in that mile or I wouldn't be writing. But to go back:

On entering the canyon I paddled bravely past the last portage on the right and into the gorge. The river narrows from a half mile to 100 feet. I suddenly felt trapped and committed. Stopped on the left after maybe a quarter of a mile and had trouble getting out on the narrow ledge with my long paddle, so I tossed it to a higher shelf where it lodged. Soon found myself in difficulty with the tricky currents and nearly flipped getting out of the kayak, which would have forced me to swim the entire gorge. Once in the water there would have been no way to regain the shore. A swimmer couldn't fight the current and would be swept downriver. Tried to abandon my plans to make a stop but couldn't reach my paddle so struggled out and lifted the boat to the safety of the ledge.

After scouting, I ran the first mile of rapids with tremendous respect—found myself upside down twice. Rolled up easily. Slammed into the cliff once and was pinned there for a lifetime on a tight turn but worked the boat forward and free with my hands–you have to hold the paddle in one and push off the cliff with the other. I'd abandoned the gloves.

Stopped again on the left, this time easily, and scouted for over a mile to a huge 45-degree drop of 30 feet or more into a boiling hell. After looking it over carefully, I decided to carry the kayak on the left. There was a seemingly easy stop and only a 100-yard portage to miss the drop. There are huge icebergs that have calved off Tweedsmuir Glacier and are running with me in the gorge. I have already hit two very hard in big water. Boat O.K. and surviving well.

As I paddled down to the portage stop in apparently quiet water, a whirlpool suddenly appeared, my boat was sucked by the stern into a perfectly vertical position, then whirled one and a half times around and plopped in upside down. I rolled up immediately and easily caught the eddy as planned, but in the wrong place. I was going to have to work my way to the extreme lower end of the eddy to get out. This I hoped to do by going along the shoreline, but I found I couldn't because of the terrific current. Consequently, I had to go out into the main current, but I went too far. Suddenly I realized I couldn't make the portage. Now I knew I had to paddle ahead! Just then an iceberg the size of my bedroom appeared alongside, charging for the drop. I hurriedly turned my boat around and paddled upstream with all my strength while sliding backward into the "falls." Missed the iceberg which went ahead, flipped, and hung upside down while the boat was tossed out of the most violent boils before rolling up. Very solid, very confident in my roll—no question of swimming. I was almost euphoric in my survival and so thrilled I had not had to portage after all, for I knew I would soon be out. Stopped and relaxed for five minutes on the shore among the icebergs. Could not check what was ahead because of a cliff, so continued without scouting.

Suddenly, I was in a frothy mess that was far worse than anything I have ever seen. I don't know how far the hair lasted and would not go back to check if I could, but I am sure it was 20 degrees down with the most gigantic waves and foam and holes on all sides of me. Very narrow—like trying to run down a coiled rattler's back, the rattler striking at me from all sides. I was shoved to the left bank about an inch from the cliff where a foot-wide eddy existed. For perhaps a mile I skidded and swirled and turned down this narrow line. I kept telling myself, "You can roll in this," but all the time I knew I couldn't. I expected to get jammed into the cliff but never touched it. Eventually, I squirted out into a pool right side up and safe, only to flip in another whirlpool before reaching shore.

I scouted on the right bank to what I hoped was the end of the gorge, about a mile below me. But I saw an immense cresting wave blocked the way, the one I had seen seven days before from the air. I checked it from a 500-foot cliff and also worked my way down to the very edge of the river. I had found a way out of the deep canyon, but there was no way I could carry my boat or supplies out on the treacherous path.

After watching the wave I felt the boat would be toppled before it could climb the crest and be tumbled sideways in the trough. My only exit would be a swim under the wave, which would leave me in the middle of the river heading for some rapids below with little chance of reaching shore. If I did, I would be afoot with no supplies since my empty boat would stay sideways in the wave. I considered abandoning everything and walking to a rescue spot but soon told myself I would eventually paddle the wave if I had to watch it for a week.

So I paddled furiously through the easiest spot to crash the roller, which was well to the right of center, accepting the risk of plummeting into a terrible hole some distance below should I fail to roll up in time. Got my paddle and body through the wave and hung on upside down, feeling my boat tear apart above me. Missed my roll and in fact found I was outside the kayak. My first instinct was to swim to the surface, but instead I snuggled back into the overturned boat. Before I could roll up, the kayak washed into the feared hole. I got scrubbed, tumbled, and shaken; rolled and missed—rolled and missed. Finally I caught a breath, calmed my nerves, jammed my knees solidly into the sides of the boat and on my sixth try made a perfect roll and popped up. I found the boat swamped and uncontrollable in the middle of the river. Only the air bladders were keeping it afloat. My body was in water to the armpits, and I was heading for a rapids far worse than Lava Falls (the worst rapids of the Grand Canyon). I made a tremendous effort to force the swamped boat to the shore, using all my reserve. Finally I reached the bank holding onto the kayak by a strap, and as I rolled out on the bank I said thanks. I found that I had torn the left thigh hook off the deck, and part of the deck as well. That had popped the spray skirt and swamped me.

Am trying to dry the boat now and fix it in a drizzle. If I can't fix it I will scout the canyon further, and if there is just the rapids to go, I will have to try it crippled. I'm not coming back. Not for $50,000, not for all the tea in China. Read my words well and don't be a fool. It's unpaddlable.

August 25, later
After finishing all my vodka and feeling better, I have the first fiberglass patch on the boat; I've used one-third of the small bottle of resin that I had for such an emergency. Erected my air mattress over the boat repair to prevent its getting wet. My tent is upstream and cozy. Outside it's about 40 degrees. I found wood for my supper fire. I have solved the riddle of this messy gorge. I flew over it when a huge rain upstream had caused it to crest. I can see the mark on the canyon here 10 feet or so above my sandbar and probably 30 feet above the water level at this time. It might be paddlable at crest, but not now. I started into the gorge at 1 P.M. and ended here on shore at 5 P.M. Total running time was probably only 10 minutes.

Slept well after a tranquilizer and a sleeping pill.

August 26
Second patch placed on the boat in the morning and both hardened well even in the cold. Deck solidly fixed by two P.M. so took off—and what a ride! There was a hole 20 feet deep at the top of the run. It was caused by a rock the size of a two-story house that had about a foot of water flowing over it. The current was sweeping by at 35 to 40 mph, and the entire river seemed to gush into the deep hole behind the rock. I'm glad I didn't drop in. I slipped by the edge but spun around and gushed down the chute backward, crushed into the cliff with my stern but didn't flip. I scouted then for two miles and found nothing else. It's a good thing because I'd had enough.

No more excitement left and I'm thankful. I did flip again in a backward vertical hole—flip no. 7. But though the next five miles of gorge were tough—the river here narrowed to 40 feet—it was nothing like the previous.

Am spending the night relaxing at the base of Vernrighe Glacier and glad I'm out. A large gull-like bird came to visit and stood around looking at me. Saw two big grizzlies today and another just now out my back door. I hope he goes by. The bears have not given me any trouble so far. Most of them I've seen from the safety of my kayak and when I shouted at them they would charge to the water's edge and stand erect. It is truly frightening to see an animal that is 10 feet high and as large as a horse growling at you, even when you know he cannot reach you.

August 27
At Dry Bay, the mouth of the Alsek, I can't find the airfield in the dark. Put up tent on huge grizzly tracks. Worn out, so no fire tonight. Nuts, fruit, candy. Today saw grizzly no. 7, a mountain goat, two bald eagles, 15 ducks. The Alsek Glacier was terrific with a whole string of ocean liners (icebergs) coming down the river.

August 28
Early up and found the local "Hilton." Got through on the radio to Layton Bennett, and he will pick me up this evening in a floatplane and take me to Juneau with my kayak strapped outside. A man from the Alaska Department of Fish and Game flew in to interview me regarding the Alsek. He said the gorge is too fast for salmon, even kings, the only huge river known where the speed of the water stops fish. Usually it's a dam or a falls.

I know the area well! Too well. I won't be coming back. Ever.

A REMINDER

Doug Ammons

Many people throughout the ages have experienced remarkable adventures, yet we are left with comparatively few classic accounts because so few are able to recapture the magic in story form. A writer might touch on the spirit of the venture, paint a thrilling action sequence, impart the shifting inner experience, or supply deft commentary on the nature of being engaged in a challenge where all the marbles are thrown and thrown hard. But rare is the account that combines all these elements, the story that foists our mind, body, and spirit into the heart of the maelstrom. Doug Ammons has accomplished this, and more, in the following story, which, for my money, is a high-water mark in the rich trove of river chronicles. I suspect Doug's passage on the river being "the vessel of all opposites" is destined to become one of the most oft-quoted paragraphs in all of adventure literature.

‡   ‡   ‡

Long before sunrise, the sky is clear—a perfect spring day. It's 5:00 A.M. and I'm driving 300 miles nonstop to the North Fork of the Payette River in Idaho. Up and down three passes and through seven river drainages, the drive is all sharp corners with guardrails and cliffs and overhangs. In the last twenty years I've ripped the rubber off four sets of tires and counted every one of those corners (17,071!) a couple hundred times. But I keep going back because it's the greatest drive in the world to the greatest river in the world, and I'm smiling a smile that just won't stop, high as the sky and flooring it the whole way, barely on the road.

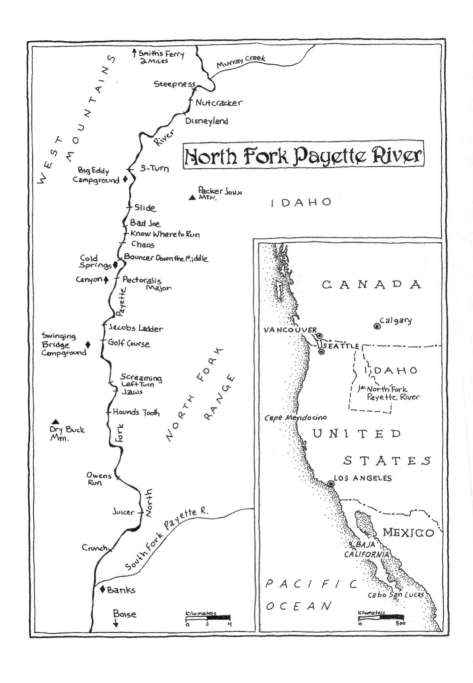

Over Lolo Pass, I'm dodging the deer and one startled bear who is munching clover beside the road. Playing chicken with a moose—I'm the chicken—and watching a beautiful sunrise through the misty fog on the Lochsa River. The water's high and cold and the sun's just up over the mountains, warm through the near-freezing air. I can see my breath when I stop for a few minutes and clamber down through the boulders. A ritual toast to the rivers of the world: "Here's to life!" I shout and drink the icy clean water, mixed from the melting of a hundred winter snows up along the divide. Then it's back up the bank and revving down the road with a spray of gravel, my eyes devouring the early morning. Every river I pass—the Lochsa, the South Fork of the Clearwater, the Salmon and Little Salmon—every damn one is pumping and high, with swells and waves rushing past. And the sky above me is deep blue and beautiful, fringed by ragged trees on the ridgeline.

It's a manic drive, and three hours later when I whip down past the Cascade reservoir, I look over and can see that all the release pipes are gushing full bore. The overflow channel is a solid flume of white shooting hundreds of feet through the air, and below the riverbed is flooded. And then I know for sure—the North Fork's going to be good.

There's an energy in the air as I fly down the highway beside the river. Down into the canyon and over the old cement bridge, peering and trying to guess the flow. What is it? 5,000 cubic feet per second? 6,000? Damn the river's high and raging. We're in for a big-water day. . . .

The North Fork of the Payette is one romp of a river. It cuts a narrow canyon straight south out of the center of Idaho from the mountains around McCall down toward Horseshoe Bend, a little north of Boise. On its way, it falls a good 3,000 feet before reaching dry rolling hills at the bottom, and most of that is in one big plunge from Smith's Ferry to Banks. It's a blue-ribbon thumper I consider the best full-on river running in the world. Ten or fifteen times as steep as the Grand Canyon of the Colorado and a hundred times as wild. To those who know it, there's no need to put a name on it: You know what somebody's talking about when they say "the North Fork."

The railroad hems the river in on one side and the highway hems it in on the other. The river has a naturally narrow riverbed, but when the highway and railway engineers started blasting the granite away with dynamite and rolling big boulders into the water, things got pretty squeezy down there. The sharp boulders look like they could decapitate you if you go upside down, and they can. The river is no more than 40 feet across in some places and it almost seems like you can touch the other side—except what rolls between is a brawling, frothing monster. The dam engineers like to keep the flow down for irrigation in the dry lowlands below, and through the summer you're usually guaranteed a good level—about 1,500 to 2,000 cubic feet per second. That's a level when the riverbed is getting filled and fast, the boulders are covered— sort of—and there's nonstop action with big ledges and breaking waves and holes. You pinball down in your kayak, getting bounced all over the river, and even the best paddlers find it disconcerting. You're not supposed to run a river that way, seat of the pants and blasting along.

At those flows, the rapids are solid class IV+ and V, and I'm talking western style, which means just about any other paddlers in the world would consider it solid class V or worse. For some of the small number of people who run "top to bottoms," the full 15 miles of Smith's Ferry to Banks, it's the pinnacle of their careers. But there's a level far beyond that because once you've been on the river when the water really gets up, you have to redefine what class V means, and normal flows just don't cut it anymore. There's a kind of absurd redefinition of reality in looking at things that way, but what the hell: you have to see it to believe it and that's just the way it is.

About 50 years ago the dam builders did their best to put a bridle on the river, building the Cascade Dam, and another dam way upstream at McCall, right at the headwaters. But there's a limit to the bridles you can put on a river like this, and in the spring when there's lots of snow in the mountains and it starts melting, there isn't much the Bureau of Reclamation can do at the Cascade Dam except open the floodgates and pray.

The highway borders the river the whole way down, and you can scout most of the run from your car. But the thing just goes and goes, and unlike most rivers, you have to take it in big bites so a little scout here or there doesn't do much good. You'll blow by the eddy you thought you could make and be in no-man's land in a heartbeat because the whole river is just one big rapid. Solid white from start to finish—15 miles of huge waves, exploding and mashing water, with the lower five considered manageable, while the upper 10 miles are another world. Every five or six years, when the water starts pumping like it is today, everything hikes up a couple notches, and all but the most serious locals stand on the bank in silence, shake their heads, and then motor off to something more sane.

I meet up with my friend Greg, taking for granted we're going to make a run. Greg's an intellectual who somehow got into paddling a long time ago, a reporter, writer, cabinetmaker, a thoughtful guy who likes a challenge, whether it's shaping a block of wood into a four-drawer dresser or taking on a hell of a river.

We park his car at the bottom and drive mine up the canyon to the top, pointing and comparing assessments of the rapids along the way. Greg and I have run the river many times, but when it rears up like this it's a different and serious animal. If it's class V at the normal flows, when it gets four or five times that much water in it—roughly 6,000 cubic feet per second—you start scratching your head. Is it class VI? Class VII? Class VIII? Who knows? When the river runs like this, at 30 or 35 miles per hour, with 12- to 14-foot breaking waves and freight-car-sized holes, numbers are meaningless. Even at the normal levels around 1,500 cubic feet per second, plenty of paddles are destroyed and boats lost or wrapped around boulders. Hard plastic boats can take a beating. Human flesh doesn't fare as well. There have been countless bones bruised deeply, teeth knocked out, stitches, dislocated shoulders, and several deaths. There would be a lot more carnage except that when the water gets way up the thing looks so damn mean that few choose to tangle with it. But to some of us the beauty is in the power of that river, rolling wild and free.

Greg and I put on at the top and paddle downstream, round the first set of corners and head into Steepness, the first rapid. On a normal river, you come up on a rapid, get out and scout, then run the thing. But here, Steepness begins with a half mile of raging whitewater—totally continuous and huge class V at this level. Exploding waves, shuddering gusts of water as we come down, two Ping-Pong balls whacked from side to side keeping pace with the cars up on the highway.

How to describe it? You close your eyes and feel the thing. It erupts, writhes underneath you, thrashing and punching at your boat. You roll with everything you can and weather anything you can't roll with. When you start out, your reflexes are always behind because everything happens twice as fast as anything you've ever experienced. No matter how quickly you react, the river's always two steps ahead. It's like playing your kid's video game, the one with the realistic 3-D images and the jet motorcycle that goes 150 miles per hour. The world whizzes by at breakneck speed, you hit a ramp and launch 200 feet into the air, hurtling a quarter mile through space, then ripping through the top of a palm tree. Uhhhhgg! That's a taste of what it's like, only the North Fork is real. And the tree isn't some soft-fronded palm, it's a 60-foot-long anvil-hard ponderosa blocking a corner of the river as you pound down straight for the thing, ready to wrap your boat or break your arms, tear your head off, and most assuredly drown you.

People think that all that power and crashing mean you must be aggressive and attack. Not so. The water is the vessel of all opposites, hard but supple, complex and simple, and you can never forget that. You sometimes get carried away by the rush, but you also have to pay close attention to each reminder, because otherwise it'll kill you. It takes a clear head and calm nerves to run a river like this. You can't fight it and can never oppose its power. All that chaotic wildness has to be worked with, smoothly, without hurry. You have to match everything you do to the mood of the water, threading yourself into its strength and beauty. If you do it right, you'll become a part of the flow of Nature herself. You don't conquer or tame that beast, you just try to blend and live with it for a little while because the river always reminds you that Nature's very big and you're very small. But there's never any malice in the water's action. It just is, and it can't be anything different. If you find yourself wishing it were something different, you have more to learn.

Greg and I run Steepness and down through Nutcracker. Then Disneyland, Double S-turn, and Slide, one after the other through the meat of the run. Huge geysering mauling drops that never stop, they just go and go, grade into each other one after the other. It's like a roller coaster crashing down a mangled, broken railway—one endless, massive derailment in action, pounding and shuddering and shaking the ground as you scout carefully along the bank for most of a mile, and then at some point you say, "I know the line," and you get in and become a part of that pounding and shuddering and shaking. It's our element and we're *on*, rapid after rapid. Bad José, Nowhere to Run, Bouncer Down the Middle, Pectoralis Major. After three hours we came to Jacob's Ladder and Golf Course, the crux of the whole run.

Jacob's is a long gradual left turn, one of the narrowest and steepest parts of the river. And the most intimidating. At 6,000 cfs, the water funnels into this flume, and when it hits the first ledges it humps up into exploding waves that break violently and completely across the river, way up into the boulders on the right bank. Miss the move through them and you'll be surfed up into the rocks and ripped to shreds. Below, the river drives down a straightaway at 35 mph to slam into a riverwide hole. If you get through that, it lunges down another huge drop and slams into this *Thing*. You could call this *Thing* a hole, but it looks like the water's gushing out of the earth itself in a huge mounding haystack the size of an eighteen-wheeler. Then, you have a half mile of Golf Course, winding, exploding, with 12-foot-deep holes and logs along the side. Enjoy. . . .

We stand at the bottom of Jacob's Ladder and scout.

"So, what would you call this?" I ask Greg.

Greg rubs his beard and hmmms and then hmmmms some more. Finally he says, "It's class six-plus. The limit of controlled navigability." A pause and another hmmmm. "I guess it might be possible to wash through something harder and survive, but. . . ." He lets the sentence dangle in the air because there isn't much point in finishing it. Then he adds, "I'm not trying it."

He waves toward the end of Golf Course, a long, long way downstream. "I'm putting in at the bottom of the whole thing."

"Well, I'm running," I say. "Watch for me."

Kayaking big water is "free soloing," like rock climbing without a rope. You push out into the current and deal with what's there, come what may. There's this great purity because it's always just a one-shot deal. You get one chance and one chance only and you have to lay your best shit on the line; in water like this it's everything you've got. So all the thinking and pondering have to come before, all the considering of safety and lines and weighing and assessing the moves. You've got to answer the question "Can I do it?" And if you say yes, then you pull into the current and *deal*.

I deal. Down the lead-in to Jacob's, cutting through the huge breaking waves and driving straight into the close-out hole. As I hit, I flatten myself on the deck with my paddle feathered out just a little so it doesn't get ripped out of my hands, and I submarine through. A quick spin back to the left and the river gives me a straight flush into the *Thing*. It's towering over my head and *thwwuuup*, I'm deep deep into the center of it—all froth and I submarine deep deep deep until I shoot out the backside. Then, spinning and cutting and rodeo-ing through all the unbelievable stuff in Golf Course. It just keeps coming and I twist and move with the coiling water. My boat is shot completely into the air again and again, punching through exploding waves cresting 10 feet overhead.

A long way down, after 80 seconds of sheer bizarre *dealing*, I pull the eddy where Greg is, panting with muscles screaming for rest. I bob there, gasping and hanging onto the branch of a tree that had toppled into the water. Greg looks upstream, then back at me.

"Commendable paddling," he says.

"Thanks," I say between pants.

We both know we're through the worst. It's still another 7 miles out of the run's 15, but we're through the hardest by far. We're feeling good, we've handled it well and everything's gone smoothly, and I let down a notch. Another mile and a half downstream, after a well-named rapid called Screaming Left Turn, we eddy out at the top of the Jaws sequence, a long rapid, the river flushing back and forth with turn after turn, piling up on one side gnawing against the rock walls, then up the other side into boulders and over ledges. There's just this one big rapid left, then we're to the lower 5 miles, and big-time class V fun to the take-out.

I've been leading nearly the whole day, paddling more aggressively than Greg. I motion for him to go ahead. He smiles, gives a little nod, and peels out. I wait a few seconds—not long enough—and paddle into the rapid 30 yards behind him.

When you head into a huge rapid, there's always this sense of disbelief. If it's truly monstrous water, the river drops off the face of the earth and all you see is a horizon line of humped-up dark water, and you feel like you're revving your car straight for the edge of a cliff. You come up on it and the whole rapid is somewhere on the other side, unseen, crashing away below and around the corners downstream. All the power of the world seethes underneath you. You feel it welling up and accelerating, pulling at you like a bronco in the stall, muscles tensing, ready for the gate to open and explode. The bronc's will is to break away and not be chained. To fight every limitation and barrier and kick and snort and go like a hellion any way it can. A nasty bronc might have a bad attitude toward you, he might feel those spurs and think and wait and set you up, and then *do* you. But this bronc is liquid and weighs thousands of tons and doesn't think and doesn't care. So you hang on the expectancy as you paddle toward that horizon line. Then you slip over it: The bronc's cut loose and out of the gate.

I follow Greg over the horizon line and suddenly we're hurtling along as fast as a runaway car down a steep mountain, bouncing and slamming and jumping. Great waves launch up before me. Whoosh! Over the top of the wave, the explosion at the crest kicking me out of the air and I balance and fly. For an instant I can see far down the river, then the water shudders with a violent twist and a surge shoves me one way, then lurches up, grabs and rips at my paddle. Greg's far ahead, popping up, then gone. Then I'm up at the top of another wave and Greg pops up, his boat skipping away to the right, and I hunker down and brace because I know that I'm about to hit a big hole. I crest the wave—and there it is—an erupting white wall that I'm instantly jammed into. It's all reflex: I get small, with my head on the deck of the boat and the paddle feathered into the hole, shoulders hunched so they won't dislocate from the force. I dive into the beast. It bucks me wildly and, like Greg, I'm shot, skipping far right across the surface of the water by a wild driving power.

It's wonderful, full on, we're cooking. Then suddenly I'm right on Greg's tail—and shocked we're so close. *Jesus! Get away*, I think, *or he'll hit a hole and my boat will break him in half.* A split-second decision. I spin the boat and try to put some distance between us. Little thoughts fly through my mind, *Get away, get away, backpaddle, spin and stroke clear.*

A big river takes any little thing you give it and hammers you over the head. A wave catches and throws me, kayak and all, 15 feet through the air to the side. I land and the water's nothing but rushing bubbles, gushing into my face and sucking at the paddle. We've still got another long corner before the crux—but anywhere in here I could slam a rock and get hosed, knocked cold, paddle ripped out of my hand. *Get up!* A quick sweep of my paddle, and I'm upright and moving. Then, *damn*, Greg shoots upward out of a hole and right across my path. If I come down on him when he's caught, I'll either kill him with my boat or he'll kill me.

I'm backpaddling again, trying to get clear, but the river is pounding down around the corner just above the crux. We have to get right—the whole left side plunges over a big ledge into this nasty, bullshit place we call the Dome Hole, one of the biggest holes on the river. I spin back right and start making my move, but out of nowhere Greg shoots in front of me again and I backpaddle to get away. Another wave explodes underneath me and I'm airborne, flying upside down way to the left. I land head down, immediately start rolling, then I'm *crushed* into a rock. Stars explode in front of my eyes and this huge, sharp cracking pain explodes in my head and shoulders and back as my body's mashed around a sharp rock cutting the water like the prow of a ship. For an instant I can feel the water crumpling me against the rock and my head's filled with lights and exploding pain and then I wash free, stunned and seeing stars with a sharp metallic taste filling my mouth.

I'm hurt bad, and know it. The water's washboarding across a shelf of boulders, piling along and slamming into every one. The line's over to the far right, and I'm way left and hurt and I know the Dome Hole is just downstream. My mind screams, *It's shallow, shallow, shallow, you'll hit again. Get up!* I crank up a roll and pain pierces my neck, shoulders, and back, and I'm just upright as my knuckles rip across the top of another boulder, tearing the skin off the back of my hand. I'm looking down at the blood sprouting bright red from the knuckles and bone but I don't have time for any of that, *No time, no time, get back right.*

The river's turning to the right and the water's piling high up onto the left bank, waves are breaking onto me and won't let me turn. I've got 40 yards, just a couple seconds to move right. I sweep hard to spin the boat. A lightning bolt of pain stabs at my head and neck and I gasp at the sharp grating of bone on bone. I sweep again and there's another bright flash and a wave of nausea as the bones run ragged and scraping across each other and a little voice says, "Broke your collarbone in half. . . ." The thought is there but it's just another fact of the millions that don't matter in a world rushing by faster than anybody can reel in.

The water doesn't stop, it never stops, and I'm washing away and my head's ringing and I'm fighting to stay upright, but the boat's slamming over the washboard rocks, skipping and ricocheting, and the boat's flexing and my head and shoulders and back are all white hot pain. *The Dome Hole*—it's just downstream. I know it's there and I'm calm but I know it's there and the whole river is ramming me right straight toward it. My balance falters, pain shooting all the way through my shoulders and down into my lower back and hips.

The metallic taste fills my mouth and I sweep a third time and there's another blast of pain. I'm not mad, not frustrated, not scared, I'm just thinking, *Make the move.* But the water is flushing my boat way left, and I'm bearing down on the corner, and suddenly I know I can't make it. I glance and see a big curling wave on the crest of the ramp above the hole and realize I've got one chance to take a stroke and maybe catch the wave enough to surf a little back to the right, away from the gut of the hole. I've got maybe a second or two watching it coming and setting my backstroke, swept up on the wave and it breaks down on me and I stroke and—nothing happens. I'm willing my arm to move, but my neck and shoulders are paralyzed and scream back at me with another explosion of pain. Time freezes, then the curling wave lifts me up, spins the boat like a feather, and flushes me backward down the ramp into the gut of the biggest hole on the river. I'm calm, so calm, looking up into the blue sky and all I can think is, *I'm in for it now.*

The water drives me down and the huge flushing plunger of the river cartwheels the boat end to end like a kid's toy. I can feel the boat airborne and I twist it strong, cranking my body to the left as the boat flies out and twists to land upright, and for an instant I'm balanced, then I'm sucked back down into the gut of the thing and can feel it driving me deep. Then the boat surges up and out of the water, rising and airborne in another cartwheel and I hang my weight back and twist and drive the boat with my knees as it flips through the air. I land up high on the backwash, I can feel I'm way high up near the balance point, and I know this is it. I dig my paddle deep into the violently bursting water and pull. I pull and pull with my bad arm as the hole yanks and rips my arms and paddle and the pain is all exploding in lights flashing through my head. Waves of nausea flush through me like the water, and my arm and back lock up again and I can't move them, I pull and pull with everything I have. . . .

And then I wash free.

My balance is almost gone. I'm fighting to stay upright, spots dancing in front of me and nausea pulsing and my whole right side has seized. That grating-bone pain pierces deep inside me. I know I'm hurt bad and I'm thinking, *If you black out you're dead.* I can barely stay upright. Another hundred yards, around the next corner, there's an eddy, the only chance I've got.

I wobble side to side, ready to flip over, everything is seizing, muscles spasming and refusing to work and half my body's gone rigid. The pain is everywhere, I can't even move my paddle on my right and so I lock my arm down against the deck and lean left and get hit again and again down through the last big holes and breaking waves of the rapid, totally at the mercy of the water, fighting to stay upright now because I'm sure I can't roll if I go under again, but I'm almost through this. I have to make the eddy, if I wash down past it I'm fucking dead because there's another big rapid below that's a half-mile long and I can't do it and can't swim. I *have* to make the eddy.

I round the corner and there's the eddy ahead with the river rushing past it. The water swirls and surges, spinning the boat strongly. The eddy line pushes out away from the bank, welling up, and I'm doing everything I can to angle and cut through it. I turn the boat as best I can, but the current spins me as I hit the eddy wall, pushing me back out into the current, and I'm swept downstream by the fast-flowing water. Have to make it. I'm concentrating and leaning on my left paddle blade, it's all I can do to weakly scull and try to time my turn. Exhausted, muscles locked, gasping, I finally get the right angle and wash into the big moving eddy. The water sloshes back and forth like it's in a huge tank, and I scull and spin over to the bank and grab onto a rock with my left hand.

I made it.

I sit there fighting to stay conscious, concentrating on a piece of driftwood in the water as the spots and nausea and the whole world swell and fade and pulse.

I made it. I fucking made it.

Greg paddles up and pulls into the eddy. "Jesus! What a rapid!" he yells out. He's half laughing, amazed at how wild it was. He hadn't seen what happened to me because he'd been too busy dealing with his own epic. Then he notices I'm bent over. "Doug, are you okay?"

"Broke my collarbone, I think. Can't move." He quickly gets out of his boat and stands in the water holding onto me. I keep concentrating on that little piece of driftwood, flipping and washing back and forth in the eddy waves near the bank. *Just stay conscious. Just stay upright.*

Greg helps me out of my boat and up the bank. We flag down a truck on the highway and cut my drytop off. Soon we're in Greg's car, heading down toward the hospital in Boise. I'm lying there with my eyes closed, letting the pain move through me, pissed off that I made the mistake of following Greg too closely and pissed off I didn't paddle the river like it needs to be paddled. I just didn't do it. And I almost paid everything for that.

At the hospital they poke me and make their CAT scans and X rays and shoot me full of Demerol. They find a dislocated collarbone, separated shoulder, ripped cartilage along my ribs and down my sternum, badly bruised shoulder blade, torn muscles from my neck to my shoulder and all down my back. The river stomped me. But I made the eddy.

That was five years ago. I've been back since and paddled the river many times. I've recovered as much as I ever will, and it's good enough,

I guess. My collarbone still pops and snaps, the shoulder still hurts. When I get tired, the muscles in my neck lock up. There are big knots in there, from all the tearing. You take your lumps and try to come away the wiser for it. I think about the accident every once in a while. Six inches to the right and I would have caught the entire force of the rock on my helmet, been knocked unconscious, and drowned. Six inches to the left and I would have taken the hit on my back and been padded by my life jacket. Life sometimes hangs on the details. You can make of that what you want.

I returned to the river with a group of friends late that fall, three months after the accident. I couldn't paddle very well, but the water was low and not nearly so difficult. I wasn't healed and hadn't been in my kayak since the pileup. After only an hour on the river I was hurting. But it was a great Indian summer day, and I love paddling and I love that river, even if it almost killed me.

As we got to Jaws, we eddied out in the swirling pool above. My buddies said, "Where's that rock? Show us that damn rock and let's dynamite the fucking thing!" One of them swung his paddle around and yelled, "I'm gonna whack the hell out of it. I'll spit on it as we go by!" I laughed and let them go on ahead, this time with plenty of room. I hung back thinking about that day, still sharp in my mind like the pain in my shoulder. I ran the rapid cautiously, well behind the others, making moves cleanly, trying to find the same boulder. I eddied out right above it—a car-sized rock, narrow and sharp on the front, cutting the water apart like the prow of a ship. I tried to imagine what I must have looked like there, pinned on the front with five times as much water bearing down, crushing me, breaking me. I remembered the franticness, the sharp bright pain, and closed my eyes with everything vivid in my mind. After a few minutes I peeled out into the current, wondering *Should I hit the thing? Should I spit on it?* But as the river washed me by I reached out my hand and ran it gently over the boulder for an instant and said, "Thanks for reminding me."

CONTRIBUTORS

Doug Ammons is a twenty-year veteran of kayaking around the world. An expert in all aspects of the sport, he particularly enjoys difficult expedition runs, and has traveled to Alaska, northern Canada, Mexico, the Himilayas, and the Andes in search of big water and unrun rivers. He has a Ph.D. in experimental psychology and works as a full-time editor for two large scientific journals. He has helped make five films for such companies as National Geographic, ESPN, and Outdoor Life, three of which have won Emmy Awards, and he has won an Emmy himself for his camera work. He has published numerous magazine articles and is currently working on two books about whitewater paddling. Doug lives in Missoula, Montana, with his wife and five children.

Richard Bangs is a world adventurer, international river explorer, and award-winning author. He is editor-in-chief of *Mungo Park*, Microsoft's online adventure magazine (http://mungopark.com). He graduated from North-western University in 1972 with an English degree, and received a master's degree in journalism from the University of Southern California in 1975. He is a founding partner of Mountain Travel/Sobek, America's oldest and largest adventure travel firm. Bangs has led first descents of thirty-five rivers around the globe. His publishing credits include more than five hundred magazine articles and twelve books, and he has produced many documentaries and CD-ROMs. Bangs lectures extensively on adventure travel, related environmental issues, and his latest exploratory expeditions.

Walter Lloyd Blackadar, M.D., New Jersey–born, Dartmouth- and Columbia-educated, moved to Idaho in 1949 to practice medicine in a place surrounded by wilderness and great hunting and fishing. Four years later he ran the River of No Return in a raft and fell under the spell of moving water, but not until 1967 at the age of 45 did he take up whitewater kayaking. Over the next eleven years he revolutionized the sport, making contributions which have never been equaled. A pioneer and adventurer, Blackadar set the standards in paddling big Western whitewater. Numerous first descents filled his paddling résumé—perhaps the boldest of which was his solo first descent of the Turnback Canyon on Alaska's Alsek River in 1971. The journals he kept on this expedition, reprinted here, are considered by many a benchmark in adventure writing. They represent one of the few pieces Blackadar published during his paddling career. Walt Blackadar drowned on the North Fork of the Payette River in the early season, 1978. A highly recommended biography of him, *Never Turn Back: The Life of Whitewater Pioneer Walt Blackadar,* by Ron Watters, is available from Great Rift Press, Pocatello, Idaho, (208) 232-6857.

Jeff Bennett is a contributing editor for *Paddler* magazine and a frequent contributor to *Canoe and Kayak* and *River* magazines. He has authored and co-authored a bevy of whitewater manuals and guidebooks, including *A Guide to the Whitewater Rivers of Washington; Class Five Chronicles; The Complete Inflatable Kayaker; The Complete Whitewater Rafter;* and *The Essential Whitewater Kayaker.*

Whit Deschner claims he was the model for Edvard Munch's famous painting, *Scream.* He began paddling in 1968 and has traveled the world extensively with his kayak and quirky sense of humor in tow. He is the author of three books: *Travels with a Kayak; Burning the Iceberg: The Alaskan Fisherman's Novel;* and *How to be a Jerk in Bristol Bay: An Abuser's Guide.* All are available from Eddie Tern Press, HCR 88 Box 169, Baker, Oregon 97814. (Or order via e-mail at: whit@pdx.oneworld.com.)

Mike Doyle was born in Flemington, New Jersey, in 1959. In 1982 he graduated from University of California Berkeley where he was a member of an NCAA championship swimming team. He has rafted and kayaked all over the United States, the Yukon, and Costa Rica. In 1985 he started Beyond Limits Adventures, Inc., now one of California's premier rafting companies. He lives with his wife and two daughters in Modesto, California.

Linda Ellerbee is an outspoken journalist, award-winning television producer, best-selling author, one of the most sought-after speakers in America, a breast-cancer survivor, and mother of two children. In the 1980s she wrote and anchored the pioneering late-night news program *NBC News Overnight,* which won the Columbia duPont Award. In 1986, she won an Emmy for Best Writing for her work on *Our World,* a weekly prime-time historical series. In 1987 she quit the networks to start Lucky Duck Productions, which is currently producing prime-time specials for HBO, A&E, MTV, ABC, CBS, and Nickelodeon. Recently, HBO signed Ellerbee, Whoopi Goldberg, and Diane Keaton to develop a twelve-hour mini-series about the women's movement of the 1960s and 1970s. She spends her personal time in New York City and Massachusetts with her partner in work and life, Rolfe Tessem, and their golden retriever Beau.

Gardner Heaton graduated *cum laude* from Cornell University in 1991, with a degree in Anthropology/South Asian Studies/Nepali Language. He works as a professional mountain guide for EXUM Mountain Guides in Jackson, Wyoming, and as a freelance illustrator and artist. He contributes often to the *American Alpine Journal;* his work was recently included in a traveling art exhibit titled "The Best of the American Alpine Journal." He is also a frequent contributor to *The Mountain Yodel: The Art, Writing, and Photography of the Climbers of Jackson Hole.*

Timothy Hillmer worked as a river guide for ten years in California, Oregon, and Colorado. His first novel, *The Hookmen* (University Press of Colorado; paperback edition published by Simon and Schuster), was the recipient of the Colorado Fiction Award, the Top Hand Award from the Colorado Author's League, and a special fiction prize from the Colorado Center for the Book. He lives in Louisville, Colorado, with his wife and two daughters where he works as a public school teacher.

Pam Houston was born in New Jersey and graduated from Denison University in 1983. Her book *Cowboys are my Weakness* was the 1993 winner of the Western States Book Award and now is published in eight languages. Formerly a hunting guide and river guide, she now lives at 9,000 feet near the Continental Divide in southwestern Colorado. Her latest book is called *Waltzing the Cat* (W.W. Norton & Company).

Joe Kane lives in Oakland, California, with his wife and two daughters. He is the author of *Savages*, about the Huaorani people of the Ecuadorian Amazon, and has contributed to *The New Yorker*, *National Geographic*, and other publications.

Tim Keggerman is a raft guide whose travels have taken him to all corners of the Earth in a never-ending search for challenging whitewater.

John Long's instructional books have made him a best seller in the outdoor industry, with over a million books in print. His recent instructional book, *Advanced Rock Climbing* (Falcon Publishing, co-authored by Craig Luebben) won the 1997 Banff Mountain Book Festival award for Best Mountain Exposition. His award-winning short stories—known for taut action and psychological intensity—have been widely anthologized and translated into many languages. A legendary performer in the sport of rock climbing, Long's achievements include the first one-day ascent of the 3,000-foot face of El Capitan in Yosemite. Long's other adventures include a Baffin Island–North Pole expedition; a coast-to-coast traverse of Borneo; discovery and exploration of the world's largest river cave in Papua New Guinea; the first descent of Angel Falls in Venezuela; and the first land crossing of Indonesian New Guinea, one of the most primitive regions in the world. He splits his time between California and Venezuela.

Michael McRae, world traveler and adventurer, is a contributing editor for *National Geographic Adventure* magazine and a correspondent and frequent contributor to *Outside* magazine. He writes for many periodicals including *Science, Natural History, National Geographic,* and *Audubon*. His forays to out-of-the-way corners of Africa, Asia, and South America have yielded a critically praised collection of nature-travel essays called *Continental Drifter: Dispatches from the Uttermost Parts of the Earth* (Lyons and Burford). He is currently working on a book called *Recent Discoveries and Deaths in Tibet's Tsangpo Gorges.*

William Nealy is a veteran kayaker whose instructional book *Kayak: The Animated Manual of Intermediate and Advanced Whitewater Technique* (Menasha Ridge Press), is widely recognized as the definitive volume on whitewater kayaking technique.

Kevin O'Brien is a photographer, writer, and filmmaker specializing in adventure sports and travel. His work has appeared in *Time, Newsweek, Sports Illustrated, Outside* and numerous other publications worldwide. He has been kayaking twenty-four years and also works as an instructor and guide. Expeditions and work assignments have taken him from the Dead Sea to the Himalayas. He lives in Hidden Valley, Pennsylvania.

Major John Wesley Powell was a U.S. geologist and ethnologist (the study of cultural origins) who in 1869 led the first descent of the Grand Canyon of the Colorado River. Prior to this he had fought in the Civil War—losing an arm at Shiloh—and worked as a geology professor. The Grand Canyon descent was technically a geological and geographical survey mission under the direction of the Smithsonian Institute; in the following years Powell led more geological and ethnological explorations in Arizona and Utah. He was instrumental in the establishment of the U.S. Geological Survey in 1879, and he served as director from 1881 to 1894. In 1879 he became director of the Bureau of American Ethnology. He died in 1902 and is buried in New York City.

James Snyder has been paddling whitewater since 1965, building custom wooden paddles since 1975, and designing kayaks since 1981. He currently works on the design team for Perception kayaks. He was a raft guide in West Virginia for nineteen years and was a pioneer of many steep creek runs, including the first descent of Quarry Run in 1977. In the 1980s he helped develop the sport of squirt boating and was the first person to do flatwater cartwheels; he subsequently wrote *The Squirt Book* (Menasha Ridge Press). In 1993 he won the National Squirt Championships. In 1998 he received the American Canoe Association's "Legends of Whitewater" award, along with Jon Lugbil. He lives in West Virginia with his wife Doris, son Nathan, and daughter Amelia.

Louise Teal is a writer who has been published in *Arizona Highways, Backpacker*, and *Mountain Bike* magazines, among others. She writes about boatwomen because she's one of them. She began working as a swamper (assistant motor boatman, as they call it) in 1972. She started rowing commercially in the Grand Canyon in 1974, and in 1978 she led the first all-women's Grand Canyon trip. The next year she worked in the Grand Canyon as a river ranger for The National Park Service. She still floats through the Grand Canyon regularly as she has for nearly twenty-five years.

Barry Tuscano, 47, of Bolivar, Pennsylvania, earns his living as a roofing contractor. Paddling class V whitewater is still a family affair for Barry, who often is joined on the river by his wife, Kitty, and their 20-year-old son, Ambrose. Barry is also active in river conservation work, serving as secretary on the board of directors for American Whitewater. American Whitewater is a river conservation group that represents whitewater boaters across the nation and publishes *American Whitewater* magazine. For more information on American Whitewater, call (301) 589-9453 or check out their website (www.awa.org).

COPYRIGHT AND PERMISSIONS